The Warha... ...e
exploits of l... ...of
powerful enemies. Now for the first time the tales
of these mythical events will be brought to life in a
new series of books. Divided into a collection of
trilogies, each will bring you hitherto untold details
of the lives and times of the most legendary of all
Warhammer heroes and villains. Combined
together, they will also begin to reveal some of the
hidden connections that underpin all of the history
of the Warhammer world.

◀ THE LEGEND OF SIGMAR ▶

Kicking off with *Heldenhammer*, this explosive trilogy
brings Sigmar to the foundation of the Empire.

◀ THE RISE OF NAGASH ▶

Nagash the Sorcerer begins this gruesome tale of a
priest king's quest for ultimate power over the living
and the dead.

◀ THE SUNDERING ▶

The immense, heart-rending tale of the war
between the elves and their dark kin commences
with *Malekith*.

Keep up to date with the latest information from
the **Time of Legends** at *www.blacklibrary.com*

More Time of Legends from the Black Library

· **THE LEGEND OF SIGMAR** ·

Book 1 – HELDENHAMMER

Graham McNeill

Book one of the Nagash Trilogy

NAGASH THE SORCERER

The undead will rise...

Mike Lee

To Janet, who saved me from Nagash not once,
but many times.

A BLACK LIBRARY PUBLICATION

First published in Great Britain in 2008 by
BL Publishing,
Games Workshop Ltd.,
Willow Road, Nottingham,
NG7 2WS, UK

10 9 8 7 6 5 4 3 2

Cover illustration by Jon Sullivan.
Map by Nuala Kinrade.

A CIP record for this book is available from the British Library.

UK ISBN 13: 978 1 84416 660 2
US ISBN 13: 978 1 84416 556 8

See the Black Library on the Internet at
www.blacklibrary.com

Find out more about Games Workshop
and the world of Warhammer at
www.games-workshop.com

Printed and bound in the UK.

It is a Time of Legends, a time of gods and daemons, of kings and heroes blessed with the power of the divine.

The arid land of Nehekhara has been blessed by the hands of the gods, giving birth to the first great human civilization by the banks of the winding River Vitae. The Nehekharas dwell in eight proud city-states, each with its own patron deity whose blessings shape the character and fortunes of its people. The greatest of them all, situated at the nexus of this ancient land, is Khemri, the fabled Living City of Settra the Magnificent.

It was Settra, hundreds of years before, who united the cities of Nehekhara into mankind's first empire, and declared that he would rule over it forever. He commanded his priests to unlock the secret of life eternal, and when the great emperor eventually died, his body was entombed within a mighty pyramid until the day when his liche priests would summon his soul back from the afterlife.

After Settra's death, his great empire unravelled, and Khemri's power waned. Now, amid the haunted shadows of Khemri's mortuary temple, a brilliant and mighty priest broods over the cruelties of fate and covets his brother's crown.

His name is Nagash.

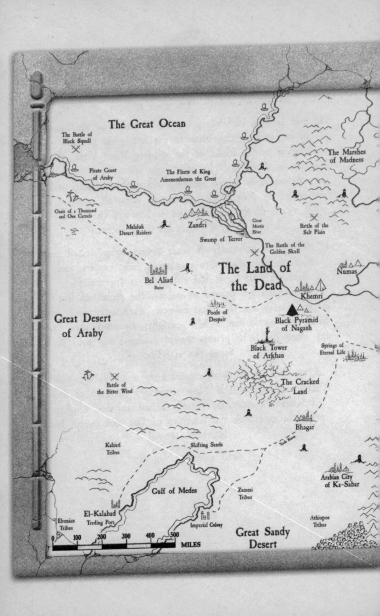

The Great Ocean

The Battle of
Black Squall

Pirate Coast
of Araby

The Fleets of King
Amenemhetum the Great

The Marshes
of Madness

Oasis of a Thousand
and One Camels

Malaluk
Desert Raiders

Zandri

Great
Mortis
River

Battle of
the Salt Plain

Swamp of Terror

The Battle of the
Golden Skull

Bel Aliad
Ruins

The Land of
the Dead

Numas

Khemri

Great Desert
of Araby

Pools of
Despair

Black Pyramid
of Nagash

Springs of
Eternal Life

Black Tower
of Arkhan

Battle of
the Bitter Wind

The Cracked
Land

Bhagar

Kahied
Tribes

Shifting Sands

Arabian City
of Ka-Sabar

Ebonian
Tribes

El-Kalabad
Trading Port

Gulf of Medes

Zamesi
Tribes

Athiopos
Tribes

Imperial Colony

Great Sandy
Desert

0   100   200   300   400   500
MILES

The Plain of Bones

Desolation of Nagash

The Sour Sea

Nagashizzar
Below which lies
the Cursed Pit

Misty Mountain

Blight River

The Broken Teeth

Battle of
the Grey Hag

The Fortress
of Vorag
Ruins

Red Cloud
Mountain

The Straits of
Nagash

Mortis Tarn

N

Cursed
Lahmia

Doom
Mountain

The Bitter Sea

Ash River

The Battle of
Phar's Legion

Battle of
the Mighty Flame

Devil's Backbone

Lybaras
Resting Place of
Queen Khalida

Gulf of
Fear

Mahrak
City of Decay

Doom
Glade
Swamp

The
Cursed
Jungle

Quatar
Palace of Corpses

Charnal Valley

Battle of
the Old Gods

Mount
Arachnos

Crater of the
Walking Dead

Temple of
Skulls

Lost Plateau

Rasetra

The Lost Hold
Karak Zorn

KEY TO MAP OF THE LAND OF THE DEAD

🏛️	Settlement	✗	Battle
🏛️	Necropolis	🌴	Oasis
⚓	Fleet	🌴	Jungle
- - -	Trade Route	🌋	Volcano
♟️	Tower Delineating Borders of Nehekhara		

BOOK ONE

◄ ONE ►

A Prayer Before Battle

*The Oasis of Zedri, in the 62nd year of Qu'aph the Cunning
(-1750 Imperial Reckoning)*

AKHMEN-HOTEP, BELOVED of the Gods, Priest King of Ka-
Sabar and Lord of the Brittle Peaks, woke among his
concubines in the hours before dawn and listened to the
faint sounds of the great army that surrounded him.
Sounds carried far in the desert stillness; he could hear
the distant lowing of the oxen as the priests moved
among the herds, and the whickering of the horses in
their corral at the far side of the oasis. From the north
came the reassuring tinkle of silver bells and the ringing
of brass cymbals as the young acolytes of Neru walked
the perimeter of the camp and kept the hungry spirits of
the desert at bay.

The priest king breathed deeply of the perfumed air, filling his lungs with the sacred incense smouldering in the
tent's three small braziers. His mind was clear and his
spirit untroubled, which he took to be a good omen on

the verge of such a momentous battle. The chill of the desert night felt good against his skin.

Moving carefully, Akhmen-hotep disentangled himself from the arms of his women and slid from beneath the weight of the sleeping furs. He sank to his knees before the polished brass idol at the head of the bed and bowed before it, thanking the shedu for guarding his soul while he slept. The priest king dipped a fingertip in the small bowl of frankincense at the foot of the idol and anointed the brow of the stern, winged bull. The idol seemed to shimmer in the faint light as the spirit within accepted the offering, and the cycle of obligation came full circle.

There was a scratching at the heavy linen covering the entrance to the chamber. Menukhet, favoured servant to the priest king, crawled inside and pressed his forehead to the sandy floor. The old man wore a white linen kilt and fine leather sandals whose wrappings rose almost to his knees. A broad leather belt circled his waist, and a leather headband set with semiprecious stones sat upon his wrinkled brow. He'd wrapped a short woollen cape around his narrow shoulders to keep the cold from his bones.

'The blessings of the gods be upon you, great one,' the servant whispered. 'Your generals, Suseb and Pakh-amn, await you without. What is your wish?'

Akhmen-hotep raised his muscular arms over his head and stretched until his hands brushed the tent's ceiling. Like all the people of Ka-Sabar, he was a giant, standing almost seven feet tall. At eighty-four he was in the prime of his life, still lean and strong despite the luxuries of the royal palace. His broad shoulders and the flat planes of his face bore the scars of many battles, each one an offering to Geheb, God of the Earth and Giver of Strength. The Priest Kings of Ka-Sabar had long been accounted as fearsome warriors and leaders of men, and Akhmen-hotep was a true son of the city's patron deity.

'Bring me my raiment of war,' he commanded, 'and let my generals attend upon me.'

The favoured slave bowed his shaved head once more and withdrew. Within moments, half a dozen body slaves entered the chamber, bearing wooden chests and a cedar stool for the king to sit upon. Like Menukhet, the slaves were clad in linen kilts and sandals, but their heads were covered by hekh'em, the fine ceremonial veils that kept the unworthy from viewing the priest king in all his glory.

The slaves worked swiftly and silently, preparing their master for war. More incense was cast upon the coals, and wine was offered to Akhmen-hotep in a golden cup. As he drank, nimble hands cleaned and oiled his skin, and bound his short beard into a queue with braided strips of glossy leather. They dressed him in a pleated kilt of the finest white linen, placed red leather sandals upon his feet, and set around his waist a belt formed of plates of hammered gold, inlaid with lapis lazuli. Wide gold bracelets, inscribed with the blessings of Geheb, were pressed around his wrists, and a bronze helmet crowned with a snarling lion was set upon his shaven head. Then a pair of older slaves placed his armour of woven leather bands around his powerful torso, and a broad necklace of gold, inlaid with glyphs of protection against arrow and sword, around his neck.

As the armourers finished their tasks a pair of veiled slaves entered the sleeping chamber with trays of dates, cheese and honeyed bread for their master to break his fast. They were followed by a pair of armoured Nehekha-ran nobles, who fell to their knees before the priest king and touched their foreheads to the floor.

'Rise,' Akhmen-hotep commanded. As the generals straightened, sitting back on their haunches, the priest king settled onto his cedar chair. 'What are the tidings of the foe?'

'The army of the usurper has encamped along the ridge north of the oasis, as we expected,' answered Suseb. Akhmen-hotep's champion was called the Lion of Ka-Sabar, and was tall even among his own people; at a crouch, his head was nearly level with the seated priest king, forcing him to bend his neck ever so slightly to show proper deference. The champion carried his helmet tucked beneath one powerful arm. His handsome, square-jawed face was clean-shaven, as was his dark-skinned head. 'The last of their warriors arrived only a few hours ago, and they appear to have suffered greatly on their long march.'

Akhmen-hotep frowned, and asked, 'How do you know this?'

'Our sentries along the northern perimeter can hear groans and fearful murmurs rising from the enemy camp,' Suseb explained, 'and there are no signs of tents or camp-fires being lit.' The priest king nodded.

'What do our scouts report?'

Suseb turned to his companion. Pakh-amn, the army's Master of Horse, was one of the wealthiest men of Ka-Sabar. His black hair was curled into ringlets and oiled, falling over his sloping shoulders, and his armour was ornamented with lozenges of gold. The general cleared his throat. 'None of our scouts have returned as yet,' he reported, bowing his head. 'No doubt they will arrive at any time.'

Akhmen-hotep waved the news away with a sweep of his hand.

'What of the omens?' he asked.

'The Green Witch has hidden her face,' Pakh-amn declared, referring to Sakhmet, the baleful green moon, 'and a priest of Geheb claimed that he saw a desert lion hunting alone among the dunes to the west. The priest said that the lion's jaws were dark with blood.' The priest king scowled at the two generals.

'These are fine portents, but what of the oracles? What do they say?' he asked. It was Suseb's turn to bow his head regretfully.

'The Grand Hierophant assures me that he will perform a divination, after the morning's sacrifices,' the champion said. 'There has been little opportunity up to this point. Even the senior priests are occupied with menial tasks–'

'Of course,' Akhmen-hotep interjected, grimacing slightly at the memory of the shadow that had fallen over Ka-Sabar and the other cities across Nehekhara barely a month past. Every priest and acolyte touched by that tide of darkness had died within moments, leaving the great temples decimated.

Akhmen-hotep was in no doubt that the foul shadow had been spawned in blighted Khemri. All of the evils plaguing the Blessed Land for the last two hundred years could be laid at the feet of the tyrant that ruled there, and the priest king had vowed that Nagash would at long last answer to the gods for his crimes.

THE PRIESTS OF Ptra greeted the dawn with the blare of trumpets. On the plain to the north of the great oasis, the assembled warriors of Ka-Sabar's Bronze Host shone like a sea of golden flames. To the east, the weathered line of the Brittle Peaks was etched in harsh, yellow light, while the endless, rolling dunes of the Great Desert off to the west was still cloaked in shadow.

Akhmen-hotep and the nobles of the great army gathered by the waters of the oasis, glittering in their martial finery, and offered up sacrifices to the gods. Rare incense was burned to win the favour of Phakth, the god of the sky and bringer of swift justice. Nobles cut their arms and bled upon the sands to placate great Khsar, god of the desert, and beg him to scourge the army of Khemri with his merciless touch. Young bullocks were brought stumbling up to Geheb's stone altar, and their lifeblood was poured out into shining bronze bowls that were then passed among the assembled lords. The nobles drank deep, beseeching the god to lend them his strength.

The last and greatest sacrifice was saved for Ptra, mightiest of the gods. Akhmen-hotep came forward, surrounded by his towering Ushabti. The priest king's devoted bodyguards bore the marks of Geheb's favour;

their skin was golden and their bodies moved with the fluid power of the desert lion. They stalked around the priest king with massive, two-handed blades gleaming in their taloned hands.

A great pit had been dug at the edge of the oasis, in full view of the gathered army, and seasoned wood brought all the way from Ka-Sabar had been piled in it and set alight. The priests of the sun god surrounded the blaze, chanting the Invocation of Going Forth to Victory. Akhmen-hotep stood before the hungry flames and spread his powerful arms. At his signal, shouts and screams shook the air as the Ushabti dragged a score of young slaves forward and cast them into the flames.

Akhmen-hotep joined the chanting of the priests, calling upon Ptra to unleash his wrath upon Nagash the Usurper. As the smoke darkened above the fire and the air grew sweet with the smell of roasted flesh, the priest king turned to Memnet, the Grand Hierophant. 'What are the portents, holy one?' he asked respectfully.

The high priest of Ptra shone with the Sun God's reflected glory. His short, round frame was clothed in a robe woven with threads of gold, and golden bracelets pinched the soft flesh of his brown arms. Upon his chest lay the polished golden sun-disk of the temple, inscribed with sacred glyphs and showing the likeness of Ptra and his fiery chariot. His fleshy face was covered in a sheen of sweat, even at this early hour.

Memnet licked his lips nervously and turned his face to the flames. His deep-set eyes, shadowed by a thick band of black kohl, betrayed none of the priest's inner thoughts. He studied the shapes in the smoke for a long time, his mouth set in a grim line.

Silence fell upon the scattered nobles, broken only by the hungry crackle of the flames. Akhmen-hotep frowned at the Grand Hierophant.

'The warriors of Ka-Sabar await your word, holy one,' he prompted. 'The foe awaits.'

Memnet squinted at the curling ribbons of smoke.

'I...' he began, and then fell silent. He wrung his podgy hands.

The priest king stepped close to the smaller man.

'What do you see, brother?' he asked, feeling the expectant stares of a thousand nobles weighing upon his shoulders. Cold fingers of dread tickled at his spine.

'It... it is not clear,' Memnet said hollowly. He glanced up at the king, and there was a glint of fear in his dark-rimmed eyes. The Grand Hierophant glanced back at the sacrificial fire. He took a deep breath. 'Ptra, Father of All, has spoken,' he said, his voice gathering strength as he fell into the ceremonial cadences. 'So long as the sun shines on the warriors of the faithful, victory is certain.'

A great sigh passed through the assemblage, like a breath of desert wind. Akhmen-hotep turned to his noblemen and raised his great bronze khopesh up to the sky. The light of the sun god blazed from its keen, curved edge.

'The gods are with us!' he cried, his powerful voice carrying over the murmurs of the throng. 'The time has come to cleanse the stain of wickedness from the Blessed Land! Today, the reign of Nagash the Usurper will come to an end!'

The assembled nobles answered with a great cheer, raising their scimitars and crying out the names of Ptra and Geheb. Trumpets sounded, and the Ushabti threw back their golden heads and roared, baring their leonine fangs at the cloudless sky. North of the oasis, the serried ranks of the great army took up the cry, clashing their weapons against the faces of their bronze-rimmed shields and shouting a challenge in the direction of the enemy camp, more than a mile away.

Akhmen-hotep strode back in the direction of his tents, calling for his chariot. The assembled noblemen followed suit, eager to join their warriors and reap the glory that awaited them. No one paid any more heed to Memnet, except his fearful and exhausted priests. The Grand

Hierophant continued to stare into the flames, his lips working soundlessly as he tried to puzzle out the portents contained within.

A MILE DISTANT, along the rocky ridge that sat astride the ancient trade road leading to far-off Ka-Sabar, the warriors of Khemri lay like an army of corpses upon the dusty ground.

They had marched night and day, burnt by sun and frozen by darkness, driven by the lash of their generals and the implacable will of their king. League after league passed beneath their sandalled feet, with scant pause for rest or food. Years of famine and privation had rendered their bodies down to little more than sinew and bone. The army moved swiftly, winding down the road like a desert adder as it bore down on its foe. They travelled light, unburdened by the weight of a baggage train or extravagant retinues of priests. When the army stopped, the warriors sank to the earth and slept. When it was time to move again, they rose silently to their feet and shuffled onwards. They ate and drank on the move, eating small handfuls of raw grain and washing it down with sips of water from the leather flasks at their hips.

Those that died on the march were left by the side of the road. No rites were spoken for them, nor were any gifts offered to propitiate Djaf, the god of death. Such things had long been forbidden to the citizens of the Living City.

The corpses withered under the merciless heat of the sun. Not even the vultures would touch them.

As the light of dawn stole across the stony earth and the warriors of the Bronze Host shouted the names of their gods to the sky, the warriors of Khemri stirred from their exhausted slumber. They raised their heads and blinked dully at the sound, turning their dust-streaked faces to the oasis and the shining army that awaited them.

A dry, rustling sound, like a chorus of swarming locusts, rose from the shadows of the dark pavilions erected behind the army's silent ranks. Moving slowly, as though in a dream, the army of Nagash rose once more to its feet.

'IT'S AS IF they're marching to their deaths,' Suseb the Lion declared, watching the shambling ranks of the enemy army descend from the ridge and form up at the edge of the shimmering plain.

The tall champion stood beside his king in the bed of Akhmen-hotep's armoured chariot, taking advantage of the slight elevation to look over the heads of their assembled troops. Double lines of archers formed the front ranks of the army, their tall bows of wood and horn held ready as the enemy slowly drew within range. The companies of spearmen, nearly twenty thousand in all, waited behind them, stretching like a wall of flesh and bronze nearly two miles long. Gaps between the companies created lanes for the bands of light horsemen and charioteers that the priest king chose to hold in reserve at the rear of the waiting host. Once the Khemri army broke, he intended to unleash his cavalry upon the fleeing warriors and slaughter them to a man.

No quarter would be asked, and none given. Such was not the usual way of war in the Blessed Land, but Nagash was no true king. His nightmarish reign in the Living City was an abomination, and Akhmen-hotep intended to erase its taint for all time.

The priest king and his bodyguard were drawn up at the centre of the battle-line, athwart the old trade road. The priests and their retinues were still streaming out of the oasis and making their way to the rear of the army, wreathed in clouds of incense and bearing the icons of their gods before them. Hashepra, bronze-skinned Hierophant of Geheb, had arrived first, and was already deep in prayer. His bare chest was striped with sacrificial blood, and his deep voice was intoning the Invocation of Unconquerable Flesh.

Akhmen-hotep studied the mass of dark figures that was flowing sluggishly onto the plain before his army. Spearmen and axe-men gathered together in ragged companies, intermingled with small bands of dusty archers. Their shambling march kicked up a haze of dust that masked the movements of other units still on the ridge. The priest king thought he saw small units of cavalry moving slowly along the ridge line, but it was difficult to tell for certain.

There was some kind of activity behind the centre of the enemy host. It looked like a mass of slaves, carrying a number of dark shapes, palanquins, perhaps, and arranging them in groups at the crest of the ridge. The sight of them sent an unaccountable chill down the priest king's spine.

Suseb sensed the king's disquiet.

'Your strategy has worked to perfection, great one,' he said. 'The enemy is exhausted, and their ranks have been thinned by their headlong march. See how far the people of the Living City have fallen! We have nearly twice as many companies at our command.' The champion pointed to the army's flanks. 'Let us order our left and right wings forward. When the battle is joined we can encircle the Usurper's army and grind them to dust.'

Akhmen-hotep nodded thoughtfully. He had counted upon this when he'd raised the banner of war against distant Khemri and called upon the other priest kings to unite against the Usurper. Nagash would not tolerate defiance. He'd shown that at Zandri, more than two hundred years ago. So, Akhmen-hotep had made no secret of his advance on the Living City, knowing that Nagash would hasten to meet him before his spark of rebellion could ignite the rest of Nehekhara. Here, then, was the fiend, hundreds of leagues from home, having pushed his army past all human endurance in a fit of tyrannical fury.

Nagash had played directly into his hands. It was like a gift from the gods, and yet, Akhmen-hotep could not shake a powerful sense of foreboding as he watched his foes array for battle.

'Have there been any reports from our scouts?' the king asked.

Suseb paused.

'None, great one,' he admitted, and then shrugged. 'Likely, the Usurper's patrols chased them into the desert during the night, and they are still making their way back to us. No doubt we will hear from them soon.' The priest king's lips drew into a grim line.

'And no news of Bhagar, yet?' he asked.

Suseb shook his head. Bhagar was the closest Nehekharan city, still little more than a merchant town, perched at the edge of the Great Desert. Its princes had pledged their small army to Akhmen-hotep's cause, but there had been no sign of their forces since the Bronze Host had begun its slow march. The champion shrugged.

'Who can say?' he said. 'They might have been delayed by sandstorms, or perhaps Nagash sent a punitive expedition against them as well. It matters little. We don't need their help against a rabble such as this.' Suseb folded his powerful arms and glared disdainfully at the Usurper's approaching warriors. 'This won't be a battle, great one. We will slaughter them like lambs.'

'Perhaps,' the priest king said. 'But you have heard the stories from Khemri as well as I. If half of what the traders say is true, the Living City has become a dark and terrible place, indeed. Who knows what awful powers the Usurper is consorting with?' Suseb chuckled.

'Look around, great one,' he said, indicating the growing assembly of priests with a sweep of his hand. 'The gods are with us! Let Nagash consort with his daemons; the power of the Blessed Land burns in our veins!'

Akhmen-hotep listened and took heart from Suseb's words. He could feel the power of Geheb burning in his limbs, waiting to be unleashed upon the foe. With such blessings at their command, who could stand against them?

'Wise words, my friend,' he said, gripping Suseb's arm. 'The gods have delivered the foe into our hands. It is time for us to strike the killing blow. Go, and take command of the chariots. When I give the signal, grind the enemy beneath your wheels.'

Suseb bowed his head respectfully, but his handsome face was lit with a joyful grin at the prospect of battle. The Lion leapt gracefully from the chariot, and immediately one of the Ushabti and a tall, keen-eyed archer took his place in the king's chariot.

Alone with his thoughts, Akhmen-hotep resumed his study of the approaching enemy force. He was a skilled and experienced general; the sight of the enemy's silent, shambling ranks should have filled him with eager joy. Once again, he tried to shake a creeping sense of dread.

The priest king beckoned to one of his runners, and said, 'Inform the Master of the Bow to begin firing as soon as the enemy comes into range.'

The boy nodded, repeating the order word-for-word, and ran off towards the battle-line.

Akhmen-hotep turned his face to the fierce light of the sun and waited for the battle to be joined.

THE WARRIORS OF Khemri poured down off the ridge like water spilling from a cup, spreading in a dark arc across the white plain and flowing inexorably towards the Bronze Host. Hollow-eyed nobles paced along behind their ragged companies, cymbals clashing and drums pounding, setting a funereal pace. Squadrons of bedraggled horsemen followed behind the footmen, slipping like ghostly shadows in and out of the dusty haze kicked up by the infantry's marching feet.

Horns wailed along the length of the opposing battle-line, barely a hundred and fifty yards distant. The archers of Ka-Sabar stood twenty yards ahead of the regular infantry: three thousand men, arrayed in three companies, with a dozen arrows per man driven into the sand by their feet. At the signal, the archers plucked the first of their arrows from the sand and fitted it to their powerful composite bows. Bronze arrowheads glinted angrily as they were aimed into the cloudless sky. The archers paused for a single heartbeat, muscles bunched along their arms and shoulders, and then a single, piercing note from the signal-horn rang out and the bowmen loosed as one. Bowstrings hummed, and three thousand reed arrows, sped by prayers to Phakth, god of the sky, fell hissing among the enemy ranks.

The warriors of Khemri crouched low and raised their rectangular shields. Arrowheads punched through laminated wood with an angry rattle. Men screamed and fell, shot through the arm or leg, or collapsed lifeless to the broken ground. The infantry slowed momentarily beneath the awful rain, but continued to press grimly forwards. Within moments of the first volley, a second was arcing skyward, and then a third. Still the enemy pressed forwards, their companies withering slowly under the steady rain of fire.

Then came the thunder of hooves, and several squadrons of light horsemen charged out of the haze towards the line of archers. The cavalrymen wielded compact horn-bows of their own, and the Khemri warriors unleashed a ragged volley as they bore down on the bowmen. Arrows sped back and forth across the killing ground. Horses and men went down in a spray of dirt and rock, but the bowmen of the Bronze Host shrugged off the enemy fire. Protected by the invocations of their holy priests, most of the Khemri arrows broke or glanced harmlessly from their bare skin.

Still the horsemen bore down on the thin line of archers, heedless of the appalling losses inflicted by the bowmen. Bronze scimitars flashed in the riders' hands as they closed in. At thirty yards the archers fired a last volley into the front ranks of the horsemen, and then turned and raced for the safety of their battle-line.

An eager cheer went up from the front ranks of the Bronze Host as they made ready for the enemy charge. The

Khemri horsemen lashed at the flanks of their mounts, but the weary horses could not catch up to the fleeing bowmen. Frustrated, they reined in less than a dozen yards from the shouting infantry, and then wheeled about and withdrew, leaving several hundred of their fallen brethren littering the battlefield.

The sacrifices of the cavalry, however, bought time and distance for the Usurper's infantry, who were almost upon their foes. With a final clash of cymbals and a rattle of hide drums the silent companies surged forwards, brandishing stone axes and short-handled maces above their arrow-studded shields. The two armies came together with a hollow crash of flesh, wood and metal, punctuated by fierce shouts and the screams of the dying.

The warriors of the Bronze Host moved back not a single step from the force of the enemy's charge. Filled with the vigour of Geheb, their patron god, they splintered shields and shattered bones, dashing their foes to the ground. Decades of pent up anger against the tyrant of Khemri found its voice in a hungry, wordless roar that reverberated from the warriors of Ka-Sabar. Akhmenhotep and the chanting priests felt the echoes reverberate across their skin and were awed by the sound.

Dust was thickening around the churning mass of warriors, making it difficult to see. Akhmen-hotep scowled, studying the rearmost ranks of his footmen. They were pressing forwards, eager to join in the killing, which he took to be a good sign. The priest king sought out the priests of Phakth. He saw them a short distance away, shrouded in plumes of fragrant incense.

'Glory to the god of the sky, who sped our arrows in flight!' he shouted. 'Will great Phakth stretch forth his hand and wipe the dust from our eyes?'

Suhket, High Priest of Phakth, stood in the centre of the chanting priests, his shaven head bowed in prayer. He opened one eye and arched a thin eyebrow at the priest king.

'The dust belongs to Geheb. If you would have it lie still, importune him instead of the Hawk of the Air,' the priest said in his nasal voice. The priest king scowled at Sukhet, but did not press further. Instead, he turned to his trumpeter.

'Sound the general advance,' he commanded.

Horns wailed, echoing up and down the line. The champions of the infantry companies raised their blood-streaked swords and shouted orders to their men. Shouting, the warriors took one step forward, and then another. Bronze-tipped spears jabbed and thrust, streaming blood, and the exhausted warriors of the Living City gave ground.

Step by step, the warriors of Ka-Sabar drove the enemy back the way they had come. They climbed over the bloodied corpses of the fallen until blood stained the wrappings of their sandals up to their ankles. Meanwhile, the companies at the far ends of the battle-line began to curve inwards, trying to surround the retreating enemy. The Khemri light cavalry harassed the flanks of the spearmen with arrow fire, but did little to slow the inexorable advance.

Akhmen-hotep gestured to his charioteer, who took up the double reins and lashed the team of horses into motion. The chariot rolled forward with a clatter of bronze-rimmed wheels, keeping pace with the advancing army.

A runner appeared from the right flank, his face flushed with excitement.

'Suseb asks permission to attack!' he cried in a piping voice. The priest king considered this for a moment, cursing the dusty haze. Finally he shook his head.

'Not yet,' he answered. 'Tell the Lion to bide his time a little longer.'

So, the advance continued. The Bronze Host moved inexorably across the plain, drawing slowly but steadily closer to the ridge line. Akhmen-hotep's chariot bounced and lurched over the corpses left behind by the fighting. The priests of the city were far behind him, hidden by the dust of the advance, while the churning haze continued to mask the fighting to the fore. He could hear the rattling of chariot wheels off to his left and right, and the nervous whicker of horses as the cavalry kept pace with the footmen. The priest king listened intently to the timbre of battle, waiting for the first signs that the enemy companies were broken and in full retreat.

Despite the steady, remorseless slaughter, the warriors of the Living City refused to break. The closer they drew to the silent, black pavilions lining the ridge, the harder they fought. They pressed against the shields of the enemy spearmen, as though the death looming before them was preferable to what waited at their backs.

WITHIN AN HOUR, the fighting was nearly at the foot of the low ridge line. From the rocky summit, the battle resembled nothing so much as the swirling edge of a sandstorm, lit from within by hard glints of flashing bronze.

Figures waited silently on the slope, watching the approaching storm. Companies of heavy horsemen waited among the dark linen tents, their banners hanging listlessly in the hot, still air. Smaller bands of heavy infantry, clad in leather armour and bearing bronze-rimmed shields, knelt stoically before the great pavilions, awaiting the call to battle.

A group of priests stood together at the centre of the line, outside the largest of the tents. Tall and regal, they wore the black robes of Khemri's mortuary cult, circlets set with sapphires and rubies adorning their shaved heads, and their narrow beards bound with strips of hammered gold. Their dusky skin was pale, and their hawk-like faces were gaunt, but dark power hung over them like an invisible shroud, causing the morning air to shimmer around them like a mirage.

These terrible men waited upon a stooped, elderly slave that crouched at their feet and watched the progress of the battle on the plain below. Blind and nearly toothless, the slave's blue eyes were clouded with milky cataracts, and his brown skin was dried and wrinkled like aged parchment. His bald head was cocked to one side, balanced precariously on his scrawny neck. A thin line of drool hung from his trembling lips.

Slowly, the wrinkled head straightened. A ripple went through the assembled priests, and they shuffled forward, their faces expectant. The slave's mouth worked.

'It is time. Open the jars,' he said, in a voice ravaged with pain and the weight of too many years.

Silently, the priests bowed to the blind slave and went inside the tent. A pair of sarcophagi stood within, carved from glossy black and green marble, fit for the bodies of a mighty king and his queen. Baleful glyphs of power were etched upon their surfaces, and the air surrounding the coffins was as cold and dank as a tomb. The priests averted their eyes from the dreadful figure carved upon the king's sarcophagus, kneeling instead before eight heavy jars nestled at its feet.

The priests picked up the dusty jars in their hands and carried them out into the open air. Each of the clay vessels vibrated invisibly in their grasp, sending a deep, unsettling hum reverberating through their bones.

Slowly, fearfully, the priests set the jars down on the uneven ground. Each vessel was sealed shut with a thick band of dark wax, engraved with rows of intricate glyphs. When all of the jars were in place, the men drew their irheps, the curved ceremonial daggers used to remove the organs of the dead for interment. Steeling their nerves, the priests cut away the wax seals. At once, the buzzing grew louder and more insistent, like the drone of countless angry wasps. The heavy clay lids rattled violently atop the jars.

Nearby, horses shied violently away from the unsealed vessels. With trembling hands, the priests reached forwards and pulled the lids away.

AKHMEN-HOTEP RAISED his hand to signal his trumpeter. Now was the time to send the chariots and horsemen forwards to break the enemy line once and for all.

All at once, the swirling haze of dust was swept away. The priest king felt a cold wind rushing over the skin of his upraised arm, goose bumps prickling his bare flesh.

The pall of dust flowed up the rocky slope of the ridge in a single, indrawn rush. For a dizzying instant, Akhmen-hotep could see the battlefield in every detail. He saw the struggling companies of enemy foot-sloggers, reduced to ragged bands of tormented warriors forced back almost to the very foot of the ridge line. Beyond them, the priest king saw the rocky slope, leading upwards to a long line of black linen tents, and squadrons of rearing, plunging horsemen.

Then he saw the priests and their tall, heavy jars. The dust formed whirling cyclones over the open vessels, and then Akhmen-hotep watched them darken, turning from a pale tan to deep brown, and then to a slick, glossy black.

A seething, whirring drone radiated down the rocky slope and washed over the combatants, sinking through armour and flesh, and vibrating along their bones. Horses bucked and screamed, their eyes white with terror. Men dropped their spears and clapped their hands over their ears to try to shut out the awful noise.

The priest king watched in growing terror as the ebon pillars stretched upwards and poured out a pall of roiling darkness that spread like ink across the sky.

◀ TWO ▶

Second Sons

Khemri, the Living City, in the 44th year of Khsar the Faceless (-1968 Imperial Reckoning)

ON THE SEVENTH day after his death, the body of the Priest King Khetep was taken from the temple of Djaf, in the southern quarter of the Living City, and borne within an ebon palanquin to the House of Everlasting Life. The palanquin was carried not by slaves, but upon the shoulders of Khetep's great Ushabti, and the king's mighty champions marched with their heads hung low and their once-radiant skin stained with ash and dust.

Throngs of mourners crowded the streets of the Living City to pay homage to Khetep as the palanquin passed by. Men and children fell to their knees and pressed their faces to the dust, and mothers wept and tore at their hair, calling to Djaf, god of the dead, to return their monarch to the land of the living. Water drawn from the River Vitae, the great Giver of Life, was cast upon the sides of the palanquin amid tearful prayers. Potters brought out the cups and bowls that had been fired on the day of Khetep's death and dashed them to pieces on the street in the wake of the priest king's passage. In the merchant's quarter, wealthy traders tossed gold coins into the dust before the cortege, where the polished metal caught the light of Ptra's holy fire and blazed beneath the Ushabti's marching feet.

By comparison, the streets of the noble districts surrounding the palace to the north were silent and still. Many of the households were in mourning, or preparing the exorbitant ransoms expected to redeem their lost kin after the disastrous defeat outside Zandri a week before. The atmosphere of sadness and dread settled over the procession like a shroud, weighing heavily on the shoulders of the devoted. Khetep had ruled over Khemri for more than twenty-five years, and through a mix of diplomacy and military prowess he'd forced the cities of Nehekhara to put aside their feuds and live together in peace. Nehekhara had enjoyed an age of prosperity not seen since the great Settra, five hundred years before.

All that had been swept away in the space of a single afternoon on the banks of the Vitae. Khetep's great army had been broken by the warriors of Zandri, and the Ushabti had failed in their sacred duty to protect the king. The news had spread across the Blessed Land like a dust storm, sweeping all before it, and the future was uncertain.

The silent procession made its way into the palace grounds, where the king's household lined the great avenue leading to Settra's mortuary temple. Noblemen and slaves alike prostrated themselves in the dust as the palanquin approached. Many wept openly, knowing that they would soon be joining their great king on his journey into the afterlife.

Settra had built his temple to the east of the palace, facing downriver where the Vitae led to the foot of the Mountains of the Dawn, and symbolic of the journey of the soul after death. The avenue led to a massive, roofed plaza, supported by ranks of huge sandstone columns that led all the way to the temple's grand entrance. The shadows beneath the broad cedar roof were cool and fragrant after the fierce, dry heat of the day. Their footsteps echoed strangely among the columns, transforming their heavy, measured tread into mournful drum beats.

A thirty foot high doorway stood open at the far end of the plaza, densely carved with sacred glyphs and flanked by towering basalt statues of fearsome warriors with the heads of owls, the horex, servants of Usirian, the god of the underworld.

A procession of solemn figures strode from the shadows beyond the great doorway as the Ushabti approached. The priests were clad in ceremonial robes of purest white, and their dusky skins were marked with hundreds of painted henna glyphs, sacred to the cult. Each priest wore a mask of beaten gold, identical to the burial masks of the great kings who lay in their tombs in the sands to the east, and wide belts of gold adorned with topaz and lapis lazuli encircled their waists.

The priests waited in silence as the Ushabti laid the palanquin down at last and drew open the heavy curtains that concealed the priest king's body from view. Khetep had been tightly wrapped in a white burial shroud, his hands folded across his narrow chest. The great king's shrouded face was covered in an ornate burial mask.

For the only time in their lives, the great Ushabti sank to their knees and prostrated themselves before someone other than their king and master. The mortuary priests ignored the mighty champions. They drew near the palanquin and carefully removed the body of their exalted charge. Two by two they bore the shrouded corpse upon their shoulders, and took it into Settra's temple, where only the dead and their eternal servants were allowed.

Once upon a time, the services of the mortuary cult were reserved for the Priest Kings of Khemri alone. Over time, their practices had spread across all Nehekhara, and grew to encompass noble families who enjoyed the priest kings' favour. Now, even the lowliest families could purchase the services of a priest to attend upon their loved ones, though the price was steep. No one begrudged the cost, even though a man might scrimp and save for a lifetime for the privilege. The promise of immortality was a gift beyond price.

The priests carried the body of the king into the depths of the great temple, through vast, sandstone chambers whose walls were covered with intricate mosaics depicting the great Pilgrimage from the East and the Covenant of the Gods, wrought more than seven centuries before. On those walls, great Ptra led the people to the great, lifegiving River Vitae, and Geheb sowed the dark earth with rich crops to make them healthy and strong. Tahoth the Wise showed the people the secrets of shaping stone and raising temples, and when the first cities had been built, glorious Asaph rose from the reeds beside the river and beguiled the people with the wonders of civilisation.

Another chamber lay beyond these wondrous halls, low-ceilinged and dark. Smooth red sandstone gave way to glossy blocks of polished basalt, joined together so cunningly that no seams between the stones were visible. The carvings were highlighted here and there with faint touches of silver dust or precious crushed pearl: landscapes of fertile plains and a wide river, presided over by a mighty range of mountains that dominated the distant horizon. The details were vague, made all the more ephemeral by the shifting light of the oil lamps that flickered around the marble bier at the centre of the room. The Land of the Dead was a beguiling image, like a mirage of the deep desert, beckoning seductively to the viewer only to fade once he drew near.

The priests laid the body of the king upon the bier, and reverently pulled away the linen shroud. Khetep's body had been cleaned by his attendants at the battlefield, and the priests of Djaf had further washed it in a solution of ancient herbs and earth salts. The great king's angular face appeared serene, though the cheeks and eyes were already sunken and there was a strange, bluish-black tint to his thin lips.

A silent procession of acolytes filed in and out of the room as the priests worked. They bore clay pots of expensive ink and fine brushes of camel hair to paint Khetep's skin with glyphs of preservation and sanctity, as well as jars of raw herbs, perfumed water and still more earth salts. Finally came a procession of four young priests carrying intricately carved alabaster jars that would store Khetep's vital organs until his eventual resurrection.

The senior priests worked swiftly, preparing the body for preservation. The priests of the city temples had declared that the coronation of Khetep's heir and his sacred marriage must proceed at sunset, only seven hours away, so there was little time before the dead king's interment. Once the burial shroud was removed, they gathered in a circle around the bier and faced the statues of Djaf and Usirian, which flanked a ceremonial doorway on the eastern wall of the chamber. The senior priest, Shepsu-het, raised his stained hands and prepared to utter the Invocation of the Open Door, the first step in securing Usirian's permission to one day return Khetep's spirit to the Blessed Land.

Just as the priest began to speak he felt a chill race down his spine. The back of his neck prickled beneath the weight of a cold, inimical stare, much as a mouse might suffer under the unblinking gaze of a cobra.

Shepsu-het turned to face the shadowy figure standing in the chamber's entrance. The other priests followed suit, and sank quickly to their knees as they recognised the figure.

Nagash, son of Khetep, Grand Hierophant of the Living City's mortuary cult, favoured the kneeling priests with a disdainful glare.

'What is the meaning of this?' he demanded in a clear, resonant voice.

The senior priests looked to one another apprehensively, their disquiet evident in the set of their hunched shoulders and furtive movements. Finally, they turned to Shepsu-het, who gathered his courage and spoke.

'Time is of the essence, holy one,' he said, his old voice muffled by the mask he wore. 'I thought you would wish us to begin the rites at once.'

Nagash considered the priest for a long moment, and then favoured Shepsu-het with a mirthless smile. At only thirty-two, Nagash was the youngest Grand Hierophant of any city in Nehekharan history, and his physical presence filled the funeral chamber. He was tall for the people of Khemri, and preferred the attire of a warrior prince to the staid robes of a priest. His white linen kilt was bound with a broad belt of fine leather, studded with rubies and gold ornaments in the shape of scarabs. Fine sandals of red leather covered his feet, and a wide-sleeved open robe covered his broad shoulders and the upper part of his muscular arms. His broad, tanned chest bore the scars of battle, earned in the wild years of early adulthood and still stark against his nut-brown skin.

He had his father's handsome features but none of Khetep's warmth, with a square chin and an aquiline nose, but a pair of eyes the colour of polished onyx. His narrow beard was bound in a queue with strips of hammered gold, in the manner of the royal household, and his scalp was shaven and oiled to a lustrous sheen.

'Once again, you demonstrate why *I* am Grand Hierophant instead of you,' Nagash said, stepping deeper into the room. He moved with a jungle cat's grace, gliding almost soundlessly across the stone floor. 'You are an old fool, Shepsu-het. I choose to attend upon my father alone.' He waved his arm at the doorway behind him. 'Begone. If I need the assistance of a pack of prattling monkeys, I shall send for you.'

The senior priests quailed before Nagash's forbidding stare. They rose quickly, as one, and shuffled out of the room. Shepsu-het went last, his expression unreadable beneath the smooth, golden features of his mask. As he departed, the figure of a young priest slipped quietly through the doorway into the chamber. Unlike Nagash, the young man was conservatively attired in a white robe and simple gold belt, but his scarred face was lit with an impudent grin, and his brown eyes were sharp and calculating.

'That one means you trouble, master,' he murmured, watching Shepsu-het disappear from sight.

Nagash stepped around the foot of the bier and folded his arms, studying the body of his dead father in detail.

'I suppose you think I should kill him,' he said absently.

The young priest shrugged, and said, 'He must be a hundred and fifty years old. There are herbs that could find their way into his wine: simple things you could find in the temple kitchens, but deadly when combined in the right way. Or an asp could wind up underfoot in the priests' baths. It's been known to happen.'

Nagash shrugged slightly, listening with only half an ear. His attention was focused on the body before him, looking for clues that would reveal how the priest king had died. Khetep's skin had a yellow tinge from the natron wash the priests had given the corpse, but it could not fully disguise the body's grey pallor. Though well advanced in years, at the age of one hundred, Khetep still possessed a measure of the fighting strength he'd enjoyed in his prime. Nagash studied the formation of the king's muscles, noting with a frown the dark lines of the corpse's veins and the body's distended belly.

'Too much wine and luxury,' he muttered. 'Your defeat was written in the sagging lines of your body, father. Your glories made you weak.'

The young priest chuckled, and said, 'I thought that was the point of glories, master.'

Khefru was the first son of a wealthy merchant family, who had enjoyed spending his father's coin on wine and games of dice. He'd got the scar that disfigured the left side of his face in a drunken knife fight outside a gaming-house. His opponent, the son of a powerful noble in Khetep's court, died a few days later. Rather than face execution, Khefru had begun a new life in the mortuary cult. He was a terrible scholar and an indifferent priest, but possessed a sharp wit and a singular bloody-mindedness that Nagash found useful. He'd chosen Khefru as his personal servant on the same day he'd become Khemri's Grand Hierophant.

'Glory is for fools,' Nagash declared. 'It's a poison that saps the will and diminishes one's resolve. Khetep learned that to his cost.'

Khefru arched an eyebrow at his master, and said, 'No doubt you would have ruled differently.'

Nagash glared balefully at the young priest. At sixteen he'd followed his father's army east through the ancient Valley of Kings, and then south towards the steaming jungles that, according to legend, had been the birthplace of their people. For three years Khetep had fought against the hordes of lizardmen that lurked there, beginning construction of the great fortress of Rasetra as a bastion against their constant raids against the allied city of Lybaras. When Khetep was stricken down with the fever, Nagash assumed command of the expedition. For almost six months he'd led his father's warriors in a merciless campaign against their enemies, finally culminating in the brutal battle that had broken the backs of the local lizard chieftains and pacified the region.

For those six months, he'd ruled like a king, and held the land in an iron grip, but when Khetep had recovered enough to begin the long trek home, he'd given Rasetra to one of his generals, and brought Nagash back to the Living City with him. The surviving members of the expedition had been forbidden to speak of Nagash's brief rule. He had been praised as a mighty warrior, but no more, and upon their arrival in Khemri the king sent

Nagash to Settra's temple to begin his studies. Now, thirteen years later, Rasetra was a small but thriving city with a priest king of its own.

The Grand Hierophant rested his palm on the hilt of the jewelled irheps at his belt.

'If noble families passed their inheritance to their firstborn, as they do in the barbarian tribes to the far north, things would be very different indeed,' Nagash said. 'Instead, fortunes are passed to second sons, and we are shut up in temples.'

'The firstborn are given to the gods, in return for the Blessed Land they have given us,' Khefru said, reciting the old saying with no small amount of bitterness. 'It could be worse. At least they don't sacrifice us, like they did in the old days.'

'The gods should take goats, and be content,' Nagash snapped. 'They need us far more than we need them.'

Khefru shifted from one foot to the other, suddenly uncomfortable. He glanced worriedly at the grim-looking statues on the other side of the room.

'Surely you don't mean such a thing,' he said quickly. 'Without them, the land would wither. The ancient compact–'

'The ancient compact sold us a bowl of sand in exchange for eternal servitude,' Nagash declared. 'The gods offered to make our fields bloom and hold the desert at bay in exchange for worship and devotion. Think on that, Khefru. They were willing to give us paradise in exchange for prayers and the gifts of our firstborn. The gods were *desperate*. Without us, they were weak. We could have enslaved them, bent them to our will. Instead, we are in bondage, giving them strength that we could better use ourselves. Real power lies here, in *this* world,' Nagash said, tapping the marble bier for emphasis, 'not in the next. Settra understood this, I think. That was why he sought the secret to eternal life. Without the fear of death, the gods would have no hold over us at all.'

'A secret that has eluded the mortuary cult for more than five hundred years,' Khefru pointed out.

'That is because our sorcery depends upon the beneficence of the gods,' Nagash said. 'All our rites and invocations are fuelled by their energies. Do you imagine they will help us escape their clutches?' The Grand Hierophant clenched his fists. 'Do not think I flatter myself when I say I possess the greatest mind in all Nehekhara. In thirteen years I have learned everything the cult knows about the process of life and death. I have the knowledge, Khefru. What I lack is *power*.'

As he spoke, Nagash's eyes grew fever-bright, and his voice rose until it was almost a shout. The intensity of the Grand Hierophant's emotions stunned Khefru.

'One day you will find it, master,' the young priest stammered, suddenly afraid. 'No doubt it's only a matter of time.'

Nagash paused. He blinked, and seemed to collect himself, and said, 'Yes. Of course. Merely time.' The Grand Hierophant glanced down at his father's body. He drew the curved bronze knife at his belt.

'Bring the first jar,' he commanded. 'I won't have Shepsu-het accuse me of failing in my duties.'

Khefru went quickly to the waiting alabaster jars and picked one carved with the likeness of a hippo. The canopic jars were made to hold the dead king's four vital organs, the liver, lungs, stomach and intestines, and were carved with glyphs that would preserve them until such time as they were needed once more.

The young priest set the heavy jar beside Nagash, and murmured a prayer to Djaf, god of the dead, before pulling off the lid. Nagash held the bronze blade over his father's belly. He paused briefly, savouring the moment.

'No sign of a wound at all,' he observed. 'Perhaps his heart gave out in the heat of battle.' Khefru shook his head.

'It was sorcery, master,' he said. 'I heard that the army of Zandri called down a spell that smote the priest king and his generals, far behind the battle-line. None of the wards laid by our priests could stop it. When Khetep fell, our army lost its heart, and the Zandri warriors hurled our men back in disarray.'

Nagash considered this, and said, 'But Zandri's patron is Qu'aph. That does not sound like the subtlety of the Serpent God.'

'Even so, master, this is what I was told,' Khefru said, shrugging.

Scowling, Nagash reached down and made the first cut, slitting the abdomen from navel to sternum. At once, the king's belly deflated, spilling a foul, bubbling flood of tarry fluid over the edge of the bier and onto the floor.

Khefru reeled back from the stinking liquid with a muttered curse. Nagash stepped back as well, frowning in surprise. After a moment, the viscous flood subsided, and the Grand Hierophant stepped carefully through the sticky pool back to Khetep's body.

Using the tip of his knife, he added four perpendicular cuts to widen the incision, and pulled one of the flaps of skin aside. The sight of what lay within caused Nagash to hiss in surprise.

The priest king's organs had been fused together by some magical force. His intestines and stomach were shrivelled into a knotted ball, until there was no way to tell where one ended and the other began. Likewise, the diaphragm and lungs had been warped into bulbous masses of diseased flesh. It was as though a great cancer had eaten Khetep from within.

The Grand Hierophant knew of no god who could do such a thing.

Gingerly, Khefru eased up to the table. When he saw what had become of Khetep, his face twisted in disgust.

'What foul sorcery could do such a thing?' he gasped.

Nagash was no longer listening. The Grand Hierophant was bending low over his father's corpse, studying the great king's twisted remains with rapt fascination. A strange, hungry gleam shone from the depths of his dark eyes.

BY NOONDAY, THE great plaza outside the palace was full of noblemen and their retinues, waiting to offer gifts for Khetep's interment and to pledge their fealty to his heir. Small tents of brightly coloured linen had been erected by the royal household to shield the nobles from the worst of the sun's heat, and slaves bustled to and fro with jugs of watered wine cooled by the cisterns deep beneath the palace. The stink of sacrificial animals hung heavy in the still air, as each of the noble families sought to outdo their rivals with lavish gifts of lambs, oxen and even a few precious horses. Nagash scowled forbiddingly at the noxious spectacle as he and Khefru made their way to Settra's Court. He knew that by the end of the ceremonies the grand plaza would resemble a stockyard on market day. The stench would linger for weeks.

The crowd grew thicker the closer they came to the king's audience chamber. A dozen of Thutep's Ushabti bodyguards lined the broad steps leading into the echoing hall, resplendent in their polished gold breastplates and gleaming swords. The faces of the devoted were young and fierce. Still little more than acolytes, their skin shone with Ptra's holy blessing, but their bodies had yet to develop the perfectly muscled physiques of the Great Father's chosen warriors. A hectic knot of palace slaves stood behind the rank of bodyguards, bearing wax tablets and rolls of fine parchment. They circled around a tall, dignified figure of middle years, wearing the gold circlet of Khetep's grand vizier.

Nagash moved effortlessly through the multitude, like a crocodile knifing through the dark waters of the Vitae. Slaves scattered from the Grand Hierophant's path and prostrated themselves on the hot, filthy ground, while their masters fell silent and bent their heads in respect. Khetep's eldest son ignored them, one and all.

The Ushabti bowed their heads in turn as Nagash glided smoothly up the sandstone steps, and the palace servants withdrew swiftly into the shadows of the court. That left only the grand vizier, who folded his hands calmly and awaited Nagash's approach.

'The blessings of the gods be upon you, holy one,' Ghazid said, bowing his head respectfully to the Grand Hierophant. Though at least a hundred and ten, the grand vizier was still lean and fit, with the quick, hawk-like energy of the desert tribes from which he was born. Legend said he'd been a bandit in his early years, but had allied himself with Khetep when the young priest king had tried to bring the desert tribes to heel. Khetep quickly found himself confiding in the bold, clever tribesman, and when the army returned to Khemri, Ghazid went with them. In short order Ghazid was named grand vizier, and he had served the royal household ever since. He proved to be an able advisor and stalwart friend to the king, and many believed that much of the city's resurgent glory could be rightly attributed to him. His keen blue eyes missed nothing, and he feared neither man nor beast. Nagash had hated him since childhood.

'Pray, reserve those well wishes for yourself, grand vizier,' Nagash said with a cold smile. 'I come to tell my brother that the rites for our great father are complete. He will be laid to rest in the Great Pyramid in just a few hours, in accordance with the wishes of the priests.' The Grand Hierophant bent his head in a semblance of respect. 'It will be yet another loss to Khemri when you go into the darkness alongside him.'

'Alas, holy one, you are misinformed,' Ghazid replied smoothly, 'no doubt due to your grief and the duties of your station. Alas, Khetep has forbidden me from accompanying him into the underworld. As he lay dying on the battlefield, he commanded that I remain to guide his son through the early days of his reign.'

'I… see,' Nagash replied. 'Such a thing is unprecedented. It is a great honour, of course.'

'And a great responsibility,' Ghazid added. His blue eyes regarded Nagash steadily. 'Times of peace and prosperity tempt otherwise reasonable people to make rash decisions.'

The Grand Hierophant nodded gravely, and said, 'Wise words as ever, Ghazid. I can see why my father valued your counsel so much.'

Ghazid waved his hand dismissively. 'Your father never truly needed my counsel,' he replied. 'If anything, he often brooded too much over his decisions. If I did anything for him, it was to prompt him to take action when the situation warranted it. Better a swift blow to kill a viper before it can rear up and threaten to strike.' Nagash's eyes narrowed thoughtfully.

'Well said, Ghazid. Well said.'

The vizier smiled, saying, 'I am pleased to be of service, as always,' he replied, bowing his head once more. He stepped aside, gesturing to the court's open doorway. 'Your brother is receiving offerings from the city's embassies as we speak. He will be pleased to hear your news.'

Nagash nodded brusquely and resumed his swift pace, passing between the massive sandstone columns supporting the roof of Settra's Court and into the presence of the towering basalt statues of Asaph and Geheb, who stood to either side of the towering doorway. Geheb stood to the doorway's right, his left hand clutching the sickle of the harvest and his right hand held up in a gesture of warding, keeping out spirits of misfortune or malevolence. Asaph held her hands crossed over her breast in greeting, her glorious face serene and inviting. Gold leaf decorated the goddess's headdress and the bracelets upon her wrist, and shone from the curved blade in Geheb's hand. The idols were a display of enormous wealth and power. The rough basalt alone had taken ten years and cost the lives of more than four thousand slaves to bring it from the Brittle Peaks to the east, but they paled in comparison to the great hall that lay beyond.

Settra's Court was a rectangular chamber more than two hundred paces long and forty paces wide, bordered by great columns of polished marble that supported a ceiling forty-eight feet above the gleaming stone floor. The sandstone walls and floor had been faced with square sections of rich, purple marble, shot through with veins of onyx and gleaming gold that glowed in the light of scores of polished bronze oil lamps situated along the length of the chamber. The air inside the grand, echoing space was cool and fragrant, perfumed with costly incense burnt in braziers near the grand dais at the far end of the hall.

In ages past, Settra's Court had been the grandest audience chamber in all Nehekhara, surpassed only by the extravagance of the White Palace at Quatar some centuries after Settra's death. In these times, the entire nobility of Khemri could fit inside the lofty space, with room to spare for their families and slaves. Today, however, the audience chamber was crowded nearly to bursting, the murmur of voices mingling together in a steady, surf-like roar that echoed in the space between the huge pillars. Even Nagash was, for a moment, taken aback by the sheer spectacle that lay before him.

During Khetep's reign his tireless efforts to unite all of Nehekhara, if not as an empire then as a confederation of allied city-states, had involved so much negotiation and statecraft that the other Nehekharan cities had been obliged to create permanent embassies within the Living City. Delegates from each of these embassies filled the hall, each of them bearing lavish gifts to accompany Khetep into the afterlife and cement their relationship with his successor. From where he stood, Nagash could see a delegation from Bhagar in their black desert robes and head wrappings, whispering to one another in the company of a dozen slaves bearing urns of rich spices brought by caravan from the south. Nearby, the golden-skinned giants of

Ka-Sabar folded their massive arms and watched the pro-
ceedings intently, beside them open chests containing
ingots of polished bronze. Farther down the hall on the
right, the Grand Hierophant spied a crowd of courtiers and
noblemen clad in the silk robes and long kilts of distant
Lahmia. Their expressions were guarded as ever, but
Nagash noted the weariness that hooded their eyes and
dulled their expressions. No doubt many of the Lahmians
had escorted Thutep's young bride up the great river to
Khemri, a difficult journey in the best of times, but all the
more gruelling when it had to be done in haste. Idly, he
wondered what other gifts the rich and decadent Lahmians
had brought to honour his dead father.

At the moment, the attention of the Lahmians, and
indeed that of nearly everyone else in the chamber, was
focused on the great procession currently making its way
towards the grand dais. Ranks of noblemen clad in plain,
white kilts and shoulder capes were being led forward,
escorted by tall Ushabti with gleaming green skin and
long, fine black hair. Nagash recognised the devoted with
a start. They were the chosen warriors of Zandri, the architect of Khemri's defeat.

Khefru had noticed the procession as well, and whispered, 'What can this mean, master?'

Nagash gestured to his servant for silence. Frowning, he
slipped quickly to the right and began working his way
through the deep shadows behind the pillars along the
great wall. Dozens of royal slaves bustled past them in the
darkness, each intent on his own business and unaware of
the personage who moved in their midst.

'Nekumet, the Priest King of Zandri, is a thoughtful and
devious man,' Nagash hissed. 'He invited the war with
Khemri over those absurd trade disputes last year, and
now he seeks to supplant us as the pre-eminent power in
Nehekhara. This is but the next step in his grand strategy.'

The Grand Hierophant moved as swiftly as his station
allowed, reaching the far end of the audience chamber in

a few minutes, where the shadows were watched over by alert, keen-eyed Ushabti. The young bodyguards bowed their heads at Nagash's approach and let him slip quietly into the crowd of viziers and courtiers in attendance at the foot of the dais.

Nagash noted at once that the viziers were troubled men. They whispered quietly to one another, their hands moving in urgent, impassioned gestures as they discussed the events unfolding before them. Impatient, the Grand Hierophant pushed his way through the crowd of grey-bearded officials until he was nearly standing before the king's throne.

The throne of the Living City was ancient, carved from an elegant, fine-grained dark wood not found anywhere in Nehekhara. Legend said it had been brought from the jungles south and east of the Blessed Land, during the mythical Great Migration, while some claimed it had been built from wood taken from the south in the early years of Settra's reign. It rested at the top of the grand dais, beneath a massive statue of Ptra, the Great Father. Reaching nearly to the ceiling, the idol was made of sand-stone plated in sheets of hammered gold. The sun god's right hand was clasped against his chest in welcome, while the left hand was held out in a gesture of warding, protecting the Priest King of Khemri from the evils of the world.

There was also a lesser throne upon the dais, set off to the right and two steps lower, closer to the floor where Khemri's citizens attended upon their king. In the early days of the Living City, Khemri's patron god was Ptra, and under the auspices of the Sun God, Settra the Great was able to forge Nehekhara into a mighty empire. This was not enough for the mighty king, however, and in time, his power and his pride grew so great that he believed that he could find a way to defy death, and reign over the Blessed Land until the end of time. That was when the city's mortuary cult was born, more than seven hundred years ago, and in Settra's lifetime its high priest supplanted Ptra's, becoming Khemri's Grand Hierophant.

The ruling house of Khemri still owed a tremendous obligation, not just to Ptra, but to all the gods of the Blessed Land. Though the people of Nehekhara first encountered the gods near where the city of Mahrak now stood, many hundreds of leagues to the east, it was at Khemri, upon the banks of the River Vitae, that they entered into the great covenant that gave birth to the Blessed Land. Ptra and the gods swore to provide a paradise for the Nehekharans to live in, so long as the Nehekharans worshipped them and raised temples in their name. In addition every noble house would provide their firstborn as a gift to the gods, to serve as their priests and priestesses. In Khemri, the firstborn child was given to Ptra as the living embodiment of the great promise sworn between men and gods.

When Settra founded the mortuary cult he risked breaking the sacred covenant that made his glorious empire possible. Since he could not give his firstborn child to the gods, he chose to honour his promise in another way, by taking a priestess of Ptra as his wife. Settra's queen, the great Hatsushepra, was a daughter of the royal court of Lahmia. Ever since, a daughter of Lahmia was wed to the Priest King of Khemri to ensure the prosperity of the Blessed Land.

The queen's throne sat empty. Khetep's wife, Sofer, was praying at the temple of Djaf in preparation for joining her husband that afternoon, but there was someone standing *beside* the lesser throne, her hand resting almost possessively on its ornately carved arm. The strange breach of decorum caught the Grand Hierophant's eye, and he glanced up at the figure on the steps, less than a dozen feet away. Nagash's breath caught in his throat.

She was very young, Nagash noted at once, still a long way off the full flowering of her beauty. Her lithe body was clad in glorious yellow silk, brought all the way from the strange land that lay across the seas east of Lahmia. Bracelets of delicate, honey-coloured amber decorated her brown wrists, and a necklace of gold and fiery rubies encircled her slender neck. She had a small mouth and a pointed nose that accentuated her high, fine cheekbones and large, almond-shaped eyes that were the colour of polished emeralds. Despite her youth, she stood beside the empty throne with great poise and dignity. She was serene and utterly radiant. In time, Thutep's betrothed might become the greatest queen Nehekhara had ever known.

Nagash had never felt beguiled by a woman at any point in his life. The thought of emotional attachment or dependency was repellent to him, and could only be a hindrance to his ambitions, and yet, the moment he saw the queen, Nagash found himself gripped with a terrible, burning desire. His hands, hidden within the depths of his voluminous sleeves, clenched into grasping claws. The thought of the horrors he could inflict on such sanctified flesh nearly swept every other ambition out of the Grand Hierophant's mind. Only the thunderous cheer of the assembled throng brought Nagash out of his cruel reverie and focused him once more on the matter at hand.

The priest king's throne also stood empty. Thutep, the heir apparent, stood at the foot of the dais before a richly dressed dignitary from Zandri. Nagash's brother still wore the ceremonial finery of a royal prince, clad in a kilt and shoulder cape of white linen worked with gold thread. Gold bracelets were clasped around his brown arms, and a circlet set with a single ruby rested upon his brow. Though he did not possess the refined features of his father and older brother, Thutep's face was expressive and his eyes twinkled with easy charm. The ambassador from Zandri, whose sea-green robes were decorated with fine pearls and smooth, teardrop-shaped emeralds, bowed deeply to the king. The ambassador's dark hair and beard were tightly curled and glistened with fragrant oil, and his face was lit with a happy smile.

Nagash scowled as he recognised many of the faces of the young men who stood in serried ranks behind the ambassador. Many of the men bore livid bruises on their limbs or chests, and several sported fresh bandages spotted with blood. To a man, their faces were downcast, their chins hanging low in shame. They were the noblemen taken prisoner in the disastrous defeat just a short month ago. Nagash grasped the nature of Zandri's plan at once, and eyed his brother speculatively.

'The people of the Living City thank Nekumet, your great king, for this expression of charity and mercy,' Thutep declared, his hands clasped across his chest as he bowed, deeply. 'Let their return signal a new era of peace and prosperity for the people of the Blessed Land!'

Cheers rang out, once more. Khefru leaned close to his master, saying, 'Zandri is giving back all their prisoners without asking even a token ransom? It's madness!'

Nagash was careful to keep his bitter dismay secret.

'Not at all,' the Grand Hierophant said. 'The gesture wasn't made for Thutep's benefit, but for the other ambassadors.' When Khefru gave his master a blank stare, Nagash shot him an irritated look. 'Can't you see? It's a carefully calculated insult, and Nekumet's opening diplomatic gambit. By making a great show of handing back our noblemen without demanding a punishing ransom, he's telling the rest of Nehekhara that we're no threat to him.' He took in the entire chamber in a sharp sweep of his hand. 'Khetep is dead, and the jackals are circling, looking to grab whatever influence they can. Zandri just leapt to the front of the pack, and Thutep is too naïve to see it.'

Suddenly, Thutep turned, as though he'd caught the sound of his name. His gaze alighted on Nagash, and after a moment, his smile widened.

'Welcome, brother,' he said, beckoning to the Grand Hierophant. 'I'm glad you were here to witness the end of

our feud with Zandri. Now the past can be put aside and
forgotten.' Nagash favoured the ambassador from Zandri
with a cold, implacable stare.

'I have come to tell you that our father's body has been
prepared for its journey,' he said to his brother. 'We will
bear him to the Great Pyramid an hour before sunset, in
accordance with the wishes of the priests.'

The ambassador heard the news and his expression
grew sombre. He bowed his head to Thutep, and said,
'Although we marched to war against your father, he
was a bold warrior and a great king, and we mourn his
death along with the rest of Nehekhara. We would
therefore humbly offer a gift on behalf of the people of
Zandri, to accompany Khetep on his journey into the
afterlife.'

Thutep received the news with a grave nod. 'Very well,'
he said. 'Let us see this gift.'

The ambassador beckoned, and a stir went up at the far
end of the procession. The former prisoners, who were
awaiting Thutep's leave to return to their families, were
brushed to either side by a knot of burly, bare-chested
slaves, dragging a trio of black-garbed figures, whom they
deposited quickly at the ambassador's feet before hurriedly withdrawing.

Nagash studied the three figures carefully. They were tall
and slender, clad in a strange combination of tattered
woollen robes and some kind of dark leather armour that
covered their torsos and abdomens. Two of them were
female, with long, white hair that hung in unkempt tan-
gles down to their waists. The male's hair was black as jet,
almost as long and equally tangled. Their skin, what little
Nagash could see of it, was whiter than alabaster. Their
features were fine-boned and delicate, with pointed chins,
sharp noses and angular cheekbones. They were beautiful,
in a strange, almost dreadful way, and for all that they
appeared fragile compared to the Nehekharans around
them, they carried an aura of menace that somehow

unsettled him. The male glanced up at Nagash. His expression was slack, and his black eyes were vacant. All three of them had been heavily drugged.

Curious whispers spread through the court. Thutep stared at the strange creatures with a mix of fascination and revulsion, as though he had come upon a clutch of cobras.

'What are they?' he asked.

'They call themselves druchii, great one,' the ambassador said quickly. 'Their ship grounded off our coast during a terrible storm only a few months ago, and they have served as slaves in the royal household ever since.'

At the sound of the word 'slave', the male druchii turned his head to the ambassador and hissed something in a sibilant, snakelike tongue. The man from Zandri blanched at the sound, but quickly recovered.

'They are a wonder, are they not?' he said. 'It is our king's wish that they attend upon Khetep's spirit in the afterlife.' Thutep was taken aback by the offer. Material goods were one thing, an outsider offering slaves for the service of a dead king was something else.

'Well, it's certainly a generous gift,' he said slowly, unwilling to give offence.

Nagash watched the entire exchange with increasing interest. What was the Zandri delegation playing at? Obviously there was much more to this than met the eye. Then he noticed one of the females steady herself and bend her head in concentration. She tried to speak, slurring the words of her chilling language, but nevertheless Nagash sensed a faint wave of power emanate from her like an icy desert wind.

He stiffened, suddenly alert. Could it be?

The Grand Hierophant turned to Thutep.

'Zandri's offer is unprecedented,' he said, struggling to keep his voice even, 'but that does not make it unwelcome. I say we should accept their gift in the spirit it was given, great one.' Thutep beamed.

'So be it,' he declared. 'The slaves should be conducted to the temple,' he said to Nagash. 'Will you see to it?'

Nagash smiled.

'I should like nothing more,' he replied.

➤ THREE ➤

The Black Vizier

*The Oasis of Zedri, in the 62nd year of Qu'aph the Cunning
(-1750 Imperial Reckoning)*

SHOUTS OF ANGUISH and fear rent the air above the battle-field as unearthly darkness rolled like a swift tide down the rocky slope and across the bloodstained sands. Akhmen-hotep, Priest King of Ka-Sabar, watched the companies of enemy infantry find new strength as the terrible shadow swept over their heads. They surged forwards against the front ranks of the Bronze Host, chopping and stabbing fiercely at the giant warriors before them. Whether their new-found ferocity was born of courage, or terror, the king could not say.

The chariot beneath Akhmen-hotep lurched backwards as the driver cursed and wrestled with his frenzied horses. The terrible, droning sound pulsed and sawed rhythmically around the struggling warriors, making it difficult to think. The priest king saw warriors in twos and threes racing past his chariot, running away from the fighting, back towards the sunlit oasis. His companies were wavering, their courage pressed to the limit by the sudden change of circumstance.

Darkness engulfed the ranks of the enemy warriors and swept over the battle line. Men cried out in terror. More and more warriors in the rear ranks of Akhmen-hotep's companies turned and fled rather than face the sorcerous shadow.

The priest king cursed and looked around in growing desperation. The tide of blackness would sweep over him in seconds. He had to act quickly and regain control of his troops before their resolve collapsed entirely.

His Ushabti bodyguards were already reacting, drawing their chariots around the priest king in a tighter defensive formation. Akhmen-hotep caught sight of his remaining messengers, standing just a few yards behind his chariot and eyeing the coming darkness with palpable dread.

'Runners!' he called out, beckoning to them. 'Here! Quickly!'

The four boys gladly raced for the safety of the chariot. Akhmen-hotep held out his hand. 'Up here! Grab hold,' he shouted above the din. As they climbed aboard, he stole a quick glance to the east, searching for Suseb's company of chariots. If the front lines broke, the Lion and his men would have to countercharge Nagash's warriors to give the infantry time to retreat and re-form their units. The chariots, however, were nowhere to be seen. The dust was rising once again, and all the priest king could see were vague shapes dashing back and forth through the haze.

There was no time to waste. He had to issue orders to his men at once, or they would take matters into their own hands. The priest king tasted bile in the back of his throat as he searched for his trumpeter's chariot. Thankfully, the man had kept his head and ordered his driver to remain close to Akhmen-hotep's left.

'Sound the call to withdraw!' the priest king shouted. Five yards away, the trumpeter nodded and put his bronze horn to his lips.

The long, wailing note rang out across the battlefield, and then the tide of unearthly shadow swept over them.

Akhmen-hotep felt a chill wind brush across his bare neck, and the air above him rustled and clattered with the whir of insectile wings. For a few moments, the priest king was blind as the spreading cloud blotted out the blazing sun, and a wave of childlike terror closed like a vice around his throat. Sounds became strangely magnified in the darkness. He heard the savage curses of his driver and the terrified panting of the horses over the clash of arms, and the shouting of warriors from the battle-line dozens of yards distant. If anything, it sounded as though the fighting had redoubled its intensity, coming from every direction at once.

The priest king's eyes gradually adjusted to the change, and details of the battlefield took shape around him. The shroud of darkness above the warriors was in constant, seething motion, which allowed just enough light to seep through so that the plain was plunged into a sort of perpetual twilight. He could see the faint gleam of the spears and helmets of the Bronze Host, still struggling with the warriors of the Usurper. His companies were giving ground, slowly but surely, but the command to withdraw had restored some of their former spirit and discipline. Still, from what the priest king could see, there were scores upon scores of stragglers staggering across the battlefield. Akhmen-hotep took heart from the fact that many of them seemed to be heading back to their companies along the line, but others were milling about in apparent shock or confusion.

All was not lost, the priest king reckoned. Off to the south, he could still see the oasis, bathed in Ptra's light. If the host could fall back to the sunlight in good order, they could stand their ground and repel the Usurper's sudden assault, but Akhmen-hotep knew they could not do it without help.

The priest king glanced down at his messengers, and asked, 'Which of you is the swiftest runner?' All four boys looked to one another. Finally, the smallest of them raised his hand.

'They call me Dhekeru, great one,' he said, with a small amount of pride, 'because I am as fleet as a mountain deer.' Akhmen-hotep smiled.

'Dhekeru. That's good.' He laid a broad hand on the boy's shoulder. 'Go and tell the priests to hurry north and join us. The gods must be with us if we are to prevail.'

Dhekeru nodded. The young boy's face was set in a determined scowl, but the priest king could feel the runner's little body trembling in his grip. Akhmen-hotep gave the boy's shoulder a reassuring squeeze, and then Dhekeru was gone, leaping from the back of the chariot and dashing off into the gloom.

The priest king straightened and tried to take stock of the battle. The battle-line was a swirling mob of silhouettes just to the north. Experience told him that they had fallen back perhaps fifty yards so far, and were giving ground quickly. More screams of terror rang through the air, and confused shouts echoed up and down the line.

Akhmen-hotep frowned. There were still more stragglers stumbling across the plain behind the retreating army. Where were they all coming from?

Then, something heavy crashed against the side of the chariot to the priest king's right, next to his bowman. The archer let out a startled shout and stumbled backwards as a figure tried to climb over the bronze-armoured side. Akhmen-hotep saw a bloody hand reach for the bowman and grab hold of his leather armour, and then, to the priest king's horror, the figure hauled back with surprising strength and pulled the archer over the side.

Horses screamed in terror. Akhmen-hotep heard the driver curse fearfully and crack his whip, jolting the chariot forwards. The priest king staggered, groping for the khopesh by his side as the silhouetted figure dragged itself further over the rim of the chariot and reached out to him. A terrible stink emanated from the attacker, and Akhmen-hotep smelled bitter blood and ruptured bowels, like a freshly killed corpse.

Then the figure drew nearer with a gurgling hiss, and the priest king peered through the gloom and realised that was exactly what it was.

It was one of the Usurper's tormented soldiers, clad only in a ragged, bloodstained kilt. Its chest was misshapen, having been crushed by the bronze-shod wheel of a chariot, and a spear point had torn open the warrior's cheek before deflecting downward into the base of its neck, leaving a gaping, bloody hole. A flap of bloody skin dangled from the side of the creature's pallid face, and the priest king could glimpse pale bone as its jaw gaped in another reptilian hiss.

Before the creature could reach him, Akhmen-hotep's Ushabti stepped between them with a liquid growl and a blur of his ritual blade. Bronze rang against bone and the undead monster fell back over the side of the chariot. Its severed head bounced once off the vehicle's wooden bed and disappeared into the darkness.

The sounds of battle raged all around them as the rest of Akhmen-hotep's retinue found itself under attack. A chariot raced past, heading south, with a trio of clawing fiends hanging from its sides. The priest king realised that one of the creatures was wearing the leather and bronze harness of his own army.

Akhmen-hotep choked back a cry of horror. Nagash's unholy powers were far greater than he imagined. The dead rose from the bloodied earth to do his foul bidding!

One of the messengers let out a terrified scream. The priest king whirled, but the boy was gone, snatched into the darkness. The other children wailed in terror, crowding towards the front of the chariot. At the priest king's side, his devoted bodyguard stood with his feet wide apart and his ritual sword raised, ready to protect his master against any foe, living or otherwise.

They heard the sound of splintering wood and the frenzied cries of maddened horses off to their left. Akhmen-hotep saw that one of the chariot drivers had lost control of his animals and the panicked beasts had turned too tightly, flipping the chariot onto its side. His stomach fell as he saw a flash of bronze cartwheel across the sand. It was the trumpeter's signal-horn. More than a dozen walking corpses were converging on the broken chariot and its stunned occupants. They reached the chariot's archer first, chopping his unconscious form to pieces with their stone axes.

Akhmen-hotep heard the chariot's driver shriek in terror, but then the Ushabti assigned to protect the trumpeter reared up among the undead warriors with a leonine roar and laid about them with his ritual sword. The giant warrior sent broken bodies spinning through the air with each sword-stroke, reaping a terrible harvest among the blasphemous throng, but more and more of the fallen warriors were closing in from all sides, brandishing bloodied weapons or reaching for the devoted bodyguard with grasping, claw-like hands.

Akhmen-hotep fought to keep his balance as his chariot turned sharply about and began to head back in the direction of the oasis. He craned his neck, trying to see what was happening along the battle-line. From what he could see, the withdrawal had ground to a halt, and his companies were being attacked from in front and behind, sowing deadly confusion through the ranks. The priest king clenched his fists in frustration; with his trumpeter gone, he had no way of communicating with his men. He thought of poor, brave Dhekeru, racing unarmed across a plain swarming with the walking dead, and his expression turned bleak.

There was nothing more he could do. Their survival rested in the hands of the gods.

* * *

BACK ALONG THE shadowed ridge, the air trembled with another seething, locust-like drone. Each of the silent tents surrounding the army's central pavilion contained an upright sarcophagus of polished basalt, attended upon by a cowering knot of dull-eyed slaves. The rising drone spurred these wretched figures to fearful action, clawing at the heavy stone lids and pulling them aside.

Serpentine hisses and cruel, hungry laughter welled up from the depths of the stone coffins, causing the slaves to fall upon their knees and press their faces to the rocky ground. Pale, black-veined hands grasped the rims of the sarcophagi, and one by one, a score of monsters who wore the shapes of men climbed from their cold beds and stepped out into the welcoming darkness.

They moved with the arrogance of princes, who knew no law but their own. Their skin was white as chalk, and their lips and fingertips were bluish-black with the stain of old, dead blood. Rings of gold and silver glittered on their clawed fingers, and jewelled circlets rested upon their alabaster brows. All of them were garbed for war, with studded leather bindings covering their torsos and skull-caps of hammered bronze.

One among them was taller than the rest, gaunt and vulture-like even in his fine armour and heavy, black cape. His tent stood at the right hand of the great pavilion, and he wore the ornate circlet of a vizier upon his bald head. The noble's cheeks were sunken, emphasising his sharply angled cheekbones and pointed chin.

Arkhan the Black looked out upon the battlefield and was pleased with what he saw. His lips drew back in a malevolent grin, revealing a mouthful of stained, pointed teeth. The Vizier of Khemri ran a blue-black tongue over those jagged points as he felt the unspoken commands of his master.

'It shall be done,' he whispered in a thin, croaking voice. Then he beckoned to a messenger waiting in the shadow of the master's pavilion. 'Go to the Master of Skulls and tell him to begin,' he told the frightened boy. Then he turned and strode swiftly to a waiting squadron of heavy horsemen formed up on the slope before his tent.

Horses and riders alike hung their heads and trembled at the undead lord's approach. Arkhan's mount was a half-mad black mare, branded with sorcerous glyphs that bound it to his will. It rolled its eyes fearfully at its master's approach, tossing its head and clashing its chisel-like teeth as the warrior climbed gracefully into the saddle. The vizier turned to his men, smiling cruelly at the way they flinched beneath his stare.

'The Bronze Host has been laid against the anvil,' he growled. 'Now comes the hammer.'

Arkhan pointed a clawed finger at his trumpeter, and said, 'Signal the cavalry to wheel right. We will charge their left flank and put them to flight.'

The Usurper's vizier drew a wicked-looking bronze scimitar from its scabbard and put his heels to his horse's flanks. It lurched forwards with a tormented squeal, and the ranks of heavy horsemen followed suit. All along the ridge-line, Nagash's immortal champions took charge of their warriors and heeded the wailing call of the trumpet.

ARKHAN'S MESSENGER RACED between the funereal tents and picked his way across the rocky summit until he disappeared behind the ridge's northern face, out of sight of the battling armies. There, along the opposite slope, waited a dozen wheeled war machines built of heavy cedar logs and ensorcelled bronze nails.

A single, dust-covered tent waited beside the ancient trade road, which ran squarely between the line of war machines and their silent crews. A short, broad-shouldered man with small, dark eyes set in a round, jowly face emerged from the tent at the boy's approach, and replied to the vizier's message with a single grunt. He was a master engineer, chosen by Nagash to master the secrets of the fearsome machines as depicted in ancient manuscripts looted from a necropolis in far-off Zandri. For his success, Nagash tore out the man's tongue so that he could not share what he had learned with anyone else.

The Master of Skulls dismissed the messenger and walked up the road. The crews of the war machines went to work at once. Some bent to the task of cranking back the throwing arm of each catapult, while others turned to the dozen large wicker baskets and pulled away their lids, revealing heaped piles of leering skulls marked with clusters of arcane glyphs.

Within minutes, the catapult arms had been locked back, and their leather baskets filled with their grisly ammunition. When all was ready, the engineer raised his hand and let out a wordless, ululating cry.

Flickering green fire burst from each of the catapult baskets, and the chief of each crew hurriedly pulled back on the lanyards. The catapult arms banged against their braces, and hundreds of fiery, shrieking skulls streaked through the darkness over the ridge.

AKHMEN-HOTEP BROUGHT his khopesh down upon the skull of one of his fallen soldiers as the corpse-thing tried to claw its way onto his chariot. The enchanted bronze sword sheared away the top of the warrior's head, splattering brain matter onto the king's bare shins. The thing collapsed, sliding from the back of the chariot, while the king's bodyguard hacked apart two more that were trying to climb aboard from the other side.

The king and his retinue had been retreating steadily across the plain, hoping to find the city priests making their way north from the edge of the oasis. Corpses assailed them from all sides. Many were crushed beneath the chariot's wheels, but others tried to leap upon the backs of the horses or get inside the chariot. The last two messenger boys had been dragged away by the undead creatures, and the horses were staggering from exhaustion and scores of minor wounds. Most of his Ushabti were still with him, as far as he could see, but they were almost half a mile away from the struggling army, and still there was no sign of Ka-Sabar's holy men.

Suddenly, the priest king heard a strange, piping chorus of unearthly cries coming from the direction of the ridge. Akhmen-hotep looked back the way they'd come, and saw a flickering rain of fiery green orbs arcing down onto the struggling companies.

The hail of screaming skulls scattered widely over the clashing armies, falling among friend and foe alike, but where the warriors of Khemri were inured to their horror, the Bronze Host was not. The grisly missiles exploded among their ranks, showering them with blazing fragments and filling their ears with shrieks of agony and despair. Beset on all sides by warriors living and dead, including the bloodied corpses of their kinsmen, the Bronze Host had been pushed far beyond the limits of its courage. Cries of horror went up from the men, and the embattled companies began to disintegrate as the warriors turned their backs upon the foe and ran for their lives.

Too late, Akhmen-hotep saw the trap that the Usurper had laid for him. Nagash had drawn his forces across the plain, through a field littered with Khemri dead, and the panicked warriors of the Bronze Host would retreat into the murderous arms of those they had already slain. The priest king's mind reeled at the disaster unfolding before him.

Just as all hope was lost, the piercing note of a trumpet sounded on the right flank, and the rumble of chariot wheels shook the ground behind the retreating army. Suseb the Lion had seen the peril as well, and he led his warriors in a sweeping charge across the battlefield. Akhmen-hotep watched as the champion and his two hundred chariots rumbled out of the haze, their scythed wheels tearing through the undead warriors caught in their path. Archers fired from the backs of the chariots, sending bronze-tipped arrows through the skulls of the slow-moving monsters as they rode past.

The chariots thundered off to the left flank, leaving a swathe of mangled bodies in their wake. Many of the army's companies were in full flight, but at least Akhmen-hotep had a chance to rally the survivors and perhaps turn the tide of battle once more, if only he could find the damned priests!

'Keep going!' the priest king called to his driver. The charioteer lashed his whip and drove his staggering horses into a trot, heading further south towards the oasis.

ARKHAN THE BLACK watched a second wave of shrieking skulls streak through the air overhead and fall upon the enemy's fleeing ranks. The centre had broken, but the flanks were still holding out against the onslaught. Somewhere behind the enemy lines he heard the wail of trumpets, and the muted thunder of chariot wheels. Was Ka-Sabar's heavy cavalry making a hasty retreat, or a desperate countercharge? At this distance, there was no way to tell.

Gripping the reins, the vizier surveyed the twenty squadrons of heavy horse massed along the western end of the ridge. Five hundred yards to the south, the left flank of the enemy army was locked in a relentless struggle with the Khemri infantry. They were heedless of the danger gathering like a cobra on the slope before them.

They would sweep down in an unstoppable wave, riding through their troops and crashing against the weakened ranks of the enemy like a thunderbolt. The infantry would break, and the slaughter would begin. Arkhan imagined the spray of hot blood against his skin, and shivered with anticipation.

Arkhan raised his curved sword and bared his blackened teeth. 'Charge!' he cried, and brazen trumpets wailed. Slowly at first, and then gathering speed in an avalanche of flesh and bronze, five thousand horsemen bore down on the unsuspecting warriors of Ka-Sabar.

Trumpets howling like the souls of the damned, the horsemen of Khemri thundered down the rocky slope towards the beleaguered companies of the Bronze Host. Arkhan the Black lashed at his enchanted mount, drawing ahead of his charging warriors in his hunger to bathe in human blood. The air rang with frenzied shouts as the heavy horsemen gave vent to their anger and fear and hurled themselves into the storm of battle.

The wings of the Bronze Host had curled inwards during the course of the battle as the warriors sought to encircle the smaller Khemri army; its battle-line curved into a long, glinting crescent, with the ends still struggling to force their opponents in towards the army's centre. This presented the charging horsemen with an opportunity to turn the tables on the spearmen of the enemy's left flank, striking the companies both from the front and the side.

The warriors of Ka-Sabar were tough and resolute fighters, however, skilled in the arts of war. Even as Arkhan's cavalry reached the base of the ridge, the enemy companies sensed the danger bearing down on them and tried to shift their lines to face the new threat. With his one good eye, Arkhan saw the ranks of spearmen waver and fragment as they tried to disengage from the relentless attacks of the Khemri infantry and prepare for the shock of the cavalry attack, but Nagash's footmen, both living and dead, drove inexorably against the struggling enemy formations. They dragged down shields and impaled themselves on spears, forcing their way among the giant warriors and breaking their cohesion still further. Seconds before impact, Arkhan saw the looks of despair on his enemies' faces as they realised that their frantic manoeuvres had been for nought.

Laughing cruelly, Arkhan led his horsemen through the thin ranks of his infantry and into the midst of the warriors of Ka-Sabar. Khemri footmen, too exhausted or too preoccupied to avoid the charge, were smashed aside by the weight of the horses or trampled beneath their hooves. Their deaths were meaningless to him, for within moments their corpses would rise and begin the assault anew.

The vizier's first blow was struck against one of his own men, his scimitar flashing down and smiting a staggering axe-man who stood between him and his chosen foe. The blade bit deep at the juncture of the man's neck and shoulder, spinning him off his feet with a scream and a welter of blood. The smell of it maddened Arkhan. Roaring hungrily he spurred his horse forward into the thicket of spears before him, his blade sweeping left and right in devastating strokes. All around him, the charge of the Khemri horsemen crashed home, fracturing the companies into knots of desperately struggling men. Swords and axes flashed, hacking down at spear hafts and crashing against the edges of bronze-rimmed shields. Spearmen fell with shattered skulls or torn throats, or clutching the stumps of severed arms. Horses thrashed and screamed, impaled on bronze spearheads or pulled to the ground by the fearsome strength of the giant warriors. To Arkhan's right, a veteran spearman grabbed the reins of a rearing warhorse and jerked its head with such power that its neck broke with a brittle crunch of bones, and then stabbed his spear through the rider's chest as the dead mount collapsed to the ground.

Even astride his powerful horse, Arkhan found himself looking his towering opponents nearly eye-to-eye. Even as they reeled from the force of the cavalry charge, they struck at the vizier from every side. A flashing spear point drove into his left side, just beneath the ribs, and another punched through his right thigh and dug into his horse's ribs. Hissing like a viper, Arkhan decapitated a man to his right and took a hand off a spearman to his left. His sword flashed and spun, scattering ribbons of steaming blood in a wide arc as he toppled one foe after another. The necromantic power burning in his veins lent him equal strength and greater speed than his enemies, and his foes toppled like wheat before the vizier's bloodstained blade.

The enemy recoiled from Arkhan's terrible might, shouting the names of their gods or crying out in dismay. A flung spear struck the vizier full in the chest, piercing his lung. He tore it free with his left hand and hurled it back with a bloody sneer, and then stood high in the saddle and began to chant in a harsh, sibilant hiss. The air around Arkhan crackled with invisible power as he spoke the necromantic spell, and the men he'd slain began to stir. Streaming blood from their terrible wounds, the dead warriors climbed numbly to their feet amid the horrified cries of their kinsmen.

The shock of the terrible charge and the fate of their fallen brothers were too much for the enemy to endure. The spearmen broke, piling back upon the company next to them and disrupting the formation in their haste to escape. Arkhan's horsemen rode the spearmen down as they tried to flee, spurring their horses forward into the press and hacking away with their blood-stained swords. The panic of the fleeing men was contagious, affecting every warrior they came into contact with. The advancing cavalry had barely reached the second enemy company when it, too, wavered and broke in the face of the onslaught. They, in turn, fell back against the third company in line, their numbers so great that even stalwart warriors were swept away in the press.

Exultant, the horsemen continued their advance, sowing terror and panic among their foes. Several squadrons had already worked their way around the growing mob of fleeing troops and had encountered a screen of light cavalry. The enemy riders fired a volley of arrows point-blank into the flanks of the Khemri horsemen, toppling more than a score of men from their saddles or sending their mounts thrashing to the ground. One of Arkhan's squadrons wheeled to face the light cavalry and made to charge them, but the horsemen of Ka-Sabar broke off at once, galloping south for the safety of the oasis.

The third company was struggling to hold together against the tide of their retreating comrades. The formation had already fragmented into large bands of isolated warriors, but these men were made of sterner stuff than their fellows, and struggled to stand their ground against all odds. Horsemen circled them like wolves, darting in and striking a few swift blows before dashing away again, but the longer reach of the spear and the strength of the men of Ka-Sabar worked to their advantage. Dead men and horses were piling up around the grim spearmen, slowing down the weight of Arkhan's charge and allowing the retreating warriors the opportunity to escape. Cursing hatefully, the vizier weighed his options. The cavalry's charge had all but spent its strength. Should he withdraw, regroup, and charge again, or summon his fellow immortals and grind these stubborn holdouts into the dust?

Arkhan hesitated, and in those few moments his opportunity was lost. With the thunder of bronze-rimmed wheels and the deadly hum of bowstrings, a dark mass of armoured chariots charged out of the haze from behind the centre of the retreating enemy army, rushing to the rescue of the wavering left flank.

Arrows buzzed through the milling crowd of horsemen, wreaking deadly havoc among their ranks, and then the scythe-armed chariots plunged into their midst. The whirling blades mounted on the chariot axles, each as long as the blade of a sword, tore through the legs of the Khemri horses, mortally wounding dozens and filling the air with their chilling screams. Great bronze scimitars flashed in the hands of the warriors riding in the backs of these heavy war machines, cutting down horsemen and walking corpses alike.

The force of the enemy charge shocked Arkhan's horsemen. The bronze-sheathed chariots of Ka-Sabar were unlike the lighter, swifter machines found in the armies of other Nehekharan cities, and in the hands of a competent commander their impact was devastating. A cheer went up from the Bronze Host at their sudden appearance, and the wavering spear companies appeared to regain a measure of their lost courage. Arkhan knew that he had to act quickly before the chariots caused so much damage that he would have to withdraw back to the ridge. The thought of facing his master and admitting his defeat was too terrible to contemplate.

Arkhan uttered a savage curse and spurred his wounded horse forward, galloping headlong into the midst of the enemy chariots. Arrows buzzed angrily around him. One buried itself in his shoulder, but he scarcely felt the blow. He was searching among the thundering war machines, seeking the champion who led them. If he could find that man and slay him it would surely dismay the rest.

He saw the man almost at once: a lean, dark-skinned giant at the forefront of the enemy attack, wielding a two-handed khopesh as though it were no more than a hollow reed. The champion was already splashed with gore, and a dozen horses and their riders lay smashed and bloodied in his wake.

Arkhan knew that this was Suseb the Lion. It could be no other. Ka-Sabar's Master of Horse was accounted as one of the greatest living warriors in all Nehekhara.

The vizier smiled coldly. He had been murdering men like Suseb for a hundred years before the Lion was even born.

Across the battlefield, the mighty champion caught sight of the vizier's dark form. The Lion's eyes widened at the sight of the pale immortal.

Arkhan raised his bloody scimitar in challenge and put his spurs to his horse's flanks.

⇥ FOUR ⇤

The Fickle Tide

*The Oasis of Zedri, in the 62nd year of Qu'aph the Cunning
(-1750 Imperial Reckoning)*

AKHMEN-HOTEP HEARD the thunder of hooves to the west
and gritted his teeth in helpless rage. Pakh-amn's light cavalry was retreating from the Usurper's sudden attack. The
shouts and screams from the far end of the battle-line had
merged into a formless, toneless roar of pure noise. It was
not the dull metal clatter of battle, but the sound of pure
butchery. If the left flank had not already collapsed, it was
teetering on the brink.

Men were pouring past the priest king's chariot in an
apparently endless flood, their faces slack with terror and
exhaustion. Behind them came an inexorable tide of walking death, a new army of undead flesh, animated by a
soulless, evil will.

He had shouted himself hoarse, trying to rally his men
and return them to the fight. At first, he enjoyed some success, collecting stragglers here and there and ordering them

back into threadbare companies, but as soon as the shambling corpses appeared, they lost their nerve once more.

Unless something could be done to hold the undead creatures at bay, the Bronze Host would be utterly destroyed, and if the fearsome warriors of Ka-Sabar were no match for Nagash the Usurper, Nehekhara was surely doomed.

There had been no sign of the priests in the long retreat across the plain. Akhmen-hotep resigned himself to the fact that young Dhekeru had stood no chance against the horrors lurking in the darkness. All that remained was to reach the oasis and make his stand, hoping that the foul stain of darkness would not spread further.

Then, a pearlescent glow flared to life, just a few yards ahead of the retreating chariot. The driver called out in alarm, but the priest king laid a reassuring hand on the frightened man's shoulder. He could hear the sound of voices mingled in a steady, determined chant.

'The priests!' he cried, his heart lifting. His message had won through after all!

Within moments, Akhmen-hotep and his Ushabti led their chariots past a line of Neru's white-robed priests, all standing fearlessly in the path of the oncoming creatures and chanting the Invocation of the Vigilant Sentinel. The pearly light of the moon goddess radiated from their skin, pushing back the darkness and giving the frightened warriors a place of refuge. Beyond the line of stalwart priests, Akhmen-hotep spied their High Priestess, Khalifra, offering prayers and sacrifice to her goddess. Farther off, he saw Memnet and the priests of Ptra, gathered in grim debate with Sukhet and the priests of Phakth.

A booming, bull-like voice rose above the distant roar of battle and the confused shouts of the retreating warriors. Hashepra, the iron-thewed high priest of Geheb, was bellowing to the soldiers of the Bronze Host.

'Darkness comes and darkness goes, but the great earth is not moved,' he called. 'Stand fast, like the mountains, and Geheb will bless you with the strength to defeat your enemies!' The power of Hashepra's voice and his stern, intimidating presence had the desired effect on the men, restoring their courage and stopping their headlong flight. Slowly, but surely, discipline was being restored, but would it be in time?

Strange, unearthly moans rose from the gloom as the first of the undead reached the barrier of moonlight cast by the priests of Neru. The creatures hesitated, raising their bloody limbs to shield their faces from the glow. They hissed and cried, but for the moment they could advance no further. Akhmen-hotep offered a prayer of thanks to the Heavenly Consort, and then directed his driver to take him to Memnet.

The priests of sun and sky put aside their heated words at the priest king's approach, but Akhmen-hotep could see the strain etched deeply on their faces. He dismounted from his chariot before it had fully stopped and rushed up to the grim-faced men.

'Thank all the gods that you got my message,' he began. Memnet frowned.

'Message? There was no message.'

'When we saw the darkness unleashed, we knew that we would be called upon,' Sukhet interjected, 'though none of us could have expected the blasphemous sorceries the Usurper now possesses.'

'I see,' Akhmen-hotep said quietly. 'What about this foul darkness? Can you not disperse it?'

'It is all we can do to keep it from spreading further,' Sukhet snapped, giving the king a sour look. 'It is no mere cloud of dust or ash, but a living thing, perhaps a swarm of beetles or locusts, marshalled by diabolical intent. It rides upon the wind, and cannot be easily swept aside.'

'Then what of the Great Father's light?' Akhmen-hotep asked the Grand Hierophant. 'Can you not invoke Ptra to burn this devilry from the sky?'

'Do you not think I have tried, brother?' Memnet said bleakly. The Grand Hierophant's face was pale, and his eyes were wide with fear. 'I have made entreaties. I have made sacrifices. I fed my body servants to the flames, but Ptra does not heed me!'

Akhmen-hotep shook his head, and said, 'You're not making sense. The covenant–'

'What the Grand Hierophant means is that we are being interfered with,' Sukhet said darkly. 'I do not know how.' He cast a worried look in the direction of the distant ridge. 'There is sorcery at work unlike anything I have ever known. It is the foulest sort of magic, the work of the devils!'

'Then you must strike at it with all the power you have available!' Akhmen-hotep said. 'Call upon the lightning! Sear the sky with Ptra's fire! Strike at the Usurper with all the wrath of the gods!'

'You don't know what you are asking,' Sukhet answered, genuinely shaken by the priest king's demand. 'The price of such power–'

'Pay it!' the king commanded. 'No cost is too great to rid the Blessed Land of such a monster! He has bled our cities white, terrorised our people and emptied our treasuries, and if we are defeated here, do you imagine that Nagash will be content with a ransom of gold, or ingots of bronze? Have you forgotten what he did to Zandri, back in the days of our fathers? That will pale in comparison to the vengeance he will wreak upon us for our defiance.'

'But the omens,' Memnet moaned. 'I tried to warn you. While the sunlight shone, we had our way, but now–'

Akhmen-hotep took a menacing step towards his older brother.

'Then make it shine again,' he snarled.

The Grand Hierophant started to protest, but suddenly a faint, skirling sound rose wild and clear above the tumult, echoing from the dunes to the west. Heads turned, searching for the source of the sound. Sukhet, whose ears were keener by the grace of his god, cocked his head attentively.

'Horns,' he said, 'but made of bone, not bronze.'

'Another trick of the Usurper?' Memnet asked.

'No, not this time,' Akhmen-hotep said. His face creased in a triumphant smile. 'The princes of Bhagar have arrived at last!'

THREE-QUARTERS OF a mile distant, hidden from sight by the Usurper's unnatural shadow, four thousand robed horsemen rode out of the blinding desert sands, hastening to the fight. The merchant princes of Bhagar had sent every fighting man they could spare to aid their allies in the struggle against Nagash, and there were no better horsemen in all the Blessed Land. In ancient times, they had been bandits, preying upon Nehekharan caravans and slipping like ghosts back into the dunes, but in the time of Settra they had been tamed and welcomed into the Empire. Since then, they had prospered as traders, but they had never forgotten their warlike ways.

The horsemen of Bhagar knew the Great Desert as a man knows his first wife. They were privy to its changing ways and its fierce temper, its hidden gifts and shadowy secrets, and yet, as they rode to the aid of Ka-Sabar, they were bedevilled again and again by fierce sandstorms and false trails that cost them precious days amid the burning sands. When their outriders caught sight of the spreading darkness staining the horizon, they had feared the worst, and pushed their fiery desert steeds to the utmost.

Led by the bold Shahid ben Alcazzar, first among equals in Bhagar and called the Red Fox by his kin, the desert horsemen plunged fearlessly into the unnatural darkness hanging over the great plain, and found themselves behind a swirling mass of cavalrymen threatening the Bronze Host's left flank. Calling upon the spirits of their ancestors, they winded their bone war horns and raced into battle. The lead riders drew short, barbed javelins from quivers hanging by their knees and let fly into the packed mass of heavy horsemen, while those further behind unlimbered powerful composite horse bows and thick, red-fletched arrows. The powerful missiles could punch through a wooden shield at forty paces, and the riders knew how to use them to deadly effect.

The sudden attack sowed death and confusion among the enemy ranks, and the squadrons of heavy horsemen scattered before the onslaught. Swift as a pack of wolves, the desert raiders wheeled about and dashed back the way they'd come, leaving a hundred dead cavalrymen littering the bloody ground. Then, after a hundred yards they stopped, turned about, and came at the enemy once more, weaving effortlessly among the heavier warhorses and toppling men from their saddles. Furious, the Khemri horsemen tried to give chase, and the desert raiders began, slowly but surely, to draw them off to the west, away from the embattled spear companies.

ARKHAN HEARD THE wailing horns of the desert riders just as he began his charge, and realised the peril his warriors were in. They were caught between two enemy forces, and if the chariots could regroup and charge his men once more, they could very well break under the pressure. Without warning, the tide of battle threatened to turn against them.

Hissing like an adder, the vizier bore down on Suseb the Lion. The champion of the Bronze Host likewise ordered his chariot forward, raising his mighty khopesh. The archer beside him raised his bow, but Suseb stopped him with a forbidding glare. This would be a battle between heroes, or so the Lion thought.

As the distance between them dwindled, Arkhan began to chant. He felt the dark power bubbling in his veins, and at the last moment he stretched out his left hand and unleashed a storm of crackling ebon bolts at the occupants of the chariot. Screams and shouts of fury answered the vizier as he veered away from the onrushing chariot and its scything blades.

After a dozen yards, he swung about and saw that the champion's armoured chariot had come to a halt. Its driver lay at Suseb's feet, his body a smoking husk, and the Lion was struggling to untangle the chariot's reins from the corpse's shrivelled hands. The champion's archer, meanwhile, leapt from the back of the chariot and stood between Arkhan and his foe. The vizier laughed at the sight and spurred his mount forward.

The bowman was a man of courage. His face was a mask of rage, but he moved with calm efficiency, drawing a long reed arrow to his cheek and letting fly at the onrushing immortal. Arkhan jerked the reins at the last minute, trying to dodge aside, and the arrow struck him in the left arm instead of burying itself in his heart.

Before the archer could draw another arrow, Arkhan was upon him. His scimitar hissed through the air, and the bowman's headless body fell forward into the dust.

The archer's death had given the Lion the time he needed, however, and with an angry cry he lashed the reins and the chariot lurched into motion once more. Suseb handled the huge machine masterfully, turning it in a tight circle, but not before Arkhan dashed past. Once again, his scimitar whirred in a decapitating arc, but the blade shivered in his hand as though he'd struck solid teak. The Lion, it appeared, ranked high in the earth god's favour.

Despite the speed of Arkhan's charge he still felt the wind of Suseb's blade slicing through the air a fraction of an inch behind him. He continued on past the champion for less than ten feet before hauling furiously on the reins. His steed tossed its head angrily and pawed at the earth as the vizier hauled it back around for another pass.

Suseb was still struggling to control the chariot with one hand while looking over his shoulder at Arkhan. He was bringing the war machine about, but too slowly. Grinning like a devil, Arkhan bore down on the Lion's back, sword poised above his head. Once again he began to chant. Wisps of foul, black vapour began to curl from the edge of his blade.

The Lion watched the vizier approach with an expression of stoic resolve. At the last moment, Arkhan's sense of triumph turned to trepidation. When Suseb let go of the chariot's reins he knew that he'd been tricked. The champion became a blur of motion, spinning on his heel and bringing his massive sword around in a whirling, backhanded blow.

It was only the immortal's unnatural reflexes that saved him. He tore at the reins, once more, and the warhorse's charge was halted for the space of a single moment. Suseb's blade fell in a glittering arc, passing before Arkhan instead of through him, and sliced through the animal's thick neck instead. The horse's headless body lurched drunkenly to the right, sending mount and rider crashing full-force into the Lion's chariot. There was the sound of splintering wood and tearing metal. Arkhan struck the side of the war machine in a bone-crushing impact and knew no more.

A CHEER WENT up from the beleaguered ranks of the Bronze Host at the sound of Bhagar's war horns. Their allies had arrived in the nick of time, just where they were needed. Akhmen-hotep felt a wild surge of hope. Could they snatch victory from the jaws of defeat?

The priest king regarded Memnet and Sukhet once more.

'You see? The gods have not abandoned us!' he said. 'Now it is up to us to show that we are worthy of their aid. Call upon their power, and let us destroy the Usurper once and for all!'

A terrible look came over Sukhet's face as he heard Akhmen-hotep's plea, but he nodded nevertheless.

'So be it,' he said in a leaden voice, and led his priests some distance away to begin the invocations.

The priest king turned to Memnet, and asked, 'And what of you, Grand Hierophant? Will the Great Father Ptra aid us in our time of need?'

Memnet stepped close to the king.

'Don't take that tone with me, little brother,' he said in a low voice. 'Did you not hear Sukhet? The gods are not soldiers to be commanded, like your warriors. They will exact a heavy price for such power, and *we* will be the ones to pay it, not you!'

The king was unmoved.

'If you fear to call upon your god, Memnet, then go and bend your knee to Nagash. Those are the only choices any of us have left.'

Memnet's face twisted into a mask of rage, so sudden and so intense that the Ushabti took a protective step towards the king, his fleshy hands clenching into trembling fists. The Grand Hierophant's jaw bunched angrily, but when he spoke, it wasn't to utter imprecations against the priest king. Instead, he began to chant in a heated voice.

Akhmen-hotep saw beads of sweat gather on Memnet's round face, and then felt a puff of hot air brush against his skin that quickly became a whirling, restless wind. The clacking, chattering cloud of darkness overhead roiled like a stormy sea. Narrow spears of fierce sunlight stabbed through the churning mass, touching the ground for an instant before the shadow swallowed them. Black, smouldering shapes fell to the earth around Akhmen-hotep and his warriors in a steadily building rain. The king realised that they were the husks of tomb scarabs, each as large as a grown man's fist.

Memnet's voice grew louder, rising over the howling wind in counterpoint to Sukhet's piercing, nasal voice. The priest of Phakth, the sky god, sounded as though he were in terrible pain.

Akhmen-hotep started as he felt his ears pop, and then he heard his soldiers cry out in fear and awe as a forked bolt of lightning crashed down on the distant ridge.

The crash of thunder that followed sounded like the end of the world.

ARKHAN'S EYES SNAPPED open at the crescendo of noise, the thunder's concussion so great that for a moment the vizier thought someone had struck him.

He was lying on his back a few yards from the twisted wreckage of his enemy's chariot. The impact of his dead horse had splintered the war machine's left wheel and flipped the heavy vehicle onto its side, and the four horses that had drawn it were galloping away in terror, dragging the broken yoke behind them. Horses and men were screaming all around him in the gloom, and his cavalry, beset from two sides, were struggling to survive.

Cursing, Arkhan struggled to regain his feet. His right leg was weak and stiff. Belatedly, he realised that a dagger-sized shard of bronze was jutting from his right thigh. He tore it free with his left hand and forced himself upright. A shudder passed through the immortal, and he felt the familiar, dreadful ache begin in his guts. The exertions and the wounds he'd received had consumed much of his master's vital elixir, and a deadly lassitude began to steal along his limbs.

Feeling a tremor of fear, Arkhan surveyed the wreckage of Suseb's chariot. Had the champion survived?

He saw the mass of wood and metal shift. Twisted bronze plates groaned and popped, and Arkhan felt a surge of dread as the Lion's head and shoulders struggled into view.

Desperate, the vizier raised his sword and chanted the Incantation of Summoning. The dark magic was fickle, resisting his control due to his weakened state, but three of Arkhan's dead cavalrymen stirred and struggled to their feet.

'Kill him!' the vizier commanded, pointing to Suseb.

The undead warriors lurched forwards. One cavalryman pulled a javelin from his chest and hurled it at the pinned champion. It struck Suseb in the left shoulder, piercing his armour but not the blessed flesh beneath. The Lion roared in anger and redoubled his efforts, pushing himself onto his knees. With his right hand, he tore a jagged piece of bronze plate from the wreckage and hurled it end-over-end at the nearest walking corpse. The impact crushed the revenant's skull, dashing it to the ground.

Cursing, Arkhan charged in alongside his remaining warriors, hoping to slay the champion before he could free himself.

One of the dead cavalrymen lunged at Suseb, chopping down at him with an axe. The stone blade glanced from the Lion's skull, leaving a shallow gash along the side of his head. The other reached for the champion's throat with bloodied hands. Suseb grabbed the empty-handed creature by the arm and hurled it into the axe-wielding warrior's path. The clumsy revenants tangled together and fell in a squirming heap, and before they could rise again the Lion snatched up his massive khopesh and cut through both bodies in a single, ringing stroke.

Sensing an opening, Arkhan leapt forwards and slashed at Suseb's face. The champion saw the blow coming and tried to twist away, but the scimitar left a deep slash across the warrior's brown cheek. The vizier laughed at the sight of the wound, but his triumph was short-lived. The Lion's khopesh flickered through the air, and the immortal darted backwards barely in time to avoid having both legs cut from under him.

With a lusty roar, Suseb flexed his powerful legs and burst free from the wreckage. His huge sword wove a deadly pattern through the air as he advanced fearlessly upon the vizier.

'Vile, godless coward,' he growled. 'It's a disgrace to stain my blade with such an unworthy foe, but I'll do it gladly if it will rid the world of you and your ilk.'

Arkhan spat a swift incantation and hurled a bolt of necromantic power at the Lion. It struck Suseb full in the chest. The champion bellowed in pain, but continued his implacable advance.

Another bolt of lightning smote the earth, this time striking in the midst of a company of Khemri warriors near the centre of the battle-line. Shouts of wonder and dismay were drowned in the peal of thunder that followed.

Then, to Arkhan's horror, a shaft of sunlight pierced his master's shroud of darkness and glinted from the Lion's blade. His cold flesh trembled at the sight, and for the first time he feared the possibility of defeat.

AN ANGRY WIND rushed northward across the battlefield, howling with the fury of a god. Lightning scourged the earth like a taskmaster's lash, clawing along the ridge line amid a growing hail of burning scarab husks. More and more sunlight made its way through the writhing cloud, striking down the walking dead wherever it touched.

Within the black pavilion, a crowd of slaves grovelled in the dust before the king's grim sarcophagus and begged for their deliverance. In the shadows at the back of the chamber, the Usurper's ancient slave turned his blind face skywards and uttered a terrible, croaking laugh.

There was a hiss of air and the grating of stone, and the lid of the king's sarcophagus slid open. A shrieking chorus of tormented spirits and a gust of freezing air washed over the terrified slaves, who raised their hands in supplication to their lord and master.

Nagash the Immortal, Priest King of Khemri, stepped from his ensorcelled coffin amid a whirling nimbus of shrieking souls. Wreathed in roiling, ethereal vapour, the master of the Living City paid no heed to the worshipful entreaties of his slaves. Green bale-fire blazed from his sunken eyes and crackled along the staff of dark metal clutched in his left hand. The faces of the four skulls that topped the fearsome stave glimmered with unearthly power, blurring the air around it.

The king's handsome, lined face and strong hands were the colour of alabaster, gleaming like polished bone from the folds of his dark, crimson robes. His bald head was covered by a skullcap of hammered gold, inscribed with strange glyphs in a tongue unknown to civilised men.

Cowering slaves scattered from the immortal king's path as Nagash turned to the smaller sarcophagus that waited beside his own. The figure carved upon its surface was serene and beautiful: a goddess of the Blessed Land in the bloom of her youth.

A cold smile bent the necromancer's thin lips. He stretched forth his right hand, and the spirits surrounding him flowed down his arm and played across the coffin's surface. The marble lid shivered, and then slowly drew aside.

A faint, tortured moan rose up from the depths of the sarcophagus. Nagash listened, savouring the sound. His smile turned cruel.

'Come forth,' he commanded. The king's voice was bubbling and raspy, wheezing up from a pair of ruined lungs.

Slowly, painfully, the figure emerged. She was clad in priceless samite, with a queen's golden headdress set upon her brow. Bracelets set with brilliant sapphires hung from her fragile wrists, wrinkling the dry, parchment-like skin beneath. She clutched her claw-like hands painfully to her withered chest, and her head was bowed beneath the weight of her royal finery. Wisps of faded, brittle hair had escaped from the folds of her headdress and curled against her sunken, yellowed cheeks. Time had eaten away the gentle curves of her face, leaving only sharp edges and a thin, almost lipless mouth. Her joints creaked like dried leather as she moved, drawn to the necromancer as though by an invisible cord.

Bright, beautiful green eyes shone like emeralds from the queen's mummified face, etched with suffering so deep that it defied human comprehension.

The slaves grew silent as their queen walked among them. They buried their faces in the dust and pressed their hands to their ears to shut out her pitiful cries.

Nagash waved his hand once more, and the tent's heavy flap was pushed aside. He led his queen into the raging tumult, heedless of the wrath of gods or men. The necromancer looked out across the battlefield, and his smile twisted into a hateful sneer.

'Show them,' he commanded his queen, and she raised her withered arms to the sky and let out a long, heart-rending wail.

AKHMEN-HOTEP FELT the change, more than a mile away. The wind and the lightning stopped in a single instant, so suddenly that the king found himself questioning his senses. Then the rustling darkness overhead seemed to swell, filling his ears with its buzzing drone, and the priests began to scream.

He had turned his back on Sukhet and Memnet when the fire and lightning had begun, leaving them to their incantations while he tried to gauge their effect upon the battle. Now he whirled at their agonised cries, and saw that both men had fallen to their knees. A shiver went down the king's spine at the look of absolute horror writ upon their faces.

'What is it?' he asked. 'In the name of all the gods, what's happened?'

For a moment, it seemed that neither man heard him. Then Memnet whispered, 'We are undone.'

'Undone?' the priest king echoed. Mounting fear tightened like a fist around his heart. 'What does that mean? Tell me!'

'The Daughter of the Sun,' Memnet groaned. The Grand Hierophant's skin was flushed, and his eyes bright with fever. Akhmen-hotep could feel heat radiating from him in palpable waves.

'Neferem?' the priest king asked, surprised. 'What of her? Does she still live?'

'He has enslaved her!' hissed the Grand Hierophant. 'Nagash has bound her, body and soul!'

The news stunned Akhmen-hotep.

'That's not possible. She's the covenant made flesh. Her spirit binds the *gods*.'

'Do not ask me how,' the Grand Hierophant said. He sounded like a frightened child rather than a living embodiment of Ptra. He stretched a trembling hand to the north. 'I can feel her, brother! You cannot imagine her pain. The things he has done to her... I cannot bear it!'

'Then we must do something!' the king declared.

'Our power cannot touch her,' Memnet cried, 'nor can the blessings of the gods be arrayed against her. Look! Even the light of Neru fails in her presence!'

Horrified, Akhmen-hotep turned his gaze to the north. Memnet was right, the Consort's potent ward had failed, and the undead were closing in once more. The acolytes of the goddess had retreated to their high priestess, their faces pale with shock. Khalifra was weeping openly, her hands clenched to her belly as though stabbed.

The king's body felt cold and leaden. With a shock, he realised that even Geheb's gift of strength had failed him.

The gods had abandoned the men of Ka-Sabar.

SUSEB'S MASSIVE SWORD crashed against Arkhan's guard, hard enough to drive the vizier to his knees. The immortal struck the ground hard and rolled aside barely in time to avoid another blurring stroke aimed at his head. In desperation, Arkhan threw a backhanded slash at the champion's ankle, but the scimitar turned awkwardly in his hand and glanced off Suseb's calf. Arkhan realised, with a shock, that the champion's blow had bent his prized blade.

Arkhan kept rolling, narrowly avoiding another cut that struck a glancing blow against his shoulder. The Lion was as swift and as strong as his namesake, his god-given gifts rivalling even those of the Ushabti. Thinking quickly, he flipped onto his back and threw out his left hand, spitting words of power. A single bolt of energy leapt from his fingers and struck the champion in the chest. Suseb let out a pained grunt, but his stride never wavered. The vizier's power was almost spent.

'You cannot escape judgement so easily,' the Lion roared. 'The time of your reckoning is at hand!'

Suseb reached the vizier in a single, swift step and brought down his terrible blade. Once again, Arkhan tried to parry the blow, but this time his weakened scimitar snapped with a discordant clang.

The immortal threw the broken blade aside and threw up his empty hand.

'I yield!' he cried, sliding his left hand behind his back to the dagger concealed in his belt. 'Have mercy, Lion of Ka-Sabar! Nagash will pay any ransom you choose!'

Suseb's face lit with righteous anger as he spoke. 'You dare to plead for mercy, servant of the Usurper? If the gods see fit to spare you, let them stay my hand!'

The Lion drew back his blade. For the briefest instant, he seemed to stagger, as though the sword was suddenly heavier than before, and Arkhan saw his opportunity. His left hand snapped up in an underhand throw, and there was a heavy *thunk*, like a knife sinking deep into wood.

Suseb paused, his mouth hanging open. Slowly, his gaze fell to the hilt of the dagger jutting from his chest. Hurled with superhuman strength, the needle-sharp blade had driven deep into his body.

The champion took a half-step forwards, his face etched with strain as he tried to draw one more breath, but the dagger had pierced the Lion's heart. Suseb's great sword tumbled from his grasp, and the champion sank slowly to his knees.

Arkhan bared his jagged teeth in a slow, wicked grin. Slowly and deliberately, he rose to his feet and picked up Suseb's blade. Then he bent down and whispered softly in the Lion's ear.

'It seems the gods have spoken,' he said.

Cries of dismay went up from Suseb's men as the vizier brought the heavy blade down on the Lion's neck. Weak as Arkhan was, it took two clumsy blows to hack the champion's head from his shoulders.

AKHMEN-HOTEP HEARD the shouts of despair from the army's left flank and knew that the battle was lost. The acolytes of Neru had fled, bearing away their high priest-ess as the marauding undead closed in. The king's Ushabti had dismounted and encircled him with bared swords, awaiting his command.

Hashepra, high priest of Geheb, approached the king. The burly priest's face was stricken, his tanned cheeks wet with tears, but his voice was as strong as ever.

'I have four companies of spearmen formed up and waiting for your orders, great one,' he declared. 'What would you have us do?'

The priest king felt cast adrift in the unnatural darkness. The foundations of his world had been torn away in a single morning, leaving him bereft.

'Save yourselves,' he said numbly. 'Order the trumpets to sound the retreat. Nagash has won the day.'

Hashepra recoiled in surprise, as though Akhmen-hotep had struck him. The priest started to protest, but there was no denying the disaster unfolding around them. Finally he nodded and went to pass the word to the trumpeter.

The Ushabti led the priest king back to his chariot and sped him away, in the direction of the oasis. Memnet had disappeared, evidently carried away by his own priests.

Akhmen-hotep caught sight of Sukhet's corpse as the chariot passed by. The priest of Phakth lay upon his back, his face a mask of despair. The living embodiment of the god of justice had slit his own throat.

AN HOUR LATER, Arkhan limped up the rocky slope in the direction of his master's pavilion. The last surviving companies of the Bronze Host had fought their way out of the darkness and fallen to their knees in the bright sunlight of the oasis. Nagash's undead minions halted at the shadow's edge, unable to pursue any further. The vizier doubted there were more than a hundred living Khemri warriors scattered across the entire plain.

Nearly a dozen alabaster-skinned figures waited hungrily outside their master's tent. They glared at Arkhan with barely concealed hatred as he brushed past his brethren and entered the master's tent unannounced.

Nagash waited within, surrounded by his retinue of ghosts and attended upon by his queen and his slaves. Three immortals knelt at their master's feet, gulping noisily from golden goblets held in their trembling hands.

Arkhan smelled the heady perfume of the life-giving elixir and fell to his knees. He crawled through the dust to Nagash's feet, the ghosts circling him, touching his skin with fingers of ice and keening in his ears.

'I bring news of your victory, master,' he said hoarsely.

'Speak, then,' Nagash said coldly.

Arkhan ran his tongue over his cold lips. The thirst was terrible. Every vein in his body was shrivelled and aching. With an effort, he continued, 'The Bronze Host is in flight, and Bhagar's horsemen have been forced to quit the field.'

'Your cavalry pursues them even now,' Nagash said.

'Even so, master, even so,' the vizier replied, raising his eyes to the king. The queen stood to Nagash's right and a little behind the necromancer. Arkhan avoided her unblinking, agonised stare. 'We should recall our horsemen at once, before they become too spent,' he said. 'The Bronze Host is in disarray, fleeing for their lives down the trade road to Ka-Sabar. At least half their number lies dead on the plain below. If we pursue them, we might destroy them utterly–'

The king shook his head.

'There will be no pursuit,' Nagash declared. 'The army must return to Khemri at once. The Kings of Rasetra and

Lybaras have risen against us as well, and even now their armies are marching through the Valley of Kings.'

Arkhan was taken aback by the news. For a moment, even his dreadful thirst was forgotten.

'What of our allies at Quatar?' he asked

'I have sent a message to Priest King Nemuhareb,' Nagash replied. 'He is marching to block the western end of the valley, and is certain that he can turn back the rebels.'

The vizier studied his master's face.

'You are not convinced,' he said.

'We must confront this rebellion from a position of strength,' the necromancer replied. 'This battle today was but the first of many. I foresee a long, bitter war to come. We must gather our allies and prepare for the storm.' A hungry glint shone in Nagash's dark eyes. 'We will deal with Ka-Sabar later. Before we are done, all Nehekhara will lie beneath our heel, and Settra's great empire will be restored!'

'From your lips to the gods' ears,' Arkhan might once have said. Now, the vizier only smiled, and asked, 'What would you have me do, master?'

'For now, drink. Then go and summon your errant horsemen. We depart for Khemri at dusk,' Nagash said, stretching forth his hand.

Ghazid, the king's blue-eyed slave, shuffled from the darkness at the far side of the tent with a golden goblet in his wrinkled hands. The vessel brimmed with a thick, crimson liquid. Arkhan's hands clenched spastically as it drew near.

The vizier tore the goblet from the mad slave's hands and gulped greedily at its contents, all thoughts of war and conquest forgotten.

◄ FIVE ►

A Storm out of the East

*The Valley of Kings, in the 62nd year of Qu'aph the Cunning
(-1750 Imperial Reckoning)*

SOMETHING WAS MOVING beyond the Gates of the Dawn.

It was almost noon. Rakh-amn-hotep, the first of his name, Priest King of Rasetra, rubbed a calloused hand over his shaven scalp and squinted in the fierce sunlight. The air shimmered in the confines of the Valley of Kings, flashing brightly against the drifting clouds of chalky dust stirred up by the movement of the allied army. The fine, glittering dust had become their worst enemy during the long, punishing march down the winding valley. It clung to the skin, clogged throats and eyes, and sawed at the axles of the chariots. From where the king stood, surrounded by his Ushabti atop a low hill just off the wide temple road, he could see great clouds of dust shrouding the narrow pass at the western end of the valley, concealing whatever dangers might be arrayed against them.

Something was out there. That much was certain. But what?

Rakh-amn-hotep hooked his blunt thumbs into the arm holes of his heavy scale shirt and tried to shift it into a more comfortable position. It had been a long time since he'd marched through the sands of central Nehekhara, and he could stand the heat, but his skin was afire from the thick layer of dust chafing beneath the weight of his armour. The priest king was a short, very stout man, with a wide barrel chest and a blunt, pugnacious face. The point of a lizardman's spear had left a permanent dimple in his left cheek, creating the illusion of a smile. He was a savage, cunning man, cruel to his enemies and relentless when his anger was aroused, and the Priest King of Rasetra was frequently angry about something. His small city, situated near the edge of the steaming southern jungles, was constantly under threat from tribes of savage lizardmen. Not a year went by when the Rasetrans weren't fending off raiding parties, or leading punitive expeditions into the wilds to burn villages and take hostages from the larger tribes.

Years of fighting against the tribesmen had left their mark on the priest king and his warriors. They wore longer, heavier kilts of thick cotton that stretched below their knees, overlaid with cured leather taken from the massive thunder lizards that crashed their way through the thick jungle growth. Their torsos were covered in thick shirts of scaly lizard hide, with overlapping, bony plates to turn aside tooth or claw. The strange armour lent Rasetrans a savage, exotic appearance, which contrasted dramatically with the simple, conventional attire of their allies.

The city of Lybaras, on the other hand, was not known for its prowess in war. Their patron was Tahoth, the god of knowledge and learning, and their wealth, such as it was, stemmed from their great academies and craftsmen rather than from fierce raids or conquest. Their nobles had little use for jewels or fine clothes, but rather, invested their fortunes in scrolls and strange tools, vessels of rare glass and arcane devices of bronze and wood.

From where the King of Rasetra stood, it was difficult to tell a Lybaran noble from a slave. Both favoured a simple, dun-coloured kilt and functional leather sandals, with a dark brown cape that hung below the waist. The only difference, Rakh-amn-hotep noted with a scowl, was the amount of glass baubles and metal trinkets the nobles carried wherever they went. Even their Ushabti were strange, their bodies bearing none of the physical blessings of the other gods, and their weapons a motley assortment of sticks, knives and coils of tightly braided rope. Only their eyes betrayed their divine nature. They were a piercing, almost luminous grey, as hard and incisive as sharpened stone. Nothing seemed to escape their notice, much less catch them unprepared.

Hekhmenukep, Priest King of Lybaras, stood amid a bustling throng of chattering viziers and nervous scribes just a few yards to Rakh-amn-hotep's right. The king was peering intently through a long, wooden tube rimmed with polished brass, balanced on the bare shoulder of a waiting slave. Hekhmenukep was tall and lean to the point of being skeletal. His kilt hung listlessly down to the top of his bony knees, and the fall of his cape only accentuated the slope of his narrow shoulders. A fine gold chain lay around the king's long neck, from which hung a strange assortment of glass discs edged in copper, silver and brass wire. He looked more like a mason than the ruler of a mighty city, Rakh-amn-hotep mused.

'Well?' the King of Rasetra demanded. 'Do you see anything or not?'

The viziers surrounding Hekhmenukep shifted uneasily at Rakh-amn-hotep's peremptory tone, but the king himself appeared unfazed.

'The sunlight turns the dust into a swirling curtain,' he said, squinting into his strange contraption. 'There are flashes of light and the occasional shadow, but it's difficult to discern what any of it means.' The priest king straightened. 'Perhaps you would care to try?' he offered, gesturing at the tube.

Rakh-amn-hotep scowled at the strange object.

'I know little about Tahoth and his ways,' he grunted. 'I doubt he would bless me with any special sight.' The comment drew a laugh from Hekhmenukep.

'There is no need for special prayers in this case,' he said. 'Merely look into the tube. The glass will aid the working of your eye.'

Rakh-amn-hotep was dubious, but the need for information spurred him to try. On the level ground west of the hill, the armies of Rasetra and Lybaras were hastily turning off the road and forming their battle-line to the shrill wailing of trumpets. Somewhere up ahead, in that swirling mass of dust at the end of the valley, was the army's advance guard of light horsemen. Half an hour ago, a rider from the advance guard had come galloping down the road with a message from his commander: enemy troops had been sighted at the Gates of the Dawn. There had been no word since. Had the light horsemen encountered a small detachment of troops and driven them off, or were they fighting for their lives against the entire army of Quatar?

He'd known from the beginning that the march down the valley would be a race against time. The Valley of Kings was an ominous place, fraught with old magics and restless spirits that haunted the tombs of the ancient Nehekharans. Nothing grew there, and the nearest water was almost a hundred leagues away. The high, sheer walls of the valley forced travellers to traverse it from one end to the other. The eastern end, known as the Gates of the Dusk, was guarded by the city of Mahrak and its army of warrior priests. The western end, known as the Gates of the Dawn, was guarded by the Tomb Guard of Quatar. Rakh-amn-hotep knew that if their campaign were to have any chance of success, they would have to reach the Gates of the Dawn before Quatar got word of their approach and moved to block the mouth of the valley. If the Tomb Guard controlled the Gates of the Dawn, the allied army would either have to risk a brutal, bloody assault or else turn around and retreat back the way they'd come. Since leaving Mahrak, the allied army had moved with surprising speed down the winding valley, thanks largely to the Lybarans' strange, floating wagons. Suspended high above the valley floor by the hot desert wind, the wagons were able to carry the army's supplies and keep pace with the troops instead of being slowed to a crawl by unruly teams of camels or oxen. The army had covered almost a hundred leagues in just the first five days, and Rakh-amn-hotep had dared to believe that his gamble would succeed.

How the gods laughed when men dared to hope, the priest king mused sourly. He strode over to Hekhmenukep's odd invention and reluctantly peered into the end of the wooden tube.

At first, all he could see was a blurry circle of white. Frowning, he started to pull away from the tube, and suddenly the image cleared somewhat. Rakh-amn-hotep grew still, and noticed that he was seeing the swirling clouds across the valley almost as clearly as if they were just a few yards away. The priest king glanced back at Hekhmenukep.

'How is it that the gods share such power without requiring something in return?' he asked.

The King of Lybaras folded his thin arms and smiled. Like a tutor addressing a young student, he said, 'Tahoth teaches us that the gifts of creation are hidden in the world around us,' he said. 'If we are clever, we can uncover their mysteries and claim them for our own. In this way, we honour the gods.'

Rakh-amn-hotep tried to make sense of this, but gave up with a shrug. When they made camp that night he would make a sacrifice to Tahoth and consider the debt settled.

When he turned back, the King of Rasetra found that he'd lost the image once more. Frowning, he carefully drew back from the tube until once again the far end of the valley came into view.

Dust and more dust, the king observed irritably. Then he saw a glint of bronze wink from the murk, a reflection from a helmet, perhaps, or the tip of a blade. Then a vague shadow darkened the haze for a fleeting instant. Large and swift-moving, it was undoubtedly a man on horseback.

'The advance guard is engaged,' he muttered darkly, 'and they're fighting on our side of the valley mouth.' Rakh-amn-hotep rubbed his scarred chin thoughtfully. Years of battlefield experience suggested what was happening behind the curtain of dust. The advance guard numbered five thousand light horsemen, more than enough to over-whelm a small garrison of unprepared infantry within the space of half an hour. Instead, they were still fighting, rid-ing madly back and forth through the thick haze rather than pushing their way through the mouth of the valley as they'd been ordered.

'Khsar flay their hides,' Rakh-amn-hotep cursed. 'The Tomb Guard has beaten us to the Gates of the Dawn.' Hekhmenukep's eyes widened in surprise.

'How is this possible?' he exclaimed. 'We moved faster than any army has ever marched, and our scouts encoun-tered no sentries along the way.'

'Who can say what powers the foul Usurper possesses?' said a sharp voice behind the two kings. 'He has ruled unjustly in Khemri for more than two hundred years. It would not surprise me if every evil thing in Nehekhara is his to command.'

The kings turned as Nebunefer the Just struggled the last few yards up to the summit of the hill and limped painfully into their midst. The elderly priest was covered in a fine dusting of grit, coating his seamed face and dulling his bronze skullcap. He was attended by half a dozen senior priests and priestesses, each one raised in the great temples of Mahrak, the City of the Gods. Each of the hierophants wore fine linen robes in a variety of rich colours, from the Sun God's gleaming yellow to Geheb's mix of dark brown and vivid green. Rakh-amn-hotep noted their fierce expressions with secret amusement. How long had the Hieratic Council at Mahrak urged restraint in the face of Nagash's mounting crimes, saying that the gods would see justice done? That was before the shadow spread from Khemri, felling thousands of priest and acolytes all across Nehekhara. Within days of that terrible event, the council was beating the drum of war. Using the Hierophants of Rasetra and Lybaras as go-betweens, they had hammered out a hasty alliance between the three cities and opened their immense coffers to finance a campaign to liberate Khemri once and for all.

Unfortunately, gold was all that the Hieratic Council seemed willing to provide. Rakh-amn-hotep had requested a contingent of Mahrak's fabled warrior-priests to accompany the allied army, but Nebunefer and his small retinue were all that the city could spare.

'If Nagash knows we're coming we could be facing the combined armies of Khemri and Quatar,' Rakh-amn-hotep growled. 'We can't possibly defeat them both.'

Nebunefer shook his head decisively, saying, 'Our spies in Khemri report that the Usurper has taken his army south to fight the Bronze Host of Ka-Sabar. The massacre of holy men across Nehekhara has spurred Akhmen-hotep to declare war against the Living City.'

Hekhmenukep nodded thoughtfully.

'That's welcome news,' he said, 'but what of the remaining cities?'

'Numas and Zandri side with Nagash, along with Quatar,' Nebunefer replied. 'Of the minor cities, Bhagar will probably follow Ka-Sabar, while Bel Aliad remains loyal to Khemri.'

'And what of Lahmia?' the King of Rasetra asked. 'Their army is as large as mine and Hekhmenukep's combined.'

'We have sent an embassy to Lahmia to urge them to action,' Nebunefer, said, shrugging, 'but so far they remain neutral.'

'Waiting to see which side gains the upper hand,' Rakh-amn-hotep grumbled.

'Perhaps,' Nebunefer said. 'Lahmia has ancient ties to the Living City. It is possible they are reluctant to take up arms against Neferem.' Hekhmenukep frowned.

'No one's seen Neferem for more than a century. Surely she's free of Nagash by now,' he said.

'No,' Nebunefer said uneasily. 'The Queen of the Dawn is not dead. We would know it if she were.'

Suddenly, a chorus of wailing trumpets echoed up and down the allied battle-line. Rakh-amn-hotep turned back to the swirling chaos at the western end of the valley. He could see the black specks of figures dancing at the ragged edges of the cloud. Scowling, he put his eye to Hekhmenukep's device to try to see who they were. For a few moments, all he could see was a panorama of boiling dust, but then he caught sight of a horseman of the advance guard. The warrior's horse was lathered and the rider was covered in dust. As the king watched, the warrior fitted an arrow to his bow and fired into the swirling dust, before retreating a dozen yards from the edge of the cloud. The same thing was happening all along the length of the dust cloud as the battered squadrons of light horse-men withdrew in the direction of their army.

Within moments, Rakh-amn-hotep saw why. A wall of white shields took shape out of the haze, growing larger and more distinct from one moment to the next. Slowly, inexorably, the first companies of the Tomb Guard advanced into the valley to meet their waiting foes.

'What is it?' Hekhmenukep asked. 'What do you see?'

For a moment, Rakh-amn-hotep could not believe his eyes.

'The King of Quatar is impatient,' he said. 'Instead of waiting for an assault, he's chosen to come and fight us here.' He shook his head in wonder. 'Nemuhareb has made a reckless mistake. With luck, we can make him pay for it.'

'How?' the King of Lybaras asked.

Rakh-amn-hotep glanced through the viewing-tube again. Strange as it was, he had to admit it was a damned useful tool. He gauged the speed of the enemy's march and reckoned they had another half an hour before the Tomb Guard was in range. The king turned back to Hekhmenukep, and asked, 'How quickly can your war machines be made ready?' The King of Lybaras looked to his viziers.

'Thirty minutes,' he said. 'Perhaps a little less. They should only be half a mile behind us at this point.' Rakh-amn-hotep smiled.

'Then we're going to get to see if they're half as clever as you claim they are,' he replied, and then called out to the messengers waiting at the bottom of the hill.

THE NEXT THIRTY minutes passed in a flurry of movement as the allied army prepared for the coming battle. Companies of archers advanced twenty paces in front of the infantry and made ready to fire. Behind them the battle-line stretched for a mile and a half across the valley, with the Temple Road running roughly down its centre. The infantry companies of Rasetra took up the army's centre and left flank, while the warriors of Lybaras took up the right. The beleaguered light horsemen of the advance guard withdrew off to the north, further reinforcing the right flank. The army's heavy cavalry waited a hundred yards behind the left flank: some two hundred Rasetran chariots, drawn by vicious, two-legged jungle lizards instead of horses. The warriors of Rasetra had been using the lizards in battle for more than a hundred years, but this was the first time they would be employed against another Nehekharan army. Rakh-amn-hotep kept them well back, hidden behind a low ridge just out of sight. His champion, Ekhreb, would lead them into battle.

Behind the left flank, the Lybarans were still wrestling their catapults into position. They had brought eight of the massive war machines with the army, and their crews were hastily readying piles of stone to load into their broad wicker baskets.

The full weight of Quatar's Tomb Guard marched against the allied force. Quatar's patron was Djaf, the god of death, and the city's warriors were justly feared for their prowess on the field of battle. Their infantry wore white-painted leather armour and carried heavy wooden shields, and their massive swords were capable of splitting a man in two with a single blow. It was said that their Ushabti bore the faces of jackals, and could kill with the lightest touch of their blades.

The Tomb Guard advanced on a wide front, with companies of archers interspersed among the heavy infantry. A large force of light horsemen and two great companies of chariots rode behind them. The light cavalry and one company of chariots swung to the north, threatening the allied right flank, while the remaining chariot company was held back in reserve, close to the Priest King Nemuhareb and his retinue.

Rakh-amn-hotep studied the enemy army carefully. The Tomb Guard was easily the size of his combined force, and had more heavy cavalry. He turned to his trumpeter.

'Signal the archers to fire when ready,' he said, and then turned to Nebunefer. 'Do you imagine the King of Quatar will follow the old customs, or will he fight us to the death?'

'It would depend on whether he has any of Nagash's lieutenants among his retinue,' the old priest said, shrugging. 'We should know soon enough once you spring your trap.'

The King of Rasetra grunted to himself.

'Assuming it works,' he muttered.

Down on the field, the archers drew back their bows and began to fire. Showers of arrows darkened the sky and fell among the warriors of Quatar, who raised their shields to protect them from the deadly rain. Here and there a warrior fell with an arrow lodged in his chest or his neck, but the rest continued to press forward. The enemy archers returned fire while still on the move, and Rakh-amn-hotep was impressed at the steadiness and accuracy of their volleys. Bowmen from both sides fell as the archery duel began in earnest.

To the right, the first of the catapults lofted its load of stones high into the air with a muffled bang. The projectiles spread out in flight, each as large as a man's head, and fell among the advancing infantry. Shields splintered and men were dashed to the ground, but the advance continued. Rakh-amn-hotep turned to Hekhmenukep.

'What of the other war machines?' he asked.

The King of Lybaras responded with an enigmatic smile. 'They will make their appearance known when they are ready.'

Rakh-amn-hotep frowned. When they were ready? What kind of an answer was that? Concealing a flash of irritation, he gestured once more to his trumpeter.

'Signal the left flank to advance,' he ordered.

The horn rang out at once. On the left flank, the warriors of Rasetra marched forward, raising their shields and readying heavy, stone-headed maces. The archers in their path fired off one last volley before gathering their unspent arrows and retreating down the narrow lanes between the infantry companies. When the last bowmen had passed, the companies closed ranks and presented a solid front to the enemy. Within minutes their shields were studded with arrow shafts as the Quatari bowmen continued their fire.

Moments later, the two forces on the left came together in a grinding crash of flesh, metal and stone. The echoing roar of battle resounded across the open ground, in counterpoint to the steady banging of the catapults off to the right. On that flank, the enemy light horsemen were trying to push around the edge of the allied lines, but so far the cavalry of the advance guard was keeping them at bay. The enemy infantry was staggering under the hail of heavy stones, but with great determination they continued to press forward. Behind them, the chariots made ready to add their power to the inevitable charge.

Rakh-amn-hotep studied the course of the battle so far and was satisfied. The troops on the left were struggling against the Tomb Guard, and the Rasetran companies were already shrinking as a steady stream of wounded men staggered away from the fight and sought safety behind their battle-line. The king looked for the Quatari reserves. The chariots were still in the rear, close to the enemy king.

Long minutes passed. The companies in the centre met with a grinding roar, while the enemy advance on the right foundered under the ceaseless bombardment. On the left, the Rasetran companies were starting to waver. Still there was no sign of the remaining war machines. Rakh-amn-hotep shot a worried glance at Hekhmenukep, but held his tongue.

Another minute passed, and the first companies on the left flank began to fall back. The Tomb Guard pushed forward, hacking relentlessly with their heavy blades. The carnage was terrible. Men fell with their skulls split or their arms hacked away, and rivers of blood stilled the clouds of dust around the struggling warriors.

The retreat on the left began to gather speed. As one company fell back, the ones on either side hurriedly withdrew as well. Within moments, the whole flank was falling swiftly to the rear.

Rakh-amn-hotep heard the faint wail of trumpets in the direction of the enemy centre. The reserve chariots were moving, bouncing quickly across the rocky ground towards the left flank. The enemy king sensed victory.

'Order the left flank to begin a general withdrawal,' he ordered.

Events on the ground, however, were moving with a speed of their own. The retreating companies were picking up speed, stumbling over themselves in their haste to escape the blades of the Tomb Guard. The enemy pressed forward hungrily, and more horns wailed as the Quatari chariots raced to join the impending slaughter.

Rakh-amn-hotep turned to the trumpeter.

'Send the signal!' he shouted.

The complex notes rang out across the battlefield. At once, the retreating companies picked up the pace and curved backwards, like a gate swinging on a hinge, to clear the path for the Rasetran chariots. Rakh-amn-hotep heard a wild, moaning cry of jungle horns as his heavy cavalry swept over the ridge and bore down on the unsuspecting Tomb Guard.

Then, a great commotion went up on the right flank. The King of Rasetra turned to see a pair of towering dust plumes rising up behind the enemy battle-line, nearly in the midst of the advancing Quatari chariots. A faint, thready hiss carried over the tumult of battle, and huge shadows moved within the cloaking dust. Then there was a rending crash, and the king watched with amazement as a chariot and its horses were hurled like toys into the air.

The Lybaran war machines had made their appearance at last.

They crawled from huge pits in the soft earth on clanking legs of wood and bronze. Steam, heated by the blessings of Ptra, hissed in bronze pipes and drove segmented legs and huge, sweeping pincers. A tail the size of a battering ram curled over each machine, lashing out and smashing chariots to flinders with each blow. Fashioned in the shape of enormous tomb scorpions, the constructs fell upon the rear of the enemy companies with disconcerting speed and power. Within moments, chariots and infantry alike were in full retreat.

On the left, the charge of the Rasetran chariots had inflicted a similar shock. The Quatari infantry staggered under the sudden counterattack, and the chariots had broken through their lines. The Quatari chariots, meanwhile had fallen into disarray, their horses terrified by the huge, fanged lizards drawing the enemy cavalry. A wild melee was in progress, but the Quatari forces were caught between the Rasetran chariots and their infantry, which had begun to advance once more.

The final blow came on the right flank. The enemy light horsemen panicked at the sight of the huge Lybaran war machines and quit the field. Seeing their opportunity, the horsemen of the advance guard swept around the Quatari flank and bore down on the enemy king and his retinue. Surrounded, cut off from retreat, Nemuhareb, Priest King of Quatar, offered his surrender.

The way to Khemri had been opened.

⊰ SIX ⊱

Death and Life

Khemri, the Living City, in the 44th year of Khsar the Faceless
(-1968 Imperial Reckoning)

IN THE WANING hours of the day, Khetep, Priest King of Khemri, was brought forth from the House of Everlasting Life to begin his journey into the afterlife. The body of the king was wrapped in strips of the finest white linen, each one marked with the Glyphs of the River and the Earth in careful, precise script to sustain Khetep's flesh against the passage of ages. The hands of the king were folded across his chest, and a long, golden chain called the ankh'ram was twined about his wrists. The chain would anchor Khetep's spirit to his body so that he could find it again after centuries in the afterlife. His gold burial mask, shaped with care during the king's life by the finest craftsmen in the Living City, shone warmly in the late afternoon light. Garlands of fragrant blossoms surrounded the king's body, filling the air with their vibrant perfume.

The palanquin was borne by eight priests clad in white robes and a cape made of fluttering linen strips that symbolised the resurrection of the flesh. Their faces were hidden behind serene golden masks, and their movements were slow and ritually precise. Thirteen white-robed acolytes followed the palanquin, their heads covered in white ash and their eyes painted black with kohl, chanting the Invocation of Going Forth Into the Dusk to the beat of hide-wrapped drums. Last of all strode the Grand Hierophant in all his funereal splendour, bearing in his left hand the great Staff of the Ages. Nagash wore the ritual white robe and cape, its fabric strips embroidered with sacred glyphs in golden thread, and a golden pectoral inscribed with the sun, the jackal and the owl. White ash covered the Grand Hierophant's face, lending an otherworldly cast to his coldly handsome features.

A silent multitude awaited the slow-moving cortege in the great plaza outside the temple. Thutep and the royal household waited upon the right side of the procession, their regal finery clashing with the rough smudges of ash that blackened their cheeks and forehead. A hundred servants waited behind the household, bearing the grave goods that would accompany Khetep into the afterlife.

All those who had served the king in life stood to the left of the procession, and would continue to provide for him in death. Two score elderly servants and scribes, all of them bearing the respective tools of their trade in neat, cloth-wrapped bundles; more than a hundred slaves, their eyes hollow and their expressions bleak; and last of all, the stoic figures of the two dozen Ushabti that had survived their king's last battle on the banks of the River Vitae. The Ushabti stood in a hollow square formation, clad in all their battle finery, their gleaming ritual swords held ready. Within the square stood the trio of barbarians that the Priest King of Zandri had given to honour the death of Khetep. The druchii were still bound in chains, their expressions dulled by the effects of drugged wine. The barbarians stood apart from one another, their heads unbowed and their dark eyes smouldering with hate.

Moving to the measured beat of the drums, the cortege made its way across the plaza and into the city proper, followed by the mournful throng. They walked in echoing silence. The shops were all shuttered and the great bazaar had been emptied; even the distant docks, normally bustling with life, were empty. The people of the Living City had paid their respects to their king in the morning, as, by ancient law, they were forbidden to witness the final journey to his crypt. The gold coins scattered by the merchants earlier in the day still lay in the dusty street, untouched by beggar or thief.

At the centre of the city the cortege turned east, making their way beyond the city walls through the Gate of Usirian into the fertile fields beyond. To the north, a flock of herons took wing from the reeds along the banks of the Vitae, paralleling the cortege for a short way and then sinking back out of sight. To the east, the land sloped gently upwards. In the distance, the largest of the tombs were already visible, crowding the horizon like the rooftops of a sprawling city. Above them all loomed the Great Pyramid, its sloping sides painted crimson by the light of the setting sun.

The road was well-kept, formed of packed sand and stone, and tended to yearly by citizens as part of their compulsory service to the king. Within half an hour they came upon the first of the shrines: a tall, basalt statue of Usiris, just a few paces off the side of the road. Offerings of food and wine had been left at the statue's feet by travellers on their way to or from the great necropolis. Further on, the procession passed shrines to Neru and Djaf, Ualatp the Carrion God and even the dreadful Sokth, God of Poisoners. Everyone had a reason to fear one god or another as they made their way into the great city of tombs.

After an hour on the road, the cortege reached the rough edge of the necropolis. The procession crested a low hill, and the plain before them was crowded with small, square tombs, built of sandstone and crudely ornamented with sacred scripts or religious imagery. These were the vaults of the poor, those who spent their entire lives saving enough coin to purchase the ministrations of a mortuary priest. One tomb might hold thirty or forty bodies: an entire extended family, stacked one atop the other like mud bricks. The vaults grew in a chaotic sprawl across the uneven ground, often built by the families themselves, on whatever plot of clear, mostly level ground they could find. Some of the crude tombs had broken open over the years, allowing vermin and scavengers to eat away at the bodies inside. Huge, black vultures glided low across the tops of the tombs, or perched on the weathered roofs and eyed the procession with frank interest as the sarcophagus went by.

The road ended, for all intents and purposes, and the cortege was forced to wind its way carefully through the maze of narrow lanes and blind alleys between the shabby crypts. It was not unheard of for citizens to become lost if they wandered too deeply into the necropolis, and those that could not find their way out by nightfall were sometimes never seen again. However, the priests knew every twist and turn of the great city, for, in many ways, the necropolis was as much their home as the House of Everlasting Life.

The further in they went, the larger and finer the tombs became. They came upon grand structures of basalt or sandstone, inscribed with glyphs of protection and engravings of the gods in all their forms. Here were entombed the families of prosperous merchants or tradesmen, surrounded by shrines and statuary that both proclaimed their piety and forced their neighbours to keep a respectful distance. Even then, the crypts were crowded as closely together as possible, filling every square foot of available space.

Finally, as the sun was casting long shadows among the jumbled stone crypts, the procession reached a great plain at the centre of the necropolis, where the great kings of old built their tombs. The black tomb of Settra rose at the centre of the plain: a massive, square structure of black marble as large as the palace in Khemri. The great king and his household were contained within, as well as slaves, soldiers, bodyguards, chariots and horses, all in readiness for the day when they would be called to walk upon the earth once more. The doors to the great tomb were made of stone plated in raw gold, and the massive walls were carved with thousands of potent glyphs and invocations against harm.

Settra's Tomb took twenty years to build, and more than two thousand slaves perished before the labour was done. Every king that followed sought to outdo him, spending vast sums to create ever larger and more lavish crypts to proclaim their greatness to future generations. Thus it was that Khetep began building his tomb from the first day he became Priest King of Khemri. The Great Pyramid took twenty-five years to complete and cost the lives of close to a million slaves. No one but the king knew how much treasure had gone to build it. On the very day of its completion Khetep had ordered its chief architect strangled and entombed in a special chamber within.

The structure dominated the western edge of the plain, rising more than four hundred feet into the air and dwarfing every tomb around it. There were eight separate levels within the pyramid and two more tunnelled into the earth below it: room enough for an entire dynasty and their households.

A broad path of white stone led to the Great Pyramid's entrance, which had been built to resemble the façade of Settra's Court. At the top of the steps waited a score of mortuary priests, like silent ghosts lingering in the shadows of the great statues of Neru and Geheb, a dozen tall urns of wine resting on the stones before them.

A dozen armed priests from the temple of Usirian stood vigil outside the tomb, their faces hidden behind gold owl-masks. As the procession came to a stop at the foot of the steps, the leader of the horex stepped forwards and called out in a loud voice, 'Who comes here?'

Nagash raised the Staff of Ages and answered, 'The king has come. His time on earth has passed, and his spirit goes forth into the dusk. This is the house where he will take his rest.'

The horex bowed deeply and stepped aside.

'Let the king come in,' their leader intoned. 'A place has been made for him.'

Silently, the palanquin bearers made their way past the guardians and up the steps into the tomb, accompanied by the acolytes who would assist the priests in completing the interment.

Nagash climbed the steps to the tomb and took his place beside the wine-bearers. The Grand Hierophant turned to the waiting throng and spread his arms.

'The king has gone into his house,' he intoned. 'Where are the faithful, who will honour and serve him for all the ages to come?'

At once, a tall, dignified figure stepped forwards from the throng and ascended the wide steps. Khetep's wife, Sofer, wore a gown of samite bound by a belt of gold set with sapphires and emeralds. Her long, black hair was bound up in tight curls and oiled, and the circlet of a queen sat upon her brow. She was no more than a hundred and twenty years old, and her face was still unlined and beautiful. The queen stood before Nagash and said, 'I am Khetep's wife. My place is by his side. Let me go in and lie with him.'

Nagash bowed his head respectfully and stretched out his hand. Khefru emerged from the crowd of waiting priests, bearing a golden goblet. He filled the cup with poisoned wine and passed it to his master. The Grand Hierophant held out the wine to his mother.

'Drink, faithful wife,' he said with a smile, 'and enter your husband's house.'

Sofer looked at the goblet and hesitated for just a moment. Then she drew a deep breath and took the poison from her son. The queen closed her eyes, drained the goblet dry, and handed it back to Nagash. Immediately, another priest came forwards and took her by the hand. He led her into the crypt, where linen wrappings and a sarcophagus awaited her.

Next came the Ushabti. Each one took the poisoned cup almost gratefully, glad to escape the accusing eyes of the living and resume their watch upon the king. Even before the last of the devoted was gone, a stir went up among the slaves as they sensed that their time was drawing near. More than one had to be dragged up the stone steps and forced to drink the sacred wine, much to the consternation of the royal household.

When the last of the slaves had been taken into the crypt it was time for the sacrifices. Once more, Nagash spread his arms before the diminished crowd, and proclaimed, 'Let us make offerings to Usirian, he who leads the souls through the darkness, so that Khetep may enjoy a peaceful journey into the afterlife.'

Nagash turned to Khefru.

'Bring forth the barbarians,' he commanded. Khefru nodded and gestured to three of the waiting priests. They quickly descended the steps and took hold of the insensate druchii. The barbarians hissed and spat like angry cats as they were dragged before the Grand Hierophant.

Khefru stepped forwards with the cup. At once, the two females began to curse at Nagash in their cruel, sibilant tongue. The male bared his teeth in a silent snarl.

'Kill us and be done with it,' he said, 'but know this: he who slays us will be cursed, now and forever more. His lands will turn to ash, and his flesh will shrivel from his bones.'

At this, Khefru hesitated, until Nagash spurred him to motion with a heated glare. The druchii made no move to resist, and when the cup was placed to their lips they drank their measure, staring Nagash in the eye all the while. One by one, they sank to the stones and grew still.

BY THE TIME the last sacrifice had been made it was nearly twilight. Thutep and the royal household were left to race north though the necropolis, guided by fleet-footed acolytes until they made their way to the river's edge. There, his bride awaited.

While the cortege bore Khetep to his tomb, a different kind of procession left Khemri in a fleet of richly appointed barges, working their way downstream to prepare for the wedding. All of the Nehekharan ambassadors were present to bear witness, as well as all the noble families of the Living City.

Thutep reached the reed-choked banks of the Vitae just as the last rays of sunlight touched the water with flashes of mellow gold. Neferem stood in the shallows, her hands crossed over her breast in greeting, a smile upon her radiant face. She was the gift of the Sun and the River, the daughter of the Earth and the bearer of beauty and wisdom. Thutep waded ponderously through the water to take her hand and lead her to shore, where Amamurti, Hierophant of Ptra, waited.

When the marriage was sealed and the covenant between the Nehekharans and the gods had been renewed, a great cheer went up from the assembled nobles, and the new king took his queen aboard the royal barge and bore her back to the celebrations that awaited them in Khemri.

No one noticed that Nagash was not among the well-wishers accompanying his brother back home. He stood in the shadows by the river bank, watching the barges pole away upriver. The white moon had risen, and bats swooped low over the shore, hunting insects. Further downstream a crocodile slid into the water with a faint splash.

The Grand Hierophant smiled faintly and made his way back to the necropolis.

REED TORCHES DIPPED in pitch hissed and spat from the sconces along the walls of the stone chamber. It was a large room, forty paces to a side, but unfinished, the walls still undressed sandstone, and the chamber completely bare except for the three bodies stretched out on the floor.

The stone door to the chamber grated open. Khefru stepped inside, holding his torch high. Nagash followed swiftly behind him.

The Grand Hierophant walked quickly to the three life-less druchii and studied them for a long moment.

'There were no problems?' he asked Khefru.

'None, master,' the priest replied with a smirk. 'I just waited until everyone had left for the city, and then dragged them inside.'

Nagash nodded thoughtfully. He knelt first beside the druchii male and pulled a tiny vial from his belt. He pulled open the barbarian's mouth, carefully, and poured two drops of greenish liquid on his tongue. Then he moved on to the first of the females. He had just finished with the second when the male drew in a great, whooping breath and sat bolt upright. The barbarian spat a stream of curses in his native tongue, and his eyes were wild as he looked around the room.

'Where am I?' the barbarian asked. He spoke passable Nehekharan, though his accent made him sound like the hissing of a cobra.

'Deep beneath the earth,' Nagash replied. 'You are in a vault in the lowest recesses of the Great Pyramid.' The barbarian frowned.

'The wine…' he began.

'You drank from a different urn than all the rest. Khefru made sure you drank a potion that created the illusion of death, rather than inflict it outright.'

'For what purpose?' the druchii asked warily.

Nagash smiled, and said, 'For what other purpose? You have something I want. I'm prepared to make a trade in order to get it.'

'What is it that we could possibly offer you?'

'The Priest King of Zandri slew my father with sorcery: dark, fearsome magic that our priests had no means to prevent.' He glanced knowingly at the barbarian. 'You performed that spell for him, did you not?'

'Perhaps,' the druchii said, smiling coldly.

Nagash glared at the barbarian, and said, 'Don't dissemble. The facts are obvious. Nekumet doesn't possess the skill to master such magic, and the effects of the spell were unlike anything I've ever seen. He persuaded you to use your sorcery to aid him in battle, and then, when he realised the true extent of your power, he betrayed you.'

'Go on,' said the druchii, his smile fading.

'Nekumet didn't want your blood on his hands. I expect you threatened to curse him, too, at some point in your captivity, so he sent you to Khemri instead. That way, we would kill you and suffer the consequences instead.'

'Clever, clever little human,' the druchii hissed, 'and all of this theatre was simply to satisfy your curiosity?'

'Of course not,' Nagash snapped. 'I want the secrets of your sorcery. Show me how to wield the power you command, and in return I will set you free.'

The druchii laughed.

'How delightful,' he said with a sneer. 'Nekumet said almost exactly the same thing. Why should I trust you?'

'Why, isn't that obvious?' Nagash asked, his smile widening. 'Because you're forty feet below the earth, in a tomb designed to kill those who wander its halls.' The Grand Hierophant folded his arms. 'I've already buried you alive, druchii. The only choice you've got left is to give me what I want.'

SEVEN

The Wrath of Nagash

*The Khemri trade road, in the 62nd year of Qu'aph the Cunning
(-1750 Imperial Reckoning)*

THE USURPER'S ARMY was more dead than alive after the bloody battle at Zedri. The bodies of the dead, animated by Nagash's sorcery, could move only in darkness, and so the host rose at sunset and marched until just before dawn, when they would pitch the tents in the centre of the army for their master and his champions. When the sunlight broke over the Brittle Peaks to the east, the rotting corpses sank slowly to the earth, until the trade road resembled nothing so much as a corpse-strewn battlefield. Meanwhile, the dwindling ranks of living horsemen and warriors ate what they could and slept in shifts, waiting for the next attack.

Although they had arrived too late to turn the tide of battle at Zedri, the horsemen of Bhagar were determined to make Nagash's army pay dearly for its victory. Moving invisibly among the dunes, the desert raiders shadowed the slow-moving host and bit at its flanks in an endless series of hit-and-run raids. They would ride out of the desert in a sudden rush, flinging javelins and firing arrows into the enemy ranks, and then turn and flee back into the desert west of the trade road before an effective defence could be organised. When Arkhan's horsemen tried to pursue, they more often than not rode into a carefully laid ambush. Losses mounted, but to the desert raiders' chagrin the dead would simply rise up and march back to the Usurper's encampment.

As the days wore on, the raiders' tactics evolved. Scouts would follow the progress of the army at night, and report back to Shahid ben Alcazzar just after dawn. The desert wolves would then strike the camp at around noontime, knowing that they would be facing less than a third of the Usurper's warriors. Sometimes they ambushed Arkhan's mounted patrols. At other times they would seize a few score of Nagash's lifeless warriors and drag them off into the sands, where they would be dismembered and set ablaze. At still other times they would strike for the heart of the encampment, attempting to reach the tents and the monstrosities slumbering within. Each time, the raiders managed to penetrate a little further into the camp.

Nearly a week after the great battle at the oasis, the Red Fox judged that it was time to strike in earnest. Five days of constant skirmishing had left Nagash's living warriors exhausted, and their numbers were only slightly larger than the numbers of ben Alcazzar's remaining horsemen. The Prince of Bhagar summoned his chieftains and laid out his plan.

Dawn on the sixth day found the army of the Usurper encamped across a rocky plain where the road passed close to the foothills of the Brittle Peaks. The desert to the west receded at this point, until the edge of the sands lay several miles distant. For the first time, the living remnant of Khemri's army was able to relax somewhat, believing that their camp was far more secure.

Behind the line of distant dunes, ben Alcazzar and two-thirds of his chieftains gathered before Ahmet ben Izzedein, Bhagar's Hierophant of Khsar. The desert prince and his chosen men bared their arms and made long cuts with their bronze daggers, letting the blood flow into a golden bowl at ben Izzedein's feet. The god of the desert was a hungry one, and his gifts were given only to those who were willing to make personal sacrifices on his behalf.

Ahmet ben Izzedein knelt before the bowl and began to chant the Invocation of the Raging Wind. Drawing his knife, he added his own blood to the bowl, and then drew up a fistful of sand and blew it in a hissing spray across the surface of the crimson pool.

At once, the desert wind stirred around the assembled warriors, raising a pall of stinging sand into the air. By the time they had leapt into the saddles of their graceful steeds the whirlwind was raging around them. Their war shouts were lost amid Khsar's hungry roar, but their bone horns cut like blades through the noise and sent the raiders sweeping over the dunes and racing across the rocky plain towards the enemy army.

The living warriors of Nagash's host saw the hissing cloud sweeping down upon them and knew what it portended. They leapt, fearfully, to their feet, reaching for their weapons or the reins of frightened horses. Trumpets blared in alarm, and the warriors of the Living City responded as swiftly as their exhausted bodies would allow. Within minutes, ragged bands of heavy cavalry were racing headlong into the storm, while spear companies formed up amid the decaying bodies of their kinsmen and prepared to receive the enemy charge.

Of all the gods, Khsar the Faceless was the least inclined towards humankind, and honoured the great covenant grudgingly at best. His gifts were often two-edged, and his worshippers called upon him only when they must. The raging storm called up by the Hierophant ben Izzedein lashed at both friend and foe, concealing the battle between the raiders and the cavalry in a hissing, knife-edged maelstrom. Riders literally crashed together out of the murk, striking at one another with a handful of frenzied blows, before pulling apart and disappearing once again. The screams of the dying were torn apart by the hungry wind, and the bodies of the dead were reduced to scoured bones within moments.

The desert raiders of Bhagar were in their element, however. With their faces hidden by their head scarves in a sign of devotion to their god, they read the shifting pattern of the winds and knew how to peer through the haze to find their foes. They rode with supernatural skill, as though their steeds could read their very thoughts. The desert horses were a breed apart, thought to be the only gift Khsar ever truly gave to his people, and they were prized above rubies by their masters. Time and again the raiders clashed with their foes, and more often than not they left a horseman of Khemri reeling in the saddle or bleeding out his life upon the ground.

Riderless horses stumbled out of the storm, galloping for the relative safety of the Usurper's camp. The spear companies watched the storm draw steadily closer and clenched their weapons fearfully. Their champions snarled orders to tighten the ranks, forming a solid wall of shields and spears in the face of the raging wind.

The sandstorm swept over the warriors in a hissing, blinding wave, stabbing at their eyes and clawing at every inch of exposed skin. The front ranks recoiled, as though from the impact of an enemy charge, but the rear ranks ducked their heads behind their shields and pushed back, keeping the line intact. Javelins flew out of the murk and fell among the ranks, sticking in shields or sinking through leather and into the flesh beneath. Men screamed and fell, their cries both painful and joyous, as though death was not so much an end as a release from the horrors they had endured.

Riders appeared like ghosts out of the storm, rearing their mounts before the shield wall and slashing down with scimitar and axe. They hacked off spearheads and dented helms, and, here and there, they bit into unprotected arms or necks. More men fell, but before their fellows could react, the riders had turned about and disappeared once more into the whirlwind.

Still, the line held, forming an arc of bronze between the storm and the silent pavilions along the road behind them. Warriors shouted encouragement to the men in front of them and leapt forward to fill the gaps left by their dead comrades. Their courage was desperate and unrelenting, each man knowing what would happen to their families at home if they failed to keep the raiders at bay.

They were so determined to stand in the face of the whirlwind that they failed to notice the silent band of raiders sweeping over the foothills to the east and charging into the opposite side of the camp. Only a handful of heavy horsemen stood in their path, and they quickly fell, riddled by arrows from the raiders' powerful horse bows. The raiders swept over the corpse-strewn ground and raced for the undefended tents just a few hundred yards away.

Shouts of alarm and strident trumpet calls rose from the centre of the camp. Slaves staggered from the tents into the bright sunlight, brandishing knives and wooden clubs in defence of their masters. The men of Bhagar cut them down like reeds, or pinned them to the earth with their barbed javelins, but the slaves' sacrifice delayed the attackers for a few, precious seconds. As the last of them fell, the air seethed with the hissing of countless wings, and the raiders cried out in dismay as a swirling pillar of scarabs spread above the cluster of tents and blocked the noonday sun.

ARKHAN HURLED THE heavy lid of the sarcophagus aside and leapt to his feet, his brain aching from his master's blistering command. The sounds of battle were very close, and the vizier understood at once what had happened. Snatching Suseb's blade from the hands of a kneeling servant, the immortal dashed out into the unnatural darkness.

Two javelins struck him at once, punching into his chest from both the left and the right. The vizier staggered under the twin blows, but stretched out his left hand and hissed a dreadful incantation. A storm of magical bolts sped from his fingertips and slashed through the mass of horsemen before him, pitching men and horses shrieking to the ground.

A desert raider swept in from the right, slashing at Arkhan with his scimitar. The vizier spun on his heel, swinging his massive bronze khopesh and cutting off the horse's forelegs. The screaming, thrashing animal crashed to the ground and pitched the rider from the saddle. The raider landed nimbly and whirled to face Arkhan, but the last thing he saw was the immortal's flashing blade as it crashed into his skull.

Javelins and arrows buzzed through the air, and the shouts of horsemen filled the air. The raiders were among the tents, striking at anyone they could find, and the screams of men and horses echoed through the darkness as the immortals rose from their sleep and joined the swirling battle. Snarling a savage curse, the vizier leapt at the enemy. Fuelled by the fire of Nagash's unholy elixir, Arkhan plunged into the reeling crowd of desert raiders before him. Men fell dead from their saddles or found themselves pinned beneath the thrashing bodies of their mounts as the vizier cut a bloody path through their midst.

Then came a rising chorus of wailing, angry cries, and an eerie green glow suffused the darkness to Arkhan's left. The ghostly chorus swelled to a maddening crescendo, quickly joined by the frenzied screams of living men. A shock went through the crowd of raiders surrounding the vizier, and then suddenly they were gone, galloping madly in the direction of the desert. Arkhan whirled, searching for the cause of their sudden retreat, and saw Nagash, surrounded by almost a score of writhing, screaming men. The necromancer's hands were raised to the sky, and his eyes blazed with baleful light as he unleashed his retinue of ghosts upon his foes. As the vizier watched, the spirits wound around the shrieking men like snakes, pouring through their open mouths and into the corners of their eyes in search of their living souls. They left behind shrivelled, smoking husks, contorted in poses of agonising death.

The sudden, unnatural darkness and the wrath of the awakened necromancer set the desert raiders to flight. The sandstorm was already receding as the worshippers of Khsar fled back to the safety of the dunes. Arkhan raised his stolen sword and jeered at the fleeing raiders. Then he nearly staggered beneath his master's wordless, furious summons.

The vizier made his way swiftly across the battlefield and fell to his knees before the king. His mind raced, trying to puzzle out Nagash's sudden fury.

'What is your bidding, master?' he asked, pressing his forehead to the ground.

'Quatar has fallen,' Nagash declared. 'Nemuhareb and his entire army have been overthrown.' The ghosts surrounding the necromancer echoed his rage, hissing like a clutch of angry vipers. 'The rebel kings have placed him under arrest and seized control of the city.'

The vizier was stunned by the news. Seizing the city? Such a thing was unheard of. Battles between kings were settled on the field of battle, and the loser paid a ransom or other reparations to the victor. Sometimes territory or other rights were forfeited, but unseating a king and taking his city was unprecedented.

'These rebels have no respect for the law,' Arkhan replied carefully, running his tongue over his jagged teeth. It also went without saying that the enemy was within a few weeks' marching distance of Khemri, far closer than Nagash's own battered army.

'They think to weaken me by depriving me of Quatar,' Nagash said, 'but instead they have delivered themselves into my hands. The Kings of Numas and Zandri will not stand for the seizure of the White Palace, and will gladly join their armies with mine to drive the rebels back across the Valley of Kings.' The necromancer clenched his fist and smiled hungrily. 'Then we will march on Lybaras and Rasetra in turn and bring them to heel. This will be the first step in building a new Nehekharan empire.'

Arkhan gazed across the battlefield at the remnants of Khemri's conscript army. Nearly all of the Living City's resources had gone into Nagash's grand design for the last hundred years. This pitiful force of infantry and cavalrymen was the most that could be mustered to challenge Ka-Sabar, and that army was a horror-stricken remnant of what it had been. The vizier knew all too well how heavily Numas and Zandri had been called upon to provide tribute to fund construction of the living god's mighty pyramid. Their armies would be in little better condition than Khemri's, and while Nagash's terrible power could bestir the bodies of fallen warriors, Arkhan could see that the exertions of the campaign had drained even the king's prodigious reserves of strength. With Rasetra and Lybaras in control of the White Palace, they were in a precarious position indeed.

'Numas and Zandri will need time to raise their armies,' Arkhan said, 'and time is something we do not have in abundance. Our foes are in position to reach Khemri even now, while these desert wolves dog our every step–'

The priest king cut him off with a cruel chuckle.

'Do you doubt me, vizier?' he asked.

'No, great one!' Arkhan replied quickly. 'Never! You are the living god, master of life and death!'

'Indeed,' Nagash replied. 'I have defied death and laid the gods low. I am the master of this land, and all that it contains.' The necromancer stretched out his hand, pointing a pale finger at Arkhan's head. 'You look about you and see calamity, our small army in tatters, surrounded by our foes, but that is because your mind is weak, Arkhan the Black. You let the world bend you to its whims. That is the thinking of a mere mortal,' he spat. 'I do not heed the voice of this world, Arkhan. Instead, I command it. I shape it to my will.'

Nagash's cold, handsome face was alight with passion. The cloak of spirits surrounding him writhed and wailed in despair, and Arkhan could feel the power of the grave radiating from the king like a cold desert wind.

The vizier pressed his face to the dust once more.

'I hear you, master,' he said fearfully. 'Victory will be yours, if you will it.'

'Yes,' Nagash hissed. 'So it will. Now rise, vizier,' he said, abruptly turning away and striding in the direction of his pavilion. 'Our foes have made their move. Now we shall counter it.'

Arkhan fell into step behind the king. Every now and then his boot would fall upon one of the desert raiders that Nagash had slain, their bodies crunching like burnt wood beneath his feet.

'Summon your horsemen,' the king said. 'You will ride at once to Bhagar and visit my wrath upon the home of the desert princes.'

The vizier nodded, fighting to keep his face from betraying his trepidation. After the bloody battle at Zedri and the constant skirmishes since, he was left with just under three thousand cavalrymen, living and dead.

'It will be a long ride through enemy territory,' he replied, dreading the idea of crossing harsh desert terrain that his foes knew all too well. He and the other immortals would have to bury themselves deep in the sand to escape the sun's merciless glare.

'You will conquer Bhagar in five days' time,' Nagash declared. Arkhan's good eye widened.

'But we would have to ride day and night,' he said, before he could catch himself.

The necromancer paid no heed to the vizier's impertinence, saying, 'You will take two of the Sheku'met along with you. Use only one at a time, to preserve their strength.'

Arkhan looked up at the swirling, chittering shadow overhead. The Jars of Night were a potent tool, but the great scarabs had to be fed a steady diet of flesh to maintain their sorcerous bond. There had been no lack of food on the battlefield of Zedri, and since then Nagash had set the scarabs to feast upon the bodies of his undead warriors. Arkhan had watched soldiers covered in a writhing carpet of beetles, still marching stolidly down the trade road as the scarabs burrowed deep into their putrefying organs and flensed the skin from their skulls.

'It will be done, master,' the vizier replied. There was nothing else to say. 'What of you and the rest of the army?'

'The Master of Skulls will take charge of the living warriors and return the army to Khemri,' Nagash said as they reached the great pavilion. Slaves prostrated themselves at the king's approach, and a pair of moaning spirits flew from the king's side to peel back the tent's heavy linen entry flap. The tortured figure of Neferem stood just inside, and when the king beckoned, the queen shuffled painfully to his side.

'I shall return to Khemri at once,' Nagash said, 'and summon the Kings of Numas and Zandri to a council of war.' The king turned to Arkhan. 'Remember, you must seize Bhagar in five days' time: no more, no less. When the moon rises on the fifth day, this is what you must do.'

The vizier listened to the king's instructions without expression. He fixed his gaze on the necromancer's glowing eyes and tried to push the image of Neferem from his mind.

'As you wish,' he said, when Nagash was finished. 'Bhagar's fate is sealed.'

The king fixed his vizier with a soul-searching stare, and seemed content to find none. 'Remember, Arkhan the

Black, go and bend the world to my liking, and you will continue to enjoy my favour.'

Then the living god raised his hand to the sky and shouted a string of rasping syllables with his ruined voice. At once, the swarm above him thrummed and spun like a gyre balanced on the necromancer's palm. The leading edges of the great shadow shrank inwards as a torrent of flashing, buzzing scarabs descended in a swirling column around Nagash and his queen. The two figures grew indistinct, and then disappeared altogether.

Arkhan felt the desert air rush past his shoulders, drawn from all directions towards the seething funnel before him. Then, in an instant, the pillar of glittering chitin leapt skywards like the cracking lash of a taskmaster's whip, drawing a column of roiling dust in its wake.

Nagash and the Daughter of the Sun were gone.

The vizier studied the empty space where the king had been, and a bleak look passed across his scarred face. Around him, slaves rose quickly to their feet and went to work striking the tents they had raised only a few hours before. Overhead, the living shadow began to constrict further as the insects, freed from Nagash's will, began to settle to the earth in search of food. The steady approach of sunlight shook Arkhan from his reverie. Slowly at first, and then with growing speed, he began issuing orders.

Within two hours the vizier and his horsemen were heading west, into the unforgiving desert. A restless cloud of hungry scarabs swirled over the centre of the column, shielding Arkhan and his immortal lieutenants from Ptra's searing light.

By mid afternoon, the army was on the march again, shuffling wearily north along the old trade road.

The companies of the dead, no longer animated by the will of their master, were left to fester in the hot desert sun. More than one weary soul looked back at the still figures and envied their fate.

* * *

A RIBBON OF seething, chittering shadow passed low over the Living City shortly after dusk. It raced over the top of the southern wall, past the huddled sentries crouching atop the battlements, and down the neglected streets of the Potter's Quarter. The rooftops of the crumbling, mud-brick homes were deserted, despite the heat of the long day, and not even dogs prowled among the piles of refuse strewn down the narrow lanes. The Merchant Quarter was likewise silent and shuttered tight. The squares of the Grand Bazaar were empty, its stalls dilapidated and its flagstones covered with sand. Only the noble districts further north showed any signs of life, where the city watch patrolled the streets in large, well-armed groups past barricaded courtyards and high walls topped with shards of broken pottery and glass. Even the sprawling complex of Settra's Palace was dark and empty of life. The only light to be seen anywhere on the horizon was off to the east, beyond the city walls, where serpentine flickers of indigo-coloured lightning crawled along the sides of a massive, black pyramid that rose from the centre of Khemri's great necropolis.

The hissing swarm of scarabs wound like a serpent towards the great palace, shedding streamers of smoking insect husks as it went. Finally, it plunged like an arrow into the great plaza outside Settra's Court and poured a flood of wriggling, dying beetles onto the silent square. Their life energies spent on the gruelling northward flight, the last of the scarabs clattered lifelessly to the ground around Nagash and his queen.

Even as the king came to earth, hundreds of slaves were hurrying down the steps from the court and abasing themselves before their master. In their wake came a pallid immortal clad in a crimson-dyed kilt and red leather sandals. The warrior's torso was wrapped in strips of banded leather armour, and wide leather bracers covered his forearms. A cape of flayed human skin fluttered in his wake as he strode swiftly up to Nagash and sank to his knees in supplication.

The priest king acknowledged the immortal with a nod.

'Rise, Raamket,' he commanded. 'How has the city fared in my absence?'

'Order has been restored, great one,' the immortal said at once. Raamket had broad, blunt features, like a rough-hewn statue, with heavy brows and a bulbous, oft-broken nose. His dark eyes held little imagination or wit, but were cold and steady as stone. 'There have been no further riots since the army went south.'

'And the ringleaders?'

'Some have been captured,' Raamket said. 'Others took their lives before we could seize them. The rest have fled the city.'

'How can you be so certain?' Nagash asked, his eyes narrowing in suspicion.

Raamket shrugged, and said, 'Because we have not found them, master. The city has been searched thoroughly, from one end to the other.' A faint smile crossed the immortal's stolid face. 'I personally questioned many of the city's merchants. They swore that many of the priests fled east, towards Quatar.'

Nagash considered the news. 'Relax our patrols,' he ordered, 'and then offer a double ration of grain for anyone that offers information on dissenters still hidden in the city. If there are any rebels left they will grow bold once they learn that the White Palace has fallen.'

Raamket's dark eyes glittered at the sudden news.

'The east has risen against us?' he asked. The savage immortal sounded pleased at the prospect.

'Lybaras and Rasetra have chosen to defy me,' the king answered darkly, 'and I suspect they are not alone.'

Nagash set off quickly towards the steps to Settra's Court, leaving the servants to surround the queen and escort her into the palace. Raamket fell into step behind his master. 'How shall we deal with these traitors?' the warrior asked.

'Send messengers to Numas and Zandri,' Nagash commanded. 'Summon the kings to attend upon me at Settra's Court in four days' time to attend a council of war. Quatar will be retaken, and then the east will drown in a sea of blood.'

Raamket smiled, revealing white teeth filed to needle-sharp points, and said, 'It will be done, master.'

◀ EIGHT ▶

Red Rain

The desert city of Bhagar, in the 62nd year of Qu'aph the Cunning (-1750 Imperial Reckoning)

ON THE MORNING of the fifth day, Arkhan's horsemen crested the dunes east of Bhagar and found Shahid ben Alcazzar and his horsemen awaiting them just beyond the green expanse of the city's caravanserai.

The vizier reined in his rune-marked warhorse at the top of the furthest dune and spat a stream of incredulous curses into the shadow-bound sky. He had pushed his warriors relentlessly, pausing only at dawn and dusk to open the Jars of Night and then seal them up again. He killed horses and men by the score along the way, returning their corpses to the ranks when their exhausted bodies could withstand no more. Still others were sacrificed to the ravening scarabs. Their bones now gleamed white in the preternatural gloom, knit together by black sorcery alone. All so that he could outpace ben Alcazzar's horsemen and strike at their home before they could mount a proper defence, and yet they had still managed to outpace him!

When he'd run out of curses to hurl at the uncaring heavens, Arkhan sat back in his saddle and took quick stock of his situation. His horsemen, almost two thousand in all, were spread in a rough arc along the line of dunes to his left and right. Five hundred yards distant, the desert raiders waited in a ragged line, grouped around the fluttering banners of their chieftains. Arkhan's advance guard, consisting of little more than two hundred horsemen, formed a thin screen in the middle ground between the two forces.

'Signal Shepsu-hur to fall back,' the vizier ordered, gesturing angrily to his trumpeter. Nodding wearily, the musician brought the horn to his lips and blew a complex series of notes. Within moments, the advance guard was withdrawing across the rolling terrain. Arkhan noted that the desert raiders made no attempt to pursue.

Shepsu-hur left his horsemen at the bottom of the dune and spurred his struggling mount up the sandy slope to make his report. The immortal was wrapped in bindings of linen and leather from neck to toe, covering nearly every inch of his exposed skin. Only his ruined face was left uncovered, revealing the terrible injuries he'd received in the battle at the palace only a few weeks before. No amount of Nagash's sorcerous elixir had been enough to seal up the gaping wounds in the nobleman's cheeks and forehead, or restore his shrivelled lips and the ragged stub of his nose. Charred bone showed through the tear in the immortal's square chin as he spoke.

'The horsemen arrived less than an hour ahead of us,' the maimed immortal rasped. 'Some of them withdrew into the city when we arrived.'

'No doubt telling their kin to flee into the desert,' Arkhan said. He knew that some of the citizens would escape; it could not be avoided. The people of Bhagar were devout followers of Khsar, and they knew the ways of the desert well. Most, however, were trapped. If they tried to run, his men would ride them down. 'How many riders?' he asked.

Leather wrappings creaked as the immortal shrugged.

'Perhaps three thousand,' he said, 'but their horses are blown. They pushed themselves past the point of exhaustion getting here ahead of us.'

'Then this won't last long,' the vizier said, nodding grimly.

Drawing his huge khopesh, Arkhan called to his trumpeter. 'Sound the charge!' he commanded. 'We will press on to the city, regardless of the cost!'

Trumpet notes sang their clarion call along the dunes, and the mass of horsemen started to move down the sandy slope. Shepsu-hur wheeled his mount and raced ahead to catch up with his squadron. Arkhan kneed his warhorse forwards at a trot, his attendants closing ranks around him.

Bhagar was a prosperous city, but a small one. Its princes had nothing to fear from bandits, and it had never been so wealthy as to attract the attention of the larger cities to the north and the east. As a result, its leaders had never seen the need to spend vast sums building a wall around the city. Now, its horsemen tried to form a living barrier against the vizier's warriors, but Arkhan could see how the proud raiders slumped in their saddles, and the heads of their magnificent horses hung low to the ground. Better for Shahid ben Alcazzar to have preserved his men, Arkhan thought. He might not have saved his city, but at least he might have lived to avenge it another day. Now the proud desert prince would die along with them.

The Khemri horsemen spread out across the rolling, sandy terrain as they reached the bottom of the dunes, the immortals leading the way, followed by the grim, silent corpses of men that had belonged to their squadrons. The living cavalrymen fell behind, unnerved by the dead comrades riding in their midst. Far ahead, the proud desert horses of their enemies tossed their heads and pawed at the sand as the scent of rotting flesh reached them.

Still, the desert raiders waited, taking no action as their foes drew nearer. Arkhan peered through the gloom with his one eye, trying to locate ben Alcazzar and his retinue. What was the prince's standard? The vizier couldn't recall.

Three hundred yards... two hundred and fifty. Maddened shouts and wailing cries went up from the immortals, and the horses quickened their pace to a canter. A shadow passed over the desert raiders as the leading edge of the scarab cloud swept over them. Arkhan watched them become forbidding silhouettes, standing starkly against the lush greenery of the caravan oasis at their back.

Then, a figure at the rear of the desert horsemen raised a shining scimitar to the heavens. It caught the last of the sunlight, flashing with Ptra's angry fire, and then Arkhan heard a faint shout that cut through the mounting thunder of hoof beats.

A hot wind hissed through the oncoming cavalry. Arkhan felt its rasping touch slide across his cheeks. Then the hissing rose to a full-throated roar, and the world disappeared in a raging maelstrom of sand.

Arkhan raised a hand to his face with a bitter curse. Horses and men screamed in surprise and fright. The sandstorm lashed at exposed skin with a million invisible knives, clothing and even leather fraying beneath its unrelenting touch. The vizier's ensorcelled mount reared and tossed its head in pain. Arkhan pulled savagely at the reins and fought to keep his seat.

The onslaught lasted only a few seconds. It crashed through the Khemri force with all the power of a cavalry charge, and when the wall of sand had swept past, the heavy cavalry was scattered and disoriented, their forward momentum lost. The next sound they heard was the deadly hum of arrows and the spine-chilling wail of the desert raiders as they charged in behind Khsar's savage wind.

Shahid ben Alcazzar was called the Red Fox for a reason. Though nearly spent, the horsemen of Bhagar were far from helpless.

A hail of arrows and throwing javelins raked the stunned Khemri force. Men and animals fell to the ground, dead or thrashing in their death throes. Then the charge of the desert raiders struck home, and bronze clashed against bronze in a swirling, furious melee.

The ferocity of the Bhagar attack might have broken the Khemri force at the outset, had the riders all been living flesh and blood, but the immortals and their dead warriors were impervious to fear and contemptuous of javelins and arrows. The living cavalrymen reeled from the attack, but the dead raised their weapons and fought on.

A trio of panicked cavalrymen raced past Arkhan's plunging mount. With a snarl, the vizier cut them down with a volley of sorcerous bolts, and then spat Nagash's dread incantation and returned their corpses to the battle. The horses' smoking bodies clambered awkwardly upright, and the blackened husks of their riders climbed back into their saddles. The cavalrymen turned their melted faces to the vizier for a moment, and then, as one, they wheeled about and charged into the fray.

With a shout, a desert raider broke free from a pair of Khemri horsemen and bore down on Arkhan, his dark eyes blazing with hate. The vizier brought his horse around and called upon the power of Nagash's elixir. His blood burned, and the attacking rider seemed to move in slow, languid motion. Arkhan swatted aside the rider's blade and then slashed open his chest as the warrior lumbered past, once more uttering the arcane incantation that would bind the dead to his bidding. The raider's blood-soaked corpse had barely struck the ground before it was moving once more, rising clumsily onto its feet and staggering off in search of its former kinsmen.

Across the battlefield, the dead rose from the ground and threw themselves at the living. The men of Bhagar cried out in terror as the bloody corpses clung to their legs, snatched at reins or struck at them with knife and fist. The raiders slashed at the undead with swords and axes, severing arms and caving in skulls, but for every corpse that fell, another waited to take its place, and the men of Bhagar had precious little strength left after their long, wild ride across the desert.

Still the battle raged, with neither side willing to give ground. The forces were intermingled, and there was no telling who had the upper hand. Arkhan looked around for his trumpeter, and found the boy on the ground a short distance away with an arrow through his eye. With a snarl, the vizier realised that he scarcely needed the horn any more. The dead would do his bidding according to his will, and there were more of them joining his side with every passing minute.

Suddenly, Arkhan heard a whistling roar off to his right, and a plume of dust and sand rose like a fist into the sky. Men and horses were caught up in it and flung through the air like toys. The vizier bared his jagged teeth. That had to be the city's Hierophant of Khsar, and ben Alcazzar would no doubt be somewhere close by. Spurring his horse with a shout, Arkhan headed towards the slowly collapsing pillar of earth with the surviving members of his retinue in close pursuit.

Once again, he called upon the power of the elixir in his blood, and Arkhan waded through a sea of turgid bodies and drifting blades. He cut down everything in his path, be it enemy or friend. Every man he slew rose in his wake and rejoined the battle, their expressions still fixed in the agonising moment of death.

After what seemed like an eternity of slaughter, Arkhan came upon a knot of desert horsemen surrounded by a rising tide of slashing, snapping corpses. The vizier recognised ben Alcazzar at once, with his black leather armour and flowing head scarf. The prince rode a fiery white warhorse whose flanks were near pink with gore, and his scimitar was red and notched nearly to the hilt. He was surrounded by a dozen of his kinsmen, who slashed and stabbed at the encircling horde with grim, silent determination. The warriors had learned that a corpse without a head would not rise again, and they plied their blades like executioners, striking down one slow-moving undead warrior after another. The mindless corpses were already being forced to climb over the mounded heaps of their fellows in order to reach their prey. Arkhan noted with surprise that two of the headless bodies near the prince had the alabaster skin of immortals.

Next to ben Alcazzar sat a brown-robed man on a dusty steed, wielding a curled wooden staff instead of a blade. As the vizier watched, the man pointed his staff at a cluster of nearby riders and bellowed an entreaty to Khsar. At once, the sand beneath the riders exploded upwards with a roar like a storm wind, hurling their broken bodies more than thirty feet into the air.

Cursing, Arkhan cast around for something he could throw. He caught sight of the body of a warhorse nearby with a javelin jutting from its side, and rode over to grab it. The barbed shaft did not come free easily, even with the vizier's more-than-human strength, but finally he held the bloodstained weapon in his hands.

There was another blast of air just a few dozen paces to Arkhan's right, sweeping up half of the vizier's retinue and crushing the life out of them. With a savage shout, Arkhan turned in the saddle and hurled the javelin at the hierophant with all of his might.

The priest saw the weapon streak towards him at nearly the last moment and raised his staff in a desperate attempt to block Arkhan's throw. Had the javelin been cast by a mortal hand, the priest might have succeeded; as it was, the hierophant simply wasn't fast enough to keep the weapon's bronze head from punching into his chest and hurling him from his saddle.

Shahid ben Alcazzar saw the priest fall, and followed the path of the javelin back to Arkhan, some ten yards away. The vizier met the prince's dark eyes, smiled, and then spoke the Incantation of Summoning.

A moment later the prince's horse reared in fright, and ben Alcazzar staggered as the corpse of the priest tried to pull him from the saddle. The two figures struggled for a moment. Then, with a savage cry, ben Alcazzar drew back his sword and buried it in his older brother's skull.

As the priest's body fell limply to the ground, the prince glanced wildly around, and saw only a sea of grasping, bloody hands and slack, lifeless faces. Some of those who reached hungrily for him were once his friends or his cousins. Finally, ben Alcazzar turned back to Arkhan and shouted, 'Enough! Stop this tide of horrors, and I will yield!' The prince reached up and tore away his head scarf, revealing the anguish etched deep into his handsome face.

Arkhan raised his hand, and with a single thought his undead warriors retreated a step and grew still. Across the battlefield, the clamour of battle abruptly tapered off. The vizier edged his horse forwards until he was just a few yards from the prince. He smiled.

'What will you give so that your people may survive?' he asked.

'Take whatever you want,' ben Alcazzar said thickly. Tears stained his tanned cheeks. 'There is gold enough in Bhagar to make you a king, Arkhan the Black. I'll pay any price you name.'

Arkhan's dark eyes glittered.

'Done,' he said, and the fate of Bhagar was sealed.

THE KINGS ARRIVED in Khemri at roughly the same time, early on the evening of the fifth day after Nagash's return. The twin Priest Kings of Numas, Seheb and Nuneb, travelled south through the fertile river lands north of the Vitae with a mounted retinue of Ushabti, viziers, scribes and slaves. They crossed the great river by ferry, arriving at the empty city docks just as the royal barges of Zandri were poling their way to shore. The viziers of the two royal parties eyed one another with diplomatic reserve, and then hissed sharp orders to their slaves to begin disembarking as quickly as possible.

Within minutes, the square began filling with horses, chariots, palanquins and scores of frantic slaves as each procession sought to gain the advantage of precedence over the other. Zandri's chief vizier took the tactical step of ordering the king's wardrobe to be left aboard his barge, saving nearly half an hour of unloading. Not to be outdone, the chief vizier for the horse lords noted the surreptitious manoeuvre and sent a message across the river that only the chariots of the twin kings should be brought across, consigning the rest of the retinue to walk the rest of the way to the palace. Gold was pressed into the palms of the ferrymen to redouble their efforts, and bargemen were pulled from their duties and pressed into service unloading the royal household. Slaves lost their footing and fell into the river, and no one could spare a moment to aid them.

In the end, despite heroic efforts and great sacrifice on both sides, the kings reached the docks at very nearly the same time. The viziers had fought to a draw, bowing curtly to one another across the open square.

It was only then that the functionaries noticed the unease of the royal bodyguards, and realised how silent and dark the Living City had become. They looked around the deserted wharves, lit only by Neru's silver glow, and wondered at all the rumours they had heard about Khemri's ageless king.

No sooner had the royal personages set foot on the docks than a single, pale figure appeared at the southern edge of the square. Raamket, approached the three kings, his cloak of flayed skin spreading like ghastly wings around his shoulders.

'Nagash the Living God welcomes you,' he said, bowing deeply. 'It is my honour to escort you into his presence.'

Before the shocked kings could offer a reply, the vizier beckoned to the twin Kings of Numas, and then turned and set off at a brisk stride towards the palace. The order of precedence had been set, and a hissed command from the vizier set the royal chariots rattling forwards across the paving stones, leaving Amn-nasir and his scowling retainers to follow as best they could.

The procession made its way down the empty streets of the noble district, wondering at the walled compounds and bronze-studded gates. At the palace, the great gates stood open, but no guards stood watch at the entrance. Likewise, the great plaza outside Settra's Court was deserted, save for swooping bats and scuttling lizards hunting among the drifts of sand. There were no trumpets to announce their arrival, nor white-robed acolytes to bless them with salt and the joyous clash of cymbals. Unnerved, the twin Kings of Numas stepped from their chariots and joined Raamket at the steps to Settra's Court to await Amn-nasir's arrival, leaving their viziers to mutter fearfully and oversee the unpacking of gifts to present to Khemri's king. The twin kings' keen-eyed Ushabti, clad in white kilts and leather armour ornamented with medallions of turquoise and gold, surrounded their royal charges and glared forbiddingly into the deep shadows surrounding the square.

Fifteen minutes later, the Zandri delegation wound its way into the plaza, and Amn-nasir joined his royal peers with as much affronted dignity as he could manage. The Priest King of Zandri was stocky and walked with the rolling gait of a lifelong sailor. At the venerable age of a hundred and twenty, his years at sea were long behind him, but his frame was still lean and strong. By contrast, the twin horse lords were tall and fey, with darting eyes and sharp, angular features. Bands of hammered gold decorated their slim arms, and their black hair was bound in identical horsetail queues. The rulers of both cities owed their wealth to trade: slaves from the wild north in the case of Zandri, and herds of fine horses raised on the plains around Numas. Together, they represented the richest cities in all of Nehekhara, and they remained so because they allied themselves with the Priest King of Khemri.

Raamket wasted no time on ceremony. As soon as Amn-nasir joined them, the vizier bowed silently and led the way past the tall pillars and into Settra's Court. The statues of Asaph and Geheb were lost in shadow, their feet covered by piles of charred and broken stone.

Beyond, the great hall was as dark as a tomb. The only light came from the Priest King of Khemri, sitting upon the ancient wooden throne and surrounded by the restless glimmer of his ghostly retinue.

Raamket stepped swiftly into the hall, his sandals whispering softly across the marble floor. The three kings stared at one another uncertainly, all thought of precedence forgotten, until by silent agreement they entered the court together with their bodyguards close behind. Their footsteps echoed in the vast space, and the Ushabti nervously fingered their weapons as they felt unseen eyes watching them from the darkness along the length of the hall.

At the foot of the dais, Raamket fell to his knees before his master. The swirling nimbus of glowing spirits regarded the three kings with empty eyes and faint, fearful moans. Their funereal glow silhouetted the lower legs of the great statue of Ptra behind the wooden throne, revealing jagged scars and pockmarks blasted into the gold-plated sandstone. To Nagash's right, the ghostly luminescence outlined the edge of the queen's lesser throne. From time to time, the ebb and flow of the unearthly light would play across the bony tip of a shoulder clad in spotless samite, or the edge of a resplendent golden headdress.

Nagash slouched upon Settra's ornate throne, resting his head on the palm of his hand in contemplation. He studied the three kings coldly, his eyes like flecks of polished obsidian. 'Greetings, kings of the north and west,' the necromancer rasped. 'The Living City welcomes you.'

The regal twins of Numas paled at the sound of Nagash's ruined voice, and could not manage a reply. Amn-nasir, older and made of sterner stuff, mastered his deep unease and said, 'Your summons came as a great surprise. We thought you were far to the south, answering the challenge of Ka-Sabar.'

'Circumstances to the east compelled my return,' Nagash replied. 'No doubt you have learned of the battle at the Gates of the Dawn.' Amn-nasir shot a sidelong glance at the twin Kings of Numas.

'There are rumours,' he admitted. 'It is said that the Tomb Guard has been overthrown, and the Priest Kings of Rasetra and Lybaras have seized the White Palace.'

'It is no rumour,' Nagash declared. 'Hekhmenukep and Rakh-amn-hotep, that treacherous son of Khemri, have broken the ancient code of warfare laid down by Settra and deposed Quatar's rightful ruler. Now they are poised to march upon the Living City.' The Priest King of Khemri straightened slowly upon the ancient throne and stared intently at his guests. 'This is no mere feud between kings. These reckless men have invited chaos upon all of Nehekhara, and we must give answer to them!'

'But… what would you have us say?' Nuneb stammered. 'Your warriors are many days away, are they not?'

'And we have neither the gold nor the time to raise an army,' Seheb added.

'It is the same with Zandri,' Amn-nasir said. 'As you know very well, great one.'

'Once a crocodile tastes human flesh, it wants nothing else,' Nagash growled. 'These outlaw kings have taken Quatar, and intend to seize Khemri next. Do you imagine they will stop there? If we do not stand together against them they will surely conquer us one by one.'

'What of Lahmia?' Seheb asked. The young king's gaze flicked nervously to the hunched silhouette upon Neferem's throne. 'Where does Lamashizzar stand?'

'Or Mahrak?' Nuneb said. 'Surely the Hieratic Council will repudiate what Rasetra and Lybaras have done.'

'The Hieratic Council,' Nagash said with a bubbling sneer. 'Hekhmenukep and Rakh-amn-hotep are their pawns. They intend to destroy me, and because you are my allies, they will supplant you as well!'

'Is this because of what you did to Khemri's temples?' Amn-nasir asked. 'Or does it have to do with the darkness that fell across Nehekhara several weeks past? The one that slew so many young priests and acolytes?'

'It is because the Hierophants of Mahrak see me as a threat to their corrupt rule,' Nagash said, his eyes narrowed angrily at the Priest King of Zandri.

'Because you are a living god?' Amn-nasir asked archly.

A flicker of triumph shone in the necromancer's dark eyes, and he replied, 'Because I have conquered death itself.'

'Be that as it may, it does not change the fact that the armies of Rasetra and Lybaras are within a few weeks' march of Khemri,' the Priest King of Zandri said, unmoved. 'The warriors of Zandri have not fought a battle in centuries. Our weapons are dulled and our armour lies in tatters.'

'Numas is little better,' Seheb said. 'Our nobles are poor, and our treasury all but exhausted.' He spread his hands helplessly. 'We would need years to rebuild our neglected army.'

The Priest King of Khemri listened to the kings, and nodded.

'Then you shall have it,' he said. 'I shall keep our foes at bay while you prepare your cities for war.'

Seheb and Nuneb glanced nervously at one another, and then looked to Amn-nasir. The Priest King of Zandri eyed Nagash warily.

'How is such a thing possible?' Amn-nasir asked.

Nagash rose to his feet and smiled mirthlessly down at the three kings. 'Go home and ask your priests, Amn-nasir. Ask how their gods used to punish those who defied them. Then consider how fortunate you are to be an ally of Khemri.'

WITHIN HOURS THE three kings were gone, heading back to their homes with their gifts still in hand and their minds troubled with thoughts of war. Darkness fell heavy upon the Living City as midnight drew near, and an ebon palanquin borne by a dozen pallid and shuffling slaves made its way from Settra's Palace through the empty streets, heading in the direction of the Gate of Usirian. To the east, the night sky was lit with strange, shifting lights and crackling lashes of indigo-coloured lightning.

Inside the swaying conveyance, Nagash sat cross-legged upon the cushions with the Staff of the Ages by his side and a great book lying open before him. Dark glyphs and arcane diagrams stood out starkly from the brittle pages of yellow papyrus, lit by the swirling aura of spirits that surrounded the King of the Living City. The necromancer traced their curving lines with a meditative fingertip, preparing for the ritual to come.

The slaves carried their master down the long road towards the necropolis, their feet slapping rhythmically on the clean-swept stones. The broad fields to the south of the road, once vibrant with grain, now lay mostly fallow. To the north, along the banks of the river, the reeds grew unchecked. The ancient shrines were abandoned and showed signs of neglect, and the slaves gazed fearfully into the darkness, wondering what evil spirits might be watching them from the shadows.

At length, they drew near to the vast city of the dead. The crowded tombs shone beneath the shifting veils of light that hung above the centre of the necropolis: strange, ominous curtains of green and purple that seemed to coalesce out of the air and twist in strange patterns above the enormous pyramid at the city's heart. Greater than Settra's Tomb, greater even than the Great Pyramid of Khemri, the sloped sides of Nagash's Black Pyramid towered above them all. Wrought from black marble quarried in the Mountains of the Dawn, the pyramid was darker than the night; indeed, the eerie storm of lights swirling above it made no reflection in its matte black surface. Ribbons of indigo lightning curled and crackled up the pyramid's four sides, coming together at its needle-pointed peak and coruscating through the sheets of colour swirling high above. Power radiated from the monument in palpable waves, washing over the surrounding tombs and down the twisting lanes of the necropolis.

The slaves bore the palanquin to the base of the ebon pyramid and sank silently to their knees, their limbs trembling not from inertia, but from pure, atavistic fear. Nagash emerged from the palanquin at once, the great book hanging in the air by his side, and strode swiftly through the monument's shadow-haunted archway.

Beyond lay a narrow corridor of close-fitting black stones, carved with row upon row of carefully ordered glyphs. No golden statues or colourful mosaics adorned the walls of the crypt, and no torch sconces broke the seamless procession of arcane symbols. The Black Pyramid was no palace to house the body of a dead king; it was built to tap the energies of the otherworld.

The vast structure held more than a hundred rooms, both within the pyramid and dug deep into the earth beneath. Terrible spells of misdirection and death had been laid upon its corridors and intersections, and all the devious arts of Khemri's tomb builders had been brought to bear to kill unwanted intruders with subtle, deadly traps. Only Nagash knew them all, and he made his way swiftly down the dark hallways and through huge, echoing chambers crowded with occult tomes and centuries of arcane experiments. He made his way towards the very centre of the pyramid, to a small room of stone that lay precisely beneath the peak of the towering structure more than four hundred feet above. The chamber was pyramidal in shape, the floor and walls each constructed of a single slab of black marble, carved with hundreds of sigils and glyphs. A vast, complex sign had been incised into the stone floor and inlaid with gold by the priest king. He had spent twenty years learning the art of its construction before hazarding the attempt. No one else could be trusted with such a delicate, precise task.

Nagash stepped carefully across the lines of the great symbol and stood in its centre. Midnight was almost at hand. At the heart of the pyramid he could sense the movement of the moons and stars overhead, moving in their careful, measured paths. Currents of dark magic, drawn through the air from the very crown of the world, swirled and seethed against the tomb's black flanks.

Raising his hands to the sky, Nagash spoke the first words of the great ritual in his broken, rasping voice.

FAR TO THE south, the sky was clear, with a vault of glittering stars high overhead. Neru, the bright moon, was sinking low to the west, and baleful Sakhmet, the Green Witch, shone cruelly overhead as Arkhan and his warriors led the people of Bhagar out onto the plain between the city and the caravanserai.

Shahid ben Alcazzar and his desert princes had been bound with ropes, along with their families and slaves, and surrounded by a cordon of undead riders. Behind them came the traders, the craftsmen, the farmers, beggars and thieves: all the people of the city, in a shuffling, heartbroken mass. They were bound in huge slave coffles that stretched for more than a mile, leading back along the trade road into the heart of the city.

The remnants of Arkhan's mounted force waited upon the plain with the city's wealth gathered in their midst: a stamping, wide-eyed herd of magnificent desert horses, the wondrous gifts of Khsar. In Nehekhara, where a noble's status was measured in part by the number of horses in his stable, the herd was practically worth its weight in gold. The princes and their sons wept openly at the sight of their beloved companions in the hands of their foes.

Ben Alcazzar walked at the head of the vast procession, surrounded by his wives and children. His face was like stone, but his dark eyes were full of pain. Any price, he had said to Arkhan upon the battlefield, with the blood of his own brother staining his hands: anything, so that his people might survive. Terrible as his fears had been, he'd never dreamt it would come to this.

Arkhan waited with his horsemen upon the plain. Less than two thousand remained, and nearly all of those were bloodied and dead. The desert raiders had fought like daemons to defend their home, plunging knives into their foes even as they died. More than a quarter of the immortals accompanying the force had been slain, their decapitated bodies buried under piles of the enemy dead. The vizier's force had been wiped out twice over, he estimated, and only dark sorcery and pure, black will had saved the day.

The desert princes were led out into the centre of the plain by the undead horsemen. The slave coffles were herded to the left and right some fifty yards distant, forming long processions of weeping, distraught figures. Arkhan nudged his horse forwards, followed by Shepsu-hur and a score of grim-faced immortals bearing naked blades in their hands. The vizier could feel the blood start to pound in his veins, a slow, relentless rhythm, pulsing like a dark tide through his brain. Words, too faint to understand, whispered dreadfully in his ears.

Arkhan reined in before Shahid ben Alcazzar. The desert prince watched him approach, and for a moment the fire of defiance lit his dark eyes.

'May all the gods curse you, Arkhan the Black,' he said in a voice grown hoarse with sadness. 'What mercy is this, turning my people into slaves?'

'At least they will survive,' the vizier said coldly, 'for a time, at least. Such is the mercy of Nagash.'

The pulse was growing stronger, rippling through his body in waves. The other immortals felt it, too, their bodies swaying in their saddles, caught in the grip of its power. Arkhan's hand tightened on the hilt of his blade.

'I have kept my promise,' he said, baring his jagged teeth. 'Now you must pay the price.'

Shahid's defiant expression faltered. He glanced down at his chained hands.

'You have taken my freedom,' he cried. 'What more must I pay?'

The words were ringing in Arkhan's ears, rasping and insistent. His vision reddened under the pounding of blood in his temples, and his reply came out as a wordless growl as he raised his sword to the sky.

Behind the vizier, bronze flashed in the green moonlight as the horsemen drew their curved daggers and plunged them into the necks of the desert herd. Horses screamed and tossed their heads, scattering ribbons of steaming blood across the sands, and still the knives flashed and fell, slaughtering Bhagar's priceless steeds.

Howls of shock and despair went up from the people of the city as they saw their horses slain. Shahid ben Alcazzar's face turned ashen at the sight. The shock of the slaughter pierced his heart deeper than any blade. Arkhan saw the light go out of the desert prince's eyes long before his sword plunged into ben Alcazzar's neck.

Screams and wailing pleas went up from the chieftains and their households as the immortals waded in among them, their swords hacking down left and right in brutal, bloody strokes. Men threw themselves in front of the falling blades, protecting their wives with their last breaths, and mothers tried to cover the bodies of their stunned and silent children. The fetlocks of the immortals' horses turned red with steaming gore.

The people of Bhagar rent their clothes and tore at their hair in misery as they were forced to witness the massacre. As terrible as the bloodletting was, worse still were the spectral figures that rose in torment from the mutilated bodies and were drawn into a swirling pillar of shrieking souls that rose into the starlit sky and sped in a twisting ribbon off to the distant north.

A HOWLING WIND stirred the space within the Black Pyramid, stirring Nagash's robes as the necromancer's ritual neared its peak. Dark magic flowed down the sides of the great crypt, drawn by the arcane symbols carved into its vast flanks, and were channelled through conduits worked cunningly into the stone. The power flowed into Nagash, and with it he reached out with his will across hundreds of leagues and seized upon the death energies of Bhagar's noble houses and their enchanted steeds. He drew their tormented spirits to him, down into the black stone of the pyramid, and fed them to the ritual he had painstakingly built.

Above the massive pyramid, the night sky grew heavy with dark, swirling clouds. Indigo lightning leapt from the black stone into the sky, kindling unholy fires deep within the boiling mist. Pain, agony and death, distilled from a thousand tormented spirits, was poured into the growing storm.

Deep in the pyramid, Nagash raised the Staff of the Ages to the stone peak above him and shouted a single, arcane syllable. There was a flash of light, and a rushing chorus of wailing souls, and then, in an instant, the roiling storm overhead vanished, leaving the world stunned and silent in its wake.

HUNDREDS OF LEAGUES distant, sentries pacing the walls of Quatar noticed the dark clouds gathering over the city from the west. Many of them were from Rasetra, and were used to the sudden storms of the southern jungle, so they paid little heed to the building storm.

Slowly and steadily, the clouds piled up over the city, blotting out the stars above. Hours later, the first, heavy drops began to fall. They pattered thickly against the stones and splashed on the helmets of the soldiers. Some turned their faces towards the sky and tasted the rain on their lips. It was warm and bitter, tasting of copper and ash. They wiped their chins and, holding up their hands to the guttering torches, they saw that their palms were slick with blood.

Red rain fell across Quatar, staining the White Palace crimson and filling the streets with puddles of gore. It fell upon the citizens sleeping on their roofs and spattered the faces of the priests who hurried from their temples and stared wide-eyed at the heavens.

The ghastly downpour lasted until a minute before dawn. When it was done, the entire city was steaming like a sacrificial altar.

By nightfall the first people began to sicken and die.

⟨NINE⟩

Secrets within the Blood

Khemri, the Living City, in the 44th year of Qu'aph the Cunning (-1966 Imperial Reckoning)

THE EMISSARY OF Quatar approached the king's throne to the beat of hide drums and the tolling of a deep, bronze bell, leading a procession of courtiers garbed in bone-coloured linen and fine, golden masks. Behind them came a score of pale-skinned barbarian slaves, naked but for colourful strips of cotton tied to their throats and arms like the feathers of singing birds. They carried open chests of sandalwood and polished bronze in their calloused hands, filled with gold coins, precious spices and other exotic treasures. It was mid-afternoon, and the air inside Settra's Court was hazy with swirling clouds of incense. The grand assembly had been in progress for more than four hours, and the city's nobles were casting impatient glances towards the dais and shifting uncomfortably from one foot to the other. Outside, a new acolyte had taken up the role of the Ptra'khaf, summoning the wealthy and powerful to attend upon their king in a sweet, singsong voice. Nagash fancied he heard a note of desperation in the young boy's call.

The Grand Hierophant moved amid the deep shadows behind the court's towering marble columns, watching the games of state play out on the grand processional before the dais. In Khetep's time, the court would have been easily three-quarters full during the monthly grand assembly, with the second sons of every noble family and emissaries from all of Nehekhara's cities in attendance. The last time the chamber had known such a throng had been on the day of the old king's interment, but, two years later, the great hall was little more than a third full. Ghazid and the king's servants had spread out the attendants from the dais to nearly the middle of the room to make the assembly seem larger than it truly was.

'Beware of nobles bearing gifts,' Khefru murmured over Nagash's shoulder. 'It looks as though old Amamurti has decided he's had enough. I wonder if he'll head back to the White Palace, or decamp to Zandri's court next?'

Near-invisible in the deep shadows, Nagash sneered in the direction of the emissary and his entourage, and said, 'Judging by the richness of his gifts, Amamurti will be boarding a barge for Zandri by sunset. He'll regret his lavishness once he reaches the coast. The old goat will have to pay dearly to gain Nekumet's favour over the embassies already camped there.'

From the moment of Khetep's death by the banks of the Vitae, Khemri's power and influence had slipped like grains of sand from the weak hands of his successor. Rasetra's envoy had been the first to take his leave of Thutep's court, amid promises of eternal goodwill and support for Khemri's policies. Then the desert princes of Bhagar had departed, followed by the envoys of Bel Aliad and Lybaras. Within months, word reached Khemri that the dignitaries had taken up residence in Zandri instead, paying homage to Nekumet's court. Slowly but surely, the locus of power was shifting away from the Living City for the first time in history, and for all his impassioned speeches and lofty ideals, Thutep seemed powerless to stop it.

Even Khemri's noble houses had begun to lose their respect for the king's authority. None of the most powerful families chose to attend the royal summons to the grand assembly. At first there had been elaborate excuses and sincere regrets, but now they simply ignored the call of the Ptra'khaf in favour of other pursuits. Many of the lesser houses had followed suit, and as the Grand Hierophant surveyed the bored-looking nobles gathered in the hall he found that he recognised less than half of them.

Not that Nagash had been a fixture in Thutep's court since his brother's ascension. For the last two years he had spent nearly every night in the secret chambers within the Great Pyramid, seeking to master the sorcerous arts of the druchii. He'd spent months learning their degenerate tongue, and hours listening to their hissing discourses on the nature of magic. Everything they told him confirmed his beliefs: the gods were not the wellsprings of the world's power. Magic permeated the land, invisible and omnipresent as the desert wind. Those that were sensitive to its touch could direct its flow, providing they had a keen mind and a potent will. So the druchii said, and yet, despite his every effort, Nagash felt nothing.

The Grand Hierophant paused beside the rounded bulk of a marble column, his handsome face hidden in shadow.

'A court full of jackals and mangy dogs,' he observed, studying the crowd with a sour expression. 'Who are these fools?'

Khefru stepped up to his master's side, and said, 'Third and fourth sons, mostly, with no prospects or inheritance. Most of them are here because of public debts or other minor crimes. Your brother requires them to attend the grand assembly to help atone for their misdeeds.' The young priest smirked. 'I know many of them quite well.'

'Such as?' the Grand Hierophant asked, his eyes narrowing thoughtfully.

'Well,' Khefru murmured. He nodded his head at a group of noblemen standing on the opposite side of the hall. 'Take that pack of rats over there,' he said. 'You won't find a worse lot of drunkards and gamblers in all of Khemri. The tall one in the middle is named Arkhan the Black. He'd cut his own mother's throat for a bag of coin.'

Nagash arched a narrow eyebrow, and said, 'Arkhan the Black?'

'If we were close enough to see his teeth, you wouldn't have to ask,' Khefru said, chuckling softly. 'He chews jusesh root like a common fisherman, and he's got a smile like a smashed wine cup. Spends most of his ill-gotten coin on favours at Asaph's Temple, and word is that he has to pay double before any of the priestesses will go near him.'

'My brother makes a mockery out of all of us,' Nagash hissed, shaking his head in disgust. His hands clenched angrily at the thought of his father's blasted corpse and the terrible power that had destroyed him: power that remained stubbornly out of his reach! Bile burned at the back of his throat at the thought of all he could do with but a *sliver* of that awful strength. He turned to Khefru. 'Any one of these will do,' he said with a disdainful sweep of his hand. 'Promise whatever you must, but be discreet.'

'I know just the person, master,' Khefru said, nodding quickly. 'You may rely upon me.' The expression on his face told Nagash that the young priest knew very well what would happen in the event that he failed.

Nagash dismissed Khefru with a curt nod of his head and the two parted ways, the young priest slipping silently into the rear of the crowd while the Grand Hierophant continued his journey through the shadows towards the great dais. The envoy of Quatar had reached the far end of the hall, and his deep, practised voice was echoing from the columns and the high, dark ceiling.

'Great King of the Living City, on behalf of Quatar I offer up these treasures and a coffle of fine northern slaves to you as a measure of our esteem. It is with great regret that we must take our leave of you, and we hope that these gifts will recommend us fondly to you in our absence.'

It was nearly mid-afternoon, and once the emissary had been given leave to depart, the grand assembly would conclude. Then, Thutep's queen would be brought forth to offer blessings upon any children born since the last new moon. Nagash planned to settle in the shadows and watch the Daughter of the Sun for a time. He had not seen her since Khetep's interment, but he thought of her often. She was exquisite, a perfect blossom tended in the temples of Lahmia since her youth, and unlike any woman he had ever known. The Grand Hierophant wondered what it would be like to possess one such as her.

Lost in his covetous reverie, Nagash failed to notice the white-robed figure waiting in his path until he was nearly on top of her. She wore the ceremonial vestments of a matron of Ptra, her stout figure entirely concealed except for her strong, wrinkled hands, which were clasped tightly at her waist. Her face was concealed behind a gold mask that glimmered faintly in the reflected light of the court's oil lamps. The matron bowed deeply at Nagash's approach.

'The blessings of the Great Father be upon you, holy one,' she said in a deep voice. The matron spoke with a Lahmian's singsong accent. Nagash scowled at the woman.

'I require no blessing from you, matron,' he replied curtly. The answer seemed to amuse the matron.

'Be that as it may,' she said. 'I stand before you on behalf of the queen. Neferem wishes to speak with you.'

'Indeed?' Nagash murmured, his handsome face betraying a hint of surprise. 'This is an unexpected honour. When am I to meet with her?'

'Now, if it please you,' the matron answered, gesturing into the darkness beyond the dais. 'She waits in the antechamber beyond the great hall. Shall I escort you there?' Nagash let out a snort.

'I was born in these halls, woman. I can find my own way,' he said, and left the matron bowing awkwardly in his wake as he strode swiftly off into the gloom. His dark eyes were pensive as he contemplated the reasons for this surprise summons. The Daughter of the Sun did not, as a rule, hold private audiences with anyone save the king.

The shadows grew deeper as Nagash passed by the great dais. Thutep was perched at the edge of Settra's throne, smiling politely at the Quatari emissary as the man continued his lengthy farewell speech. A small crowd of bodyguards and functionaries waited upon the king's pleasure in the darkness just past the dais. Nagash moved swiftly past them and approached a trio of wide-spaced stone doors set into the chamber's far wall. Statues of the gods stood watch beside each of the doorways: Neru at the door to the far left, Ptra in the centre, and Geheb to the right. A pair of Ushabti stood guard at the centre door with their huge ritual swords in their hands, their skin glowing softly with the sun god's blessing. A matron waited with them, poised and patient. She bowed gracefully as Nagash came forwards, and she spoke quietly to the devoted, who nodded solemnly and stepped aside. The Grand Hierophant acknowledged the matron with a passing glance and pushed the stone door open.

The antechamber was small and brightly lit, with more than a dozen oil lamps guttering in niches from the sandstone walls. Fine Lahmian rugs, imported from the Silk Lands to the east, covered the floor, and the air was thick with a haze of pungent incense. Low divans had been arranged in a loose circle in the centre of the room, all facing towards a cushioned chair ornamented in gold leaf. Neferem, Daughter of the Sun, sat facing the door, her back straight and her arms resting lightly on the arms of her chair. She wore the dazzling golden headdress of Khemri's queen, and a broad pectoral of gold studded with gemstones and lapis lazuli lay upon her breast. Her eyes were shadowed with dusky kohl, and her skin shone like bronze in the firelight. She smiled slightly as Nagash approached, and the Grand Hierophant was surprised to feel his pulse quicken in response. A fool like Thutep did not deserve such a wife!

Nagash approached the queen, taking note of the half a dozen matrons resting upon their knees at a discreet distance on the far side of the room. He bowed smoothly before the Daughter of the Sun.

'You summoned me, holy one?' he said.

'The blessings of the Great Father be upon you, Grand Hierophant,' Neferem replied, in a voice as dark and rich as honey. She spoke with the musical accent of the Lahmians, and her every movement was graceful and poised. The queen indicated a divan to her right. 'Please, sit. Would you care for wine, or perhaps some food?'

'I do not partake of wine,' Nagash said. 'It clouds the senses and corrupts the mind, and I can abide neither.' The Grand Hierophant settled on the edge of the divan. 'But I thank you, nonetheless.'

Across the room, the matrons shifted uncomfortably, but the queen was unruffled.

'My husband was speaking of you the other day,' she began. 'He has seen very little of you since your great father's death.'

Nagash shrugged. 'My brother and I have never been close,' he said, 'and my duties with the cult demand much of my time.' His eyes narrowed thoughtfully. He had been careful to conceal his trips to the Great Pyramid these last couple of years. Was it possible Thutep was spying on him?

'I certainly understand the demands that gods and men place upon the priesthood,' the queen said with a knowing look, 'and as the Grand Hierophant of Khemri's

Mortuary Cult your influence extends beyond the Living City, to liche priests all across Nehekhara. Some might even say your power rivals that of the Hieratic Council in Mahrak.' Nagash smiled faintly.

'All men die, holy one,' he said. 'That alone is the source of our influence.' He waved his hand dismissively. 'The great mysteries of life and death occupy my interest. I have no time for the petty politics of the priesthood.'

Once more a stir went through the silent matrons. Neferem studied the Grand Hierophant for a moment, resting her chin on the tips of her fingers, and said, 'But the kings of Nehekhara rely upon priests for their insight and wisdom, do they not?'

'Some more than others,' Nagash observed. 'The Priest Kings of Lahmia are notably indifferent to the demands of their holy men, for example.'

'That depends upon the advice, I think,' the queen countered, 'and its source.' Nagash folded his arms across his chest and regarded Neferem coolly.

'And what advice would you have me give, holy one?' The Daughter of the Sun smiled at him.

'Your brother has a bold vision for the Blessed Land,' she said. 'Your father brought an era of peace and prosperity to Nehekhara. Thutep wants to build upon that and unify the land once more.' Nagash arched an eyebrow at the queen.

'He would restore Settra's empire?'

'Not an empire,' Neferem said, 'a confederation of equals, bound by ties of trade and mutual self-interest.' Her eyes glittered with passion. 'We are all one people, Grand Hierophant, bound to the gods in a covenant of faith. The Blessed Land belongs to all of us. Settra's empire only hinted at the glories we could achieve once our rivalries were put aside.' The Grand Hierophant let out a derisive snort.

'You would have the people of Khemri believe that they are the equal of those flea-bitten horse thieves in Bhagar? It's outrageous!' Neferem straightened in her seat, and her beautiful face took on a haughty cast.

'They *are* equal,' she said, 'and both cities could profit from such an understanding. What has Nehekhara gained from centuries of warfare except stagnation and death?'

'Death is the way of the world,' Nagash said. 'Why should a man trade for something when he can seize it instead?' The Grand Hierophant rose to his feet. 'Khetep understood this. The Priest Kings of Nehekhara yielded to his authority because he was a great general, and they feared the might of his army.'

'And look at how long his achievements lasted after his death,' Neferem answered. 'Khemri's court is all but emptied. Fear can compel men, but it cannot bind them together for long.'

'Not without constant reinforcement,' Nagash hissed. 'Thutep surrendered what authority Khemri possessed when he chose not to seek revenge against Zandri for the death of our father.' He gestured sharply in the direction of the court. 'The great houses disdain him, and he does nothing. At this point, I would not be surprised if more than one of them was plotting against him. How does he expect to forge a grand confederation of kings when he cannot manage his own court?' The queen stiffened.

'And what would you have him do?'

'What I wish is not relevant,' Nagash snapped. 'If Thutep hopes to rule over Khemri, he must spill his share of blood. Heads must roll, both here and abroad. That is how cities grow wealthy and powerful, not because they went to their neighbours and begged for aid.'

Neferem's jaw tightened fractionally at Nagash's contemptuous tone, but her voice was steady as she spoke. 'I can't deny that my husband's vision grows harder to achieve with each passing day,' she said. 'We are not blind to Zandri's ambitions, Grand Hierophant. I hoped that you could be persuaded to intervene on your brother's behalf. If the other cities would agree to help form a united front against Nekumet–'

'To what end? So they could throw away their swords and become a nation of merchants?' Nagash's lip curled in distaste. 'And you thought I would lend my voice to such foolishness? You insult me, holy one.'

Neferem's face grew still.

'Then I regret having given offence,' she said neutrally. 'I shall take up no more of your time, Grand Hierophant. My husband had spoken to me at length of your brilliance, and I know what it is like to put aside ambition and serve the needs of a temple. I had hoped to give you a role in shaping the future of Khemri.' The Grand Hierophant bowed deeply to the queen.

'For me to shape the future of Khemri I would require a crown,' he said coldly. 'For now, that privilege belongs to the Priest King of Zandri.'

Nagash turned on his heel and took his leave of the queen. The startled whispers of the matrons followed after him as he returned to the shadows of Settra's Court. While he had been with Neferem the grand assembly had concluded, and the hall buzzed with the murmur of voices as the young nobles of the city hurried out into the sunlit afternoon in search of better entertainment. A handful of nervous young mothers clutched their babes at the foot of the great dais, awaiting the blessing of the Daughter of the Sun. Thutep was already gone, having exited the court through Neru's door at the rear of the chamber.

The great dais was deserted. Nagash paused nearby.

'A crown,' he murmured thoughtfully, looking up at Settra's throne.

Unnoticed by the dwindling crowd, Nagash climbed the stone steps and stood beside the ancient chair. He rested his hand on the arm of the throne and contemplated the backs of the milling nobles, his eyes full of dark and terrible thoughts.

THE DRUCHII WARLOCK frowned at the centre of the chamber's stone.

'You're certain this faces directly north?' Malchior said in his sibilant tongue. Nagash glanced up from the pages of the book.

'Of course,' he said. 'The pyramid is precisely aligned with the four corners of the earth. It's vital to maintaining the aura of preservation within the tomb. Have you no understanding of geomancy in your homeland?'

'Geomancy,' the warlock sneered, 'how quaint.' He stepped forwards and laid a black-gloved fingertip against the sandstone. 'Never mind the fact that this material is a poor conductor of magic. Marble works far better.'

Nagash scowled at the pale-skinned figure. Two years of imprisonment had done little to blunt the arrogance of the three druchii. Once they had accepted the terms of Nagash's agreement they had quickly demanded everything from fine foods to books and other entertainments, which they seemed to regard as nothing more than their due. The Grand Hierophant had humoured them, within reason. Over time, their prison had expanded to include more than a dozen adjoining chambers, and he had taken pains to furnish them so that they would enjoy some measure of comfort.

The great chamber where he had first revived the druchii had become their work room, and the margins were crowded with bookshelves, tables and chairs. Nagash crouched in the centre of the space, with a large, leather-bound book open before him. The thick pages were covered in copious notes dictated by the druchii and copied down in Nagash's hand. Since he had begun his training, Nagash had committed everything he'd been taught to paper, both for his own reference and to ensure that his tutors remained honest. A horsetail brush and a small pot of ink sat on the floor beside his knee.

'Marble, and gold,' Drutheira hissed. The lithe, white-haired witch was lounging like a sunning cobra on a low divan across the chamber, tracing a set of Nehekharan glyphs with an elegantly pointed fingernail. 'This cursed land is too far from the north. I can barely sense a glimmer of power here.'

'Perhaps it is this pyramid,' Ashniel said, raising her dark eyes from the book she was reading and regarding Nagash hatefully. The druchii straightened, extending her slim white arms over the reading table in a catlike stretch. 'We should be teaching you out in the open air, not shut up in this awful barrow.' Nagash grunted in amusement as he reached for the brush and ink.

'So the lion said from the hunter's pit,' he replied. 'Perhaps the fault lies in your perceptions, druchii; the pyramid is a potent focus for mystical energies. The mortuary cult has interred our kings in such crypts for centuries to maintain the invocations of restoration.'

Within the first few days of their imprisonment, the barbarians seemed to have appointed roles for themselves. Malchior took on the lion's share of Nagash's tutelage, setting a difficult and demanding pace of lectures and exercises. Drutheira assisted Malchior during the more complicated lessons, but preferred to focus her energies on more physical pursuits, and despite repeated failures, her attempts at seduction continued unabated. Meanwhile, Ashniel treated the Grand Hierophant with nothing but contempt, keeping to her books and reading voraciously about Nehekharan culture, religion and, most importantly, the construction of their crypts.

It was clear to Nagash from the beginning that Malchior and Drutheira were meant to distract him, each in their own ways, while Ashniel kept to herself and looked for a way to free them from Khetep's tomb. The hateful witch had been careful to cover her tracks, but not quite careful enough, and Nagash and Khefru had found evidence that Ashniel had managed to breach the first layer of traps surrounding their apartments and was making slow but steady progress exploring the lower level of the crypt. The battle of wits, keeping one step ahead of the witch by changing the location and nature of the traps, had become a diverting pastime for Nagash and his favoured servant.

The Grand Hierophant dipped the brush in the black ink, consulted the tome open before him, and began to paint the sigil on the floor.

'You are certain this will work?' he asked, tracing the complicated lines with care.

'I am certain of nothing in this place,' Malchior growled. The warlock folded his arms and watched the sigil take shape on the stone floor. 'Drutheira is right, this land is a desert in more ways than one. The winds of magic are very weak, scarcely stirring the aether, and, as I've said often enough, your kind has a feeble grasp of magic at the best of times.'

The warlock let the implication of his statement hang in the air between them: you may not be capable of this. Nagash clenched the brush tightly in his hand and focused on crafting the sigil.

'If this does not work, what then?' he asked curtly. Malchior shrugged.

'There is nothing else,' he said. 'This ritual isn't even an accepted part of our magical lore. It's the sort of thing practised by shade-casters and gutter witches, who lack the will to harness the winds of magic.' He spread his hands. 'If this attempt fails, the fault lies with you, human. I've tried everything I can think of.'

Then, a murmur of voices echoed from the passageway beyond the work room. Nagash glanced up from his work as Khefru entered the room with a hooded figure in tow.

'Here he is, master,' Khefru said with a bow. 'Allow me to present Imhep, of the House of Hapt-amn-kesh. He should serve your purposes in every particular.'

The hooded figure swayed slightly on his feet. Imhep reached up and bared his head with shaking hands. He was young, only sixty or so, with large, watery eyes and a receding chin. A short, black wig sat askew on his shaven head.

'It is an honour, Grand Hierophant,' he said in a slightly slurred voice. 'Your servant said you requested me personally?'

'Did you drug him?' Nagash asked, frowning at Khefru.

'Well… yes,' the young priest replied. 'I thought it prudent, all things considered.' The Grand Hierophant glanced worriedly at Malchior.

'Will that cause problems?'

The notion seemed to amuse the druchii, who said, 'That depends on how much effort you intend to put into your lesson.' He pointed to the flowing black lines. 'Just be careful that the fool doesn't scuff your hard work with his plodding feet.' Imhep was glancing around the dimly lit chamber with befuddled interest, taking special note of the two witches.

'What… That is… How may I be of service to you, holy one?' he asked. 'My friend Khefru mentioned a reward of some kind.'

'He has debts,' Khefru interjected. 'Imhep is something of a gambler, you see.'

Nagash eyed the young noble closely, noting the lack of rings or other jewellery, and the man's worn kilt and sandals.

'I take it he's the sort that loses a great deal. Won't his debtors inquire after him?' Khefru shrugged.

'Perhaps, but what will they learn? No one saw me with him, master. I was most careful.'

'We had some very fine wine,' Imhep said, his slack face quirking into a grin. 'Where was that again, friend Khefru?'

Nagash bent and finished the sigil with a few deft strokes of his brush, and then beckoned impatiently to his servant.

'Bring him here,' he said, 'but be careful of the glyphs.' Khefru took Imhep's arm and led the drugged man across the room as though he were a child.

'Mind your step,' he told the noble as they approached the edge of the sigil. 'That's it. Right into the centre.'

Imhep swayed drunkenly in the middle of the circle, forcing Nagash to grip his arms and hold him steady.

'Forgive me, holy one,' the young man said with a chuckle. 'I'm not certain how much help I am going to be at the moment. As I said, it was very fine wine.'

'Get that cape off him,' Malchior commanded. At a nod from Nagash, Khefru darted forwards and jerked the cape from Imhep's shoulders, revealing the noble's narrow, bony chest.

'Careful!' Imhep barked. 'That's my good cape! I'll be needing that back.' The warlock paced slowly around the edge of the sigil.

'Where are the implements?' he asked. Imhep turned his head at the sound of Malchior's voice.

'What's the barbarian saying?' he asked.

Khefru reached into his belt and drew out a pair of long bronze needles. The young noble's eyes widened.

'Merciful Ptra! What are those for?'

Malchior glided like a snake towards Khefru, his eyes glinting. He reached out and delicately pulled them from the priest's grip.

'Yes,' he murmured. 'These will do.' He turned to Nagash. 'Hold him.'

Nagash seized Imhep's lower jaw and wrenched his head around, until they were looking eye to eye. The noble let out a startled cry, which turned to a scream of agony as the druchii stepped inside the sigil and drove the first needle into Imhep's lower back.

The young noble collapsed to his knees, shrieking in agony. Nagash watched as Malchior put his free hand against the side of Imhep's head and bent it to the side, exposing the tendons of the noble's thin neck. With a hungry smile, the warlock plunged the second needle into the juncture of shoulder and throat, and Imhep's entire upper body went rigid. Malchior worked the needle deeper into Imhep's chest.

'Remember our discussions on nerve clusters and their uses,' he said dispassionately. 'This will keep your subject alert and suffering, but unable to interfere.' Nagash looked into Imhep's eyes, drawn by the gleam of pain radiating from their depths.

'And the suffering is important?' he asked.

Drutheira chuckled.

'It is not *vital*,' she admitted, 'but it is certainly entertaining.' The warlock frowned at the interruption.

'We were speaking of sandstone earlier,' he said. 'Some physical objects channel and store magic better than others, but none work so well as flesh and bone. Humans, as I said, have a poor grasp of magic, but like all living things, their bodies accumulate power over time.' Malchior traced a fingernail across Imhep's cheek. 'Can you feel it?' he asked.

Fascinated, Nagash reached out and laid a hand on the noble's forehead. He cleared his mind and tried to employ the techniques the warlock had taught him. After a moment, he shook his head, and said, 'I feel nothing.'

Malchior smiled.

'Touch your fingers to the needle, then,' he said.

The Grand Hierophant's gaze fell to the needle jutting from Imhep's torso. Tentatively, he reached out and laid a finger on its round end. The noble stiffened, his eyes widening in pain.

The metal trembled against Nagash's fingertip. It was cold to the touch… and then he felt it, like a faint thread of fire pulsing against his skin.

'Yes,' Nagash whispered. 'Yes…' A terrible, hungry light grew in his eyes. 'At last.'

The warlock loomed over Imhep's shoulder, his face lit with ghastly joy.

'Give me your knife,' he said.

Nagash's hand fumbled at his belt. The pulse of power sent a tremor through his frame, quickening along with Imhep's pulse. He handed over his curved knife without hesitation, ignoring Khefru's quiet protest. Malchior pulled away the noble's wig and cast it aside.

'Now we shall draw that power to the surface,' he said, laying the point of the knife against Imhep's scalp. 'Hours of agony will shape it, and strengthen it as your victim struggles to survive. When the time is ripe, we will cut his throat and his life force will pour over your hands. Then your education will begin in earnest.'

Slowly, carefully, the druchii began to cut into Imhep's skin. Nagash watched the warlock work. After a moment, he turned a page in his book and began to make careful notes.

◄ TEN ►

Tidings of War

Ka-Sabar, the City of Bronze, in the 63rd year of Ptra the Glorious (-1744 Imperial Reckoning)

THE WIND FROM the east in the City of Bronze was called Enmesh-na Geheb, for it was the eastern quarter of the city that contained the majority of Ka-Sabar's complex of foundries. The Breath of Geheb reeked of cinders and the smell of scorched copper, as ingots of ore carved from the Brittle Peaks were melted in great crucibles and combined with bars of nickel to produce high-quality bronze. For centuries Ka-Sabar had been known as a city of industry, and had made its wealth by trading everything from belt buckles and wheel rims to fine swords and scale armour. In these dark days the demand for her goods was greater than ever. The city's furnaces lit the eastern skies by night, and her smithies were shrouded in a perpetual mantle of acrid smoke. Heavily armed caravans made their way down the trade road from Quatar bearing chests of gold and silver, and returned laden with swords and axes, scale shirts and shields, bronze-tipped spears and baskets of arrowheads. Rasetra and Lybaras were spending enormous sums, much of it borrowed from the Hieratic Council in Mahrak, to equip their growing armies. Akhmen-hotep's viziers were stunned at the huge influx of wealth, but the king understood the desperation that drove such furious spending. He, too, had been feverishly rebuilding his shattered forces after the devastating defeat at Zedri, six years earlier. So long as that unholy monster Nagash ruled over the Living City, not a single soul in Nehekhara was safe.

News of the slaughter at Bhagar had arrived with the first of the desert city's hollow-eyed refugees, less than three weeks after Akhmen-hotep had returned to Ka-Sabar. For weeks the city was paralysed with terror and grief, and its citizens looked to the north with mounting dread as they awaited the arrival of the Usurper's nightmarish horde. Then a messenger travelled the trade road bearing letters from the Kings of Rasetra and Lybaras. They had risen up against the Usurper and taken Quatar by storm, and were poised to liberate Khemri! Akhmen-hotep swiftly drafted a letter declaring his support for the western kings and then spent the rest of the day in the Temple of Geheb, thanking the gods for his people's deliverance.

A month passed with no news as Ka-Sabar mourned its dead sons and contemplated the future. Akhmen-hotep sent one messenger after another to the White Palace, seeking word from his new-found allies. None returned. Finally, after six long months, the king despatched a small force of his Ushabti and a squadron of horsemen to Quatar to learn what they could.

Two months later, the Ushabti returned, on foot, bearing a tale of horror and despair. On the very night of the slaughter at Bhagar, the skies above Quatar had wept blood, and within days the entire city was consumed by a plague the likes of which the Blessed Land had never known before. The sickness struck man and animal with equal ferocity, maddening them with a violent, savage fever. Within a week the city was consumed in an orgy of murder and destruction. The allied armies were decimated, torn apart from within as entire companies succumbed to the fever and turned upon their fellow warriors. The Kings of Rasetra and Lybaras had been forced to flee the city, abandoning their armies for the safety of Mahrak at the other end of the Valley of Kings. According to rumour, they intended to raise more warriors and return with a contingent of warrior priests from the Hieratic Council to cleanse the city and resume the advance upon Khemri, but as the months turned to years, it became clear that the priests at Mahrak could not find a way to counter the curse that had befallen the city.

Akhmen-hotep had no doubt that Nagash was the source of the terrible plague. The thought chilled him to the depths of his soul. Grimly, the king began to rebuild his shattered army and prepare for the worst.

Nagash did not stir from Khemri in the wake of the terrible plague. Although the armies of his enemies had been devastated, it appeared that the Usurper's army had fared little better. To make matters worse, a season of terrible sandstorms had risen from the Great Desert and swept across central Nehekhara, making travel all but impossible for weeks on end. The result was a stalemate of sorts. A tattered remnant of the western armies still held the White Palace at Quatar, while Nagash was free to work his evils in the Living City. The fate of the Blessed Land hung in the balance as both sides raced to rebuild their devastated forces and start the war anew.

THE VIZIER ROSE slowly into view as he ascended the sandstone steps leading to the council hall, his robes fluttering in the hot wind blowing across the city from the east. Slanting beams of sunlight shone on the functionary's bronze skullcap and glittered from the gold rings adorning the man's wide, scarred hands. He bowed low to the king and the small group of nobles who sat or paced around the windswept chamber.

'The emissary from Mahrak has arrived, great one,' he said.

Akhmen-hotep turned at the sound of the vizier's rough voice. He was pacing, as was his wont, striding along the wide flagstones beside the short, squat columns that supported the eastern edge of the council hall's roof. The chamber had no walls, resting as it did atop the royal palace in the centre of the city, which was itself at the summit of one of the Brittle Peaks' many foothills. The King of Ka-Sabar could look out across the width and breadth of his domain, from the forges spread in a smoking crescent to the east to the brooding stone temples of the gods that filled the Priests' Quarter to the west. A fine layer of soot coated the round sides of the eastern columns, and swirling drifts of sand and grit blew across the small chamber's stone floor, reminding the king and his nobles of the earth god whom they worshipped.

The king's chair, a massive thing made from pieces of petrified wood and heavy bronze fittings, faced the stair from the far end of the room. A score of smaller chairs were arrayed in a rough circle before it, reserved for the city's major nobles and the king's closest allies. Less than half were occupied.

On the left hand of the king's chair sat Memnet, the Grand Hierophant of Ptra. On the right slouched Pakhamn, the king's Master of Horse, along with half a dozen young sons of the city's noble families. A great many of Ka-Sabar's great lords had not returned from the debacle at Zandri, and the mantle of leadership had fallen on largely inexperienced shoulders. Neither Khalifra, the Priestess of Neru, nor Hashepra, the Hierophant of Geheb, were in attendance, and the king felt their absence keenly. The emissary's sudden arrival had left Akhmen-hotep with little time to gather his advisors, and the religious leaders were rarely seen outside their temples these days. The new Hierophant of Phakth, a priest named Tethuhep, had not been seen in public at all. His spokesman claimed that Tethuhep was occupied with prayers for the defence of the city, but Akhmen-hotep suspected that Sukhet's successor was not yet ready to assume his official duties.

Truth be told, Pakh-amn and Memnet were in little better shape. It was plain to Akhmen-hotep that both men had been deeply scarred by the horrors they had witnessed six months before. The Grand Hierophant was a gaunt, hollow-eyed figure, his face aged beyond his years since the fateful battle. Though still a powerful and influential figure in the city, Memnet had grown increasingly distant and withdrawn with each passing year. Pakh-amn had suffered even worse since his return to the city. Akhmen-hotep had made no secret of the young noble's precipitous withdrawal from the battlefield, and his early return to Ka-Sabar, more than three days ahead of the king, caused many in the city to question Pakh-amn's courage. For more than a year after the battle he was absent from the king's court, and rumours circulated that he had turned to the milk of the black lotus to escape the pain of his disgrace. He, too, was sunken-eyed and brooding, his fingers trembling as he held a cup of wine with both hands.

Akhmen-hotep studied the council for a moment, and then nodded gravely to his vizier.

'Bring him forth,' the king commanded. The vizier bowed once more and withdrew down the stairs. Less than a minute later they heard the measured tread of the king's Ushabti, and four of the devoted rose into view, escorting a very old priest, who wore the vibrant yellow robes of a servant of Ptra. Despite his advanced years, the emissary moved with surprising confidence and strength, and his dark eyes were keen and bright. His gaze fell upon Memnet, and the Grand Hierophant leapt from his chair as though stung.

'Nebunefer! The blessings of Ptra be upon you, holy one,' Memnet stammered. The Grand Hierophant clutched at his hands and bowed deeply. 'This is an unexpected honour–'

Mahrak's emissary forestalled Memnet with an upraised hand.

'Be still,' he commanded roughly. 'I haven't come to inspect your coffers, Grand Hierophant. I bring tidings to your brother the king.' Nebunefer inclined his head respectfully to Akhmen-hotep. 'Blessings of the Great Father be upon you, King of the Bronze City.'

'And to you,' Akhmen-hotep replied neutrally. 'It has been some time since an emissary arrived from the City of Hope. Do the desert storms scourge Mahrak as well?' Nebunefer arched a thin eyebrow at the king.

'The storms are our creation, great one. The Hieratic Council has gone to great lengths to keep the blasphemer in Khemri at bay so that you and your allies can recover from your terrible losses.' The king considered Nebunefer for a moment.

'We thank the council for its aid,' he said carefully. 'Does this mean that Mahrak is ready to send its warrior-priests into battle against the Usurper?' Nebunefer gave the king a terse shake of the head.

'The time is not yet right,' he replied. 'The Kings of Rasetra and Lybaras have raised new armies and are ready to resume the crusade against the blasphemer.'

'Ah. I see,' Akhmen-hotep said. 'So the Hieratic Council has at last cleansed Quatar of its terrible curse?' The emissary paused.

'The plague has been allowed to run its course,' he replied. 'Many of the city's noble families survived, including Nemuhareb and the royal family, as well as a few hundred soldiers that had been quartered inside the White Palace, but the rest suffered terribly.' Akhmen-hotep nodded gravely.

'The caravans from the north brought terrible stories: streets covered in ash and human bones, houses barricaded from within and filled with mutilated bodies, and Charnel pits filled with burned skulls. In truth, Quatar is a city of the dead.'

'And so the monster's army grows,' Pakh-amn said, raising his red-rimmed eyes to stare at the emissary. His voice was little more than a croak, and his teeth were stained a dark blue from years of drinking the milk of the lotus. 'The dead in their tens of thousands are his to command, priest. Quatar is under siege even as we speak!' For a brief moment Nebunefer was taken aback by the vehemence in Pakh-amn's voice.

'The Hieratic Council has heard the stories of the battle at Zandri,' he said, 'and steps have been taken to put the citizens of Quatar beyond Nagash's reach. The surviving members of the city's mortuary cult worked day and night to seal the dead into carefully warded tombs in the city necropolis.' The emissary turned his attention back to the king. 'What is more, the accounts of fighting at Zandri and Bhagar tell us that either Nagash or one of his so-called immortals must be present to raise the bodies of the dead, and he will not have that opportunity at Quatar.' The king clasped his broad hands behind his back and looked out across the eastern quarter of the city, feeling the breath of Geheb against his skin.

'You said that Rasetra and Lybaras have raised new armies.'

'Rasetra marches for the Valley of Kings even as we speak. Rakh-amn-hotep has mustered every warrior his city possesses, and even includes companies of savage jungle beasts in his army. Hekhmenukep and the warrior-engineers of Lybaras have emptied their fabled arsenals and are hastening to Quatar with a legion of dreadful war machines to counter the blasphemer's undead horde. Within the month they will be encamped outside Quatar, and will march upon the Living City as soon as the signs are propitious.'

Pakh-amn muttered darkly into his wine cup and took a long swallow. Akhmen-hotep shot the nobleman a hard look, but said nothing. Instead, he drew a deep breath and turned to Nebunefer.

'What does the Hieratic Council want from Ka-Sabar?' he asked. The emissary smiled faintly at the king's frank manner.

'Our spies in Khemri have reported that Nagash has not been idle since he laid his curse upon Quatar. He has bent the Kings of Numas and Zandri to his will and emptied his coffers to raise a mighty army. They are marshalling on the plains outside the Living City, though the constant storms have slowed their movements considerably.' Nebunefer paused. 'It is possible that the army is intended for Ka-Sabar, great king, but the council thinks it more likely that they will head for Quatar first and seal off the Valley of the Kings.' Akhmen-hotep nodded.

'Nagash is no fool,' he said. 'If he can hold Rasetra and Lybaras at bay by seizing the Gates of the Dawn, then he can deal with us at his leisure.' The king considered the situation. The size of the eastern armies would work against them on the march, slowing their progress almost to a crawl. The armies of the Usurper, on the other hand, were closer to Quatar, and could move with much greater speed. Nagash did not have to burden himself with food and water for his troops, after all. The thought sent a shudder down the king's spine.

'The next few weeks will be crucial,' Nebunefer continued. 'Rasetra and Lybaras must safely cross the Valley of Kings. Once they have reached the plains beyond, the advantage in battle will be theirs. Thus, we must take steps to draw Nagash's attention away from Quatar for a time.' A heavy silence descended upon the council chamber, broken only by the hissing breath of the god. Memnet glanced fearfully from his brother to Nebunefer.

'What would you have us do, holy one?' he asked in a wavering voice.

'We propose attacking Nagash from an unexpected quarter,' the emissary replied, his dark eyes glinting. 'For all his supposed genius, the blasphemer is also a petty and arrogant king. Any defeat, no matter how small, is an insult to his overweening pride, and he will be compelled to respond.' Nebunefer spread his hands. 'The Bronze Host is in an ideal position to launch such a blow.' Akhmen-hotep frowned at the man.

'And where would you have us strike?' he asked.

'At Bel Aliad, on the other side of the Great Desert.'

Pakh-amn let out a choking sound, spraying wine over the rim of his tilted cup. The haggard nobleman's gasping coughs quickly dissolved into mirthless laughter as he lurched drunkenly from his chair. Many of the council's young noblemen looked to one another in embarrassment and dismay, but some few joined Pakh-amn in laughter, believing they understood the point of the joke.

'A daring plan from a bunch of cowering priests,' Pakh-amn spat, fixing Nebunefer with a hateful glare. 'Your precious council sits on perfumed cushions and leaves us to do battle with the armies of the damned! You've heard stories of what happened at Zandri, but you weren't there! The sky didn't boil with darkness over your head! Your friends weren't turned into hissing, clawing corpses!'

Akhmen-hotep took two long strides across the council chamber and smote the Master of Horse on the side of the head. The nobleman was knocked from his feet, his empty goblet clattering musically across the stones. Swords flashed as the king's Ushabti stepped forwards, ready to act upon Akhmen-hotep's command.

'Shame me once more, Pakh-amn, and I will kill you,' the king said coldly. 'Now begone. The council has no further need for you.'

At a nod from the king, the four Ushabti stepped forwards and surrounded the nobleman. Pakh-amn climbed unsteadily to his feet, rubbing his hand over the red welt left by the king's open hand. With a last, hateful look at

Nebunefer, the Master of Horse was escorted swiftly from the hall.

The king waited until Pakh-amn had disappeared from sight before bowing his head to the emissary.

'My apologies,' he said. 'Ka-Sabar means no insult to our honoured allies. That said, surely you must appreciate the... challenges... of such an undertaking. As you said, Bel Aliad lies on the other side of the Great Desert. Travelling around it would take months, and would bring us dangerously close to Khemri along the way.'

'We do not propose travelling around the desert, but through it,' Nebunefer replied. 'There are ancient routes across the sands that caravans used to travel in centuries past.'

'Many of the oases along those routes have long since dried up,' the king said, 'and they would not have been enough to support an army in any case.' The emissary smiled.

'The desert holds more secrets than you know, Akhmenhotep. The bandit princes of Bhagar could and did move large bands of horsemen across the desert virtually at will, and we know that there are almost a hundred Bhagarite refugees here in the city. Put the question to them, great one. They can lead you across the desert.'

'Why should they?' the king asked. The question took the priest aback.

'Why? For revenge, of course,' he said. 'Nagash must pay for what he did to Bhagar. Do you not agree?' Akhmenhotep ignored the emissary's question.

'And if we attack Bel Aliad, what then?' he asked.

'You occupy the city for a time,' the emissary said. 'Loot the homes of the noblemen and the spice markets. Slay those who support the blasphemer in Khemri. When word reaches the Living City that you have conquered the city, Nagash will be forced to order his army to move against you. From Bel Aliad you could threaten the city of Zandri, and that is something that he cannot allow. By the time his warriors arrive, you will have already disappeared back into the desert, and the blasphemer's army will have been drawn hundreds of leagues in the opposite direction from Quatar.'

Nebunefer's proposition deeply unsettled the king. Occupy the city? Loot its riches and slay its leaders out of hand? That was the way of barbarians, not civilised Nehekharans, but the Usurper had done far worse at Bhagar, and would not stop there. As king, he had a duty to defend his people, regardless of the cost. He could only hope that the gods would forgive him when it came time for his soul to be judged. Akhmen-hotep turned to his brother. 'What say you, Grand Hierophant?' he asked.

Memnet blanched under the king's searching gaze. The Grand Hierophant was but a shadow of his former self. Gone was the proud, confident religious leader that six years ago had demanded vengeance for the deaths of his fellow priests. He had come away from the battlefield at Zandri a changed man, wounded to his very soul by what he had seen and done. He had grown distant from the king since then, and had never spoken of the price he'd paid for calling down the fires of his god against the Usurper.

The Grand Hierophant tucked his hands into his sleeves and once more glanced fearfully from the king to Nebunefer. With an effort of will, he gathered his courage and said, 'Lead us, oh king, and we will follow.'

Akhmen-hotep drew a deep breath and nodded gravely. Outside, the breath of the god fell still.

'Then it is decided,' the priest king said. 'Sound the trumpets and call forth our warriors. The Bronze Host marches once again to war.'

— ❮ ELEVEN ❯ —

The Game of Kings

Quatar, the White Palace, in the 63rd year of Ptra the Glorious (-1744 Imperial Reckoning)

RAKH-AMN-HOTEP, PRIEST KING of Rasetra, clenched the railing of the sky-boat with his scarred, stubby fingers the moment he heard the warning grumble of the wind spirits overhead. Sure enough, there was a crackle of canvas and the huge air bladder contracted along its thirty-yard length, pitching the wooden hull of the sky-boat downwards like a ship cresting the peak of a towering wave. The king bit back a startled shout as the craft descended in a swift, graceful arc out of the Valley of Kings and over the crescent-shaped wall of the Gates of the Dawn.

Standing at the prow of the sky-boat, Rakh-amn-hotep felt hot, chalky wind buffet his face and watched the dusty ground race past with terrifying speed. They were past the fortifications sealing the western end of the valley in less than a minute, and through teary eyes he could see the gleaming stones of the Temple Road winding down the gentle slope towards the city of Quatar. The walls of the city and the central palace were a faint cream colour, Ptra's blessed sun having bleached away much of the ghastly red stains left by Nagash's cursed rain. If the god was kind, within another ten years there would be no sign of the nightmare that the Usurper had inflicted upon the city.

The great plains of central Nehekhara stretched beyond the city, a vast, rolling vista of sandy soil marked with trade roads in lines of white stone. To the king's relief, the air bladder overhead swelled once more in answer to the chorus of chanting priests at the craft's notional stern, and the sky-boat levelled out several hundred feet above the ground. Fighting to control his lurching stomach, the king could see the sharp-edged flanks of the Brittle Peaks stretching in a vast line to the north and south, and the broad ribbon of the life-giving River Vitae winding off to the west, towards the distant sea. The southern flank of the river was bordered with a thick band of vibrant green, while to the north stretched the rich fields of the Plains of Plenty, where the horse lords of Numas tended their herds and harvested the grain that fed much of Nehekhara.

To the king's relief, he saw no columns of dust or swarms of metal-clad figures making their way across the plains towards Quatar. The rolling plains were empty, all the way to the glinting, mist-wrapped Fountains of Eternal Life, many leagues to the north-west. Nagash's armies still had not stirred from the fields outside Khemri, which lay hidden behind a smudge of ominous purple clouds just at the edge of the north-west horizon. For the moment at least, Quatar and the forces encamped outside it were safe.

A vast, orderly camp had sprung up in the wide fields west of the city. Lines of dun-coloured tents were laid in neat rows, organised by company and arrayed around a central square containing parade grounds, supply tents and portable smithies. Neat columns of unhitched chariots filled an open square near a makeshift horse corral, and three adjoining fields were filled with huge, hulking shapes wreathed in tendrils of steam and thin wisps of darker sacrificial smoke. Rakh-amn-hotep saw huge cata-pults, war scorpions and towering giants made of carved wood and bronze plates. The army of Lybaras had arrived with all its strength, and it was a fearsome sight to the battle-hardened king.

The air spirits hissed and grumbled overhead, and with a creak of timbers and a groan of cables the great sky-boat swung around and began to descend. Rakh-amn-hotep saw that they were making for a large plain to the south of the Temple Road, less than a mile from the perimeter of the Lybaran camp. Three other sky-boats were already grounded on the sandy plain, unloading jars of supplies to long lines of waiting slaves. The sky-boats were hidden beneath the vast bladders of canvas, which contained the air spirits that kept the craft aloft. Built from modified river boat hulls, they hung beneath the bladders from a web of stout cables thicker than a man's arm. Each hull could carry a huge amount of cargo in its holds, including an entire company of soldiers, if their stomachs were up to the trip.

When the Lybaran sky-boat had found the Rasetran army a week ago and offered to carry Rakh-amn-hotep ahead to Quatar, the king had left much of his baggage behind and loaded the boat with a mixed company of Ushabti and heavy infantry. Their frightened cries and queasy groans had been a never-ending source of amuse-ment to the sky-boat's small crew. The king didn't envy the slaves who would be given the task of washing out the cargo holds.

The craft sank in a slow, graceful arc towards the field, drifting slightly south and gliding to a stop with a crunch of sand and gravel, just like a river boat sliding up to the shore. By the time that one of the boat's acolytes had thrown a rope ladder over the side, the first of the king's Ushabti were staggering up onto the deck and turning their faces gratefully to the sun. Smothering a wry grin at their discomfort, the king ordered his troops to disembark first. He did not have long to wait.

During the disembarkation, a trio of chariots arrived from the city, driven by members of Hekhmenukep's royal household. One of the king's viziers climbed carefully down from the lead chariot and waited patiently for Rakh-amn-hotep to descend from the sky-boat. He bowed low as the King of Rasetra stepped clear of the ladder.

'My master the Priest King of Lybaras sends you greetings, great one,' the vizier said. 'He asks you meet with him in the White Palace, where he would offer you some refreshment after your journey.'

The stout king planted his feet on the sand and swayed drunkenly. His body felt like it was still falling through the air, and his knees were as weak as a newborn's.

'Lead on,' he said with a distracted wave, and tried to concentrate on walking the ten yards to the waiting chariots without pitching forwards onto his face.

Once the king and his Ushabti were aboard, the chariots wheeled around in a tight circle and clattered across the landing field towards the Temple Road. The ride smoothed out considerably once they reached the road's stone surface, and soon the drivers had their horses dashing down the road at a ground-eating canter. After the heady rush of air travel the pace seemed sluggish to the men of Rasetra.

Within half an hour the stained walls of Quatar loomed before the chariots, and Rakh-amn-hotep saw that the city gates were open and empty of traffic, even though it was early afternoon. Only a handful of warriors stood guard upon the walls, and the king noted that they wore the dun kilts of Lybaran soldiers rather than the bleached white of Quatar's tomb guard.

He had heard that the city had suffered greatly in the grip of Nagash's foul curse, but Rakh-amn-hotep had no idea what that truly meant until the chariots passed through the open gate and onto an empty street that had once led to the city's bustling marketplace. The houses and shops lining the road were covered in a fine layer of white ash, and many doorways were streaked with soot from fires set during the plague. Piles of desiccated refuse lay heaped in the narrow alleys or along the sides of the street, but there were no animals rooting through the mess in search of a meal. A heavy pall of silence hung over the scene, muffling even the rattle and squeak of the chariot wheels. The acrid reek of burnt wood and charred flesh permeated the still air. Far off to the north-east, pillars of grey smoke rose languidly into the sky as the priests of the mortuary cult committed still more corpses to Ptra's cleansing flames.

The plague had been over for more than a year, and the survivors were still dealing with the bodies that had been left behind.

They rode on through the empty bazaar, stirring up clouds of ash and dust, and then through the Merchants' Quarter. Here the king's experienced eye saw the telltale signs of past violence. Many of the homes had been looted by bands of maddened plague victims, and piles of broken furniture and shattered pottery lay in drifts outside the smoke-stained doorways. Ominous stains against the walls of some homes hinted at the dire fates of their owners.

As bad as the destruction was in the Merchants' Quarter, the noble districts beyond had suffered even worse, as though the citizens pinned the blame for their misery squarely on their king and his supporters. All of the homes had been broken into and burned, and even the walls of some estates had been torn open by frenzied work with picks and spades. Walls had been toppled and roofs had fallen in when their wooden supports had finally burned through. Some time in the past, workers had cleared a path through the debris in the centre of the street, and the chariots were forced to ride single file past mounds of broken bricks and charred, splintered wood.

It was only when they were nearly upon the stained walls of the White Palace that they came upon the first signs of life. The grand structure, built to rival then ultimately surpass the glories of Settra's palace in Khemri, was surrounded by small ornamental parks and wide squares set with fountains that were fed by springs running beneath the city. The parks were filled with weathered, ash-covered tents and ramshackle huts made from crumbling mud bricks, and gaunt, hollow-eyed figures in tattered robes clustered wearily around the dust-covered fountains, washing clothes or filling jugs with water. The few survivors of the plague years watched the chariots roll past with expressions of misery and dread.

The White Palace rose like an island of stability amidst the squalor and despair of Quatar. Though its walls still bore the stains of Nagash's vile curse, the palace had been completely untouched by the chaos and savagery that had gripped the rest of the city. Warriors of Quatar's royal household stood guard at the palace gates, garbed in white leather armour and bearing their huge, curved swords. They bowed their heads gravely as the chariots rolled past, and the procession continued on down a wide avenue lined with towering statues of Djaf's jackal-headed servants. To the west, Rakh-amn-hotep could see the white bulk of the mortuary temple, while to the east rose the forbidding Palace of the Dusk, the temple to the God of Death. The palace lay ahead, a sprawling structure faced with white marble that towered like a sphinx above every other building in the city.

Rakh-amn-hotep's escort carried him down the wide avenue and into a small square that opened before the palace's wide steps. There, arrayed in serried ranks ten men deep, waited a company of warriors clad in the heavy scale armour of Rasetran infantry. A tall, broad-shouldered warrior whose skin glowed with the might of the sun god stood at their head. The champion raised his sword in salute as the chariots approached, and as one, the warriors let out an exultant cheer at the sight of their king.

The chariots reined in before the assembled troops, and Rakh-amn-hotep ordered his driver to turn around so that he could better see and be seen by the Rasetran warriors. Smiling fiercely, the king raised his arms in greeting.

'Stalwart souls!' he cried. 'It has been too long since I have seen your faces, and I rejoice to see you in such fine spirits. For six long years you few have held this city in the face of calamity. For six long years you alone stood between the monster at Khemri and the kingdoms of the east. All of Rasetra knows of your brave deeds! Your names have been spoken with honour in the temples, and your families have been richly rewarded by my hand in gratitude for your service. Our brothers and cousins are on the march, shaking the earth with their fury. Soon they will stand among you, and we will march east to finish the work we started so long ago!'

Once more, the warriors let out a great cheer and clashed their maces against their shields in salute. Their faces split in proud smiles to hear of the king's esteem, and only the hard look in their dark eyes hinted at the ordeal they had been forced to endure. Ekhreb, the king's champion and commander of the detachment, sank to one knee as the king descended from the chariot.

'None of that, by the gods!' Rakh-amn-hotep declared, waving his hand impatiently at his champion. 'For all that you and your men have faced, you should never be asked to bow to another man again.' The king strode forwards and gripped the champion's arms, nearly dragging the taller man onto his feet.

'Welcome back, great one,' Ekhreb replied in a deep voice. The champion was powerfully built, blessed with the strength and vitality of one of Ptra's favoured sons. His face was wide and his jaw square, and his dark eyes glinted beneath a heavy, jutting brow. Sunlight shone on his shaven head, and gleamed from the gold rings in his ears.

His wide mouth quirked in a wry grin. 'Six years is too long to be without your presence.'

'You are too kind, my friend,' Rakh-amn-hotep replied.

'Not at all. We thought you'd be back within the year. In fact, you said something along those lines just before you left.'

'It's possible that I might have been a bit optimistic in my estimate.'

'We came to that same conclusion after the fourth year or so.' The two men chuckled, and then the king's expression turned serious once more.

'How bad was it?' he asked quietly. The grin left Ekhreb's face, and his expression turned bleak as he struggled for the right words. Finally he sighed.

'It was terrible,' he said. 'None of us will lead virtuous lives after this. There is no hell that the gods can make that could equal what we faced here in Quatar.' Rakh-amn-hotep grimaced at the look in his champion's face. He looked over the ranks of jubilant men at Ekhreb's back.

'Is this all that remains? Barely a company of men out of forty thousand souls?' The champion nodded.

'Only the gods know how many deserted and headed for home during the early months. We tried to stop them, but once the fever took hold of the populace it was all we could do just to stay alive. The Lybaran army was all but destroyed within the first six months. We survived only because we fell back and shut the palace gates against the mob.' Ekhreb shrugged. 'Would that I could regale you with tales of courage, but the truth is that we hid behind these walls and prayed for our survival. Eventually we realised that the plague couldn't find its way into the palace.' Rakh-amn-hotep frowned.

'Why was that?' he asked. Ekhreb's expression darkened.

'We wondered about that as well,' he said. 'In the end, the only explanation that made any sense was that Nagash didn't want it to. Nemuhareb fears that the Usurper has a special fate in mind for him and his family.' The king's frown deepened.

'Has Nemuhareb caused any trouble?' Ekhreb shook his head.

'None,' he said. 'He is a broken man, drowning his nightmares in wine and the milk of the black lotus. We're the only reason he hasn't been deposed.'

'I'm surprised there is anyone willing to take his place,' Rakh-amn-hotep muttered darkly. 'How many citizens are left?'

'The gods alone know,' Ekhreb replied. 'Less than a thousand, for certain. We have search parties combing each district of the city, and we're still finding bodies. The city is one vast tomb. It will take generations for the city to recover, if at all.' The king nodded.

'I can see why the Lybarans chose to camp outside the walls,' he said.

'What of our own army?' the champion inquired. 'When will they arrive?'

'It will be some weeks yet,' the king said with a sigh. 'We were still several days from the Valley of Kings when the Lybaran sky-boat found us. It's been slow going, all the way from Rasetra. We've got sixty thousand infantry and horsemen, plus another twelve thousand barbarian troops and their thunder lizards.' Rakh-amn-hotep shook his head. 'I never should have let Guseb talk me into bringing the lizards along. So far, they've been more trouble than they're worth. Fortunately, it appears that Nagash is in no hurry to march on the city, which had been my greatest cause for concern.'

'You can thank Hekhmenukep and Nebunefer for that,' Ekhreb said.

'Nebunefer?' the king asked, his eyebrows rising in surprise. 'What's that old schemer doing back here?'

'He arrived with the Lybarans,' the champion replied, 'and then left almost at once for Ka-Sabar. Rumour has it, they've hatched a plan to keep Nagash distracted while we marshal our forces.'

'I'm not sure I like the sound of that,' the king said, scowling up at the palace. 'Come on, old friend,' he growled, beckoning to Ekhreb. 'Time to find out what our allies have been up to while I've been away.'

THE BLACK TOWER rose like a blade of stone in a swirling sea of sand. Just on the edge of the Great Desert, it was constantly assailed by the storms that howled across the hot dunes. The great blocks of basalt that comprised the tower's outer surface had been smoothed to a mirror finish by the scouring sand. The sound it made against the stone was like the hissing of a hundred thousand hungry snakes, seeking the slightest crack or flaw to work their way inside.

Yet, work on the tower continued, even in the teeth of the raging wind. Day and night it went on. An army of slaves shaped stones and carried them to the base of the tower, where still more labourers dragged them up a vast, spiral ramp that wound sinuously around the tall spire to a height of more than two hundred feet. The ramp was made of wood and hides, and lashed together with thick coils of rope, and it wavered and trembled appallingly in the storm. It had collapsed many times, toppled by raging gales of wind or sawn through by the abrasive sand, and each time, scores of labourers were crushed beneath the weight of fallen timbers and splintered stone.

The lucky ones did not rise again. Most, however, pushed aside the fallen beams or clawed their way out through the sand, digging with ragged hands or the pointed tips of finger bones. Some squirmed right out of the ragged scraps of flesh and muscle that had once clothed their gleaming bones. Their strength was born of pure, relentless will, lashing at their trapped souls like a scourge.

The people of Bhagar did not know hunger, or pain, or fatigue. The last of them had died more than three years before at the feet of Arkhan's black tower, fitting the foundation stones into place. The breath of their god raged impotently around them, scourging their bodies and hollowing out their eyes, and yet the tower continued to grow.

Constructing the tower had been an idea of Arkhan's for some time, dating back to the early construction of his master's mighty pyramid. When he found himself in possession of several thousand slaves after the conquest of Bhagar, the vizier saw his opportunity. While his master focused on raising his armies at Khemri, Arkhan proposed building the citadel to guard the city's southern approaches against another attack from distant Ka-Sabar, or perhaps even a revolt in the Spice City of Bel Aliad. The Undying King considered this, and agreed.

In truth, Arkhan wished to distance himself from Nagash for an entirely different reason: namely, the king's life-giving elixir. He chafed at the power that Nagash had over him by virtue of that terrible draught, but still its sorcerous formula eluded him. If he were to continue to serve the king from his seat at the black tower then Nagash would have no choice but to show the vizier how to craft the elixir for himself, or so he had thought.

Every six months a courier arrived from Khemri bearing a sealed chest that contained six vials of the elixir, just enough for one drink per month. The privation left him weak and thirsty all the time, and despite his best efforts he could never save enough of the liquid to study its properties for any length of time.

For the first two years after the slaughter at Bhagar the slaves had dug deep into the rocky soil with crude picks and shovels, creating the first of the tower's many floors more than fifty feet underground. Arkhan summoned stonemasons from Khemri to guide the slaves in their work, while his undead horsemen stood watch from the surrounding dunes. Later, the slaves were sent back to their home city and set to work demolishing their homes for the stone needed to shape the tower's foundation.

The deepest of the underground vaults was set aside for Arkhan. Although nothing like the grand eminence of his master's marble crypt, the chambers served the immortal's immediate needs. It had taken most of a year to move his household from the Living City to the distant tower due to the raging storms, and many loyal servants perished along the way. The rest he killed with poison as soon as they arrived. They waited upon him in the gloom of his sanctum, their shrivelled bodies wrapped in robes of blackest linen and wrought with arcane sigils of preservation.

Arkhan was within his inner sanctum, poring over scrolls of arcane lore and studying the ruby depths of one of his precious vials of elixir when he heard a faint, hissing rustle in the dark corners of the room. For the briefest instant he thought that the questing sand had finally found its way inside the black tower, driven by the implacable hate of Khsar the Faceless, whose people Arkhan had murdered. Pure terror coursed through the immortal's veins. Then, in a flash he snatched up a guttering lamp and advanced across the room, banishing the deep shadows before him.

Lamplight glittered on shining black carapaces. Scarabs were pouring from cracks in the stonework and flowing in a seething carpet across the sanctum's floor.

Arkhan took a step back, clenching the vial of elixir tightly in his hand as he prepared to cast a fiery incantation. The scarabs came together in the centre of the chamber, leaping into the air with a dry clatter of wings and swirling into a seething, glittering cloud.

The words of the incantation died upon Arkhan's lips as the cloud took on a familiar shape.

'Loyal servant,' said a voice from the depths of the rustling cloud. It was born of scraping mandibles and buzzing wings, scrabbling legs and dusty carapaces, but its identity was unmistakeable. Stunned, Arkhan bowed before the visage of Nagash.

'I am here, master,' the vizier said, tucking the vial into his sleeve. 'What is your command?'

'Our enemies march against us once more,' the necromancer said. The vague outline of Nagash's face turned towards the vizier. 'New armies are gathering at Quatar, and the Bronze Host crosses the Great Desert to strike at Bel Aliad.'

'Crossing the desert? Impossible!' Arkhan exclaimed. 'The storms–'

'The storms are the work of the craven priests of Mahrak,' Nagash hissed. 'They hope to hinder our efforts and conceal the movements of their troops. Even now, refugees from Bhagar are leading the warriors of Ka-Sabar along the secret pathways of the desert tribes. They will reach Bel Aliad within a fortnight. They do not know, however, that there is a traitor in their midst, one who has worshipped me for many years, since the defeat at Zedri. He will deliver the Bronze Host into our hands, and then the City of Bronze itself!'

Arkhan's mind raced as he considered the sudden turn of events.

'My warriors stand ready, master,' he said. 'What would you have us do?'

'Take your undead horseman and ride for Bel Aliad,' the necromancer said. 'Once you arrive, this is what you must do.'

The necromancer told Arkhan of his plan in hissing, crackling tones. The vizier listened with his head bowed low, contemplating the downfall of Akhmen-hotep and the people of Ka-Sabar.

◄ TWELVE ►

Designs upon a Crown

Khemri, the Living City, in the 44th year of Geheb the Mighty (-1962 Imperial Reckoning)

THE SLAVE GIRL knelt on the stone floor in the centre of the magical circle, her body rigid with agony as Nagash intoned the Incantation of Reaping. Only two days before, she had arrived in the Living City on a slave ship from Zandri, taken in a raid on the barbarian lands to the far north. Bright blue eyes stared up at Nagash in mindless terror. Her mouth gaped wide in a frozen shriek of pain, revealing fine, white teeth and a squirming tongue. Her shoulders trembled as she struggled for breath. The Grand Hierophant had been careful to allow her muscles just enough flexibility for her to breathe enough air so that she could remain conscious and alert. It had taken many months and countless experiments before he was capable of such precise control.

Nagash's powerful voice echoed from the stone walls of his sanctum beneath the Great Pyramid as he continued the remorseless, savage chant. He spoke in Nehekhem, not in the debased, snake-like tongue of his prisoners. His knowledge of their barbaric magic had grown in leaps and bounds in the three years since he'd slain that hapless fool Imhep. The spilling of blood, the unwinding of a living spirit from its bindings of flesh and bone, these things were second nature to him now.

The words of the ritual rang like the tolling of a bell, rising in tempo as Nagash focused his will upon the slave girl's labouring heart. Her heartbeat began to hammer in time with his chanting voice, and the air between them crackled with invisible power. The Grand Hierophant clenched his fists and felt the warmth of the girl's life force against his skin. His voice rose to an exultant shriek as the chant rose in tempo, and wisps of smoke began to curl from the slave's pale skin. Her trembling ceased. Veins stood out starkly at her temples and along the sides of her throat. Nagash felt the beat of her heart rise to a glorious crescendo. Then her body gave a single, violent spasm and exploded into a column of hissing green flame.

Nagash plunged his hands into the seething inferno, feeling the power race along his skin as he seized the slave girl's throat. With an inhaled breath and an exertion of will, he drew her life force into him. His veins burned, and her final cries rang soundlessly along his bones. It was over in a moment, and her body, drained of every dreg of power, collapsed in a heap of steaming bones at Nagash's feet.

This was but a prelude, a gathering of strength for the real work that was about to begin. Wrapped in ethereal mist and glowing with unholy energy, the Grand Hierophant stretched out his arms once more and turned his attention to the wooden cage just a few feet beyond the edge of the magic circle. Dusky figures stirred inside, half-hidden by the shifting shadows cast by the room's guttering oil lamps. They were siblings, a young man and a woman in the full bloom of youth and of noble birth, whom Khefru had found in the wine houses near the docks. The discovery had been a stroke of luck. Nagash's requirements for his next experiment had been very specific, and he had been forced to wait months for the pair to fall into the young priest's clutches.

With the last syllables of the Incantation of Reaping still echoing in the chamber, Nagash began his next ritual. The first phrases were simple enough, serving to focus the Grand Hierophant's concentration, but grew swiftly in cadence and complexity as the first stages of the transformation began.

He had learned very quickly that there were limits to the power of a human soul. When Imhep breathed his last and poured out his lifeblood onto Nagash's hands, the Grand Hierophant felt his veins turn to fire and believed himself a god, but that wondrous energy faded all too quickly. A single human life could fuel a minor druchii spell, but no more. Malchior had responded to his frustrations with a shrug. A soul was but a puff of breath compared to the wild winds of magic that fuelled the druchii's greater rituals.

The warlock had known this all along. It was yet another of the barbarians' devious traps. Malchior could fulfil the letter of their agreement by teaching Nagash the incantations and rituals of druchii magic lore in the full knowledge that the Grand Hierophant would never amass enough power to attempt the more potent spells. Such an effort would require scores, if not hundreds of souls, a process that was far too unwieldy to perform in a single rite, and on too large a scale to avoid notice by Thutep and the city nobles. No doubt Malchior hoped that Nagash's lust for power would tempt him to recklessness and self-destruction. Instead, the Grand Hierophant began to apply his new-found powers in another direction, namely the accumulated arcane lore of Settra's mortuary cult.

For more than two thousand years, the cult of eternal life had plumbed the dark mysteries of life and death. Their ancient tomes were filled with theoretical rituals to harness the soul and manipulate the invisible workings of flesh and bone. Until now, however, their practical rites were minor in comparison to those of the druchii, because the liche priests depended on the gifts of the gods to fuel their incantations. All that had changed when Imhep had poured out his lifeblood over Nagash's hands.

This new incantation was based upon an older rite found in the cult's body of arcane lore. Nagash had spent the better part of a year altering and refining the ritual to suit his plans. Now he would put it to the test.

The arcane chant rolled like thunder from Nagash's tongue, driven by the energies stolen from the slave girl. He focused on the two shadowy forms crouching at the far end of their cage and extended his hands towards them. At once, the young siblings collapsed to the floor, moaning in fear and pain. Power flowed from his fingertips and played across their naked forms.

Nagash performed the incantation for nearly an hour, until the last vestiges of stolen energy sped from his fingertips. As the rite concluded, he spoke a single name.

'Shepresh,' he said, and lowered his arms. Silence fell, punctuated by soft, choking sounds from inside the cage and the swish of an ink brush from the corner of the sanctum to Nagash's left.

Khefru continued to note his observations in a huge, leather-bound book for several long minutes after the rite was completed. Nagash's erstwhile tutors were absent. Since he had begun to apply his new-found abilities to the lore of the mortuary cult, the Grand Hierophant found that he required the presence of the druchii less and less. Soon, Nagash suspected that their long-term arrangement would finally come to an end.

The young priest made a final note with his brush and glanced up at his master.

'Was the rite successful?' he asked. Nagash spared a final glance towards the mewling figures at the bottom of the cage and waved dismissively.

'It is too early to tell,' he said, striding carefully from the circle. 'The transformation has only begun to take root. I shall know more when I return later tonight.' The Grand Hierophant folded his arms across his chest. 'Have you seen to the preparations inside the city?'

Khefru nodded gravely as he capped the ink-pot and set his brush aside. The past six years had taken a toll upon the former noble. Though still very young by Nehekharan standards, the priest had grown haggard and sunken-eyed in service to his master's increasingly dangerous pursuits. His face was sallow and puffy from too many nights spent in wine houses searching for his master's victims, and he'd taken to shaving his head to conceal the streaks of grey that had begun to sprout at his temples. The long scar on the left side of his face cut a jagged white furrow across his fleshy cheek.

'All is in readiness, master,' he replied. 'The house has been made ready, and the slaves know their tasks.' Nagash studied Khefru warily.

'You sound reluctant,' he said. Khefru closed the tome carefully and lifted it from the writing table.

'It is not for me to say, master,' he answered, returning it to a shelf laden with similar volumes.

'True enough,' the Grand Hierophant replied. 'Tell me, nonetheless.' The young priest considered his words carefully.

'What you are contemplating is reckless,' he began. 'These men are cowards and fools. They will betray you in an instant—'

'They will have far more to gain from me than from my brother,' Nagash cut in. 'Just as you did, if you recall.'

'That's not how they will see it,' Khefru persisted. 'They have no power, no wealth or influence. Thutep and the great houses would crush them, and they know it. No amount of persuasion will convince them otherwise.' Nagash smiled coldly.

'Persuade them? Hardly. When the time comes, they will have persuaded themselves.'

Khefru's gaze drifted to the cage at the far side of the room. His expression grew strained.

'Haven't we tempted fate enough?' he asked. 'I've lost count of all the people we've killed. Rumours are starting to spread through the river districts.'

'Fate?' Nagash spat. 'Fate is a notion that weak minds use to excuse their failures.' The Grand Hierophant stepped close to the young priest. 'Have you grown weak, Khefru? Our work has only just begun.' The young priest met Nagash's eyes, and his face went pale.

'No, master,' he said quickly. 'I'm not weak. Command me, and I will serve.' Nagash studied Khefru's face for a long moment.

'Let us go, then,' he said, and turned away.

Khefru watched the Grand Hierophant leave the dimly lit chamber and begin the long, winding trek to the surface. A wet, gurgling cough came from the deep shadows within the cage. With a last, dreadful look at the squirming forms inside, the priest hurried quickly after his master.

IT WAS APPROACHING midnight in the world beyond the crypt. Neru hung, bright and full, above the vast necropolis, limning the stone structures in ghostly silver light and creating pools of inky blackness in the narrow lanes between, while Sakhmet, the Green Witch, shone baleful and red just above the eastern horizon. Nagash and Khefru made their way alone among the houses of the dead, listening to the chatter of jackals among the poorer crypts to the south-west. They encountered no dangers on their trek to the distant road. In times past it was not unknown for gangs of thieves and grave robbers to prowl among the vast city of tombs, but that had come to an end within the last few years. Rumours abounded in the city that something dark and terrible had taken root in Khemri's necropolis, and those who braved its streets after dark were never seen again.

The Grand Hierophant had certainly not lacked for subjects in the early days of his studies, nor had his tutors lacked for entertainment.

They walked in silence along the mortuary road, past neglected shrines half-covered in sand and marked with bird droppings. Bright moonlight painted the slopes of the distant dunes and silhouetted the broad sweep of a heron's wings as it took flight from the river bank to the north. A pack of jackals followed the pair a short way from the necropolis, their low-slung forms loping along the crests of the dunes and their eyes shining like polished coins as they studied the two men. With every mile, the scavengers edged closer and closer to the pair, until finally Nagash turned and fixed the largest of the pack with a challenging glare. The pack leader held the necromancer's stare for a few moments, and then let out a ghoulish, yapping cry and disappeared over the crest of a sand dune with the rest of the pack close behind.

The gates to the Living City were shut for the night, but the Grand Hierophant was allowed in without so much as a challenge. By ancient tradition, the priests of Settra's cult were allowed to come and go through the Gates of Usirian at any time of the day or night, owing to their duties among the crypts outside the city. Beyond the gate, the streets of the Temple district were quiet. Distantly, the two men could hear the faint chants of the priestesses of Neru rising from their temple compound as they went about their nightly vigil, warding Khemri from the spirits of the wastes.

Just beyond the temple district, Khefru led his master to a predetermined alley, where a palanquin and eight nervous-looking bearers waited. Nagash was ushered quickly inside and the bearers set off at once, making their way into the Merchant's District and turning north, where wine houses and dens of vice lined the side streets just south of the city's wealthy neighbourhoods.

Here the streets were still well-travelled, even at such a late hour. Groups of drunken men staggered to and from the taverns and gambling houses, or crouched outside the shops and passed jars of beer or played games of dice. Young, grubby-faced children ran along the lanes, offering to help the drunkest souls find their destinations, and relieving them of their coin along the way. Fights broke out as dice games grew heated or drunken arguments got out of hand. Small bands of dour city watchmen prowled the area armed with lanterns and stout, bronze-capped staves, scattering the worst troublemakers with angry shouts and sharp blows to the offenders' shoulders and legs.

The palanquin made its way unnoticed among the late-night revellers and scowling watchmen, finally turning right down a narrow alley close to Coppersmith Street. Khefru jogged ahead of the palanquin to a recessed door lit by a small, hanging oil lamp. The priest rapped softly as the bearers lowered the palanquin to the ground. With a rattle of bolts, the door swung open just as Nagash emerged into the night air. Glancing warily up and down the dark alley, the Grand Hierophant stepped quickly through the doorway into a small, rubbish-strewn court-yard. Two of Nagash's household slaves bowed low to their master and quickly secured the door behind him.

The Grand Hierophant took in the courtyard with a single, disdainful glance. Sand covered the cracked flag-stones, and weeds grew in the stagnant water of a long-dead fountain. Rats scuttled through the shadows along the foot of the pockmarked walls.

'This hovel was the best you could find?' he asked Khefru.

'You wanted anonymity, did you not?' Khefru said archly. 'Would you have preferred a manor in the noble districts, in full view of every gossiping slave and meddlesome widow?' He surveyed the decaying home with a satisfied nod. 'Places like this are common near the seedier quarters. Nobles or traders buy them up and use them for trysts, and then sell them off again when the mood suits them. The locals see people come and go from them at all hours and don't think twice, and it's just down the street from some of your guests' favourite haunts.'

'Fine, fine,' Nagash snapped. He turned to the two slaves. 'Are all in attendance?' he asked.

'The last arrived an hour ago, master,' one slave said as he shot the last bolt home.

'No doubt they've drunk most of the wine by now,' Khefru said darkly. 'Not a good way to begin a conspiracy, master.' The Grand Hierophant ignored the priest's impertinence.

'Take me to them,' he commanded the slaves.

Nagash followed the two men across the courtyard and through an open doorway, into a narrow, unfurnished corridor lit by a pair of guttering oil lamps. More slaves were bustling up and down the passageway, bearing empty jars of wine or platters of half-eaten food. The sound of a muffled voice emerged from the far end of the corridor, followed by raucous laughter.

The slaves led the Grand Hierophant down the passageway and through a series of small, empty rooms cluttered with bits of broken furniture. Each room was more brightly lit than the last, until Nagash found himself in a well-lit antechamber adjoining the house's large common room. The buzz of voices and the clink of metal cups sounded from the other side of a pair of curtained doorways on the opposite side of the antechamber.

Nagash waved the slaves aside and, with a brief glance back at Khefru, he straightened his robes and stepped quietly through the nearest doorway.

Unlike the rest of the house, the common room had been richly appointed with furnishings from the Grand Hierophant's apartments at the royal palace. The floor was covered in fine rugs made in distant Lahmia, and fine divans set with silk cushions had been arranged in a rough circle around an imposing chair made of dark, polished wood. A dozen young noblemen lounged on the divans or sprawled on the rugs, drinking wine and picking at scraps of fish or fowl from copper plates laid out among the revellers. The aromatic smoke from expensive incense curled from braziers in the corners of the room.

Heads turned as the Grand Hierophant entered the room. Faces flush with wine and ribaldry wore expressions of bemusement, and then surprise, as the guests recognised the man who had come late to the feast.

Nagash stepped forwards, pausing beside the chair of dark wood reserved for the dinner's host. As the drunken voices fell silent, the man reclining in the chair straightened with a chuckle.

'What now? Will we have dancing girls?' he asked, glancing over his shoulder. 'With skin as pale as moonlight and hair as black as–' His lecherous smirk turned to wide-eyed shock as he saw who stood beside him.

Nobleman and priest stared at one another for a long moment. Then Arkhan the Black began to laugh. The Grand Hierophant's expression turned grim.

'Do I amuse you?' he asked in a quiet voice. Arkhan smiled, revealing his ruined teeth.

'We were speculating who our mysterious host might be,' he said, lapsing once again into laughter. 'Raamket thought it might be another attempt by the king to keep us out of the wine houses.' He raised his glass to Nagash. 'And here you are.'

Raamket, a dark-eyed brute of a man with the face of a dockside brawler, glared daggers at Arkhan. The other nobles burst into drunken laughter at their friend's discomfort. Another noble, a man named Meruhep, fished a baby eel from a bowl in his lap and studied it in the lamp light.

'Our friend Raamket seems to know a bit too much. Perhaps we have a spy in our midst!' he said, tilting his head back and noisily slurped the eel down.

More laughter filled the room. Nagash waited in silence until the merriment died away. He eyed Arkhan coldly. After a moment, the nobleman's smirk faded and he rose sullenly from the chair. Nagash settled gracefully into the seat.

'A crude attempt at humour, but the sentiment is accurate,' the Grand Hierophant said. 'In fact, the reason you are here is because you know firsthand how misguided and dangerous my brother's rule has become.' Arkhan snorted into his wine cup.

'The only danger I can see is death by boredom,' he said. 'Those Grand Assemblies get more excruciating by the month.'

'My brother treats you all like children,' Nagash said. 'It's humiliating, not just for you, but for Khemri as well, because it reveals to the world that our king is a weak man.'

'What would you do in his place?' Meruhep asked with a smirk. 'Drag us all into the bazaar and cut off our hands?' The Grand Hierophant ignored the question.

'Thutep has convinced himself that humans are innately compassionate and charitable,' he said. 'He thinks that if you sit through enough royal courts the virtues of civic responsibility will seep into your heads like drops of cool water. He fancies that he can persuade the kings of Nehekhara to put aside centuries of warfare out of enlightened self-interest and the temptations of trade.' The words dripped like venom from Nagash's tongue. 'And how has our city profited in the last six years? The great houses of Khemri ignore his royal summons whenever they see fit and act according to their own interests. Entire neighbourhoods in the noble districts lie empty because the embassies of our brother cities have been seduced away by Zandri. The City of the Waves has usurped Khemri as the greatest city in Nehekhara for the first time in centuries. And for what? So that Thutep can negotiate lower grain prices with Numas and import rugs tax-free from Lahmia.

That is what we have traded our pre-eminence for, beads on an abacus.'

Several of the nobles shifted uneasily at the vehemence in Nagash's speech. One of the men, a handsome, easygoing rake named Shepsu-hur, leaned back on his divan and eyed the Grand Hierophant warily.

'If things are as dire as you paint them, holy one, why haven't the great houses moved against Thutep?' he asked. 'Wasn't that how your dynasty came to exist in the first place?'

Nagash gave Shepsu-hur a sharp glance, but then a reluctant nod. Khetep had been of royal blood, but he was not the son of Rakaph, the previous king. When Rakaph had finally died his wife, Queen Rasut, had defied ancient law and claimed the throne for a short time, fearing that the kings of Numas or Zandri would try to supplant her infant son and claim the city for their own. Ultimately, the Hieratic Council of Mahrak managed to persuade Rasut to yield the throne and return to Lahmia, where she died a short time later. Khetep, Rakaph's trusted vizier, was appointed to rule the city as its regent until Rasut's son reached adulthood.

Within a month of Rasut's death, her young son died of a sudden fever, and Khetep became Priest King of Khemri.

'For the moment, the current situation favours the great houses,' Nagash continued. 'Under my father's rule, their power and influence were kept in check, but now they can flout the king's law and build their fortunes however they choose.' He shrugged. 'No doubt in time one of the houses would believe itself strong enough to seize the throne, but they will never get the opportunity. Zandri means to become the pre-eminent power in Nehekhara, but for that to be possible, Khemri must be forever broken. King Nekumet is gathering his strength even now. In a short time, perhaps a few years, he will grow bold enough to march against us. When that happens, the Living City will bow its knee to Zandri and forever become its vassal.'

The assembled noblemen did not know how to respond to Nagash's bald declaration. Many looked to their wine cups or glanced surreptitiously at their fellows. Only Arkhan ventured a reply.

'These are grim tidings indeed, holy one, but what do you expect us to do about it?' he asked. 'We have no power, wealth or influence.' The nobleman gave the Grand Hierophant a ruined grin. 'I suppose we could challenge Nekumet to a drinking contest, or a game of dice. How would that be?' Raamket glowered at Arkhan.

'I wouldn't try,' he muttered. 'I've seen the way you throw dice.'

The room erupted in gales of laughter at Arkhan's expense. The nobleman bared his blackened teeth and snarled drunken oaths at his friends, and for a few moments all the talk of kings and conquests was forgotten. Nagash simply sat, patient and unblinking as a snake, until finally the laughter died and the faces of his guests were solemn once more.

'Power is a fluid thing,' he continued, as though the interruption hadn't occurred. 'It changes hands more easily than one might think. Surely my brother is a prime example of that.' Nagash studied each of the assembled nobles in turn. 'You are powerless now, that is true, but that could change.' Arkhan leaned forwards, setting his cup on the floor.

'You could arrange such a thing?' he asked.

The Grand Hierophant smiled coldly. 'Of course,' he replied. 'The old ways are coming to an end. Khemri will have a new king, and he must be served by cruel and ruthless men, men who are not afraid to bloody their hands and make people fear the Living City once more.' Nagash studied his assembled guests in turn. 'You can be wealthy and powerful beyond your wildest dreams, if you are the ruthless men I seek.' Meruhep noisily slurped down another eel.

'You're a fool if you think you can become king,' he sneered. 'You're a priest. The Council at Mahrak would never allow it.'

'Those frauds have no power over me!' Nagash snarled, his hands clenching the grips of his chair. 'Their authority is a lie, and one day I will cast them into the dust. They have bound us to the will of the false gods for long enough!'

The young noblemen stared wide-eyed at the Grand Hierophant, too shocked to speak. Meruhep shook his head disdainfully, fishing about in the bowl at his lap. After a long moment, Arkhan broke the silence.

'I am a ruthless man, holy one,' he said quietly, 'but you knew that already, or else I would not be here.'

'I am as well,' Raamket said heatedly. 'See if I am not.' Shepsu-hur chuckled softly.

'I can be ruthless when the mood takes me, holy one,' he said.

One by one, the other nobles added their voices to the chorus. Arkhan had been correct, Nagash had chosen each man carefully, based on recommendations from Khefru. For all their youthful bravado, they were desperate and wretched men, deep in debt and lost in their vices. The promise of wealth and power tempted them beyond reason, and none of them had much to lose beyond their wasted lives.

Only one man held his tongue. Meruhep's expression turned more and more scornful as the cacophony around him grew. He set his bowl aside, sloshing wine and limp eels onto the floor.

'You are all fools!' he snapped, glaring angrily at his fellows. The young noble pointed angrily at Nagash. 'He has no power! His cult is a sham, made to satisfy the vanity of a king. Do you think the great houses will sit idly by and let him depose his brother? Do you imagine even Thutep will be merciful when he learns of this? No. Your heads will sit atop spikes outside the palace.' Meruhep turned back to Nagash. 'And believe me, the king will find out, one way or the other. These things never remain secret for long...'

The young noble stopped in mid-sentence, his brow furrowing. For a moment, it looked as though he'd lost his train of thought, and then his eyes widened and he doubled over with a gasp of pain that quickly gave way to agonised screams.

Men scrambled to their feet with surprised shouts. Some threw their wine cups to the floor, fearing some kind of poison. One man, a distant cousin of Meruhep, tentatively approached the stricken noble's side, but stopped dead when he caught the look on Nagash's face. The Grand Hierophant was staring intently at the writhing nobleman, his lips moving in a silent recitation.

Shepsu-hur caught the look on Nagash's face as well. His gaze fell on Meruhep, and his eyes widened in horror.

'Blessed Neru,' he said, pointing to the floor. 'The eels!'

The assembled nobles followed Shepsu-hur's gesture. Meruhep's overturned bowl lay in the centre of the floor, and a knot of boiled eels writhed and snapped like a clutch of snakes in the spreading pool of wine.

Cries of horror and dismay filled the common room, and the young men recoiled in terror from Meruhep's thrashing body. Within seconds, his screams turned to gurgling, gasping cries, and blood began to soak through his linen robes. His movements became uncontrolled, turning into death spasms as the eels chewed through his abdomen.

Within a few minutes, Meruhep was dead, lying in a pool of his bodily fluids. Long, pale shapes squirmed through the blood and bile, falling still one by one. When the last of the creatures had returned to lifelessness, Nagash raised his eyes to the shaken crowd.

'No doubt you all understand the need for secrecy in this endeavour,' he said calmly. He beckoned to the shadows at the corners of the room, and slaves rushed forwards to drag Meruhep's body away. 'For the moment, you need do nothing but wait.'

Nagash raised his hand again, and Khefru appeared from the antechamber. The young priest carried a roll of papyrus in his hands.

'At present, all I need from you are your names,' said Khefru. 'Write them down on this scroll, along with the names of any other noblemen whom you believe can be persuaded to our cause.'

Khefru went to Arkhan first, handing over the papyrus and reaching for an ink brush tucked into his sleeve. The nobleman was staring at the trail of blood left behind by Meruhep's corpse with a mixture of avid interest and revulsion. With an effort, he tore his gaze away from the nightmarish scene and glanced at the blank papyrus.

'Do we… do we sign this in blood?' Arkhan asked hesitantly. The question surprised Nagash.

'Blood?' he said archly. 'Certainly not. What do you take me for, some kind of barbarian?'

HOURS LATER, NAGASH emerged from the decrepit house and directed the palanquin bearers to return to the necropolis. They did so fearfully, their footfalls echoing down the city's deserted streets. It was nearing the hour of the dead, when Neru's light was nearly gone and the spirits of the wastes could roam the land in search of prey. Sakhmet burned brightly, just above the western horizon, and the bearers kept throwing frightened glances over their shoulders, as though the Green Witch was dogging their heels. When they finally returned to the Great Pyramid, Khefru had to promise to double the men's wages to keep them waiting among the jackal-haunted tombs.

Nagash noticed none of this. He rose from the palanquin without a word and dashed swiftly inside the huge tomb. The oil lamps were still burning inside his sanctum. He snatched one up and rushed forwards, holding it high above his head and banishing the shadows that concealed the contents of the wooden cage on the opposite side of the room.

Mewling cries of terror greeted Nagash as he reached the enclosure. Yellow light gleamed from the wide, maddened eyes of a young man, who had pressed his trembling body into the furthest corner of the cage to try to escape the fate that had befallen his sister. Her body lay almost at the Grand Hierophant's feet, surrounded by a pool of congealing blood and bodily fluids. Her skin had swollen like a sausage and then burst, spilling a foul slurry of cancerous flesh and reeking blood onto the stone floor. The stained bones amid the gore were the only indication that the corpse was even human.

Nagash fumbled quickly at the lock securing the cage door. Then he reached in and seized the young man by the hair. He dragged the screaming figure out of the cage like a butcher selecting a kid for the slaughter, and examined every inch of his naked body.

The Grand Hierophant smiled. The young man, Shepresh by name, was completely unharmed. The curse that had slain his sister had not touched him, despite the noble blood they shared.

Still smiling, Nagash dragged the mewling figure into the ritual circle to begin the Incantation of Reaping once more. Then, Khefru entered the room, carrying the rolled-up papyrus they'd brought from the meeting.

'The names!' Nagash said, stretching out his hand. 'The names! Bring them here!'

The hour of the dead was at hand, and there was terrible work to be done.

◄ THIRTEEN ►

The Two-edged Blade

Bel Aliad, the City of Spices, in the 63rd year of Ptra the Glorious (-1744 Imperial Reckoning)

THE BHAGARITE HORSEMAN raced effortlessly down the narrow lanes of the army camp, glimmering like a ghost in the predawn gloom. Silver bells attached to the leather tack of the desert horse made a strange, unearthly counterpoint to the animal's drumming hoofbeats, sending a shiver of dread through the warriors of the Bronze Host as he raced towards the centre of the camp. New recruits rose from their bedrolls and stumbled out into the horseman's wake, wondering what all the urgency was about, while the veterans shared grim looks and reached for their whetstones, or began making last-minute repairs to their armour.

The Bronze Host of Ka-Sabar was encamped at the western edge of the Great Desert, their tents spilling in a great crescent from the mouth of a narrow wadi that had sheltered them for the last ten miles of their trek. The journey across the dunes had taken many weeks, even with the unerring guidance of nearly a hundred Bhagarite riders. They marched by night and took shelter during the searing heat of the day, and within the first week even the strongest warriors looked out across the endless expanse of sand and feared that they would never find their way out again. Their guides were as good as their word, however, and the Bronze Host was never more than three days from a desert oasis or a hidden cache of sealed water jars, preserved food and even feed for their horses. The guides entered each oasis and opened each cache with an eerie, keening wail, drawing their knives and slicing their cheeks in an offering to their faceless, hungry god. By the time the army reached the far edge of the desert their guides were pale and wide-eyed, shivering as though with fever and muttering prayers to Khsar under their breath.

The Bhagarites had guided the army to a rocky plain just a mile from the Spice Road that ran along the western edge of the desert, little more than five miles from Bel Aliad. As the warriors of the Bronze Host stumbled onto the plain like men woken rudely from sleep, the Bhagarites wrapped themselves in funereal robes of the purest white and wound their headscarves round their heads in the complicated arrangement called the Eshabir el-Hekhet, the Merciless Mask. They prepared to avenge their slaughtered kin in an orgy of righteous bloodshed.

The order to attack had not come. Instead, Akhmen-hotep ordered the army to make camp and offer prayers to the gods. They had just completed a gruelling trek across the merciless sands of the Great Desert, and even the Bhagarites reluctantly admitted that the army could stand to wait a day and regain some of its strength.

One day passed and then two. A third day came and went, and still the army did not stir. The Bhagarites grew restless. Did the priest king not realise that sooner or later a caravan or a shepherd could stumble across the camp and send a warning to their foes? They tried to make their case to the king, but Akhmen-hotep was unmoved. He sent the riders from the camp, ordering them northwards to scout the terrain and bring back news of the city and its people.

Five days after the army's emergence from the desert, a Bhagarite horseman was riding for the king's tent as though the howling spirits of the waste were hot upon his heels.

The rider came upon Akhmen-hotep and his generals as they were beginning their morning prayers. A young bull, one of five precious animals brought with them across the desert, had been sacrificed to Geheb. Hashepra, the Hierophant of the Earth God, was standing before the kneeling noblemen, his muscular arms outspread and the bloody sacrificial knife held high. Two young acolytes, neither one more than twelve years old, held the great bronze bowl with trembling hands to catch the dying animal's blood.

Heads rose curiously at the sound of the hoofbeats, and the king's Ushabti rose to their feet and formed a forbidding line in the rider's path. The Bhagarite reined in a discreet distance from the bodyguards and leapt gracefully from the saddle.

'Great king!' the horseman cried. 'Your camp has been discovered! The warriors of Bel Aliad are assembling on the plains south of the city and making ready to attack!'

Startled shouts and calls to battle rang out from the assembled nobles, some even going so far as to dash off across the camp to ready their warriors for the coming battle. Among their number, only Akhmen-hotep remained on his knees, his hands held out in supplication and his head bent in prayer. Those noblemen nearest the king eyed Akhmen-hotep, worried, uncertain what they should do.

Among them was Pakh-amn. The Master of Horse was still out of favour with the king, but Akhmen-hotep insisted that he be brought along when the army marched on Bel Aliad. By ancient custom, the Master of Horse was one of the king's chief generals in times of war, and Akhmen-hotep had commanded that all the old traditions be upheld. For his part, Pakh-amn had performed his duties with cold-hearted diligence and devotion.

The Master of Horse took in the unfolding scene and drew a deep breath.

'What is your command, great one?' he asked stiffly. His cheeks were still hollow and his eyes sunken from the touch of the lotus, but his voice was sober and strong.

Akhmen-hotep did not answer at first, his lips moving in a silent prayer. He passed his hands over his face and across his shaven scalp, as though washing himself clean of fear and doubt.

'We shall finish making our obeisance to Geheb,' he said quietly, 'and then we shall summon the Grand Hierophant and offer sacrifices to Ptra so that he will guide us to victory.' As he spoke, the king bent his head to Hashepra. The hierophant nodded and beckoned to his acolytes, who brought forward the wide, brimming bowl. Pakh-amn's stained lips pressed into a thin, angry line.

'Time is of the essence,' he said. 'The enemy could be upon us within the hour. Since they willingly serve the Usurper, I doubt they will trouble themselves with lengthy prayers to the gods.'

'All the more reason for us to demonstrate our devotion,' the king replied calmly. 'We are not fighting for glory, or for gold. We are fighting to defend the Blessed Land, and to honour the covenant between gods and men.'

'The warriors of Bel Aliad will not appreciate the distinction,' Pakh-amn said sourly, 'when they are scattering our disorganised companies and setting fire to our tents.' Unperturbed, Akhmen-hotep accepted the sacrificial bowl and raised it to his lips. When he passed it back to the acolytes his chin was wet with blood.

'What happens today is the will of the gods,' the king said. He looked pointedly at the waiting acolytes. 'Will you show your devotion to the Earth God, Pakh-amn, or do you intend to continue the debate and delay the army further?'

Pakh-amn glared hotly at the king. He started to reply, but caught himself at the last moment, and instead reached impatiently for the red-rimmed bowl. Casting apprehensive glances to the north, the rest of the assembled nobles followed suit.

THE EARLY MORNING sunlight rested like a red-hot iron across Akhmen-hotep's face and neck. Around him, the Bronze Host surged forwards to the tramp of thousands of feet and the heavy beat of drums. The air above the army was thick with swirling dust that coated a man's throat and gummed up his eyes. They were three miles north of camp, advancing in a steady, if ragged line towards the City of Spices and its waiting army. As it happened, Pakh-amn's fears had been for naught. Although the warriors of Ka-Sabar had taken more than two hours to form up and make ready to depart, the army of Bel Aliad was no faster. By the time the two armies came within sight of one another the defending army had managed to travel just a single mile.

They came together on a rocky plain bordered by the Spice Road to the west and the desert fringe to the east. Akhmen-hotep could just see the walls of Bel Aliad rising along the horizon to the north. The fighting men of the City of Spices were advancing in rough order, slowly but surely driving back the hundred Bhagarite horsemen who were trying to screen the Bronze Host's approach. Bel Aliad boasted its own light horsemen. The city had been originally founded by exiles from Bhagar, after all, more than four hundred years past, but their mounts were ordinary animals bought from Numas, rather than gifts from the desert god. Their squadrons advanced in fits and starts, wheeling across the plain like flights of angry birds before racing back to the safety of their advancing army. The desert horsemen retreated slowly but steadily, greeting the enemy movements with derisive jeers and the occasional bowshot.

The main body of the enemy army numbered eight thousand strong, or so the Bhagarite scouts claimed: a large force, but like their light cavalry, it lacked quality. Bel Aliad was the smallest city worthy of the name in all of Nehekhara. To defend itself from desert raiders and to protect its numerous merchant caravans, the city's princes spent a fortune maintaining a standing army of sell-swords and hired thugs. Their bowmen were drawn from the fearsome sea archers of Zandri, and their two large City Companies were bolstered by four thousand northern mercenaries, hired from the barbarian tribes and brought south aboard chartered merchant ships to take up arms under Bel Aliad's banner.

The barbarians were huge, stinking, hairy brutes, clad in matted furs and long, oily tunics cinched with wide leather belts around their waists. Though primitive and ignorant of the proper arts of war, these mercenaries were fearsome fighters with shield and spear, or wielding deadly, leaf-shaped bronze swords brought from their rugged homeland. Leading the army were the merchant princes and their retainers, who disdained the cavalry tactics of their ancestors and instead fought from the back of light, swift chariots like other civilised armies.

Against this army the Bronze Host could muster only four thousand men, plus the hundred Bhagarite horsemen who had served as their guides. Six years had not been enough time for Ka-Sabar to restore its shattered forces, for the heavy infantry companies of the City of Bronze demanded lengthy training and conditioning to fight with spear, shield and scale armour. Akhmen-hotep had managed to field only two full infantry companies, plus a large force of five hundred chariots and a thousand trained bowmen. The rest of his army was comprised of loose companies of warrior-aspirants who had been pressed into service as improvised light infantry. Each aspirant carried only a small, round shield, a short sword and a quiver of light, barbed javelins, identical to the hunting weapons that many of them had used as children. They had been drilled relentlessly on the training fields outside the city, but no one knew for certain how effective they would be on the field of battle.

When the Bronze Host had left Ka-Sabar, it had been generally hoped that they would not see action at all. Now the companies were ranged just ahead and to the sides of the slow-moving heavy infantry, each man holding a javelin loosely in his hand. The army's bowmen formed a long line behind the heavy companies, their bows strung and ready, while behind them came the army's chariots.

The army of Bel Aliad had come to an unsteady halt across the plain, and was re-forming its companies. Two lines of mercenary archers were far out in front, their arrows placed and ready to fire. Behind them crowded noisy mobs of barbarian warriors, their faces painted with blue and red dyes and their shaggy faces alight with the prospect of bloodshed.

At the sight of the Bronze Host, the mercenaries began to clash their weapons against the rims of their shields and howl like a pack of hyenas, filling the air with strange war cries spoken in their guttural tongue. Akhmen-hotep thought he could see the standards of the City Companies, beyond the milling barbarians, and a roiling plume of dust that had to come from the army's chariots. Bel Aliad's light horsemen crowded around the army's flanks, threatening to charge once again at the thin line of Bhagarite cavalry occupying the middle ground between the two armies.

Raising his hand, Akhmen-hotep ordered the army to halt. Trumpets sounded, and the king turned and leapt from the back of his armoured chariot. His Ushabti joined him at once, ringing the priest king in gleaming bronze. Pakh-amn dismounted his chariot nearby and hastened to the king's side, along with his other generals, members of his retinue and Ka-Sabar's religious leaders. Hashepra was garbed for war, clad in bronze scale armour and bearing his customary hammer, and Khalifra, high priestess of Neru, carried a blessed spear in her slender hand. Only Memnet was unarmed, his face pale and waxy in the fierce light of day.

The king waited until the assembly had gathered and nodded gravely.

'The blessings of the gods be upon you,' he said to them. 'The day of battle is upon us, and so far, all is proceeding as expected.' Pakh-amn folded his arms.

'You mean to say you planned this?' he asked. 'Instead of sweeping down on Bel Aliad and taking it by storm, you wanted to fight their army in the open field, where their greater numbers would tell against us?' Akhmen-hotep eyed the Master of Horse coldly.

'You expected us to steal upon Bel Aliad like thieves in the night and slaughter its citizens while they slept? That is the way of the Usurper, Pakh-amn. We will fight the men of Bel Aliad according to the proper rules of war, as the priest kings have done since the time of Settra. Quarter will be given if asked, and ransoms will be claimed.' A stunned expression crossed Pakh-amn's face, followed by one of dawning comprehension.

'That's why you tarried in camp for so long,' he said scornfully. 'You wanted them to discover us. Why didn't you just send a messenger inviting them to battle? Wouldn't that have been the civilised thing to do?' Hashepra took a step towards Pakh-amn, glowering forbiddingly at the young nobleman.

'You forget yourself once again,' he warned. 'Here, on the field of battle, you can be slain outright for such talk.'

'No doubt that would suit the king well,' Pakh-amn snapped, 'but it won't change the truth of what's before us. Have you all forgotten what happened at Zedri? The old ways are gone! If we don't accept that, Nagash will destroy us!'

'The old ways are all that separate us from that monster!' the king cried. 'If we abandon our beliefs and fight like the Blasphemer, how are we any better than him?' He raised his fist to the sky. 'So long as we live, the old ways survive! So long as I draw breath, the Blessed Land lives within me.' Pakh-amn's dark eyes glittered with contempt, but he bowed to the king.

'Lead on, then,' he said, 'for so long as you live.'

Hashepra growled angrily and began to raise his hammer, but the king stopped him with a raised hand.

'Return to your chariots!' he commanded his warriors, and then turned to the assembled hierophants. 'Remain here and summon the powers of the gods to aid us,' he said. 'If Bel Aliad has truly turned to Nagash, there will be no priests among them. Your blessings may well turn the tide in our favour.' Khalifra folded her arms regally, but her face was lined with strain. The beautiful priestess seemed to have aged decades since the terrible battle at the oasis.

'We will give what we can,' she said gravely. Hashepra folded his powerful arms and nodded as well.

'If Bel Aliad has turned to Nagash, they won't need priests,' Memnet said in a leaden voice. 'They will have the Usurper's power to call upon.' The king looked his older brother in the eye, and a bleak look came over his face.

'Then we will have to trust in courage and god-given bronze,' he said. 'That is all any man can do.'

Akhmen-hotep considered his gathered generals, particularly his belligerent Master of Horse. The defeat at Zedri had left wounds that ran deeper than flesh. He knew that the confidence of the army was shaken, nearly to the point of rebellion. Pakh-amn in particular had been badly scarred by what he had seen. Could he be trusted? For a fleeting moment, Akhmen-hotep was tempted to remove the Master of Horse from his position and send him back to camp, but immediately he realised that doing so would send the wrong signal to the rest of the army. If they saw that the king's faith in them was so shaken that he would arrest one of his generals, their resolve might vanish like wax under the midday sun. He had to believe that there was still strength in the old ties of duty and piety, that the covenant between men and gods was still strong, and that there were some things in the world that not even Nagash the Usurper could sweep aside.

Drawing a deep breath, the king made his decision. He beckoned to his trumpeter. 'Order the Bhagarites to probe the enemy horsemen to the right,' he said, 'and then withdraw to the rear by way of the desert.' Hashepra frowned as he listened to the king's order.

'You would deprive us of our light cavalry at the start of battle?'

'Our guides have clad themselves in white once more, and wear the Merciless Mask,' Akhmen-hotep said. 'They hunger for vengeance, but I will not allow our cause to be tainted by a massacre of innocents. The Bhagarites will have to bide their time until Nagash and his immortals are made to account for their crimes.'

The trumpeters raised their curved, bronze horns and blew an intricate series of notes. As the sounds faded, the king turned to Pakh-amn.

'I will lead half the chariots forward, comprising the centre of the army,' the king said. 'When we start to move, and the dust fills the air, take the remaining half and head for the left flank. Take care to conceal your movements behind the aspirant companies, so that the enemy does not suspect you are there. I'll draw the attention of the prince and his chariots. Wait and watch for the opportune moment to strike.'

Pakh-amn stared into the king's eyes, and seemed to understand what Akhmen-hotep was giving him. He nodded slowly.

'I will not fail you, great one,' he said.

'Then return to your chariots,' the king ordered, 'and may the gods grant us victory.' As the generals and the king's retinue raced to their posts, Akhmen-hotep turned to the hierophants. 'Will the gods lend their favour today, holy ones?' he asked quietly. 'I drank deep of the bull's blood this morning, and yet I felt nothing. Geheb's strength does not burn in my veins.'

Memnet refused to meet his brother's eyes.

'I warned you,' he said softly. 'I told you at the oasis that there would be consequences for presuming upon the power of the gods.' Hashepra gave the Grand Hierophant a sour look, and then bowed his head to the king.

'Fear not, great one,' he said. 'Geheb has not forgotten his favoured sons. You will feel his presence among you as you race forth to battle.'

Khalifra touched the king's muscular arm and smiled warmly.

'Neru is always with us, great one,' she said. 'Her light ever burns in the darkness. Do not fear.'

The Priest King of Ka-Sabar bowed to the holy ones, and his heart felt light. Smiling, he turned and strode quickly for his chariot, trailed by his leonine Ushabti. With every step, his doubts and fears were swept away by the measured tramp of feet and the clatter of arms and armour. The clamour of the battlefield beat against his bones like a drum. For a moment, he was able to forget the horrors he had witnessed, and the great suffering that the Blessed Land had witnessed in the course of his life. For a moment, he was back in the times of his father, and his father's father, waging war for wealth and power, and the glory of his gods.

Akhmen-hotep climbed aboard his heavy chariot and grasped the hilt of his gleaming sword. He signalled his trumpeter with a flourish.

'Order the army to advance!' he called.

Trumpets called across the battlefield, and as one the companies of the Bronze Host began to move. As the king's chariot lurched forwards with a rumble of bronze-rimmed wheels, Akhmen-hotep stood tall and surveyed the disposition of his and the enemy's forces. The City Companies of Bel Aliad were mustered behind a rough line of four large mercenary bands. Between the two large infantry units Akhmen-hotep could see a profusion of banners, no doubt adorning the chariots of the merchant princes and their leader: Suhedir al-Khazem, the Keeper of the Hidden Paths.

To the far right of the enemy line, Akhmen-hotep could see a swirling smudge of dust. The Bhagarites were withdrawing towards the desert, hopefully drawing the enemy light horsemen on that flank along with them. Mirroring the Bel Aliad formations on the other side of the plain, the two heavy companies of the Bronze Host marched at the centre of the battle-line, and in between them advanced half of Ka-Sabar's feared chariots. Pakh-amn and the other half of the chariot force were already on the move, shifting off to the left behind two marching companies of aspirants. Still further back came the host's company of archers, still hidden from the enemy's view.

The warriors of the Bronze Host continued forwards, advancing slowly but steadily. The king peered off to the left, trying to catch a glimpse of the enemy light cavalry on that side, but he couldn't see them. Shouted warnings from the ranks of the infantry companies brought the king's attention back to the front, and he saw a cloud of dark, flickering reeds arcing high into the sunlit sky ahead of them. Men cursed and raised their round-topped wooden shields, and the warriors in the chariots crouched low behind the bronze-clad walls of their machines. The arrows fell, whirring malevolently through the air, and Akhmen-hotep felt his skin prickle with heat as the blessings of Geheb came upon him.

Bronze arrowheads cracked against shield faces or smacked into scale and leather armour. Men grunted and stumbled beneath the fearsome rain, but the warriors plucked the arrows from their vests and tossed them contemptuously aside. Shafts struck their tanned skin and glanced aside, turned by the power of the God of the Earth. Cheers went up from the Bronze Host as they discovered that Geheb was with them. Akhmen-hotep bared his teeth and signalled to his trumpeters again.

'Order the aspirants forward!' he cried. 'Archers, make ready!'

Two signals rang out along the length of the host, and were answered by lusty shouts from the young men of the aspirant companies. Javelins ready, the lightly armoured warriors quickened their pace, jogging swiftly across the plain towards the mercenary archers and footmen. The Zandri bowmen, shaken by the failure of their first volley, made ready to fire again, while the barbarian troops howled like beasts and shook their weapons eagerly as they watched the light infantry approach.

The enemy bowmen fired off one more volley, and then swiftly retreated down prepared lanes between the barbarian mobs as the aspirants drew near. At sixty paces, the javelin throwers quickened their pace. At fifty, they drew back their arms and hurled a shower of barbed weapons at the waiting barbarians. The javelins fell among the mercenaries, sticking into shields or punching through furs and thick tunics. Men roared and fell to the ground, clutching at the wooden shafts.

At forty paces, the aspirants drew more javelins from their quivers and let fly, and then again at thirty. At twenty paces they cast again. Then, they turned tail and ran back in the direction of their lines. Jeers and obscenities followed, until, seventy paces away, the aspirants turned, drew more javelins, and advanced once more. Flights of javelins fouled the mercenaries' shields, inflicted terrible wounds and killed a few score men, and again, just as the aspirants were nearly within reach of the barbarians' weapons, they turned and ran.

On the fourth such attack Akhmen-hotep heard trumpets and the sounds of battle off to his left. The enemy light horsemen had intervened on that flank, attempting to run down the light infantry companies. In the centre and on the right, however, the barbarians had taken all they could stand. Prodded to the point of distraction, the mercenaries abandoned all sense of discipline and charged forwards, eager to strike back at the javelin throwers.

Their job done, the aspirants turned tail and kept on running, drawing the barbarians across the plain towards the heavy infantry of the Bronze Host and the bowmen behind them.

Akhmen-hotep raised his sword.

'Archers, make ready!' he ordered. The king watched as the line of mercenaries rushed towards his companies in a seething wave of flesh and bronze. At fifty yards he brought down his blade. 'Fire!'

A rain of deadly arrows leapt from the rear of the Bronze Host and fell among the charging mercenaries, sowing death through the swarming mobs. Men fell by the hundreds, and for a moment the pursuit faltered in the face of mounting casualties. The mercenaries were more than two hundred yards away from the rest of their army, however, beyond the reach of their bowmen and the support of the City Companies. Trumpets blew urgently from the midst of the enemy chariots, vainly trying to call the warriors back and re-form their disorganised companies, but Akhmen-hotep was not about to give them the chance.

The Priest King of Ka-Sabar threw back his head and gave a fierce shout.

'Warriors of the Bronze Host! Strike now, and redeem your honour! For the glory of the Earth God, charge!'

The earth shook with the roar of two thousand voices and the thunder of hooves as the army of Ka-Sabar sprung its trap.

◄ FOURTEEN ►

The Bloodstained Sands

The Western Trade Road, near the Fountains of Eternal Life, in the 63rd year of Ptra the Glorious (-1744 Imperial Reckoning)

'SOMEONE IS SIGNALLING,' Ekhreb said, straightening gracefully from the low, leather-covered divan and gesturing with his wine cup at the sky.

Rakh-amn-hotep glanced up from his maps with a weary grunt, squinting into the dust-stained air. The Kings of Rasetra and Lybaras had made their midday camp in the shelter of a pair of dunes just off the side of the western trade road, drawing the huge, creaking wagons of the Lybaran court into a defensible circle beneath the shade of a small grove of palm trees. Within the circled wagons the Lybaran servants had spread thick rugs over the sandy ground and set out tables and divans for the comfort of the kings and their generals. When the King of Rasetra had first laid eyes on the massive wagons he'd sneered quietly to Ekhreb about the soft ways of Hekhmenukep and the Lybaran nobles, but after more than a week on the march to Khemri, the bellicose Rasetran had to admit that there were far worse ways to conduct a campaign.

For all their zeal to reach the Living City and cleanse the Blessed Land of Nagash and his minions, the movement of the allied armies had been dreadfully slow. It had taken almost two weeks for the Rasetran army to make its way along the Valley of Kings, even with the help of the Lybaran sky-boats, and once the two armies were united at Quatar, the march slowed nearly to a crawl. The heavy catapults and other war machines crafted by the Lybarans frequently broke down, requiring hours to replace warped axles or broken wheels, and the jungle auxiliaries of the Rasetran army could only face the searing heat of the desert for short periods of time before they had to rest and take on more water.

The allied armies stretched back along the trade road for many miles. Like an inchworm, the tail end of the host would leave its camp in the morning, and by evening it would be settling into the camp of the army's lead elements from the night before.

At such a slow pace, the kings and their retinues rose from their furs at dawn, lingered over their morning meals and devotions and got a start on the business of the day while the troops marched slowly past. When the last elements of the army came into view by late afternoon, the court would spend an hour or two consulting with the commanders of the rearguard and baggage train. Then, as the sun set behind the veil of dust to the west, the camp would travel for a few hours and catch up with the army's lead companies.

According to Rakh-amn-hotep's original estimations, the allied armies should have been on the outskirts of Khemri by now. As it was, they were still roughly two days' march from the Fountains of Eternal Life, little more than halfway to their goal. The two forces, and the Rasetran auxiliaries in particular, were consuming supplies at a staggering rate, especially fresh water. The huge thunder lizards had to be literally doused with it at regular intervals to keep their thick skins from drying out, to the point that their handlers had been on half-rations for days so that they could keep their charges alive.

'What now, by all the gods?' Rakh-amn-hotep grumbled, peering up at the silhouetted bulk of the Lybaran skybox. The contraption was very small by comparison to the great sky-boats: a box, slightly smaller than a chariot, suspended by cables from a spherical bladder filled with air spirits. The whole thing could be loaded into the back of one of the huge Lybaran wagons, and was drawn out each time the kings made camp. The box was kept tethered to a pair of wagons by a length of stout rope, and raised to a height of more than a hundred feet.

The Lybarans kept a trio of boys up in the box at all times, scanning the countryside for miles with their clever seeing-tubes and watching for messages from the army's vanguard. As Rakh-amn-hotep watched, one of the boys raised a platter-sized dish of polished bronze and caught the rays of Ptra's glorious light, aiming a series of brilliant flashes off to the west. After a moment, the boy lowered the signalling device and the lookouts watched intently for an answer. Ekhreb took a sip of wine and wiped the sweat from his eyes.

'Perhaps it's just the cavalry reporting that they've reached the springs,' he said. The king snorted in bitter amusement.

'Your optimism never ceases to amaze me,' he said. Ekhreb shrugged philosophically.

'I survived six years at Quatar. Nothing much worries me any more.'

'That's right. Rub some more salt in the wound,' the king growled. He levered himself to his feet and shrugged his heavy scale coat back into place. 'You keep going on like that, and I'll petition the Grand Hierophant to make you priest king instead of me. Then I could go live the carefree life of a king's champion.'

'Gods forfend!' Ekhreb said in mock horror. 'You're far too ugly to be a proper champion.'

'Don't I know it,' the king said with a chuckle. His grin faded as one of the boys climbed fearlessly over the edge of the skybox and slid nimbly down one of its long ropes. The young messenger disappeared from sight behind one of the hulking wagons, and Rakh-amn-hotep made his way across the expanse of rugs to await the boy's arrival next to the Lybaran king.

As he did nearly every day of the march, Hekhmenukep sat before a low, broad table covered in sheets of papyrus inscribed with all manner of arcane diagrams and invocations. Half a dozen of his retainers crowded around the edges of the table, deep in discussions about strange subjects of engineering or alchemy, while the king studied the diagrams through one of his bronze-rimmed disks and made annotations with a fine-haired ink brush. A slave knelt at Hekhmenukep's left, holding a wine goblet for the king's refreshment, while another stirred the air above the royal scholar's head with a fan made of peacock feathers. He seemed entirely at ease, immersed in a world of ratios and calculations. Rakh-amn-hotep felt a bitter surge of envy at the Lybaran's detachment.

Hekhmenukep glanced up from his work just as the messenger wound his way nimbly past the parked wagons and raced past the watchful Ushabti into the king's court. The Lybaran king glanced bemusedly from Rakh-amn-hotep to the wide-eyed boy.

'Yes? What is it?' he asked.

'There is a sun-sign from Shesh-amun,' the boy said, referring to the Lybaran champion in charge of the allied vanguard. 'He says: enemy horsemen east of the sacred springs.'

'Damnation,' Rakh-amn-hotep growled, his scarred hands clenching into fists. 'Is the enemy present in strength?' The messenger took a step back at the king's fierce tone.

'A thousand pardons, great one. He did not say.'

'Shesh-amun wouldn't have reported otherwise,' Hekhmenukep said calmly. The news did not please the Rasetran king. He turned to Hekhmenukep.

'I thought you said that the Bronze Host was drawing Nagash's army to Bel Aliad,' he said

'Indeed,' the Lybaran king replied, and then gave a thoughtful shrug. 'Perhaps Nagash chose to split his forces instead. If so, that could still work in our favour.'

'If we were in possession of the sacred springs, I would agree with you,' Rakh-amn-hotep growled. 'As it is, our stocks of water are very low. If we don't get to the springs very soon, the heat will kill our troops quicker than Nagash could.'

Hekhmenukep frowned. 'How long?' he asked.

The Rasetran king bit back a surge of irritation. How could he not know the needs of his own army?

'A day or two. Certainly no more,' Rakh-amn-hotep declared, 'and it's nearly mid-afternoon now.' The king began to pace across the rugs, considering his options. If they were very, very lucky, the enemy cavalry was nothing more than a scouting force, or the vanguard of the Khemri army. Reaching a decision, he glanced back at the Lybaran king. 'I'm going forward to take command of the vanguard and see what we're facing,' he declared, and then turned to Ekhreb. 'Gather up a mixed force of light infantry and bowmen, plus all the horsemen you can lay your hands on, and join me as quickly as you are able,' he ordered. Ekhreb nodded, rising swiftly to his feet.

'What is your plan?' the champion asked.

The question seemed to amuse the Rasetran king. 'My plan?' he said. 'I'm going to head down the road with all the warriors I can muster and kill every living thing between me and the springs.' He slapped Ekhreb on the shoulder. 'Don't tarry, old friend,' he said, and hurried from the camp, shouting for his charioteers in a gruff voice.

* * *

WARNING SHOUTS ROSE above the clamour as trumpets wailed across the battlefield and Bel Aliad's barbarian troops let out a ragged, hungry shout. Akhmen-hotep hefted his notched and bloodstained khopesh and bellowed hoarsely, 'Here they come again! Make ready!'

Horns blared, signalling the Bronze Host and the distant priests, and with a clatter of metal and wood the infantry companies made ready once more. The battle had raged for hours, ebbing and flowing across the corpse-strewn plain. Akhmen-hotep's plan to put the barbarian mercenaries to flight with a single, swift charge had failed, and despite heavy losses the barbarians had refused to break. They fought with a reckless courage that bordered upon desperation.

More than once over the course of the bloody battle, the king wondered what fearful things the merchant princes had told them about their overlord in Khemri. Had it not been for a timely charge by Pakh-amn's chariots on the left flank, the army would have been surrounded during the first attack. The Master of Horse had proven his worth time and again over the course of the day, driving off cavalry attacks and saving the light infantry on his flank from utter destruction.

Except for the discipline and skill of the veteran companies of the Bronze Host, the battle would have already been lost. Time and again they withstood showers of deadly arrows and the crushing weight of the barbarian infantry attacks. The enemy mercenaries had been reduced to four ragged companies, and the fire from the Zandri archers had dwindled, suggesting that they were running low on arrows.

A unit of light horsemen still lurked at the edge of the enemy's right flank. They had already caught Akhmen-hotep's light infantry in two surprise charges and mauled them severely, and were watching for another chance to strike. The king regretted having sent the Bhagarite horsemen to the rear and had despatched a messenger to recall them, but that had been nearly two hours ago, and they had yet to reappear.

As the weary veterans closed ranks and readied their spears, Akhmen-hotep caught sight of a ripple of movement across the battlefield. Bel Aliad's chariots and its two City Companies, which had been held in reserve since the battle began, were marching forward in the centre of the enemy battle-line. It was late in the afternoon, and his troops were exhausted, as were the enemy mercenaries. The merchant princes had come to the conclusion that the next attack would decide the battle. Looking over his battered troops, the king thought that they were probably right.

'Messenger!' Akhmen-hotep cried, and a boy dashed up to the side of the king's chariot. 'Tell the archers to concentrate their fire on the City Companies,' he ordered. The runner repeated the order word-for-word and dashed off to the waiting bowmen. For a moment, the king debated on sending another messenger back to the priests, to beg for one more appeal to the gods, but he changed his mind with a shrug. The gods were not blind. They could see how desperate the situation was. If they withheld their power the war was already lost. The king swept his blade down in a wide arc.

'Forward!' he called to his men, and the formation of chariots began to move. They were a few dozen yards behind the main battle-line, positioned between the two veteran companies. The gap was currently being covered by a small company of light infantry the king had shifted over from the left flank. The weary aspirants felt the chariots approaching and gratefully withdrew. Their capes were torn and bloodstained, and many of them carried bent or splintered javelins recovered from the bodies of the slain. A few raised their weapons in salute to the king as they filed past the advancing chariots and went into reserve.

The clamour of the enemy troops grew louder as the barbarians picked up the pace. Their savage nature drew them to battle like moths to a flame, and they began to outstrip the measured pace of the City Companies. Then the first volley of arrows from the Ka-Sabar archers hissed overhead, plunging in a deadly rain among the enemy infantry. Men staggered, pierced through their thin leather vests or bronze skullcaps. The screams of the wounded galvanised the mercenaries, who had suffered one terrible volley after another for most of the day. Their hoarse war cries turned to frenzied screams as they broke into a wild charge, hoping to come to grips with their enemies before the archers could fire again.

Men shouted orders among the veteran companies, and the Bronze Host steeled itself to receive the charge. Akhmen-hotep felt a glimmer of hope as the mercenaries broke ranks with the city troops. He watched the advancing chariots carefully, waiting to see how the merchant princes would react. The line of war machines hesitated for a moment, and then a ragged chorus of war-horns sounded and the chariots surged forwards, trying to lend their weight to the mercenaries' attack.

Akhmen-hotep smiled fiercely. It appeared that the gods were smiling on them after all. The king studied the pace of the charging enemy troops, waiting for the moment when the mercenaries had committed to their attacks.

The enemy infantry swept in from left and right, converging on the solid ranks of bronze-armoured spearmen. They ignored the aspirants, having learned from bitter experience that the javelin men would only fall back in the face of their charge and leave them exposed to further arrow fire. For their part, the aspirants waited patiently, hefting their barbed weapons. Once the melee began, they would rush in and hurl their shafts point-blank into the mercenaries' flanks.

The two forces came together in a thunderous crash of wood and metal. Both veteran companies staggered under the impact, but the strength of Geheb filled them, and they bore up beneath the assault. Barbarians fell beneath the Host's stabbing spears or were dashed to the ground by bronze-rimmed shields, but they pressed forwards in a bestial frenzy, hacking with notched axes and blunted blades. Though their limbs were hard as teak and their bodies clad in fine bronze scales, here and there a foe-man's weapon would find its mark, and a warrior of Ka-Sabar would topple to the ground.

In that moment of contact, while the barbarians were focused on the enemies before them and the City Companies were struggling beneath a hail of arrows, the chariots of the merchant princes were in the middle ground between the two forces, alone and unsupported. Akhmen-hotep grinned fiercely and raised his sword.

'Charge!' he ordered.

Trumpets wailed, and with a fierce shout the heavy chariots of the Bronze Host thundered forwards, passing between the struggling infantry companies and crashing into the mingled flanks of two barbarian companies. Heavy, bronze-rimmed wheels and scythe-like blades tore through the milling troops, crushing limbs and splitting torsos. Bowstrings hummed as archers fired into the howling mass of warriors. At such close range the powerful arrows punched clean through their targets and often struck the man next in line. Noblemen and Ushabti lashed out at the mercenaries with their curved swords, striking down at their exposed heads and shoulders and inflicting terrible wounds.

The barbarians gave way before the fearsome charge within moments, retreating away to either flank of the terrible chariots, and Akhmen-hotep drove them onwards, through the enemy battle-line and directly at the advancing merchant princes. The nobles of Bel Aliad saw the huge bronze war machines bearing down on them and their formation came to a panicked halt, like a caravan in the face of a sudden, vicious sandstorm. Though greater in number than the chariots of Ka-Sabar, they were far lighter and no real match for the veteran warriors of the Bronze

Host. Several noblemen around the edges of the formation tried to turn their machines around and scurry out of the way of the oncoming wall of flesh and metal, while others surged forwards in a bold display of resolve. The result was disorder and chaos, robbing the formation of much of its strength at a critical moment.

Arrows snapped back and forth through the air as bowmen of both formations traded shots. One arrow struck the lip of Akhmen-hotep's chariot and ricocheted, striking him in the hip. The king swatted the arrow away as though it were a stinging fly. Horses and men screamed as other arrows found their marks, but the sounds were lost in a swirling, crashing roar as the formations came together.

Akhmen-hotep heard his charioteer let out a warning yell, and the chariot swerved to the right. An enemy chariot swept past, almost too fast to follow. The scythe-like blade fixed to the hub of the heavier Ka-Sabar chariot struck the enemy machine in the flank and ripped the wicker hull apart in a shower of splintered reeds. The bowman in the chariot let fly a wild shot that snapped past the king's head, and then they were lost in the dust of the swirling melee.

The battlefield shook with the clash of arms and the screams of the dying. To Akhmen-hotep's left, the Ushabti in his chariot lashed out with his ritual sword at a passing enemy machine, his fearsome strength slashing open the enemy chariot's hull and chopping apart its driver. Off to the right, lost in the haze, there was a splintering of wood and a broken chariot wheel soared through the air behind the king's speeding chariot.

Akhmen-hotep leaned against the front of his chariot and tried to make sense of the confusion around him. He searched for the blurry shapes of banners, trying to find Bel Aliad's leader. One quick challenge could end the battle, if the merchant princes still possessed a shred of honour.

A rumble of wheels thundered in from the right, and a Bel-Aliad chariot charged out of the dust. The charioteer angled his machine expertly, passing the king's vehicle on the right quarter. The archer in the back of the chariot drew his bow and fired, just as Akhmen-hotep lashed out with his sword. The arrow struck the king at the rounded part of his shoulder, punching through the bronze scales and sinking deep into the flesh beneath, but not before the king's sword had sliced through the charioteer's right arm. The man let out an anguished scream and fell onto his side, causing the horses to veer suddenly to the left and flip the chariot over.

The king pulled the arrow free with a snarl and cast it aside, feeling hot blood spread across the inside of his armour. As near as he could reckon, they had penetrated nearly all the way through the enemy formation. He heard a distant, surf-like surge of noise, to his left, but it was too far away to matter to the king at that moment. He glanced wildly in every direction, looking for a sign of the enemy leader.

There! Off to the right and a few dozen yards ahead, he spied a knot of stationary chariots flying a profusion of brightly coloured banners. It had to be the enemy prince and his bodyguards. Akhmen-hotep brought them to the attention of his charioteer by gesturing with his sword, and the man swung the war machine around. They bore down on the enemy like a hurled spear, aimed directly for the chariot in the centre of the group.

The prince and his retinue saw the danger at once, but there was little time to get their horses moving. Two of the bodyguards tried to push forwards and bar Akhmen-hotep's path, but their horses could not get moving quickly enough. Instead, the king's chariot struck the prince's machine like a thunderbolt, smashing the wicker hull to pieces and flipping it onto its side.

Akhmen-hotep leapt from the still-moving chariot and rushed towards a tall, lean warrior clad in burnished bronze armour and desert robes of brilliant yellow and blue. His men, an archer whose arm had been clearly broken in the crash and his unarmed charioteer, both threw their bodies into the king's path, but Akhmen-hotep hurled them aside like children. Still, it bought the prince enough time to draw his blade and prepare for the king's attack.

The prince of Bel Aliad was a brave man, but no warrior. His scimitar slashed at Akhmen-hotep's face in a clumsy, backhand blow that the king smashed contemptuously aside. His return stroke blurred through the air and came to rest against the prince's throat.

'Yield to me, Suhedir al-Khazem,' Akhmen-hotep growled, 'or prepare to greet your ancestors in the afterlife.'

The prince swayed on his feet. His sword fell from his trembling hand.

'I yield. By all the gods, I yield!' he said, sagging to his knees, as though overcome by a terrible burden, and reaching up to pull away his yellow head scarf. The prince's face was youthful but haggard, gaunt and pinched with strain. 'Spare my people, great one, and all the riches of Bel Aliad will be yours!' Relief washed over the King of Ka-Sabar, but he kept his expression stern and inscrutable.

'We are not monsters,' he said to the prince. 'You have dealt with us honourably, and we will treat you in kind. Signal your men to cease fighting, and we will discuss terms of ransom.'

The prince called to his trumpeter, and gladly gave the order. From the look on the man's face, Akhmen-hotep thought that he was happy to have lost the battle. He no longer had to heed the orders of the monster that crouched on the throne at Khemri.

Horns sounded again and again, cutting through the din of battle. It was several long minutes before the clamour subsided and the dust began to settle. A cheer went up from the Bronze Host, and then was suddenly cut short by confused shouts and angry cries. Bemused, Akhmen-hotep looked to the prince, but Suhedir al-Khazem looked mystified as well.

The rumble of a chariot approached hurriedly from the north-west. Within moments Akhmen-hotep spied Pakh-amn's battered chariot racing towards them across the battlefield. As he drew nearer, the king could see the stricken expression on the young noble's face.

'What is it?' Akhmen-hotep cried as the chariot rumbled to a halt. 'What has happened?' Pakh-amn looked in dread at Suhedir-al-Khazem, and then addressed his king.

'The messenger has returned from camp,' the nobleman replied. Akhmen-hotep frowned.

'Well? What of it?' he asked.

'He could not find the Bhagarite horsemen,' Pakh-amn said in a grim voice. 'The camp guards said they never arrived.'

The king was confused for a moment.

'But where else would they go?' he began, and then his blood ran cold. Slowly, he turned, casting his eyes to the north, in the direction of Bel Aliad. Suhedir al-Khazem, listening to the exchange, let out a despairing cry.

The first tendrils of smoke were rising above the distant City of Spices.

◄ FIFTEEN ►

Lessons in Death

Khemri, the Living City, in the 45th year of Ptra the Glorious
(-1959 Imperial Reckoning)

THE GREAT ARCHITECTS of Khemri had spared no expense to provide for the late King Khetep's every spiritual need in the afterlife. They built vaults within the Great Pyramid to hold tall jars of grain and dried fish, candied dates, wine and honey. There were rooms filled with luxurious furnishings, and chests of cedar wood packed with rich garments for the king to wear. Another chamber held a brace of mummified falcons and the king's favourite bow, in case he wished to go hunting in the fields of paradise. Still other chambers contained the king's mummified horses, and a great chariot made of bronze and gilded wood.

There was even a long, low chamber containing a fine river boat, complete with mummified oarsmen, in the event that the mighty king desired to ply the great River of Death.

The finest chamber of all was built far above the king's burial vaults, set in the very heart of the Great Pyramid. There, the architects had built a glorious throne room, complete with soaring columns and flagstones of polished marble. A noble dais stood at the far end of the throne room, and upon it stood a single throne, wrought not of wood but of darkest, polished obsidian. Flanking the throne stood towering statues of Ptra and Djaf, their faces stern, but their hands raised in welcome.

More statues were interspersed among the columns that ran to either side of the chamber: Neru and Asaph, Geheb and Tahoth, all of the gods of Nehekhara, each one awaiting the arrival of the dead king's spirit. For the throne at the far end of the room was not meant for Khetep, but for Usirian, the baleful god of the Underworld.

It was in this great hall that Khetep would come to be judged by the gods. If he had lived a virtuous life, he would be allowed into the golden fields of paradise. Otherwise, Usirian would drive the king's spirit into the howling wastes of the Underworld, there to suffer for all time, or at least until such time as the mortuary priests could summon back his soul and return him to the land of the living.

It was here that Nagash would summon his noble allies, more than forty in number, and, presiding from Usirian's black throne, he would work to undermine his brother's tenuous rule. If Arkhan, Raamket or the other young nobles were discomfited by the necromancer's profound display of sacrilege, none of them were foolish enough to share it. There was also the fact that he had kept his word and made them all very rich, very powerful men.

It had been three years since they had signed their names in that run-down house off Coppersmith Street, and in that time a terrible plague had swept through the great houses of Khemri. The sickness literally dissolved its victims from the inside out over a period of days or sometimes weeks. Vast fortunes were paid to the temples of

Asaph and Tahoth to cure the sick, but the best that the priests could manage was to prolong the agony of the afflicted. No one survived the plague's touch, and the healers could not fathom how the sickness spread. Slaves, guards and functionaries were untouched, and only those born of noble blood seemed to be at risk. All, that is, except for those whose names were written on Nagash's list.

As the death toll mounted and the great houses became decimated, many vital positions in Thutep's court, some of which had been kept in the same family for centuries, were left vacant. Finally, the desperate king had little choice but to hand these titles to the only noblemen who still answered the call to the Grand Assembly. Khemri's fortunes were fading all too quickly. Other than a brief show of esteem from the other great cities upon the birth of his young son Sukhet five years before, the Living City had been all but forgotten by its peers.

'How fares the caravan trade?' Nagash asked, studying the assembled nobles over steepled fingers. The braziers in the great throne room had been lit, casting long fingers of light past the towering columns and throwing the ominous shadows of the stone gods across the marble flagstones. Khefru moved silently among the necromancer's allies, providing refreshment to those who wished it.

Shepsu-hur plucked a goblet of wine from the priest's wooden tray as he went past. Thutep had named him master of the gates, which gave him responsibility over levying taxes on the merchant caravans that came and went from Khemri. This included the river traffic from Zandri and the grain shipments that came south from Numas.

'Prices have nearly doubled in the bazaar,' he said, sampling the wine. 'Grain, spices, bronze: traders from every city are making life hard in the marketplace.'

The necromancer nodded.

'Zandri's work,' he declared. 'King Nekumet is tightening his fist around us. He's convinced the other kings to raise tariffs on exports to Khemri in order to choke off our trade.' Nagash turned his gaze to Raamket. 'No doubt it has increased smuggling tenfold.'

Raamket folded his thick arms. The burly nobleman had been appointed master of rods, making him responsible for the City Watch. With Nagash's help, Raamket had quickly used his authority to establish control of Khemri's criminal gangs as well.

'The gangs on the docks and the south gate district are doing a brisk trade,' he said with a chuckle. 'They plan on passing the goods on to the traders in the marketplace at half again the normal rate, a bargain these days, but the gangs will grow rich off it.' Nagash shook his head.

'No,' he said. 'Inform the gangs to sell their goods at the same price as the foreign traders. It serves our purpose for the city to suffer for a while.' Raamket frowned at the news.

'They won't want to hear that,' he said.

'If they won't listen, then relieve them of their ears,' the necromancer said. 'When the time comes for Thutep to yield his crown, it would be... preferable... if the populace supported his removal.' He turned to Arkhan. 'What is the mood of the people at present?'

Arkhan waited until Khefru approached, and then took a goblet. He drained half of the wine in a single draught and glowered at the rest. As master of the levy, it was his responsibility to maintain the yearly census and ensure that every adult citizen fulfilled his annual civil service. In times of war, he would also be required to marshal the spear levies that would form the bulk of Khemri's army.

'The rumours are circulating, as you requested,' he said. 'The great houses are being punished by the gods for permitting Thutep to bargain away Khemri's pre-eminence. It didn't take much effort to get people to start repeating it.'

Shepsu-hur sipped his wine thoughtfully. 'If we make the people think that the plague is the work of the gods,' he said, 'won't that drive them into the arms of the priesthood? I thought that was something we didn't want.' Nagash smiled coldly.

'They can give the priests all the coin and devotion they wish,' he said, 'so long as the holy men are helpless to stop the plague.' The necromancer leaned forwards upon the ebon throne.

'Thutep's time on Settra's throne has nearly run its course. The people are restive. A few more weeks of hunger and destitution and they will be ready for my brother to fall. For now, we must recoup our strength and prepare for one last outbreak of the so-called plague. This time, the sickness will spread beyond the great houses and afflict the city merchants. That should be sufficient to ignite the fires of unrest.' Nagash waved a dismissive hand. 'Tomorrow is the new moon. Return here at midnight with your offerings and we will perform the Incantation of Reaping.'

With that, the audience was at an end. The noblemen drained their goblets and set them on the marble floor. Then, they retired from the echoing chamber without a word. Moments later, only Khefru remained, dutifully picking up goblets and setting them on a wooden tray balanced upon his hip. Nagash studied his servant thoughtfully.

'There is something you are not telling me,' he said. Khefru shook his head.

'I don't know what you mean, master.'

'I can see it in the stiffness of your posture and the way you carefully avoid my gaze,' the necromancer said coldly. 'Don't insult me with your pitiful attempts at subterfuge, Khefru. It would not be wise.'

A faint shudder caused the young priest's shoulders to tremble. He paused for a moment, collecting himself, and then set down the wooden tray and straightened. 'I fear you are growing too bold, master,' he said. 'Thutep isn't as blind or as foolish as you think. The disappearances are gaining more and more attention. Your supposed allies are dragging dozens of victims off the streets each month for your rituals–'

'Arkhan and the rest must learn the rudiments of the necromantic arts if they are to be useful to me,' Nagash growled, cutting him off, 'and the curse requires a great deal of power to maintain it through the turning of the moon.' The necromancer shifted irritably upon the throne. 'The energy dissipates too quickly. It's like filling a wine jar using one's bare hands.'

'But the risk...' Khefru began, spreading his hands helplessly. 'Your allies are growing too bold. They're seizing the first victims they come upon, and many of them have families who take note of their disappearance. I know for a fact that people have gone to the temples begging for a formal inquiry. It's only a matter of time before a wealthy merchant or a neighbourhood full of grieving families pays the priesthood enough to start a serious investigation. After that it's only a matter of time before the king becomes involved.'

'And what of it?' Nagash snarled. 'We've spent the last three years stripping away the king's power. The great houses are all but extinct, and my men control all the vital functions of the city. If anything, I expect we could find a way to turn the inquiry to our own ends, embarrassing the priesthood as a pack of corrupt, meddling fools.' As he said this, Nagash saw Khefru blanch. The necromancer leaned forward intently. 'Ah. Now I see the heart of it. After everything we have learned, everything we've done... you're still afraid of the priesthood.'

'No... no, it's not them,' Khefru stammered. His sallow face grew pinched with fear. 'I fear no man in this world save you, master, but what of the gods? We've cheated Djaf and Usirian of dozens of human souls. By now, their wrath must be very great.'

'And yet they have done nothing,' Nagash said scornfully. 'Do you know why? Because we stand to usurp them of their power. We are plumbing the secrets of life and death, Khefru. Without the fear of dying, and the threat of judgement, the gods will lose their hold over mankind.'

'Yes. Yes, I see all that,' the young priest said, his knife-scar accentuating the pained look on his face, 'but we're not immortal yet. Death still waits for us, and beyond that, divine judgement. We... we've done awful things, master. There is no hell in Usirian's teachings terrible enough to suit our crimes.'

'Leave such things to me, Khefru,' Nagash said coldly. 'All things in due time. For now, we must focus on taking Thutep's crown. Do you understand?'

Khefru nodded reluctantly. 'I understand, master.' He bowed quickly, and returned to his work. The young priest gathered up the wine cups and made for the side passage that led down to the lower levels, where Khetep's crypt and Nagash's study were located. Just as he reached the columns along the north side of the room, he paused.

'One more thing, master,' he said. 'Your guests have made a great deal of progress exploring the crypt over the last few days. I believe Ashniel has almost found the way out. Should I introduce the next set of traps?' Nagash leaned back upon the throne, his face lost in thought.

'Leave that to me as well,' he said.

THE BRAZIERS HAD been left to burn out in the Great Pyramid's grand throne room. Nearly four hours past midnight they gave off a sullen red glow that lent the huge chamber an ominous blood-hued cast. The ruddy light scarcely reached above head-height along the towering stone columns, and pooled on the broad steps of the great dais.

Silence stretched through the chamber's chill air, broken only by the furtive sounds of burrowing tomb beetles.

Then there was a faint sound, like the whisper of skin across stone, and a thin hissing that nearly resolved into words.

Dark forms moved in the shadows beyond the columns on the north side of the room. The sibilant whispers rose again, like a conversation between a trio of vipers. Then a lithe shape glided from the darkness and stepped into the centre of the throne room. Pale hands reached up and pulled back a black cotton hood, revealing the sharp-edged features of Ashniel, the druchii witch. She turned slowly in place, as though trying to deduce where the chamber was in relation to the rest of the huge pyramid, and how close she might be to freedom.

Within moments, Ashniel was joined by her companions. Drutheira had her hood back, letting her white hair tumble across her narrow shoulders. Her ethereal beauty had been transformed into a tight mask of strain, and she clutched an improvised dagger chipped from a broken shard of obsidian. Malchior limped along in her wake, cursing softly under his breath. The shaft of a barbed dart jutted from the druchii's left thigh, and every step left a small pool of blood gleaming upon the marble. Clearly, Ashniel's mastery of the crypt's many traps still left something to be desired.

The three druchii came together and whispered once more, clearly arguing about which way they should go. Then a cold voice echoed from the darkness, transfixing them with its predatory intensity.

'You're very close,' Nagash said from the darkness surrounding the ebon throne.

Cloth whispered against stone as the necromancer rose to his feet and slowly descended the steps into the ruddy light. In his left hand he held the Staff of the Ages, and his dark eyes were intent upon the barbarians. Nagash smiled, a gesture devoid of warmth or humour.

'Shall I tell you which direction to go?' he asked, pointing to the doorway at the far end of the hall. 'When the spirit of the dead king was judged and accepted into paradise, he could leave the Great Pyramid and travel to the afterlife. So the architects built a long, sloping corridor there, to facilitate his passage.' Ashniel gave Nagash a look of purest hate.

'A pity that a spirit has no need for an actual door,' she hissed. 'The passageway is purely symbolic, and ends at a stone wall.' She drew herself to her full height and sneered at the necromancer. 'I've spent a great deal of time reading about your people's bizarre burial rites.' The witch turned and pointed into the shadows along the chamber's southern wall. 'There will be another doorway there, leading into the upper vaults. Beyond that will be the corridor to the outside.'

Nagash inclined his head mockingly. 'The passage awaits, witch. All that stands between you and your freedom… is me.' He spread his arms expansively. 'Defeat me with your sorceries, and you may go free.'

Malchior took a limping step towards the dais. 'What kind of trick is this?' he spat, but the movement was nothing more than a feint. Quicker than the eye could follow, the warlock threw up his hand and hissed a stream of liquid syllables that caused the air to crackle with magical power.

Nagash reacted without hesitation, bringing around the Staff of Ages and chanting an abjuration just as a bolt of blue-white light shot from Malchior's hand. The destructive spell leapt at Nagash. Then it seemed to unravel midway to its target as it encountered the necromancer's counter-spell and dissipated with a thunderous *crack*!

As the ragged tendrils of sorcerous energy washed over him, Nagash switched tactics, thrusting his open hand forwards and barking out a spell. There was a flash of heat, and darts of glimmering fire stitched the air between the necromancer and the druchii. The barbarians scattered, deflecting the magical bolts with counter-spells. The darts etched molten craters in the marble flagstones and blew fragments from the towering stone columns that flanked the throne room.

Ashniel circled to Nagash's left, spitting out a blasphemous incantation and hurling a bolt of hissing blackness from her open hands. Nagash turned it aside with another quick counter-spell. It struck the Staff of the Ages and deflected past the necromancer with a thunderous roar, striking the ebon throne of Usirian and melting it into a steaming puddle of liquid rock.

Malchior struck Nagash a moment later, hitting the necromancer in the side with a spear of crackling energy. Nagash, still focusing on his counter-spell, was able to dissipate most of its power, but the rest of the spell's energy raked across his ribs like a lion's claws, and set his robes ablaze.

The necromancer staggered. With a roar, he barked a stream of syllables. The fire licking at his robes guttered and went out, channelled into a whipcord of flames that he unleashed upon Ashniel. The witch severed the stream of energy with contemptuous ease.

Suddenly, a storm of whirling shadows surrounded Nagash. A pale figure emerged from the darkness, appearing to dance past the necromancer, and fiery pain tore through the necromancer's arm. Nagash whirled, but Drutheira was already out of reach, vanishing into the magical darkness with a hateful laugh. Blood poured down his arm from a gash left by the witch's dagger.

The air in the chamber quivered with the crash and roar of sorcerous power. Another bolt of power tore through Drutheira's cloak of shadow, and Nagash felt his entire left side explode in pain as the spell grazed his hip. It spun him around like a child's toy, nearly pitching him from the dais. He landed hard on his right side, sparing him from a stream of crackling darts flung by Ashniel.

Nagash bit back the pain that clawed at his nerves and tried to collect his wits. The druchii were far more experienced with sorcery than he was, but he'd thought that without raw magic – the winds of magic, as they called it – to draw on, he would be able to counter their spells with ease. Clearly, the barbarians hadn't shared everything they knew. Nagash, however, possessed secrets of his own.

Once more, the inky shadows closed in around him. The necromancer abandoned his counter-spells and clutched the staff with both hands, watching for a telltale flicker of pale skin.

Drutheira seemed to dance through the darkness towards him, approaching Nagash from the side. He let her draw close, and then lashed out at her with his staff. The witch saw the blow coming and tried to leap aside, but the necromancer caught her right ankle and caused her to stumble. She fell with a screech, rolling painfully down the stone steps of the dais.

As she fell, Nagash rose to one knee and barked out a counter-spell that scattered the shadows like smoke. His throat was tight and painful and his body was starting to tremble from strain. Immediately, he felt a sense of pressure against his skin and he brandished the Staff of the Ages in front of him as bolts of power struck him from the front and the side. Claws of fire tore at the side of Nagash's face, and he was deafened by twin concussions that hammered at his body. Agonising pain lanced into his chest, as though iron fingers tore deep into the flesh and muscle beneath his skin.

For a dizzying instant Nagash wavered on the edge of unconsciousness. He clawed his way back by sheer force of will and sought out the wounded figure of Malchior, still standing at the centre of the throne room. Clenching his right fist, the necromancer began to chant.

Nagash knew that the barbed spike in the warlock's leg was tainted with poison, a painful, debilitating venom that was even now coursing through the druchii's veins. Somehow the warlock was able to continue fighting despite the agony of the poison, but now the necromancer enhanced its virulence tenfold. The druchii stiffened in mid-chant, his muscles tightening like cables beneath his skin. Foam burst from the warlock's mouth, and he toppled over and began to writhe across the cratered stone, until a flurry of searing bolts from the necromancer's fingers tore the druchii's body open like knives. Boiling blood spattered across the floor, and the warlock's flayed body stilled.

Nagash wasn't finished with Malchior yet. He tasted blood as he spat the Incantation of Reaping and consumed the warlock's soul. Malchior's life essence flowed into him like a river of ice, banishing the pain of his wounds and filling his veins with power.

Drutheira lay at the foot of the dais, doubled over in pain. She had landed on her right arm, which was bent at an awkward angle. With a snarl, Nagash jabbed a finger at her and spat a vicious spell. The witch threw up her good arm and screamed a counter-spell, but the force of the necromancer's attack struck her like a desert storm. Drops of blood appeared on the witch's pale skin, spreading rapidly as her flesh was stripped away in twisting ribbons by a furious magical wind. In the blink of an eye the witch was shredded, her entrails spread in a gory fan behind her steaming bones. Once again, Nagash chanted the Incantation of Reaping and ate the barbarian's life essence.

A bolt of searing power smashed into the necromancer, but Nagash scarcely felt it. The energy dissipated like smoke, cancelled by the inrush of power from Drutheira's soul. He turned to Ashniel, who still stood near the chamber's southern wall, and unleashed a rippling string of magical bolts. The witch countered his attacks with fearsome speed, deflecting many of the bolts and dissipating the rest. Crackling detonations split the stones and sent puffs of dust into the air around the druchii, but Ashniel was unharmed.

With a screech, the witch struck back. Nagash felt the dais beneath him start to shift and give way. He focused his will on the stones, which were turning black and melding together like the maw of a gaping pit. The necromancer barked a counter-spell and poured his newly gathered energies into the incantation, fixing the stones once more into solidity.

Before Ashniel could launch another attack, Nagash unleashed another torrent of bolts at the witch. Once again, she deflected them with almost casual skill. More concussions reverberated across the chamber, sending razor-sharp flecks of stone whickering through the air.

Ashniel staggered beneath the onslaught, but she gave the necromancer a malicious smile.

'A clever trick, human,' she shouted, 'but those two were amateurs compared to me. Your attacks are potent but clumsy, and your energies are finite. I can counter your spells indefinitely, and when you have exhausted yourself, I will make a new pair of gloves from your hide.'

Nagash's face twisted in rage and he began to chant again. A wild, howling wind rushed from the necromancer, roaring down the dais towards the witch. Ashniel threw up her hands and the wind curled around her. The flagstones beneath her feet erupted in fragments, and the sharp echoes of splintering stone filled the air.

'You see?' she said with a laugh. 'Your spells can't touch me.'

Nagash drew a deep breath. The power of the druchii souls was fading, leaving his throat feeling raw and torn.

'What makes you think that spell was meant for you?' he croaked.

Ashniel's smile faltered. Her eyes narrowed warily, and with a hiss like an angry cat she whirled to see the cracked and splintered feet of Asaph, goddess of love.

Baffled, she spun back to Nagash, just as the head of the goddess landed on her. The stone head, the size of a chariot, smashed to pieces, crushing the druchii to a pulp.

Nagash uttered the Incantation of Reaping one last time, and drank deep of Ashniel's life essence. Pain faded, replaced by the cold bliss of triumph.

The necromancer surveyed the scene of carnage. Veils of dust hung in the air, tinged red by the banked light of the braziers.

'My thanks for the lesson,' Nagash said with a smile.

◄ SIXTEEN ►

The Creeping Darkness

*Bel Aliad, the City of Spices, in the 63rd year of Ptra
the Glorious (-1744 Imperial Reckoning)*

By THE TIME Akhmen-hotep and his warriors reached Bel
Aliad, the Bhagarite horsemen had killed every living
thing they could. Bodies lay in heaps along the narrow
streets, cut down as they tried to flee the swift-riding
desert raiders. When the panicked citizens fled into their
homes the merciless Bhagarites flung torches and looted
oil lamps through the windows and waited with their
bows at the ready. Old men, women and children lay huddled by the doors of their homes, pierced by arrows and
spears. The Bhagarites had waded into the slaughter until
their white robes and the withers of their horses were
drenched in innocent blood.

The stench of spilled blood hung heavy in the air, even
in the famous Spice Bazaar. The brightly coloured
awnings of the spice market had been slashed apart, and
a king's ransom worth of exotic herbs had spilled from

broken urns and been trampled into the dirt. Bel Aliad had been cast to ruin in the space of a single afternoon. The desert raiders had cut out its heart to answer for all that they had lost, and now, the horsemen sat their mounts and stared dumbly at the horror they had wrought, their sword-arms hanging limp and their dark eyes empty of thought or feeling.

Akhmen-hotep strode heavily into the Spice Bazaar, surrounded by his Ushabti and Pakh-amn's light horsemen. They'd left their chariots at the edge of the town, for there had been no way to guide the heavy war machines down the streets without riding over Bel Aliad's massacred people.

The king's bloodstained sword quivered in his hand as he saw the milling figures of the horsemen. Rage and despair flooded through Akhmen-hotep, and when he tried to speak all he could manage was a wordless roar of anguish that echoed in the corpse-strewn square. The desert horses shied at the terrible sound, tossing their heads and backing away from the advancing king, but the Bhagarites stilled the animals with leaden voices and slid from the saddles with funereal grace. They walked a few steps towards the king and carefully laid their swords on the ground beside their feet.

Some of the men reached up and tugged their headscarves loose, baring their necks, while others pulled open their gore-spattered robes and revealed their heaving chests. They had avenged their murdered kin, and now prepared to join them in the afterlife.

At that moment, Akhmen-hotep would have gladly obliged them. He stared into their dead eyes and felt sick with fury.

'What infamy is this?' he cried. 'These people did nothing to you! Do you imagine your loved ones are pleased with what you've done? You've murdered mothers and their babes! This is not the work of warriors, but of monsters. You're no better than the Usurper!'

The imprecation struck the Bhagarites like the lash of a whip. One of the horsemen screeched like a desert cat and snatched up his blade, but he took no more than two steps towards the king before one of Akhmen-hotep's Ushabti stepped forwards and cut him down. The king's bodyguards swept forwards in a single mass, their ritual swords flickering, but they were halted by a commanding shout, not from Akhmen-hotep, but from Pakh-amn, the Master of Horse.

'Stay your hands!' the young nobleman shouted. 'The lives of the horsemen are for the king to take, not your own!'

True to their oaths, the devoted paused, awaiting their master's order. Akhmen-hotep turned at the sound of Pakh-amn's approach, glaring up at the nobleman as he reined in his horse beside the king.

'Do you mean to plead for their lives, Pakh-amn?' he snapped. 'Their lives are forfeit for what they have done!'

'Do you think me blind, great one?' the nobleman shot back. 'I have seen the slaughter just the same as you, but their executions must wait if you and I hope to see Ka-Sabar once more.'

Akhmen-hotep bit back a savage reply. As terrible as it was to hear, Pakh-amn was right. Without the Bhagarites they would never find their way back across the trackless sands of the Great Desert, and the king's duty to his people came before all other considerations. Justice for the people of Bel Aliad would have to wait.

'Seize them,' he told the Ushabti in a hollow voice. 'Take away their horses and their swords, and return them to camp.'

The Ushabti lowered their blades reluctantly, but did as the king commanded. The desert horsemen offered no resistance as their hands were bound behind their backs with rope taken from their saddles, and strange hands took hold of the bridles of their sacred horses. As far as they were concerned, their lives were at an end.

'We should take them back by a circuitous route,' Pakh-amn suggested. 'Lest the city nobles catch sight of them. I'll round up some troops and see about putting out the fires.' Akhmen-hotep nodded heavily.

'What will I tell Suhedir al-Khazem?' he asked, unable to take his eyes from the torn and twisted bodies filling the square.

The Master of Horse drew a deep breath. 'We will say that some of our horsemen got carried away during the battle and that there was some looting. Nothing more. If we tell them the truth there will be a riot.' Even battered and disarmed, the city nobles and the surviving members of the City Companies made for a large body of men, and the terms of ransom that the king offered meant that they would be held in camp under minimal guard. The barbarian mercenaries would be chained into slave coffles and marched back with the army: such were the wages of war in the Blessed Land.

Akhmen-hotep considered this, and nodded. The prince and his men would have to be told the truth eventually, but not today. He did not have the heart for it.

'See to it,' he said wearily, and waved Pakh-amn away.

The king stood alone in the blood-soaked square as the Bhagarite horsemen were led away and Pakh-amn snapped orders to his horsemen. His broad shoulders sagged, and Akhmen-hotep sank to his knees among the bodies of the innocent.

'Forgive me,' he said, bending down to press his forehead to the hot stones. 'Forgive me.'

THE SETTING SUN was red as fresh blood as it sank behind the mists above the Springs of Eternal Life. The hazy white clouds roiled slowly in the hot air, winding in thick tendrils around the tops of the high dunes just a few miles distant from where Rakh-amn-hotep stood. He was coated in a paste of sweat, dust and grit from the swirling cavalry skirmishes of the late afternoon, and his left shoulder ached from the sting of a horseman's arrow that had penetrated a few inches past the heavy scales of his armoured vest. His throat and nostrils were caked with mud, and it felt as though his eyes would stick shut if he closed them for more than a few moments. To his tired mind the mists seemed to curl and stretch towards him like the welcoming arms of a lover. He longed to feel that cool, clean touch, but it remained just out of his reach, guarded by a long, thin line of Numasi horsemen and Khemri spears.

The enemy force stretched along the base of a line of low dunes running roughly southwards, with their left flank standing astride the Western Trade Road that led to the Living City. The bulk of the enemy cavalry had withdrawn to the north side of the road, no doubt to discourage flanking efforts in that direction. The Numasi cavalrymen were devils on horseback, almost the equal of the desert princes of Bhagar, and despite being significantly outnumbered they'd got the better of the Lybarans in most of the day's skirmishes.

Rakh-amn-hotep had pressed them hard, believing at first that the Numasi cavalry was no more than a large scouting party sent to gather intelligence on the situation at Quatar. The enemy had retreated slowly but steadily in the face of his advance, sometimes wheeling and dashing forwards to unleash a volley of arrows or clash swords with a squadron of Lybarans who pressed too close. He had been certain that they would eventually break off and retreat north and west once the day was nearly over, but now he realised bitterly that the horsemen were merely a vanguard like his own, and they'd held him up just long enough for the rest of their force to form up for battle.

The majority of the Lybaran cavalry was arrayed in a broad crescent to either side of the Rasetran king: close to three thousand light cavalry and a striking force of fifteen hundred heavy cavalry. The heavy horse was situated to the king's left, still relatively fresh at the end of the day.

Rakh-amn-hotep had kept them and his Ushabti in reserve, unwilling to wear them out on constant pursuits when he might have need of them later. To the king's right, the horses of the light cavalry squadrons waited with their heads drooping and their flanks dappled with foam. Their riders poured precious water from the leather flasks at their hips onto thick cotton rags and held them up for their weary mounts to lick.

Rakh-amn-hotep scowled up at the lowering sun. There were perhaps two hours left before sunset. If they could not find a way to break through the enemy line it would mean another day out in the sands, consuming the last of the army's water. The Usurper's troops appeared to number at least fifteen thousand men, including the two thousand Numasi cavalry they'd skirmished with earlier, mostly light infantry and a few companies of archers. The Rasetran king would generally be tempted to put his faith in Ptra and try a massed charge, but the majority of his force was all but exhausted. Did they have enough strength left to break the enemy line?

The king turned and beckoned to the commander of the Lybaran contingent, who stood with his retinue only a few paces away. Shesh-amun was one of Hekhmenukep's staunchest allies, and despite his advanced years he carried himself with a young man's strength and vigour. He was lean and rangy like old leather, his skin burned almost black by long decades labouring under the desert sun. The champion was a bluff, forthright man who did not suffer fools gladly, and didn't think so much of himself that he couldn't be persuaded to listen to reason. The Rasetran had warmed to him at once. Rakh-amn-hotep leaned over the side of his chariot as Shesh-amun approached.

'We need to get past these jackals,' the king said quietly. 'Are your men up to one more fight?'

'Oh, they'd welcome the chance to fight someone that doesn't wheel away and run at the first sign of trouble,'

Shesh-amun growled. 'Those Numasi horse thieves have got their blood up, but I suspect that was the whole point.' The champion turned his head and spat into the dust. 'They're willing, and the horses, too, but don't be surprised if they start dropping dead if the fight goes on too long.' The Rasetran king nodded grimly.

'Well, promise them all the water they can drink, if only we can break through and reach the springs. Maybe that will keep them alive a few moments more.'

'I'll pass the word,' Shesh-amun said. Just as he began to turn away, a horn sounded beyond the dunes to the east of the weary horsemen. The champion peered off into the distance. 'Are you expecting someone?' he asked. Rakh-amn-hotep straightened and looked eastward. Sure enough, a winding ribbon of dust was rising from the direction of the trade road.

'Indeed I am, but I'd nearly given up on him,' he said. 'Reinforcements are coming,' the king told Shesh-amun. 'Ready your men for action.'

The champion bowed quickly and hastened off to spread the word. Minutes later Rakh-amn-hotep heard the rumble of hooves, and a squadron of light cavalry raced over the dunes to join the line of weary horsemen. Tired cheers went up from the vanguard as the reinforcements began to arrive, and the king waited for the sight of Ekhreb's chariot among the column of troops. He saw it at once, bouncing along in the light cavalry's wake. Rakh-amn-hotep raised his sword in greeting, and the light chariot angled off the line of march and reined in beside the king.

'I left you back at camp three hours ago!' Rakh-amn-hotep shouted to the champion. 'Did you get lost? All you had to do was follow the damned road!' Ekhreb leapt from the back of the chariot and reached the king in two quick strides.

'That's rich,' the champion replied mildly. 'You, lecturing me about arriving late. I marshalled six thousand men for you on two hours' notice. Shall I send them back to camp?'

'Don't be churlish,' the king replied. 'I can have you beheaded for that, you know.'

'So you've said,' Ekhreb replied. 'Many, many times.' Rakh-amn-hotep caught sight of a company of Rasetran light infantry jogging over the dunes to the east.

'What have you brought me, exactly?' he asked.

'A thousand light horsemen, four thousand light infantry, and a thousand of our jungle auxiliaries,' Ekhreb said. 'I thought the scaly-skins might strike some fear into the enemy's hearts.'

'No archers?' the king asked sharply. The champion made a visible effort not to roll his eyes.

'You said nothing about bowmen, great one.'

The king bit back a sarcastic reply. Ekhreb was right, after all.

'We'll have to rely on the bows of the light cavalry then,' he muttered. Ekhreb folded his arms and stared at the distant enemy line.

'Not much of a force,' he said. 'It seems that Akhmen-hotep's diversion was successful.'

'Perhaps,' the king replied, 'but it doesn't need to be very large, so long as they keep us from the springs.' Rakh-amn-hotep studied the enemy dispositions and made his plans. 'Form the infantry into line right here,' he told his champion, 'and put the auxiliaries on the right.' Then he beckoned to Shesh-amun. When the Lybaran arrived, he told him, 'Pull your light horsemen back over the dunes behind us, and start circling around to our right, towards the road.' Shesh-amun frowned.

'But they'll be expecting that,' he said. The king waved his concerns away.

'Sometimes we must give the enemy what he's looking for,' he told the champion. 'Don't commit your men to pitched battle unless you must. Just push as far as you can around the edge of their line. I'll give you ten minutes to get your riders moving before we advance.'

Though clearly still doubtful, Shesh-amun bowed to the king and began shouting orders to his troops. Ekhreb had already passed the king's commands to the allied reinforcements. The light infantry companies were already forming a rough line before the allied cavalry, and the dark green shapes of the jungle auxiliaries were moving between the king's chariots and the Lybaran light cavalry. The lizardmen were huge, hulking creatures, their scaly skins tattooed in strange spiral patterns that stretched across their rolling muscles. They carried massive clubs in their taloned hands, made of heavy pieces of wood studded with jagged chips of glossy black stone. Human skulls hung from rawhide cords around their naked waists, and their powerful, wedge-shaped heads bore a fearsome resemblance to the great crocodiles of Nehekharan legend. The trained warhorses rolled their eyes and shifted nervously at the creatures' acrid stink, but the lizardmen paid them little heed.

As the infantry were forming up for battle the light horsemen on the right flank began to slowly withdraw over the dunes to the east. Rakh-amn-hotep expected some kind of reaction from the enemy line, but the Usurper's troops made not a sound.

Ekhreb folded his muscular arms and surveyed the troops' movements with a practised eye.

'Where do you want me?' he asked the king.

'You?' Rakh-amn-hotep grunted. 'I want you right beside me, of course. That way you can't claim you got lost heading to the battle.' Ekhreb gave the king an arch expression.

'I live to serve, great one,' he said wryly. 'What now?' Rakh-amn-hotep counted off the minutes in his head.

'Order the centre and the left flank forwards,' he commanded. 'The heavy cavalry will charge along with the infantry.'

The champion nodded and passed the orders at once. Trumpets sounded, and the ragged line of warriors raised their shields and marched towards the foe, followed by the light horsemen a dozen yards behind. Across the broken ground between the two armies, the enemy bowmen waited in two long skirmish lines before the infantry companies. As the king watched the distance between the two forces shrink he found himself wishing for a few Lybaran sky-priests to spoil the enemy's aim. The thought stirred a faint twinge of suspicion in the king's mind: where were the enemy sorcerers? He'd heard the stories of what had happened at Zedri, years before. Now that his forces had been committed, he found himself wondering what terrible surprises the Usurper's army had in store.

The air darkened above the closing armies as the enemy bowmen loosed their first volley. The Rasetran infantry quickened their pace at once, throwing up their wooden shields against the deadly rain. The shower of arrows struck their targets with a dreadful rattle of bronze against wood. Men screamed, and gaps showed in the advancing companies, but the rest pressed on. More arrows flickered through the air as the light horsemen returned the enemy fire, shooting high over the heads of the advancing infantry. Far to the left, a low rumble began as the heavy cavalry spurred their mounts into a ground-eating canter, and the enemy companies on that flank lowered their glinting spears to receive the inevitable charge.

The enemy bowmen fired a second volley and then withdrew to safety as the Rasetran warriors bore down upon them. Rakh-amn-hotep nodded thoughtfully.

'All right,' he said to Ekhreb. 'Order the auxiliaries to attack.'

Ekhreb called out, and a heavy drum answered, beating out a low, dreadful cadence. With a hiss like a desert wind, the company of lizardmen rose from their haunches and loped towards the enemy battle-line, covering the ground swiftly with their long strides. The air filled with screeches and dreadful, warbling cries as the jungle warriors advanced, and Rakh-amn-hotep was pleased to see the troops on the left waver at the sound.

All along the battle-line the warriors of the opposing armies crashed together in a resounding clatter of wood and bronze. The screams of the dead and dying carried clearly above the din, and badly wounded men began to break away from the struggling companies and stagger back the way they'd come. On the left, the heavy cavalry thundered home against the enemy shield wall, flinging broken bodies back onto their fellows as they drove a wedge into two of the enemy companies. Swords flashed down in brilliant arcs, splitting skulls and cleaving torsos, and frenzied horses reared and lashed at the screaming throng with their terrible hooves.

On the right, the lizardmen leapt at their foes with a bloodcurdling chorus of hissing screeches and inhuman wails. Their scaly skin turned aside all but the strongest spear-thrust, and their war clubs smashed wooden shields and bones alike into ragged splinters. The king watched the enemy infantry reel in terror from the onslaught, but the majority of his attention was focused on the light horsemen still further down the right flank. Their horses were rearing and screaming at the scent of the strange lizardmen, but as yet they held their position at the opposite end of the road. A few of the cavalrymen loosed wild shots into the frenzied creatures, to no discernible effect.

Minutes passed, and the fighting continued. The enemy forces had wavered under the initial ferocity of the allied attack, but they had regained their resolve and their greater numbers were beginning to tell against the Rasetran infantry. The heavy cavalry on the left were being slowly surrounded by a sea of roaring, stabbing warriors and were trying to extricate themselves from the mob. The infantry companies on the left and in the centre were being driven back by the sheer weight of their foes. Only on the right were there still signs of success, as the lizardmen took a terrible toll of the lightly armoured humans. Rakh-amn-hotep, however, knew from experience that the lizardmen could not sustain such efforts for long, especially in this searing heat. Before too much longer they would start to falter, and he would have to pull them back or risk seeing them overwhelmed.

Then the king caught a glimpse of movement further to the right. A squadron of the enemy cavalry was wheeling away, heading further off to the north. A minute later another squadron followed, and then another. They had spotted the flanking movement by the Lybaran horsemen and were moving to counter the attempt, leaving the battered infantry on the right without any support.

Rakh-amn-hotep smiled and drew his sword.

'Time to end this,' he growled. To Ekhreb he said, 'The Ushabti will advance upon the right,' pointing his sword at the junction where the enemy right met the centre. 'Push through and drive for the springs!'

As one, the Ushabti shouted the name of Ptra the Glorious and raised their gleaming blades to the sky. With a peal of trumpets the company started forwards, gathering speed as the charioteers lashed the flanks of their horses. As they rumbled forwards the chariots altered their formation, stretching into a wedge aimed like a spear at the vulnerable point of the enemy line.

The earth shook beneath the thundering wheels of the war machines. Rasetrans in the rear ranks of their struggling companies saw their king approach and raised their voices in a lusty cheer that spurred the efforts of their fellows. For a brief moment the allied line surged forwards a single step, and then the chariots smashed into the battle-line. Light infantrymen were smashed aside by teams of charging horses, or trampled beneath hooves and bronze-rimmed wheels. Bowstrings snapped as archers in the chariots fired point-blank into the massed enemy troops, and the armoured figures of the Ushabti reaped a terrible harvest with their huge, sickle-shaped swords. Rakh-amn-hotep chopped down with his sword and smashed a screaming warrior's skull. Then he swept aside the jabbing point of a spear.

'Keep going!' he roared to his charioteer, and the man cracked his whip with a will, shouting to Ptra to strengthen his arm.

The infantrymen reeled from the impact, and the battle-hardened Rasetrans pressed the advantage, driving the wedge still deeper into the line. The enemy troops on the right flank were cut off from their neighbouring companies and left to the mercy of the ravening lizardmen, who tore heads from the dead and dying and crushed them in their terrible jaws. Without the support of the light cavalry, the spearmen began to waver, and a moment later their resolve failed them and they began to run, stumbling and clawing up the slope behind them. The jungle warriors gave chase, hissing and screeching their savage war cries.

Rakh-amn-hotep roared in triumph.

'Wheel right!' he ordered, and slowly the chariots began to press upon the unprotected flank of the companies in the enemy centre. Arrows scythed into the sides and rear of the enemy formations, and panic took hold. When the enemy warriors saw that their left flank had crumbled they turned and ran, and within minutes the slopes were swarming with fleeing troops. The Rasetrans snapped at their heels like wolves, slaying every man they could reach. Exhaustion alone held back the struggling allied troops, and was all that kept the retreat from becoming a blood-soaked rout.

Relief and a sense of triumph flooded the king's tired body. The battle had lasted less than half an hour, judging by the height of the sun. Ptra's burning orb had vanished into a pool of crimson light along the western horizon. With luck, the king thought, the vanguard would reach the life-giving pools by nightfall.

The Rasetran infantry clambered up the slope after their foes and disappeared over the summit of the dunes. For the cavalry and the chariots it was harder going, as the sands gave way beneath the plunging hooves of the horses. Rakh-amn-hotep was busy contemplating how he would press the pursuit with fresh elements of the army's light cavalry when his chariot finally crested the rise, and slid to an awkward halt.

Rakh-amn-hotep threw out a hand to steady himself at the sudden stop, a curse halfway to his lips, when he realised that the entire allied pursuit had pulled up short. The survivors of the enemy army were running pell-mell across a wide, rocky plain, in the direction of the springs, And, with a cold sense of realisation, the king saw why.

Across the broad plain, arrayed at the very edge of the mist-wrapped springs, stretched a line of infantry and bowmen that ran from one end of the horizon to the other. The bloody sunlight shone on thickets of spears and round, polished helms, tens of thousands strong. Huge blocks of heavy cavalry waited beyond the line of spears, and smaller squadrons of light horsemen prowled along the front of the battle-line like packs of hungry jackals.

'In the name of all the gods,' Rakh-amn-hotep whispered in awe. Now he understood. The enemy force he'd just defeated was just the vanguard for the Usurper's main host.

Ekhreb reined in his chariot alongside the king. 'What do we do now?' he called.

Rakh-amn-hotep shook his head at the legions of silent warriors waiting across the plain.

'What can we do?' he said bitterly. 'We must retreat and carry news back to the rest of the army. Tomorrow we must summon all our strength and fight for our very lives.'

BOOK TWO

◄ SEVENTEEN ►

Attack and Retreat

Bel Aliad, the City of Spices, in the 63rd year of Ptra
the Glorious (-1744 Imperial Reckoning)

THE DATE WINE was thick and cloyingly sweet. Akhmen-hotep grimaced as he raised the cup to his lips and took another draught. Inside the king's tent, the air was cold and still. No oil lamps had been lit, nor were there any coals banked against the night's chill. Only a pair of wide-eyed slaves attended upon the king, kneeling fearfully at either side of the tent's entrance.

Akhmen-hotep's tent faced west, letting in long, slanting beams of moonlight as the linen entry flap was pulled aside. Outside, the camp was quiet save for the distant music of Neru's acolytes as they performed their midnight vigil. The king raised his eyes to the round figure silhouetted in the moon's cold radiance.

'What do you want, brother?' he asked, in a voice roughened by many cups of wine.

Memnet did not reply at first. The Grand Hierophant stood in the entryway for a few moments, letting his eyes adjust to the gloom, and then shuffled wearily inside and settled in a chair close to the king. He gestured, and a slave crawled swiftly across the sandy floor to press a cup into the high priest's hand.

'I thought you and I could share a drink,' Memnet said thoughtfully, sniffing at the strong smell of the dates. He made a face. 'No water for the wine?' Akhmen-hotep took another sip.

'I do not drink it for the taste,' he said quietly.

The Grand Hierophant nodded, but said nothing. He took a tentative sip of the wine, before saying, 'You cannot blame yourself for what happened. It's the nature of war.'

'War,' Akhmen-hotep growled into his cup. 'This is not war as our fathers knew it. This… this is grotesque!' He drained the dregs and glared at one of the slaves, who crawled forwards with a fresh jug of wine. 'And the harder we fight, the worse it becomes.' He turned abruptly, causing the slave to slosh the syrupy wine over the king's hand.

'What is happening to us, brother?' Akhmen-hotep asked. His handsome features were etched with despair. 'Have the gods forsaken us? Everywhere I turn, all I see is death and ruin.' He held the brimming cup before him, his dark eyes bleak. 'Sometimes I fear that even if we do defeat the Usurper, we'll never be free of his taint.' Memnet stared into his cup for some time. He took another sip.

'Perhaps we are not meant to be,' he said quietly. The king grew very still.

'What do you mean?' he asked.

Memnet did not answer at first. His expression grew haunted, and Akhmen-hotep saw how ravaged his features had become since that fateful day at Zedri. The priest's face was like an ill-fitting mask, resting uneasily upon his skull. He took a deeper draught of the wine and sighed heavily.

'Nothing is eternal,' he said at last. 'No matter what we believe.' The high priest sat back in his chair, turning the polished cup in his hands. 'Who remembers the names of the gods we worshipped in the jungles, before we came to the Blessed Land? No one. Not even the oldest scrolls in Mahrak speak of them.' He glanced up at the king. 'Did they abandon us, or did we abandon them?' Akhmen-hotep scowled at his brother.

'Who knows?' he said. 'That was a different age. We are not the people we once were.'

'That is my point,' the high priest said. 'You ask if the gods have forsaken us. Perhaps it would be better to ask if we have grown estranged from them. Nagash may be the herald of a new age for our people.'

'How can you say that?' Akhmen-hotep snarled. 'You, of all people!' Memnet was unfazed by the king's accusatory tone.

'The role of a priest is about more than making sacrifices and collecting tithes,' he said. 'We are also the bearers of deeper truths. That is the charge that the gods lay upon us.' His gaze fell to the shadows upon the ground. 'Those truths are not always pleasant to hear.'

Akhmen-hotep considered this as he peered into the depths of his cup. Despair ate at him, draining the colour from his face. Then, slowly but surely, his expression hardened. His brows drew together and his lips pressed into a thin, determined line.

'I will tell you what I think,' he said slowly. 'I think that the truth is what we make of it. Else, why would we have need for kings at all?' He raised the cup to his lips and emptied it in one long swallow, and then held the empty vessel up to his eyes. His fist tightened, the tendons on the back of his scarred hand growing as taut as cords as he slowly crushed the metal cup. 'Nothing is preordained, so long as we have the courage to fight for what we believe.' He tossed the lump of metal onto the ground. 'We will cast down the Usurper and drive his spirit into the wastes where he belongs. We will make this land right again, because I am the king and I command that it be so!'

Memnet raised his eyes to the king and studied him for a long moment. His eyes were like dark pools, depthless and inscrutable. A ghost of a smile flitted across his face.

'I expected no less from you, brother,' he said.

The king made to reply, but faint sounds beyond the confines of the tent made him pause. He scowled, listening intently. Memnet cocked his head to one side and listened as well.

'Someone is shouting,' he said.

'Not just one,' the king answered thoughtfully. 'Perhaps it is Pakh-amn, leading his soldiers back into camp. They've been putting out fires in the city all evening.' The Grand Hierophant stared at the dregs in his cup.

'Keep a close eye on that one, brother,' he warned. 'He grows more dangerous every day.'

Akhmen-hotep shook his head dismissively, saying, 'Pakh-amn is young and proud, to be sure, but dangerous?' Yet even as he said it, he recalled the tense confrontation just before the battle today. *Lead on then. For so long as you live.*

'He has regained some of the respect he lost at Zedri,' the high priest said. 'His cavalrymen cheered his name when the battle was done.'

'And what is wrong with that?' the king asked, though he could not help but feel a twinge of apprehension.

'The Master of Horse has made it plain that he opposes the war against the Usurper,' the Grand Hierophant said. 'Who can say what he might do if he found himself in a position of influence over much of the army?'

The shouts were still distant, but growing more intense by the moment. Finally the king could stand it no longer.

'What would you have me do, brother?' he asked, reaching for his sword. 'Pakh-amn served me well on the battlefield today. I have no reason to suspect him.'

'Nor will you, if he is clever,' Memnet pointed out. 'Watch him closely. That is all I ask.'

Akhmen-hotep glowered at the priest. 'Bad enough that we must guard against the schemes of the Blasphemer,' he growled. 'Now you would have me question the honour of my noblemen.'

Before Memnet could reply, the king snatched up his sword from a nearby table and strode swiftly out into the cold night air. With an effort of will he tried to banish his brother's dire observations from his mind as he hurried in the direction of the voices, flanked by four Ushabti who had been standing guard outside the king's tent.

The shouts carried easily in the chill air, coming from the western edge of the camp. Akhmen-hotep quickened his pace at the sounds of alarm that were spreading among the tents of the Bronze Host. Men were stumbling out into the darkness, their armour half-on and their weapons in their hands. A flash of movement to the king's right drew his eye. He saw a pair of Neru's acolytes stumbling down an adjoining lane, half-carrying a third acolyte between them. Their ceremonial garments were speckled with blood. Muttering a curse, the king broke into a run.

As he drew near the edge of the camp, Akhmen-hotep began to encounter groups of panicked men running the other way. Their kilts were stained with dust and soot, and their faces were pale with fright. The men were blind to the presence of the king in their midst, rushing past him like a flock of startled birds, intent on nothing more than running east as quickly as they could.

Five minutes later the king found himself at the edge of the sprawling camp. He came upon a scene of chaos and confusion. A nobleman on horseback was shouting orders and trying to control his plunging mount at the same time, while a small group of warriors was pulling open the crude enclosure holding the barbarian prisoners they'd taken in battle. A second enclosure, built to contain the imprisoned members of Bel Aliad's City Companies, had already been opened, and the prisoners were milling around the moonlit plain in confusion.

Akhmen-hotep ran up to the shouting horseman, realising at the last moment that it was Pakh-amn.

'What is going on?' he shouted up at the Master of Horse.

Pakh-amn twisted in the saddle and stared wide-eyed at the sudden appearance of the king. 'They're coming!' he said hoarsely.

'What?' the king asked. He looked around, trying to make sense of the scene. 'Who is coming?' The young nobleman eyed the throng of milling prisoners and cursed under his breath. He leaned down until his face was just inches from the king's.

'Who do you think?' he hissed. 'The people of Bel Aliad have risen in their multitudes, great one. They set upon us as we were leaving the city and killed a third of my men. The rest of us ran the entire way back to camp, but even so, we haven't much time. The dead are rising from the battlefield, too, and are heading this way even as we speak.'

Akhmen-hotep felt his blood turn to ice as he heard the news. 'But there were no sorcerers in the city,' he protested numbly. 'Suhedir al-Khazem swore an oath on it.'

'Go and see the carnage at the city gates if you don't believe me,' Pakh-amn snarled. 'Old men with their stomachs torn open, mothers with slit throats and trampled children. They came at us out of the side streets and alleys and tore my men apart with their bare hands!'

The king's shock melted beneath the young noble's acid tone. He glowered up at the Master of Horse, and replied, 'Even so, we have the wards. The priests of Neru–'

'Are dead or dying,' Pakh-amn shot back. 'They were ambushed a short while ago as they walked their circuit. We heard hoof beats off to the north, probably light horsemen armed with bows. Neru's holy wards have no power over a flight of arrows.'

The king gritted his teeth at the news, remembering the trio of wounded acolytes he'd seen earlier. He considered the unfolding situation quickly, and his heart sank at the realisation that he'd been caught in the jaws of a trap. The battle they'd fought earlier in the day had only been a prelude, meant to wear his men out and swell the numbers of the enemy's forces even further. The king drew a deep breath.

'It's good that you thought to free the prisoners,' he said heavily.

Pakh-amn bared his teeth. 'If the gods are good, the fiends will go for them first and give us time to get out of here,' he hissed. The nobleman's cold-blooded tactic took the king aback.

'We'll form up the host here,' he said, 'between Bel Aliad and the camp. Perhaps we can find some spare weapons and arm the City Companies–'

Forgetting himself completely, Pakh-amn glowered at the king.

'Are you mad?' he snapped. 'Even had we the time to form up the army, the men are exhausted and the horses are blown, and the dead won't bother forming into companies and marching to battle. They'll lap around our flanks and swarm like ants over the camp.'

'Then what would you have me do, Master of Horse?' Akhmen-hotep growled threateningly.

Pakh-amn blinked at the king's tone, perhaps realising how far he'd overstepped his bounds.

'We must flee,' he answered, his voice more subdued, 'right now, while there's still time. Gather the Bhagarites and see if they can lose us among the sands.'

The king's lip curled in distaste, but there was some sense in the young noble's words. If he offered battle he risked playing further into his enemy's hands. The thought of such an ignominious flight went ill with the king, but they'd done what they'd come to do. They'd fulfilled their obligation to their allies. Now, their only obligation was to themselves and their city.

To the king's left, a group of barbarians began to shout, pointing off to the west and babbling in their guttural tongue. Akhmen-hotep stepped away from Pakh-amn's horse and peered westward.

At first, it seemed as if the broken plain was slowly undulating, like sluggish waves along the surface of a river, but as the king's eyes adjusted to the shadows he could make out round, drooping heads and slumped shoulders, dark and tattered beneath Neru's silver light. A shambling mob of figures limped and lurched its way silently towards the camp. Some brandished axes or spears, while others reached for their distant prey with bare and bloodied hands. The leading edge of the horde was less than a mile away, advancing at a slow, relentless pace. Akhmen-hotep felt their mindless hunger like a cold blade pressed against his skin.

The men of the City Companies saw the undead creatures too. Some of the men called out tentatively to the approaching figures, thinking that their kin had come to pay the ransom for their release.

In a few more minutes the slaughter would begin, and panic would spread like a desert wind through the camp. If they were to have any chance to escape at all, the king knew that they would have to act quickly. Sick at heart, the king turned back to Pakh-amn.

'Go and rouse your horsemen,' he told the young nobleman. 'You'll have to be our rearguard as we try to withdraw.'

Pakh-amn stared at the king for a long moment, his dark eyes hidden by shadow. Finally he gave a curt nod and kicked his horse into a gallop. The king watched the Master of Horse disappear deeper into the camp, and then began issuing orders to his bodyguards.

'Rouse the company commanders at once,' he told them. 'Tell them to muster their troops and gather everything they can carry. We move out in fifteen minutes.'

The Ushabti bowed quickly and raced off into the darkness. Akhmen-hotep looked around and saw that the mercenaries were already gone, fleeing pell-mell off to the south. The warriors of Bel Aliad were heading westwards in a ragged mob, calling out to figures that they vaguely recognised among the approaching horde.

Burning with shame, Akhmen-hotep said a short prayer to Usirian, that their souls might find their way safely into the afterlife. Then he turned and raced for the centre of the camp.

THE WALKING DEAD of Bel Aliad were methodical in their work. They stumbled after their screaming kinsmen, dragging them to the ground and stabbing them with spears or tearing them open with tooth and claw. The warriors of the City Companies fled in every direction, but they were weary from a long day of battle and terrified beyond reason at the sight of the bloodstained monsters that had once been their wives and children. Some tried to fight, taking up rocks or pieces of wood and striking in vain at the tide of relentless corpses. Others tried to hide amid the broken ground, cowering behind boulders or burying themselves in drifts of sand, until clumsy, grasping fingers closed around their throats. Still others begged for mercy, appealing to those among the horde whom they knew by name. In every case, the result was the same. The men died, slowly and terribly, and then, within minutes, they rose anew and joined in the hunt.

When the men of the City Companies were no more, the undead army combed the darkness for the pale-skinned northmen. The hulking barbarians swore wild oaths and called upon their rough-hewn gods as they fought, smashing skulls and breaking bones even as cold, dry teeth closed upon their throats. For all their struggles, the horde claimed them as well.

The last to die were the city's proud rulers. They stumbled from the empty camp of the Bronze Host and found their people waiting for them on the broken plain. Silently, reverently, the dead of Bel Aliad surrounded the princes and tore them limb from limb. Suhedir al-Khazem was eaten alive by his three daughters, watching in mute, insensate horror as they dug their fingers into his abdomen and tore his entrails free.

All the while the Bronze Host of Ka-Sabar was fleeing further and further into the desert, carrying only what the weary soldiers could sling upon their backs. They moved in silence, casting fearful glances back at their abandoned tents and wondering when the first packs of shambling corpses would find their trail, and the long hunt would begin.

Sitting atop his rotting horse on a sand dune to the north, Arkhan the Black watched the army retreat into the merciless desert, and smiled. For a moment, just before the city's dead reached the enemy camp, he'd feared that Akhmen-hotep would offer battle instead of retreating. That would have complicated his master's plans. Fortunately, the doomed king had chosen to enter the trap instead.

The immortal waited with deathless patience until the last of the enemy warriors had vanished across the rolling hills of sand. Then he nudged his dead mount forwards with a creak of old leather and a rattle of bones. At once, his squadron of skeletal horsemen followed, their harnesses rattling hollowly in the waning moonlight.

◄EIGHTEEN►

Sealed in Stone

Khemri, the Living City, in the 45th year of Ptra the Glorious
(-1959 Imperial Reckoning)

THE WAILS OF drugged and terrified victims created a shrill counterpoint to the furious chants echoing in the great throne room deep within the Great Pyramid. Nagash stood within a carefully marked ritual circle, not far from where the barbarian witch Drutheira had met a gruesome end not twenty-four hours before. Khefru had worked frantically to clear away the bodies, and then find an unmarked part of the floor where he could inscribe the ritual circle. Only the remnants of Asaph's shattered head, and the grisly remains beneath, still remained as proof of the magical duel waged on the previous night.

The braziers were burning brightly, and clouds of incense hung above the gathered nobles. All forty of Nagash's allies were in attendance, in two groups of twenty. While a score of the noblemen stood around the perimeter of the circle and joined in the invocations, the rest kept a close watch on the waiting sacrifices. Many of the victims were slaves, bought in the market near the docks that very day. Others were drunkards or gamblers, who had the misfortune of being in the wrong place at the wrong time when one of Nagash's men passed by. Their senses were dulled by wine or black lotus root, or numbed by the mild narcotic mixed with the burning incense, but even so they could not help but be aware of the terrible fate that awaited them.

Nagash led each ritual, his powerful voice rising to a crescendo as the victim caught within his grip began to burn. He drank deeply of their souls and wove the energy into the greater incantation that he'd begun hours earlier, feeding the curse that continued to plague the noble-born of Khemri. Beneath his ritual robes his torso was bandaged from his shoulders to his waist, and his cheeks were burned from the touch of the druchii's sorcery. His arms, particularly the one that Drutheira had cut, ached down to the very bone. It was all he could do to move them, much less grip each squirming slave and tear free his soul. What sustained him was the memory of his victory over his erstwhile tutors, and the knowledge that the throne he'd coveted for so long was nearly within his grasp. Another week, perhaps two, enough time for the plague to claim the last of the city's high nobility and provoke the angry citizens to riot, and he would be ready to make his move.

The victim within his hands went limp, his screams dwindling to a breathless whimper as his body burst into a hissing plume of green flame. Nagash felt the sorcerous fire lick up his arms and threw back his head in exultation as the young man's lifeforce passed through him. Not for the first time, he felt the heady, fleeting rush of youth and wondered if there might be some way to make that vigour his own.

Nagash scarcely felt the slave's body crumble to ash in his hands. He added the stolen life-force to the fabric of the curse and brought the Incantation of Reaping to a conclusion. The necromancer swayed slightly, drunk from the taste of so much power. By his count they had sacrificed half of the night's bounty so far.

'You are dismissed,' he told the men standing around the circle. 'Go and send the others to me.' Then he beckoned to Khefru, who waited in the shadows near the dais. 'Wine,' he commanded.

The servant approached with a small jug and a goblet made of beaten gold. Nagash snatched the jug from Khefru's hand and raised it to his lips. He drank deep, slaking his burning thirst.

'Better,' he said huskily, handing the jug back to his servant. The vessel fell through Khefru's slack fingers and smashed upon the stones, mingling wine with the piled ash of the sacrifices.

'Clumsy fool!' Nagash snarled. 'Sop it up at once. Drink it down if you have to! If your act of carelessness breaches the ritual inscriptions...' The necromancer paused, suddenly noticing the look of dumb horror on the young priest's face. Nagash cuffed his servant on the ear. 'Have you not heard a single thing I've said to you?' Khefru's sallow face had turned pale. He pointed a trembling finger at the knot of wailing victims.

'That girl there,' he said. 'The young one, with the gold circlet around her arm.'

Nagash scowled irritably at the huddled mass of wretches. After a moment, he caught sight of the one to whom the priest referred. She was very young, supple and strong, with a slightly exotic cast to her eyes. He reckoned a girl like her must have been worth her weight in silver on the block.

'What of her, damn you?' he asked.

'She's no slave,' Khefru said, his voice thick with dread. 'Can't you see? She's Lahmian. I've seen her before. She's one of the queen's personal servants!' The news gave Nagash pause.

'Surely not,' he said, studying the girl more closely. 'Perhaps she was taken in a raid, part of some caravan bound for Lybaras, or possibly even Mahrak.'

'No!' Khefru moaned. 'I've seen her at the palace! What slave would be put on the block with a gold circlet still around her arm?' Forgetting himself, the priest gripped Nagash's left arm. 'I warned you about this, time and again! Someone, perhaps Shepsu-hur, perhaps Arkhan, got lazy and careless, and took the first person that caught his fancy, and now we're undone! The queen won't rest until she's learned who took her maid!'

Nagash shook off Khefru's panicked grip. He beckoned impatiently to the second group of nobles, which, interestingly, contained both Shepsu-hur and Arkhan.

'Quickly!' he snapped. 'Bring her first, the young one, with the gold circlet on her arm. Now!' Khefru's eyes widened in horror.

'You can't mean to kill her?' he asked. The necromancer's hands clenched into fists.

'Do you imagine we can send her back to the palace, after all she's seen?' he hissed. 'Gather what's left of your courage, you simpleton. We've almost reached the end. In another week, two at most, none of this will matter any more.'

To Nagash's surprise, Khefru refused to yield. 'You can't do this!' he said. 'I won't–'

Before he could say any more, a fierce shout rang across the throne room from the south side of the chamber, followed by cries of surprise and fear from among Nagash's minions.

The crowd along the south side of the chamber seemed to recoil from a fierce, golden radiance that shone between a pair of columns at the midpoint of the room. Nagash saw Arkhan, who was leading the second group of noblemen and dragging the young maid by the arm, glance to his right and turn pale with shock. Weeping in relief, the maid tore loose from Arkhan's grip and ran towards the light.

Nagash turned on his heel and dashed up to the dais, climbing the cracked stone steps until he could see over the panicked, milling mob. At once, he found himself staring into the angry eyes of his brother, Thutep.

The young king was dressed as though for war, armoured in a bronze breastplate and woven leather bands that covered his arms and legs. He carried a gleaming khopesh in his right hand, and the golden headdress of Settra rested upon his brow. Thutep was surrounded by a dozen of his Ushabti, and it was from them that the golden light of Ptra shone like a lamp, chasing back the room's dreadful shadows. The devoted were armed and armoured, too, and their handsome faces were set into masks of righteous rage. Within the protective circle of the bodyguards, a few paces behind the king, stood the regal figure of Hapshur, the High Priestess of Neru. The priestess clutched her slender staff of office and gazed angrily at the tumult that surrounded her. On Thutep's left side, the queen's young maid knelt at the king's feet, her forehead pressed to the flagstones.

When Thutep saw his brother, his handsome face twisted into a mask of grief-stricken rage.

'Ghazid tried to warn me about you,' he said to Nagash, his powerful voice cutting through the clamour like a knife. 'He said you were a threat, not just to me, but to Khemri. And gods, now I see that he was right all along!'

Nagash smiled coldly at the king. 'That was your trouble all along, brother. You were always too sentimental, too afraid to hurt those around you. You wanted to be loved,' he sneered, 'but for a king to rule, he must be feared.'

The necromancer spread his arms wide, encompassing the entire chamber. 'No one in all of Nehekhara fears you, brother. Least of all me.'

'Heretic!' Hapshur cried, brandishing her staff at Nagash. 'You are an abomination before the gods, and a traitor to your priesthood! The hour of your reckoning is at hand!'

Thutep pointed his curved sword at Nagash, and said, 'There is no escape, brother. Companies of the City Watch surround the pyramid, and we know where all the exits lie. In the name of Ptra, the Great Father, you and your followers are under arrest. When the sun rises tomorrow you will be put on trial for your crimes in the temple square at Khemri, and the servants of the gods will pass judgement upon you.'

Moans of despair rose from Nagash's minions, but the necromancer felt only a rising tide of icy rage.

'You would have a reckoning then, brother?' he said. 'So be it.'

The necromancer flung out his hand and spat a string of arcane syllables, unleashing a torrent of sizzling, glowing darts that streaked over the heads of his men and chewed Hapshur apart. The high priestess let out a single, lingering shriek as her body was shredded by sorcerous teeth. Thutep and his bodyguards were all caught in the fine spray of blood and minced flesh.

'Destroy them!' Nagash commanded.

Faced with such a display of power, his men did not hesitate to obey. The noblemen drew knives and swords and rushed at the king's bodyguards from all sides, but despite heavily outnumbering the dozen glowing bodyguards, Nagash's men were completely outmatched. Blessed by Ptra with superhuman speed and strength, not to mention a lifetime devoted to mastering the arts of combat, the young devoted met the noblemen with a fierce shout of joy and began a terrible slaughter.

As young and relatively inexperienced as the Ushabti were, their skill and ferocity were appalling. Noblemen fell like ripe wheat, most cut down before they could even lay a single blow. Unless something was done, the battle would be over in moments.

Nagash hissed the Incantation of Reaping and drank in the life energy of the slain noblemen. With their raw souls bubbling in his veins, he threw out his hands once more and unleashed spell after spell, hurling bolts of pure darkness into the tight circle of bodyguards. Each bolt found a mark, sinking effortlessly through the armour of the devoted and rending flesh and muscle beneath. The Ushabti staggered beneath the blows, but fought on, sustained by their vows to Ptra.

The necromancer's minions grew more cautious, focusing their efforts on the most wounded bodyguards. An Ushabti reeled as one of Nagash's bolts peeled back the right side of his face. Sensing an opportunity, one of the noblemen lunged forwards, hacking his blade into the bodyguard's throat. Even as the devoted fell, his sword licked out in a backhanded swipe that cut his attacker in half, and the two men died at nearly the same moment.

Nagash reaped the dying nobleman's soul and continued to punish the devoted with a barrage of lethal magic. When the Ushabti surged forwards, trying to use Nagash's men to shield them from his spells, he opened pits of shadow at their feet. When the survivors reeled back to safer ground, he speared them with bolts of sizzling black flame. It wasn't just Nagash that the Ushabti had to worry about, for Arkhan and a few of the more magically adept nobles joined in too. They flung darts point-blank into the beleaguered Ushabti, striking them from unexpected directions and creating more opportunities for their fellow nobles.

Thutep stood his ground through it all, shouting encouragement to his men. More than once he tried to join the fight, only to be pushed back by his men. Their courage and devotion were a wonder to behold, but one by one the devoted were overwhelmed. Within minutes after the fight began, the last Ushabti succumbed, his sword buried in the chest of another of Nagash's men.

The surviving noblemen clambered over the bodies of their dead compatriots and closed like jackals around the king. Thutep glared defiantly at the necromancer's henchmen, his sword held ready. On impulse, he glanced down at the girl, still cowering at his feet, and murmured a quick command. Fleet as a deer, she leapt thankfully to her feet and raced into the shadows behind Thutep, fleeing to the surface and safety.

It was the last free act that Thutep ever made. At that moment, Nagash cast a powerful spell that gripped his brother's mind in a vice. He stiffened, his face growing slack with horror as Nagash exerted his will over the king.

The necromancer's henchmen saw the king's transformation and stayed their hands. Most reeled back in exhaustion, grateful beyond words that the battle was done. A circle of torn and bleeding corpses surrounded the king and his fallen bodyguards. Slightly more than half of Nagash's men were dead, and the rest counted themselves lucky not to be among them.

Nagash descended from the dais, still pinning his brother in place by sorcery and the weight of his prodigious will. He approached his brother, his cold features lit with triumph. The necromancer stood before Thutep, his eyes blazing. Slowly, deliberately, he reached up and lifted away the king's royal headdress.

Thutep's body trembled with outrage, but he could not make his muscles obey. The necromancer smiled.

'Go on,' he said. 'Strike me down. You still hold your sword. All you need is the will to use it.' Nagash took his time arranging Settra's headdress upon his brow, and then reached down and took Thutep's sword hand by the wrist. 'Here. Let me help you.'

He raised Thutep's sword arm and placed the curved edge of the khopesh against his throat. 'There. All you need is a simple flick of the wrist and you'll slice open the artery. What could be simpler than that? Go on. I won't stop you.'

Thutep's entire body trembled. His eyes were wide and unblinking, his face flushed with effort. A single tear coursed down his cheek. The khopesh did not move.

Nagash sneered in disdain.

'How pathetic,' he said, and turned away. 'Seize him, and follow me.'

All at once, the force gripping the king vanished. Thutep, still straining at his bonds, all but fell into the arms of Nagash's minions. His sword was plucked from his hands and his arms twisted behind his back. The king hung limply in their grip as the noblemen followed Nagash from the hall.

THEY TOOK THE king through the north passage, down into the depths of the pyramid where their father Khetep was laid to rest. The dead king's crypt was one among many, set aside for not only his wife, his bodyguards and his servants, but for his children as well. The Great Pyramid was meant to house not just one king, but an entire dynasty.

Nagash led the way into the crypts, lighting the path with a pale grave-light that seemed to emanate from his skin. Thutep quickly realised what was happening, and began to struggle with his captors.

'You can't do this, brother,' he said. 'The people won't permit it! You're a priest, consecrated to the gods. You can't sit upon the throne!'

'I am consecrated to no god, brother,' Nagash spat. 'I served the will of Settra, king of kings, but that time is past. Tonight, a new era has been born. It's a pity you won't see its glories unfold.'

Thutep only struggled harder, until two men had to take hold of each of his arms and drag him along the dank stones.

'You're mad!' he cried. 'The other kings will rise against you! Can't you see that?'

'I understand the political realities far better than you, little brother,' Nagash snapped. 'Let them come. I will be ready for them.'

Nagash paused. They had come to the end of a long passageway, lined with smooth, blank walls. The architects had left them unadorned on purpose, so that after Thutep died a host of artisans could come and create elaborate mosaics that would depict the glories of his reign. At the end of the passageway stood a narrow doorway, flanked by two stone horex. A huge slab of stone rested against the wall to the right of the opening.

The necromancer's light penetrated some way into the burial chamber, revealing a small room with more bare walls and a pedestal intended to hold the king's sarcophagus. Nagash gestured, and his men shoved Thutep inside. He landed hard against the stone pedestal and whirled, his expression still defiant.

'Do you have the nerve to kill me with your own hand, brother?' he snarled. 'Or will you stand there in the corridor and send in your jackals to finish the job? The gods do not countenance the murder of a king. It has been that way since the dawn of civilisation. By striking me down, you will damn yourself.'

Nagash only laughed while his men went to work around him.

'I have no intention of killing you, brother,' he said. 'Nor will any of my men raise a hand against you. I wouldn't dare, but not for the reason you might think. You see, there's another law I have to be wary of, even older than the one you described: the one that says that a man's murderer is forbidden to marry his widow.'

The look of shock and anguish on Thutep's face was priceless. Nagash savoured every moment of it, right up to the point that Arkhan and his men pushed the stone slab into the doorway and buried the king alive.

━◄ NINETEEN ►━

Blood and Water

*The Fountains of Eternal Life, in the 63rd year of Ptra
the Glorious (-1744 Imperial Reckoning)*

THE PRIESTS WERE kept busy throughout the night as the
army prepared for battle. Neru's acolytes paced the
sprawling perimeter of the allied camp, raising their eyes
to the face of the goddess and filling the cold air with song
to keep the spirits of the wastes at bay. Around the
campfires, hammers clattered against bronze as warriors
made last-minute repairs to chariots or mended their
battle-harnesses. Men prayed as they worked. Some called
upon Ptra to drive their enemies before them, while
others beseeched mighty Geheb to lend them the strength
to overcome their foes. Still others made worship to
ashen-faced Djaf, God of Death, praying that their blows
struck clean and true. The rattle and murmur of the
enormous host mingled with the cries of oxen, goats and
lambs as the priests led their charges from the sacrificial
pens and dragged them before red-stained altars in the

centre of the camp. The clamour of the army ebbed and flowed across the sands like the restless breath of a vast, elemental beast.

The army of the Usurper waited little more than three miles away, across rolling dunes and a broad, rocky plain. Small campfires flickered among the hundreds of dark tents, and from time to time the nervous whicker of a horse would reach the ears of the allied sentries, but otherwise the enemy camp was eerily still.

At the centre of the vast encampment, ringed by scores of watchful Ushabti, Rakh-amn-hotep listened to his scouts' reports and contemplated the field of battle for the coming day. Long after he'd dismissed his captains to their tents, the king perched on a camp stool and brooded over the large map arrayed before him, studying the positions of his and his enemy's troops. From time to time his champion, Ekhreb, would rise from his chair near the entrance to the large tent and fill the king's empty cup with a mix of herbs and watered wine. At the far side of the tent's central chamber the King of Lybaras reclined upon a dust-stained divan. The papyrus sheets resting in his lap fluttered slightly as Hekhmenukep snored, his chin resting upon his narrow chest.

Two hours before dawn the army's slaves rose from the cold ground and began preparing the morning meal. Bowls of grain porridge were passed out to the thousands of grim-faced warriors, along with a palm-sized piece of unleavened bread and a single cup of water. Among the tents of the noblemen, those who could bring themselves to eat breakfasted on bread and olives, goat's cheese and river fowl. Their wine was thick and resinous, for no water could be spared to thin it.

Half an hour before sunrise, as the sky was paling to the east, the army began to muster. Horses thundered down the camp's narrow lanes as the kings despatched the first orders of the day to their companies. File leaders bellowed orders to their troops, drawing them from their tents and forming them into lines. The rumble of man-made thunder and a furious shriek of steam sounded in the north-eastern quarter of the camp, setting the Rasetran cavalry rearing and stamping in fright as the Lybaran war machines stirred to life. Six huge figures reared slowly into the brightening sky, their heavy armour plates grating and groaning as they shifted against one another.

The earth shook as the giants climbed ponderously to their feet. Their faces, carved from wood and sheathed in burnished copper, bore visages meant to win the favour of the gods: a snarling hound's face, in honour of Geheb; the cunning, enigmatic jackal favoured by Djaf; or Phakth's haughty, cruel falcon. The warriors of Rasetra and Lybaras stared in awe as the great engines hefted massive stone maces and took their first steps towards the battlefield. Few noticed that the army's war scorpions were nowhere to be seen. Like their patron, Sokth, the stealthy machines had slipped away in the night, leaving only piles of churned sand to show where they had been.

The stirring of the war machines brought answering bellows from the south-eastern quarter of the camp, as the living war machines of the Rasetran army raised their armoured snouts and challenged the distant giants. The thunder-lizards were massive, humpbacked creatures, with squat legs the size of tree trunks and powerful, lashing tails that were knobbed at the end like maces. The beasts were sluggish in the early morning chill, despite sleeping on sands heated by the warmth of a score of blazing fires. Their handlers, lean, agile lizardmen from the southern jungles, prodded the creatures to their feet with long, spearlike sticks and clambered up their sides into howdahs of wood and canvas fitted to their armoured backs. Packs of lizardman auxiliaries crowded the field around their massive cousins, whispering to one another in their hissing, clacking tongue. Some showed off the bloodstained skulls they had taken in battle the day before, inviting their fellows to taste the trophies with flicks of their dark, forked tongues.

Just as the first rays of sunlight broke over the far horizon, a chorus of trumpets pealed from the centre of the camp and the infantry began to move. The forward edge of the battle-line, twenty thousand men, formed into ten companies stretching nearly five miles from north to south, advanced under the watchful stares of their noble commanders and the leathery curses of their file leaders. The cavalry rode in their wake: eight thousand light horsemen, five thousand heavy horse and two thousand chariots, plus another twenty thousand reserves and auxiliaries. Behind them, striding through swirling clouds of dust, came the titanic war machines of Lybaras and the bellowing thunder lizards of Rasetra. Last of all came the multicoloured processions of the army's priests: servants of Ptra and Geheb, Phakth and Neru, and even priests of Tahoth the Scholar in their gleaming vestments of copper and glass.

The armies of the East marched to battle with the rising sun at their backs and the shadows of night retreating before them.

The bow of the sky-boat pitched and rolled as the sun churned the air above the rolling dunes, making Rakhamn-hotep glad that he had resisted the urge to eat a hearty breakfast before heading for the battle-line. Beside him, Hekhmenukep swayed like a palm tree in a storm, relaying instructions to his signallers as easily as if he were reclining in his tent back at camp. The King of Rasetra gripped the bow rail in one white-knuckled hand and resolved not to embarrass himself in front of the scholar-king.

Scores of Lybarans crowded the decks of the sky-ship as it floated along behind the advancing army. Four teams of signallers lined the ship's rails, clutching their dish-shaped bronze reflectors and periodically gauging the angle of the blazing sun. Behind them, a company of archers sat crosslegged down the centre of the deck, their long bows resting within easy reach as they chatted or played at games of dice. At the stern, surrounding the sky-boat's complicated set of rudders, two dozen young priests chanted invocations to the air spirits that kept the vessel aloft. Farther off to the east, trailing well behind the advancing army, came the remainder of the Lybaran sky-boats, the seven stately craft casting long shadows across the rolling terrain beneath their keels.

Two hundred feet below, the allied army advanced steadily across the broken plain towards their waiting foe. At such a distance, none of the rumble and clatter of an army on the march reached Rakh-amn-hotep's ears, which only served to deepen his unease.

'I feel like a spectator up here,' he said, half to himself. He glanced at Hekhmenukep. 'Are you certain this will work? What if the army can't read our signals?' The King of Lybaras gave Rakh-amn-hotep a condescending smile.

'There are Lybaran signallers with every company,' he said, as though reassuring an anxious child. 'We have spent centuries refining this system in elaborate games of war. It cannot fail.' Rakh-amn-hotep stared thoughtfully at the Lybraran king.

'How many times have you used it in a real battle?' he asked. Hekhmenukep's confident smile faltered a bit.

'Well…' he began.

'That's what I was afraid of,' the Rasetran king growled. For a fleeting moment he considered asking Hekhmenukep to be set down with the rest of the army, but having orders issued from the ground *and* the air would only increase the risk of confusion. Scowling, he turned his attention to the battlefield below and tried to work out the enemy's dispositions.

From Rakh-amn-hotep's vantage point, the army of the Usurper was laid out before him like tokens on a battle-map. Companies of blue-clad Zandri archers formed a skirmish line some fifty yards in front of a veritable wall of enemy spearmen, anchored on the trade road to the north and stretching for more than four miles in a shallow crescent to the south. The enemy companies were less numerous, but individually larger than the allied formations, five ranks to the allies' three. The king spied still more companies held in reserve behind the front rank, reinforcing the enemy centre and right. As near as he could reckon, the combined forces of the Usurper outnumbered the allied infantry by more than twenty thousand men. Large squadrons of Numasi light horsemen prowled along the flanks of the enemy army, alert for any attempts to sweep around the battle-line, and a large block of heavy horsemen waited behind a set of dunes along the enemy's left flank. Two more formations waited at the rear of the Usurper's force, but they were cloaked in the mists rising from the Fountains: chariots, or perhaps even catapults, the king surmised.

'Seventy, perhaps eighty thousand troops,' Rakh-amn-hotep mused. 'It appears that Ka-Sabar's diversion to the south wasn't as successful as we hoped. That must be all the fighting men of Khemri, Numas and Zandri combined.' He leaned against the rail, studying the formations more carefully. 'Still no tents, as reported at Zedri. Where are the Usurper and his pale-skinned monsters?' Hekhmenukep considered this.

'Perhaps they are hidden in the mists surrounding the fountains,' he suggested.

'Perhaps,' Rakh-amn-hotep agreed. 'At Zedri, he revealed himself only when his army was on the verge of defeat. It's possible that he thinks he can carry this battle on the strength of his army alone.' The king folded his arms and scowled at the enemy troops.

'No. There's more to it than that. Something is wrong here, but I can't put my finger on it.'

Hekhmenukep joined the Rasetran king at the rail and spent several long moments surveying the broken plain. Finally he said, 'Where are the bodies?'

'Bodies?'

The Lybaran king indicated the plain with a sweep of his hand, and said, 'This is where you fought the enemy vanguard yesterday, correct? You told me that there were hundreds of dead from both sides.'

'More on their side than ours,' Rakh-amn-hotep interjected.

'But what happened to the bodies?' the Lybaran asked. 'The plain should be covered in bloating corpses and flocks of vultures, but there's nothing there.' Rakh-amn-hotep considered this.

'That's it,' he said at last. 'Yes, it must be! Nagash used his damnable sorcery to animate the dead and...' He swept his gaze across the battlefield, looking for clues. 'He could have marched them into the mists to conceal them as a reserve force.'

'Why not simply bury them in the ground where they fell?' Hekhmenukep suggested. 'Then they could spring up behind us as our companies advanced.'

The Rasetran king shook his head, and said, 'The ground is too rocky to allow it, and we'd see the churned ground from here besides.' Once again, he studied the enemy's dispositions. 'The enemy has reinforced its lines in the centre and on their right, leaving the left flank relatively weak. They want us to throw our weight against the left, drawing us forwards as their companies retreat, and then counter-charge with their heavy cavalry to stop us in our tracks. That leaves us overextended and weak on their right flank, ripe for a counter-attack from the south.' Rakh-amn-hotep pointed off into the dunes beyond the enemy's right flank. 'The dead are waiting out there in the sands,' he declared. 'That's what Nagash is planning. I'd wager my life on it.'

Hekhmenukep considered this, before saying, 'I can't fault your reasoning, but how do we counter it?'

'We shift the bulk of our reserves to the south,' the Rasetran king ordered. 'Alert the commanders to watch for counter-attacks. Then we see about turning the tables on the Usurper's forces to the north.'

Rakh-amn-hotep began to issue instructions to the waiting Lybaran signallers, his commands growing swifter and more assured as the pieces of his battle-plan fell neatly into place. Within minutes the signal-men were at work, flashing messages to the troops on the ground, and the Rasetran king grinned fiercely as the allied army went into action.

EVEN WITH THE wonders of the Lybaran sun-signals, rearranging the dispositions of the allied army took up much of the morning. Huge clouds of dust churned above the plain, masking the movements of the allied companies as they headed to their new positions. Other than a few desultory probes from enemy light horsemen to the south, the Usurper's army made no move to interfere with the allies' manoeuvres.

Rakh-amn-hotep sipped watered wine from a golden goblet as the army completed its final adjustments along the great plain. Hekhmenukep waited alongside the Rasetran, contemplating the waiting enemy forces.

'Four hours, and they've barely moved,' he said. 'It's as though we don't matter to them at all.'

'Oh, we matter,' Rakh-amn-hotep said, 'but it doesn't profit them to come out and challenge us. Remember Nemuhareb's mistake at the Gates of the Dawn? He could have sat and defended the fortifications at the gates and probably driven us back, but his pride got the better of him. Nagash knows that time is on his side. He's got the fountains at his back. All he has to do is hold us at bay, and the heat will do his work for him.' The Rasetran took another sip of wine. 'That's why we have to risk everything on one, fierce assault,' he said. 'We break through his lines with our first attempt, or probably not at all. Each successive attack will be weaker than the one before.'

A signaller on the starboard rail flashed an acknowledgement to the forces on the ground. The nobleman in charge of the team strode quickly to the waiting kings and bowed deeply, before saying, 'All is in readiness, great ones.'

Rakh-amn-hotep nodded.

'Very well,' he said, and smiled at Hekhmenukep. 'Time to roll the dice,' he said, turning to the signaller. 'Send the order to begin the advance.'

The command was passed among the men, and within moments all of the bronze discs were flashing the signal in hot bursts of light. The kings heard the wail of war-horns on the plain below, and with a muted roar the vast battleline of the eastern armies began their attack.

RAKH-AMN-HOTEP HAD SHIFTED the entire weight of the allied infantry southwards, arraying them against the centre and right flank of the Usurper's host. Ten thousand Rasetran warriors marched in the front ranks, striding shoulder-to-shoulder with their broad wooden shields raised before them. Their dark faces were painted in vivid streaks of yellow, red and white, in the manner of the barbaric lizardmen, and fetishes of feathers and bone joints were bound to the heads of their stone maces. At the rear of each company marched groups of Rasetran archers, clad in heavy, ankle-length coats of lizard hide. Each archer had a slave who paced alongside him, carrying bundles of bronze-tipped arrows so that the bowmen could draw and fire on the move.

Smaller companies of Lybaran light infantry marched behind the Rasetrans, armed with heavy swords and hatchets. They advanced close behind the heavy infantry, like jackals pacing behind a pride of desert lions. Their task was not to confront living foes, but to wield their blades against the bodies of fallen warriors, both allied and friendly, who were left in the wake of the army's advance. Still farther east, the infantry reserves of the army were arrayed in a crescent covering the advancing army's southern flank, watching for signs of a surprise attack from the dunes.

As the battle-lines advanced, the Lybaran catapults went into action, sending rounded stones the size of wagon wheels arcing over the heads of the allied troops. The projectiles ploughed into the packed ranks of the enemy infantry, crushing everything in their path amid sprays of splintered wood, flesh and bone. The screams of wounded and dying men rose above the muted tramp of marching feet.

When the allied companies were two hundred yards from their foes, the feared Zandri archers drew back their bows and darkened the skies with volley after volley of arrows. Bronze arrowheads crackled against the shields of the Rasetran infantry, or buried deep into their thick, scaly coats. Here and there a warrior fell as a reed shaft found its way through a chink in their heavy armour, but soon the Rasetran archers were returning fire against the Zandri bowmen, and the intensity of the enemy fire began to subside.

The enemy archers gave ground before the advancing allied host, continuing to fire until they had exhausted their small store of arrows. Then they retreated behind the safety of their battered infantry companies. The Rasetrans continued their slow, steady advance, conserving their strength in the blistering heat, until the two armies came together in a slow, grinding crash of arms and armour. The enemy infantry met the allied warriors shield-to-shield, jabbing at their foes with long, darting spears, while the Rasetrans hammered away at the lightly armoured troops with their brutal stone-headed weapons.

The hard-bitten jungle warriors sowed terrible carnage among their less-skilled foes, their armour shrugging off all but the strongest blows. The enemy line bowed beneath the onslaught, but before long the heavy infantry began to tire beneath the weight of their gear and the heat of the sun, and the advance began to falter. Enemy reserves streamed to the centre and right, shoring up the Usurper's battleline.

* * *

'THE ADVANCE IS faltering,' Hekhmenukep said. 'Your men can't keep this up for much longer.'

Rakh-amn-hotep rested his hands against the rail of the sky-ship and nodded. He could clearly see that the push on the centre and the enemy right could not succeed, for the heavy infantry was trying to force its way into a veritable sea of enemy troops. The attack had done its job, however, drawing off much of the Usurper's reserve troops, leaving the enemy left flank even more vulnerable than before. The enemy commanders on the ground could not see the concentrations of the opposing armies as he could, and, with the advantage of his god-like vantage point, he knew exactly where and when to strike. Had his foe been anyone else, the Rasetran king might have pitied him.

'Any sign of attack from the south?' he asked.

Hekhmenukep shook his head, saying, 'Nothing yet.'

'Then they've waited too long,' Rakh-amn-hotep said. Satisfied, he turned to the signallers. 'Signal for the attack on the enemy left to commence.'

DOWN ON THE battlefield, the Lybaran scholar-priests read the winking signals and raised their hands to the towering figures before them. Singing incantations and carefully worded commands, they unleashed their charges upon the enemy line.

Timbers creaked and giant mechanisms rattled and groaned as the six giant war machines lumbered forwards against the enemy's left flank. Packs of huge lizardmen and their lumbering war beasts loped in their wake, filling the air with furious shouts and ululating war cries.

The skirmish line of enemy archers faltered at the sight of the advancing war machines, and when the first volley of arrows clattered harmlessly against their wood and bronze frames, the bowmen beat a hasty retreat behind the dubious safety of their spearmen. The Khemri infantry held its ground as the giant engines approached, perhaps trusting in their Eternal King to deliver them.

The giants covered the intervening distance in a few dozen strides and waded into the packed warriors, hurling broken, screaming bodies skywards with every sweep of their legs. Their huge maces swept down like pendulums, carving bloody swathes through the press. Frantic, screaming warriors hurled themselves at the giants, stabbing their spears into the joints between the engines' heavy plates, but their weapons could not penetrate deep enough to hit their vulnerable joints. The war machines never slowed, driving steadily deeper through the shattered enemy companies, and into the deep, bloody furrows ploughed by their feet came the wild lizardmen, who fell upon the stunned warriors with their savage, stone-tipped mauls.

Panic raced like a sandstorm through the enemy's left flank, and the Usurper's broken line reeled backwards in the face of the overwhelming assault. As the Khemri champions tried to re-form their retreating companies the ground beneath them exploded in a shower of rock and churned sand as the Lybaran war scorpions sprang their ambush. Terrified warriors were chopped to pieces by bronze-edged pincers or crushed to pulp by the scorpions' lashing stingers. Within the space of a few minutes, organised resistance collapsed as the Khemri spearmen lost their courage and fled westwards.

As the enemy's left flank collapsed, receding from the giants in a swift-flowing tide, the air overhead was rent with unearthly shrieks and arcs of flickering green flame that rose from catapults concealed in the mist to the rear of the enemy host. Clusters of enchanted, screaming skulls rained down upon the striding giants, shattering against their wood-and-bronze plates in bursts of sorcerous fire. Within moments, two of the huge machines were wreathed in flames as burning fragments found their way through gaps in their armoured plates and ignited their vulnerable skeletons. Their advance slowed as the building heat softened their bronze gear wheels and ate at their bones. Thick copper cables snapped under the building stress, lashing like giant whips and bursting the engines apart from within. A giant with the jackal-headed visage of Djaf died first, blowing apart in a shower of jagged metal and splintered wood as its steam vessel burst in a thunderous explosion. A falcon-headed giant fell next as its bronze knee joints broke apart, toppling the machine forwards onto a dozen retreating Khemri spearmen. Horrified, the Lybaran priests chanted frantically to their war machines, commanding them to withdraw, but not before two more of the giants were struck multiple times and set on fire.

Devastating though the barrage was, it was not enough. As the last two surviving giants withdrew, the lizardman auxiliaries pressed their attack amid the lashing war scorpions, and the enemy's left flank continued to disintegrate. Farther west, trumpets sounded as the Numasi heavy horse were ordered into action to try to save the day.

HEKHMENUKEP UTTERED A stream of vicious curses as the fourth giant shuddered to a stop and blew apart, showering the battlefield with fragments of molten metal.

'I told you they weren't suited for this kind of battle!' he said in dismay. 'The giants were meant as siege weapons, to break down the city walls once we reached Khemri!'

'If we break the Usurper's army here, a siege will be unnecessary,' Rakh-amn-hotep snapped. 'Your machines served us well. The enemy flank is shattered, and victory is within our grasp.' The Rasetran king pointed westward. 'Unleash your sky-boats on the enemy's catapults and take your revenge, Hekhmenukep. It's time to strike the killing blow.' With that, he turned to the signallers and began issuing a third string of orders to the troops on the ground.

The King of Lybaras shook his head sadly at the burning wreckage littering the battlefield to the north-west.

'Such a terrible waste,' he said, watching decades of labour turn to ash before his eyes.

THE NUMASI HORSEMEN knew that something had gone terribly wrong by the frantic sound of the trumpets calling them to battle. Spurring their horses, they crested the ridge to the east and saw devastation and disaster unfolding before them. Undaunted, they closed ranks and charged into the teeth of the enemy advance.

Eight thousand of the finest heavy cavalry in Nehekhara swept down upon the marauding lizardmen, their spear points glittering balefully in the noonday sun. Like an avalanche of flesh and bronze they bore down on the howling barbarians, until the last moment, when the galloping horses caught the acrid stink of the lizardmen and recoiled in confusion and fright. Horsemen cursed and fought their suddenly panicked mounts, and chaos spread through the cavalry's ordered ranks just as the charge crashed home.

Huge lizardmen were dashed to the ground, impaled on spear points or trampled by frenzied horses. Some of the barbarians pulled the screaming animals down with them, their reptilian jaws clamped around the horses' necks. Men were smashed from their saddles by stone mauls or dragged to the ground by powerful, clawed hands. The huge thunder lizards bellowed and lashed at the cavalrymen with their massive tails, crushing man and horse alike.

Like two maddened beasts, the formations tore at one another in a wild, swirling melee. The lizardmen and their war beasts were individually more powerful and resilient, but they were also vastly outnumbered. The master horsemen of Numas quickly regained control of their mounts and pressed their advantage against the barbarians, using the speed of their horses to launch coordinated attacks against their slower foes. One after another, the barbarians sank to the ground, their thick hide pierced by dozens of spears.

Tormented past endurance by the spears of the horse-men, one of the thunder lizards let out a panicked roar and turned tail, thundering back the way it had come. Herd beasts at heart, the rest of the massive creatures fol-lowed suit, chasing after their retreating cousin. The Numasi cavalry, severely mauled by the fight, staggered to a halt and tried to re-order their scattered formation, until an ominous rumble to the east warned them of impend-ing doom.

The Rasetran chariots, two thousand strong, rumbled across the plain at the spent Numasi horsemen. Arrows fell among the exhausted heavy cavalrymen, pitching war-riors from their saddles and killing horses. Filled with dread, their commanders ordered the cavalry to withdraw in the face of the onrushing chariots in the hope of buy-ing time to organise a countercharge, but in short order the withdrawal turned into a full retreat as the decimated warriors lost their courage in the face of the enemy's relentless advance.

Behind the charging Rasetran chariots, five thousand Lybaran and Rasetran heavy cavalry raced across the plain and turned southwards, driving into the enemy's centre. Struck in the flank by the massed cavalry charge, the enemy companies wavered, and then broke. Trumpets sig-nalled frantically from the rear of the Usurper's army, and the remaining reserves rushed forwards to form a rear-guard and cover the army's retreat. Overhead, the sky-boats of Lybaras glided past the fleeing enemy troops, heading for the Usurper's catapults. As they passed above the siege engines, warriors hurled baskets full of stones and sharp pieces of metal over the side, raining destruc-tion down upon the war machines. Panicked by the sudden, deadly rain, the catapult crews broke and ran, fleeing into the concealing mists of the fountains.

Across the plain, the armies of the east raised their bloodied weapons and cheered, shouting the names of their gods into the pale blue sky. Behind the exhausted heavy infantry, the warriors of Lybaras continued their grim work, plying their heavy blades across a vast field littered with the bodies of the dead.

CHEERS RESOUNDED FROM the decks of the sky-boat as the enemy's beleaguered rearguard withdrew under a steady hail of arrow fire into the fountains' concealing mists. Hekhmenukep turned to his ally and bowed in admiration.

'The victory is ours, Rakh-amn-hotep,' he said. 'Your strategy was without flaw.'

The Rasetran king shrugged. 'Who couldn't triumph with machines such as this at their command?' he said, rapping a knuckle against the rail of the floating vessel. 'I could see the enemy's every move laid out before me, as if I was playing a game of Princes and Kings. Perhaps we've found the answer to Nagash's vile sorcery at long last.'

On the plain below, the allied cavalry was pacing after the retreating enemy like a pack of wolves, edging closer and closer to the swirling clouds and their promise of sweet, life-giving moisture. Hekhmenukep gestured towards the horsemen with a wave of his hand. 'Will you order a general pursuit?' he asked.

Rakh-amn-hotep shook his head. 'Much as I would like to ride the enemy into the ground, our troops are tired and half-dead of thirst,' he said, 'and we must see to the bodies of the dead before we press on.' He nodded towards the swirling mists. 'We'll press forwards with the cavalry, seize the fountains, and tend to our wounded by the sacred springs.' The Fountains of Eternal Life, an ancient gift from the Goddess Asaph, were legendary for their healing properties, and only the great River Vitae was more revered in Nehekharan lore. Hekhmenukep nodded in agreement.

'Now that the sky-boats have emptied their holds we could press ahead with the horsemen and take on water while the rest of the army deals with the dead and wounded,' he said. The Rasetran king considered this.

'A reasonable plan,' he said. He waved to the nearest sig-naller. 'Send word to the cavalry and the chariots to continue the advance.'

Orders were relayed to the horsemen and the seven sky-boats drifting at the edges of the mists. As the kings' vessel pulled alongside, the entire armada began a graceful descent into the pearly white clouds. Men crowded around the rails of each ship, eager for the first, blessed caress of cool, damp air.

Rakh-amn-hotep watched the mist rise past the keel of the sky-boat and sweep silently over the rails. It wound around his outstretched arms and passed like a veil across his face, but instead of feeling life-giving moisture against his parched skin, he felt only dry, dead air and the smell of dusty smoke against the back of his throat. Hekhmenukep coughed, and other members of the crew cried out in bewilderment.

Moments later, the sky-boat sank through the layers of mist and broke into open air, less than a hundred feet above the ground. Rakh-amn-hotep blinked his dry, stinging eyes and looked out across the great, hilly basin and its silvery pools of sacred water. What he saw filled him with horror.

The great basin, wrought by a holy union between Asaph and mighty Geheb, contained dozens of irregular pools, lined by winding paths covered in rich, green moss. The sacred, silver waters had been defiled, however. Each pool had been filled with the rotting corpses of the men slain in battle the previous day. Billowing stains of blood and bile desecrated Asaph's life-giving pools, covering their surface in a scum of foulness and corruption. The retreating warriors of the Usurper's host were filing back across the basin. Their former panic had subsided, and their companies were slowly re-forming as they withdrew down the once-sacred paths.

Men fell to their knees aboard the sky-boat, stricken dumb by the enormity of Nagash's crime. Hekhmenukep's hands trembled upon the rail.

'How?' he stammered, unable to tear his gaze away from the desecration. 'How could he do this?'

Rakh-amn-hotep could not answer. No words could suffice.

A vast sea of tents lay across the great basin, surrounded by companies of heavily armoured swordsmen. Concealed from the sun by the fountains' tainted vapours, Nagash's pale-skinned immortals stood in plain view, surrounding a great black tent that crouched like a spider at the centre of the camp.

The Rasetran king stared down at the distant gathering of monsters, and in that instant he felt the weight of a vast and soulless regard, like a cold knife pressed against his skin. For the first time in his life, the warrior-king felt truly afraid.

Then, from the midst of the pale immortals, a whirling column of darkness soared high into the air. It struck the swirling clouds and spread outwards, like a pool of boiling ink. As the leading edge of the wave sped towards the drifting sky-boats, Rakh-amn-hotep heard the rising buzz of locusts.

'Turn us around,' he said breathlessly. 'Do you hear? Turn us around! Hurry!'

Men began shouting all around the king as the swarm of ravening insects swept over the sky-boat. Rakh-amn-hotep staggered, feeling thousands of tiny legs scrabbling at his skin as the wave washed over him. They battered his face, clawing at his eyes and biting at his face. He roared in anger and revulsion, sweeping futilely at the swarm with his arms. Stinging pain lanced across his bare hands and wrists. He staggered backwards and fell to the deck, crunching hundreds of hungry insects beneath him.

Above the raging drone of the swarm and the scream of terrified men, the Rasetran king heard a crackling, tearing noise overhead. Blood streaming down his face, Rakh-amn-hotep clawed the insects from his eyes long enough to glimpse a roiling carpet of locusts ravaging the great bladder that kept the sky-boat aloft. As he watched, the canvas split and unravelled like a rotting carpet, releasing the air spirits trapped within.

There was an ominous creaking of timbers, and then Rakh-amn-hotep felt his stomach lurch as the sky-boat plunged to the ground.

◄ TWENTY ►

The Long, Bitter Road

The Great Desert, in the 63rd year of Ptra the Glorious
(-1744 Imperial Reckoning)

THE SKELETAL HORSEMEN attacked again just before dusk, riding down upon the retreating army with the blood-red sun at their backs. The desiccated horses and their riders seemed to glide across the sands. Their bodies, baked by the desert heat, were nothing but tattered leather, bone and cured sinew, and together they weighed not much more than a living man. Warriors at the head of the column barely had time to shout a warning before the first arrows struck home.

Screams and hoarse cries from the head of the army stirred Akhmen-hotep from his stupor. He and the survivors of the army had been on the march since midnight, fleeing ever deeper into the desert after the nightmarish attack outside Bel Aliad. The enemy cavalry had harried them every step of the way, sweeping through the disordered column at will and leaving a trail of dead and wounded men in their wake. Barely thirty in number, the undead horsemen weren't numerous enough to cause widespread destruction, but what they lacked in numbers they made up for in tireless, hateful determination. Fearful of being overtaken by the vengeful dead of Bel Aliad, Akhmen-hotep had kept the army on the march, all through the night and into the searing heat of the day. Now they staggered drunkenly across the sands, delirious from exhaustion and the merciless lash of the sun.

The king raised his head at the clamour from the front of the host.

'Shields!' he yelled hoarsely as the first of the enemy riders came into view. The skeleton's mount was in full gallop, and Akhmen-hotep could see its shoulders working through ragged holes in its hide and hear the faint slap of its cracked hooves against the soft ground. Ribbons of parchment-like skin flapped like gory pennons from the rider's bleached skull as it raced along the length of the column. Its recurved horn bow was held at the ready. As the king watched, the horseman drew back the string in one smooth motion and loosed an arrow as it shot past one of the army's remaining chariots. There was a blood-curdling scream and one of the chariot's horses collapsed to the ground.

Cursing through parched lips, Akhmen-hotep staggered towards the galloping rider. Shouts filled the air around him, but the king paid them no heed. All that mattered to him at that moment was stopping the damned monster before it killed another of their horses. Roaring in frustration and anger he raised his heavy khopesh and swung at the skeletal rider, but the horseman was still out of reach. His blow went wide and the raider swept past, readying another arrow for a victim further down the line.

'Here I am!' Akhmen-hotep cried as the rider galloped away. 'Turn about and face me, abomination! Slay the King of Ka-Sabar, if you dare–'

Suddenly the king felt a powerful hand clamp around the back of his neck, and he was hauled backwards off his feet as though he were nothing more than a child. A weapon hissed through the air. Akhmen-hotep smelled musty leather and bone dust, and then he heard a terrible *crunch!* Something sharp struck his cheek and glanced away, and then he saw the smashed pieces of a skeletal horse and its rider tumble across the sand in front of him.

'Have a care, great one,' the deep voice of Hashepra, Hierophant of Geheb, rumbled in the king's ear. The huge priest sidled backwards, his hammer at the ready, drawing Akhmen-hotep along with him. 'Master yourself, lest you shake the confidence of your men. We're in a tough enough position as it is.'

Akhmen-hotep struggled against the roar of impotent rage building in his throat. Another enemy horseman rode past, his body pierced by arrows. As the king watched, the creature drew one of the long shafts from its chest, fitted it to its bow and fired it at a living horse. The strange, almost absurd image filled the king with frustration and despair.

'By all the gods, how are we to fight these things?' he whispered hoarsely. 'Every man we kill rises again. Every kinsman we lose turns his dead hands against us.' With an effort, he planted his feet and twisted out of Hashepra's grip. 'And for every one of these monstrosities we slay, ten more spring up in its place.' He turned to the hierophant. 'Tell me, priest, how does a man defeat a foe as numberless as the sands?'

The Hierophant of Geheb stared into the king's eyes for a long moment, and Akhmen-hotep saw a reflection of his own despair in the priest's face.

'The gods alone know,' he said at last, and then he turned away. 'Come back to the chariots, great one. The enemy has passed us by for the moment. It will be dark soon, and there is much for us to discuss.'

Akhmen-hotep watched the priest trudge wearily back to the line of battered chariots less than a dozen yards away. The bleak look in Hashepra's eyes had chilled him to the bone. 'The gods know,' he said, and tried to draw some strength from the words. 'The gods know.'

Dazedly, the king joined Hashepra back at his chariot. During the chaos of the retreat, the war machines had been pressed into service as makeshift wagons to carry whatever supplies they could salvage from the camp, as well as providing transport for wounded priests and nobles. Two figures rested uneasily among sacks of grain and jars of water in the back of the king's chariot. Khalifra, High Priestess of Neru, had been made as comfortable as possible among the cargo. The stub of an arrow jutted from her left shoulder, and her face was drawn and feverish as she slept. Memnet sat beside her, his sallow features bathed in sweat. The fat priest had a damp cloth pressed against Khalifra's brow.

'We must make camp soon,' Memnet was saying as Akhmen-hotep approached. 'The men and animals are past exhaustion. If we continue any further we will kill more men than the enemy will.'

'If we stop, the enemy will attack us in strength,' the king said wearily. 'They will overwhelm us.'

'We don't know if there are any more of them out there besides the damned horsemen,' Hashepra said. 'Great one, we have to stop sooner or later. Better now while we've still got the strength to defend the camp.'

'Also, we must take stock and see how many men we have left,' Memnet pointed out. 'Not to mention our supplies.'

'And we must talk to the Bhagarites,' Hashepra continued. 'We will need to find a supply cache or an oasis soon.'

'All right, all right,' Akhmen-hotep said, raising his hands in surrender. 'We'll camp here, and move on before first light tomorrow. Pass the word to the men.'

With the decision made, the king's strength seemed to leave him. His limbs felt as heavy as lead, and at that moment he wanted nothing more than to crawl into the dubious shade beneath the chariot and sleep. Hashepra began issuing orders to a group of messengers waiting nearby when the sound of hoofbeats approached them from the rear of the column.

Akhmen-hotep whirled, thinking Nagash's horsemen had decided to turn around and strike them again, but even as he raised his blade the king saw that both horse and rider were figures of flesh and blood rather than leather and bone. As the horseman drew near, Akhmen-hotep saw that it was none other than Pakh-amn, and it occurred to the king that he hadn't seen the Master of Horse since the attack the night before.

'Where have you been?' he asked without preamble as the young nobleman reined in his exhausted mount beside the chariot. Pakh-amn's face betrayed a flash of irritation at the king's tone.

'I've been organising a rearguard and taking stock of our situation,' he replied curtly. 'I thought you might like to know the state of our army, great one.' Hashepra bridled at the young noble's peremptory tone, but Akhmen-hotep forestalled him with a wave of his hand.

'Well. Let's have it then,' he said to the Master of Horse.

'We've got two thousand five hundred men left, more or less,' the young noble said, 'though close to a third of them are wounded to one degree or another. No one has any camp gear to speak of, though perhaps a quarter of the men managed to escape camp with a couple of days' worth of food stuffed into their belt-pouches.' Pakh-amn nodded in the direction of the chariots. 'Hopefully you enjoyed better luck with the baggage train before we fled.'

'That remains to be seen,' Akhmen-hotep replied. 'What about the Bhagarites?' Pakh-amn's expression turned grim.

'Whether it was the will of the gods or Nagash's own design, the Bhagarites suffered dearly during the night,' he answered. 'Some of the men swear that the skeletal raiders went out of their way to kill the desert bandits. Out of the hundred that accompanied us from Ka-Sabar, less than twenty remain.' He shrugged. 'Perhaps if they'd still had their swords when the attack began, they could have better defended themselves.' Hashepra's face darkened with rage.

'It's time someone knocked some manners into you, boy,' he said quietly.

'Enough, holy one,' Akhmen-hotep declared. 'Remember what you said about setting an example for the men. The Master of Horse offends no one but his ancestors with such petty behaviour.' Pakh-amn let out a derisive snort.

'Petty?' he said. 'I merely speak the truth. If the king is not strong enough to face it, then he's no true king at all.'

'There is truth, and then there is sedition,' Memnet said. 'The king could have you executed for such talk, Pakh-amn.'

The Master of Horse glared at the Grand Hierophant, and said, 'I can think of perhaps a thousand men who would disagree with your opinion, priest.'

Akhmen-hotep stiffened. Suddenly, Memnet's warning from the night before echoed in his mind. *Who can say what he might do if he found himself in a position of influence over much of the army?*

If he gave the word, Hashepra would strike the young nobleman down with a single blow from his hammer. Just as the command rose to his lips, Pakh-amn turned to him and said, 'Forgive me, great one. Like you, I'm very tired, and my nerves are on edge. But I am happy to say that all is not yet lost.'

'And how is that?' the king asked.

'I have been speaking to the Bhagarite survivors,' the nobleman said. 'They know of a supply cache a day's ride from here.'

'A day's ride is two or more days on foot,' Hashepra countered. 'Half the army will be dead before we get there.' Pakh-amn nodded.

'Unless we empty the chariots and send them ahead to gather supplies,' he said. 'I could take the remaining

Bhagarites as guides and outriders, plus a few hundred picked men. Then in a day's time you march with the rest of the army and meet us halfway back on the return leg. It would be difficult, but not impossible.'

Akhmen-hotep paused, rubbing at the grit surrounding his eyes as he tried to think through the nobleman's plan. It seemed sound... if he could trust the Master of Horse. Could he risk sending off all his chariots and most of his guides under Pakh-amn's command? Even if he chose someone else to lead the expedition, how could he know for certain if the man wasn't one of Pakh-amn's sympathisers? The Master of Horse could then slip away in the night and join his compatriots, leaving the army to its fate and returning safely to Ka-Sabar.

The king looked to his brother for advice. Memnet said nothing, but the look in his dark eyes spoke volumes. Akhmen-hotep sighed and shook his head.

'We can't risk the chariots, or the guides,' he said. 'We'll ration our supplies and head for the oasis as best we can.'

Pakh-amn's eyes widened at the king's decision, but then his jaw clenched in anger.

'So be it,' he said tightly, 'but men will die needlessly as a result. You will regret this decision, Akhmen-hotep. Mark my words.'

The nobleman spun on his heel and strode swiftly to his horse. Akhmen-hotep watched him go, debating the idea of ordering Pakh-amn's arrest. Would arresting him prevent a mutiny, or provoke one?

The next thing he knew, Hashepra was gently shaking his shoulder.

'What shall we do, great one?' the hierophant asked.

Akhmen-hotep shook himself, as though waking from a dream. Pakh-amn's galloping horse was already a long distance away, heading back to the rear of the host.

'Make camp,' the king said dully. 'Then pick some men you trust and have them go over the supplies. We'll start rationing right away. Send runners looking for any servants of Neru that might have survived. We could use a ward to protect the camp once it gets dark.' Hashepra nodded.

'And then?' he asked. The king shrugged.

'Then we try to survive the night,' he said in a hollow voice.

SENSATIONS SLOWLY PENETRATED the darkness: throbbing pain in his chest, shoulders and back, and then the swelling roar of thousands of shouting voices. Cool, slightly oily water lapped against his lower legs, caressing his parched skin. For an instant, his brain was seized with competing sensations of pure terror and giddy relief.

After a moment, the cacophony of noise surrounding Rakh-amn-hotep resolved into the familiar noise of the battlefield. Wounded men screamed all around him, begging for help, while off in the distance hundreds of men shouted lustily for the blood of their foes. The Rasetran king realised in a daze that they were probably referring to him.

Blinking slowly, the king found himself lying on his stomach at the edge of one of the great sacred pools. He couldn't remember how he'd got there. The last thing he knew, he'd watched the sky-ship's air bladder come apart, and felt the deck drop away beneath him as the great craft plunged earthwards.

Wincing, Rakh-amn-hotep got his hands underneath him and tried to push himself upright. A stabbing pain lanced through the right side of his chest. More than likely, he'd cracked a rib at some point during the crash. No doubt he'd been thrown clear when the wooden hull crashed to the ground. By the gods' own grace he'd just managed to clear the deep pool at his feet. Had he landed three feet shorter he would have surely drowned in Asaph's sacred water.

No, not sacred any more, the king corrected himself. With a hiss of revulsion he jerked his feet from the corpse-choked water and wiped at the oily residue of human rot clinging to his skin. This close to the water the stench of corruption was tangible, coating the back of Rakh-amn-hotep's dry throat.

Coughing raggedly, the king rolled over and tried to take stock of his surroundings. The wreckage of the sky-boat lay just ten yards or so away, its shattered timbers partially covered by a tattered shroud of canvas and a carpet of seething, chewing insects. To his horror the king saw struggling figures buried beneath the mass of locusts. One lifted a hand skywards, as though beseeching the gods for help. Three of the man's fingers had been gnawed down to the bone.

Few of the other Lybaran sky-boats had fared any better. Rakh-amn-hotep could see broken hulls scattered across the eastern curve of the great basin, and dozens of dazed and injured men were trying to escape the wreckage.

To the west, waves of sound reverberated across the basin from the massed warriors of the Usurper's host. From what the Rasetran king could tell, the retreating companies had fetched up against Nagash's hidden reserves, and the Usurper's immortal champions were angrily re-forming their ranks. The great mass of disordered troops was the only thing standing between the allied survivors and Nagash's eager companies. That would change in a matter of minutes.

Rakh-amn-hotep staggered over to a group of Lybarans crawling away from the ruins of his sky-boat.

'Where is your king?' he asked hoarsely. 'Where is Hekhmenukep?' When the stunned crewmen stared wordlessly at him, the Rasetran applied his sandal to their backsides. 'On your damned feet!' he ordered. 'We have to get out of here, but no one leaves until Hekhmenukep is found!'

The king's commanding voice sent the crewmen scrambling back the way they'd come, hurriedly searching around the wreckage of the sky-boat.

'Get the wounded moving!' Rakh-amn-hotep called after them. 'Any men who can't move must be carried!'

As the crewmen searched, the king turned his attention to the survivors of the other sky-boats. Many flocked to the sound of his voice, and he put them to work as well. Large swathes of torn canvas were gathered off the ground to provide crude litters for the most seriously wounded, and the king began sending small groups eastwards as soon as they were organised.

'Over here!' one of the Lybarans called, waving frantically. 'He's here! The king is here!'

Hekhmenukep was lying only a few yards from the smashed prow of the sky-boat. Miraculously, he had escaped the ravages of the locust swarm, while two men who had come to earth a few feet closer to the crash had been reduced to glistening skeletons. When Rakh-amn-hotep reached the king, two of Hekhmenukep's subjects were trying to help him to his feet. The Lybaran ruler was pale and hunched with pain, and flecks of bright red foam tinged the corners of his mouth. Rakh-amn-hotep muttered a curse.

'A rib has pierced one of his lungs,' the veteran warrior said. 'Set him on a piece of canvas and get him back to the army as quickly as you can. Don't worry too much about his comfort. Right now, speed is what matters.'

As the crewmen hastened to obey, the air shook with the bellow of war-horns and the mingled voices of thousands of eager warriors. Across the basin, the Usurper's army was on the move once more.

The Rasetran king growled like an old, scarred hound. They had run out of time.

'Get moving,' he said to the remaining men. 'Help the wounded as much as you're able. Now, go!'

The Lybarans needed no further urging, fleeing for their lives in the face of the advancing army. In moments, the king stood alone, in the face of the Usurper's distant horde. Beaten but unbowed, he turned his back on his foes and headed off after his men.

Behind him, the Usurper's warriors let out a wordless roar of bloodlust and surged forwards, breaking ranks in their eagerness to catch up to the Lybarans. The enemy warriors were more than half a mile away, and were forced to follow the twisting trails that surrounded the poisoned fountains, but the same could be said for Rakh-amn-hotep and his men, many of whom could barely move. With every passing moment, the bestial sounds of pursuit grew louder in the king's ears.

Then, up ahead, Rakh-amn-hotep spotted horsemen wending their way carefully among the pools. They were Lybaran light horsemen, the leading edge of the pursuit force that had followed the retreating enemy companies into the basin. As he watched, the horsemen helped their fellows onto the backs of their horses and began to head back the way they'd come. The litter bearers had no choice but to struggle onwards with their burdens, but now they marched under the protective gaze of the light horsemen.

One of the cavalrymen spotted Rakh-amn-hotep and spurred his horse forwards with a shout. He reined in alongside the king and slid from the saddle without hesitation.

'Your champion waits with the Rasetran chariots yonder,' he said breathlessly, nodding his head in the direction of the mists to the east. 'Take my horse, great one. The enemy is nearly upon us.'

Rakh-amn-hotep glanced back the way he'd come and was shocked to see enemy spearmen less than a hundred yards away. 'Get back in the saddle,' he ordered. 'Two can ride as well as one. Besides, I'm like to fall off if I try to ride this beast by myself.'

The cavalryman leapt gratefully back onto his horse's back and with an effort helped the king up behind him. An arrow hissed through the air off to their right, and then another. The horseman hauled on the reins and spurred his mount away from the advancing host. He wove his mount through the press of retreating figures with great skill, occasionally splashing through shallow pools to circumvent larger knots of men.

Many minutes later they reached the far end of the basin and its tendrils of swirling mist. A hundred Rasetran chariots waited there in a kind of rearguard, their narrow wheels and considerable weight preventing them from penetrating further into the basin's rough terrain. Ekhreb waited nearby, ordering litter bearers to load their charges aboard the chariots as they arrived. The champion's expression relaxed considerably when he saw his king approaching.

Rakh-amn-hotep dropped gracelessly from the saddle and clasped the cavalryman's wrist in thanks before walking over to Ekhreb.

'The damned Usurper was a few steps ahead of us all along,' he snarled. 'The battle on the plain was just meant to exhaust us and use up the last of our water. Now he's poisoned the only water source for fifty miles. If we stay here his reserves will break us by nightfall, and then there will be a slaughter.' Ekhreb listened to the dire assessment calmly.

'What would you have us do?' he asked. Rakh-amn-hotep gritted his teeth.

'We retreat again, damn it. Back to Quatar, though the gods alone know how we're going to make it. Nagash will pursue us. He'd be a fool not to. We'll draw him against the walls of the city and try to break him there.'

'What if the Usurper is still thinking a few steps ahead of us?' the champion asked. Rakh-amn-hotep scowled at the champion.

'Well, if it makes you feel any better, we'll all probably be dead of thirst long before that becomes a problem.' he said. Ekhreb chuckled in spite of himself.

'Now look who's the optimist,' he said, and lead the king to his waiting chariot.

* * *

THE TENT FLAPS of heavy canvas swept aside, allowing only the weak grey light of the misty basin into the gloom of Nagash's tent. Raamket hurried inside, grateful to escape even the faint glimmer of Ptra's searing rays. Most of his body was shielded by leather wrappings and armour, leaving only his head and hands exposed. His cloak of human skin fluttered like vulture's wings in his wake as he approached the Undying King and sank to one knee.

'The enemy host is withdrawing, master,' the immortal said. 'What is your command?'

Nagash sat upon the ancient throne of Khemri, displaced from Settra's palace for the first time in centuries. The king's brooding figure was wreathed in the sepulchral tendrils of his ghostly retinue, their faint cries weaving a fearful threnody in the oppressive shadows. The necromancer's vassal kings waited upon Nagash's pleasure: Amn-nasir, the once-proud King of Zandri, sat in a low-backed chair at Nagash's left and drank wine laced with the black lotus, his expression haunted. The twin Kings of Numas sat next to one another on the necromancer's right, whispering apprehensively to one another. At the rear of the tent the Undying King's marble sarcophagus sat beside his queen's. Neferem's sarcophagus was shut. Ghazid, the necromancer's servant, knelt beside the stone coffin and stroked its polished surface with a trembling, wrinkled hand, whispering in a thin, reedy voice.

The Undying King rose to his feet amid a swirl of tormented spirits and strode to the opening of the tent. With a gesture, the mantle of spirits glided forwards and pulled the tent flap aside.

Nagash stared from the shadows into the failing light of day and smiled.

'We march to Quatar,' he declared, 'where we will grind these rebel kings beneath our heel.'

◄ TWENTY-ONE ►

The Elixir of Life

Khemri, the Living City, in the 46th year of Ualatp the
Patient (-1950 Imperial Reckoning)

THE PRIEST KING of Khemri folded his arms and scowled at the large parchment map spread before him.

'Where are they now?' Nagash asked of his vizier.

Arkhan the Black moved quickly around the corner of the long table and stood beside the king. The nobleman referred quickly to a note scrawled on ragged parchment, and then traced his finger along the length of the Great Trade Road, west of Khemri.

'According to the latest reports from our scouts, the Zandri army is here,' he said, pointing to a spot approximately a week's march from the Living City.

The other half a dozen noblemen attending upon the king, including the thuggish Raamket and a weary-looking Shepsu-hur, leaned over the table to better hear Arkhan over the sound of voices and the shuffling of pages in the King's Library. Traditionally a silent, solitary haunt for the king and the royal family, the library occupied almost an entire wing of the palace. In his youth, Nagash spent many years poring over ancient tomes in the library and prowling through the dim, dusty archives in the wing's sub-levels. Now that he was king, the large sandstone chamber had become his chamber of office, where he conducted much of the business of the kingdom.

Though it was already well into the evening, the room was crowded with scribes, messengers and harried-looking slaves, all going about their business under the disapproving glare of the library's senior clerk. It had been much the same for days, ever since the Bhagarite trader had arrived at the palace with valuable news to sell: King Nekumet of Zandri had mustered his warriors and was preparing to liberate the Living City from the clutches of Nagash the Usurper. For the first time in eighteen years, Khemri was at war.

News of the impending attack had not come as a great surprise. Indeed, Nagash had been expecting such a move for quite some time and had been making the necessary preparations. The news of Thutep's fall had spread across Nehekhara like a storm wind, prompting cries of outrage and dismay in the palaces of the other great cities.

It was not so much the act of removing Thutep that was so abhorrent, for the young king had been widely viewed as foolish and naïve, but the fact that Nagash had violated the covenant of the gods by claiming the crown. As firstborn, his life belonged to the gods, and thus he had set a dangerous precedent that the other kings could not abide. To make matters even worse, he had forbidden Thutep's wife, Neferem, to join her husband in the afterlife, as custom demanded, jeopardising the covenant and offering a grave offence to the gods.

Nagash had lost count of the number of angry delegations sent from the holy city of Mahrak to demand his immediate abdication in favour of Thutep's son.

Meanwhile, he suspected, the Hieratic Council had been sending envoys to the other cities in the hope of raising an army to remove him from the throne by force. Until now, however, the Kings of Nehekhara had preferred to bide their time and hope that the gods, or more likely, Khemri's angry populace, would step in and save them the expense of a costly military campaign.

For nine years, the gods had been strangely silent, and the people of Khemri had accepted Nagash's rule with a kind of stunned passivity. His rise to power marked the end of years of plague, and had ushered in an era of calm and stability. The king replenished the ranks of the nobility by elevating prominent members of the merchant class, and suppressed crime through quiet arrangements with the city's criminal elements. Dissenters were quickly identified and dealt with quietly by Raamket's agents, allowing the king free rein to pursue his immediate goals.

Nagash had known from the first that it would only be a matter of time before King Nekumet felt strong enough to march on Khemri. Now the labour of the past few years would be put to the test.

'What have we learned about the composition of the army?' the king inquired. Arkhan consulted his notes again.

'Our scouts report eight thousand foot soldiers, a mix of regular spear companies and barbarian auxiliaries, as well as two thousand archers and fifteen hundred chariots.'

Sidelong stares and uneasy murmurs passed among the noblemen. The Zandri army was nearly twice as large as Khemri's. Nagash nodded thoughtfully.

'King Nekumet has assembled an ideal force to combat ours' he said. 'Clearly his spies have kept him well-informed.' He glanced up at Raamket. 'What of our own troops?'

'The last of our spear companies and archers left the city by mid-afternoon, as you commanded,' the nobleman said. 'The light horsemen and chariots are finishing their final preparations even as we speak.' Nagash acknowledged the report with a curt nod, and then turned to Shepsu-hur.

'And what of your forces?' he asked. The handsome nobleman gave the king a rakish smile.

'All stands in readiness,' he said easily. 'We can leave at any time, great one.'

Nagash studied the map for a few moments more, and then nodded in satisfaction.

'There is nothing more to discuss, then,' he said. 'The cavalry will depart in two hours, as planned. Shepsu-hur, you will leave Khemri an hour after midnight. Be at the rendezvous here,' the king continued, indicating a point along the banks of the River Vitae, 'by dawn.'

Shepsu-hur bowed to the king, and the rest of the noblemen took this as their cue to depart. Arkhan quickly rolled up the map of Nehekhara and departed with a hasty bow. Two hours left precious little time to make ready, and there was still much to be done. Nagash dismissed them from his mind at once, returning his attention to the books and parchments that had been covered by the vizier's map.

Books and scrolls on architecture lay atop a broad sheet depicting a monumental pyramid, larger by far than even the Great Pyramid. The pyramid contained more than a dozen levels of carefully arranged chambers, more than half of which penetrated well below ground level, and the margins of the architectural plan were filled with precise measurements and lists of materials that would go into the pyramid's construction. Tonne upon tonne of black marble, plus hundreds of pounds of silver and jars of crushed gemstone.

The cost of the building materials alone would beggar the great cities of Nehekhara twice over. Yet every bit was absolutely vital, in Nagash's estimation. Based on everything he had learned from the druchii, plus the observations of his experiments over the last decade and a half, it would take nothing less to draw the winds of dark magic to Nehekhara and store their power for his use.

The cost of such an undertaking did not concern him, but was a relatively trivial problem, as far as Nagash was concerned. What confounded him, time and again, were the calculations of labour that would be required to build such a massive edifice. The king traced a fingertip along a series of figures in the lower margin of the plan, arriving once again at the inevitable conclusion: *two hundred to two hundred and fifty years.*

Nagash placed his palms on the tabletop and revisited his calculations once again, trying to find a way to complete his grand design in less than a single lifetime. So keen was his concentration that it was several long minutes before the king realised that the library chamber was completely silent.

Frowning, the king glanced up from his work to find Neferem and her retinue of maidens standing in the centre of the room. The Daughter of the Sun was dressed in her royal finery, complete with the ceremonial headdress and heavy golden sunburst worn by Khemri's queen. Her green eyes were limned with kohl, and her lips had been dusted lightly with crushed pearl, but such adornments seemed cheap compared to Neferem's natural beauty. Not even the cold glare of contempt she focused on the king detracted from her tremendous presence.

Everyone in the chamber: slaves, scholars, even the querulous senior librarians, had fallen to their knees and bent their heads to the floor in her presence.

'Leave us,' Nagash commanded, and the attendants hastened from the room.

The king studied Neferem appraisingly. After almost twenty years she had fully blossomed into the legendary beauty the gods had meant for her to be, and despite himself Nagash felt the hunger of desire all the more keenly.

'I see you've finally put off those damned mourning robes,' he observed. 'You look like a queen once more. Does this mean you've changed your mind?'

Neferem ignored the king's question.

'I want to see my son,' she said. Her voice had deepened over the years, roughened by an ocean of bitter tears.

'That's out of the question,' Nagash said coldly.

'You're taking Sukhet to war with you,' the queen replied, her voice quavering with barely repressed anger. 'He's still just a child, you soulless monster.'

'I'm well aware of Sukhet's age,' the king replied. 'Believe me, I would just as soon leave him here, for he will no doubt be a burden on my retinue during a very difficult campaign, but you give me little choice. How else can I guarantee you won't do something stupid while I'm gone?'

Neferem's eyes shone with tears. Defiantly, she held them back, and spoke with as much dignity as she could muster.

'My place is with my husband,' she said. 'You of all people should know that.'

'You will join him in time, never fear,' Nagash replied. 'How quickly that happens depends entirely on you.'

'I will never marry you!' Neferem cried. The tears came. Hot with rage, they traced streaks of black down her perfect cheeks. 'Your pathetic obsession sickens me. Hold me prisoner in this palace for another hundred years and it will only deepen my hatred of you.'

Nagash was around the table and halfway to the queen before he knew what was happening. His hand was raised, ready to strike. Neferem's maids wailed in terror and despair, lunging forwards to put their bodies between Nagash and their beloved queen. The Daughter of the Sun never flinched, but simply glared at the king as though daring him to strike her.

The king went completely still, legs frozen in mid-stride. He breathed deeply, and forced his fist to unclench.

'Shut up, you braying cows!' Nagash snarled at the whimpering maidens, and then stared hard at the queen. 'Your feelings for me do not matter in the least,' the king said through clenched teeth. 'And we shall see how stubborn you are after fifty years have passed, and your son has forgotten everything about you.' He inched closer. 'The choice is yours, Neferem. Submit to me, now or later.'

A shudder, born of anger and sorrow combined, wracked the queen's body. Black tears fell from her cheeks and spattered on the stone floor, but Neferem did not yield.

'Let me see my son,' she said again. 'Please. Let him have his mother's blessings before he leaves for war.'

Nagash regarded her for a moment, considering her request. He took another step closer, his face mere inches from Neferem's. He looked into the queen's eyes and smiled.

'Sukhet has no need of your blessings,' he said softly. 'He will be at my side the entire time. Think on that while we are away, Neferem, and be content.'

Two HOURS LATER, the last elements of Khemri's small army departed from the Living City in a fanfare of trumpets and the thunder of hooves. Arkhan the Black was given command of the squadrons of light horsemen, while Nagash rode at the head of the chariots, manned by the recently elevated noble sons of the new great houses. By the king's side stood Sukhet, a solemn-looking child of fifteen years who wore his father's ill-fitting armour as he rode into battle. Out through the city's western gate they went, down the Great Trade Road, in full view of however many spies King Nekumet had inside the city. Delegations from the city's temples watched the king depart, their blessings unspoken. Nagash had made no offerings to the gods before leaving for war, nor had he requested the company of the priesthood to support the army. Such a thing, as far as they knew, was unprecedented.

On into the deep desert night they rode, making good time down the broad, paved roadway. It wasn't long before the swift-moving horses caught up with the tail end of the army's infantry. Nagash called a brief halt to impress upon the company commanders the need to make the upcoming rendezvous on time, and then the cavalry pressed on.

An hour after midnight, the horsemen reached the main camp of the Khemri army, close by the banks of the River Vitae. There the king conferred one last time with Arkhan, who would assume command of the entire cavalry force, and then there was nothing to do but wait for the coming dawn.

Shepsu-hur arrived exactly on time, just as the first rays of light were breaking across the Brittle Peaks to the east. The huge, broad-bellied cargo haulers wallowed like hippos on the wide river, their hulls and long, spider-like oars backlit by the rising sun. No sooner had the first of the cargo ships pulled up to shore than the king gave the order to embark.

Over the course of the day, four and a half thousand men struggled through the shallow waters along the riverbank and climbed aboard Shepsu-hur's fleet. By late afternoon all fifteen ships were loaded, leaving just the light horsemen and chariots behind. Arkhan and the cavalry would continue west along the road to harass King Nekumet's forces and hold the attention of his army.

Four nights later, the fleet of cargo haulers slipped unseen past the watch-fires of the Zandri army and continued on to the sea.

THE SHIPS FROM Khemri reached the mouth of the River Vitae at just past dawn of the sixth day and nosed out into the heaving, blue swells of the Great Ocean. From there, it was only a few miles to the harbour of Zandri. The cargo haulers worked their way past the breakwater in a disorderly mob and made for the first empty piers they could find. The bleary-eyed harbour master and his apprentices didn't know what to make of the sudden arrivals at first. Were they part of a slaving expedition or a trading fleet that had arrived ahead of schedule? The ships flew no flags, and were no different in design from the coastal trading ships that Zandri used. So the harbourmaster scratched his head and checked his records, and the first ships had already tied up and were disembarking troops before he realised what was happening and sounded the alarm.

The Khemri army took the city by storm. With its entire army far off to the east, Zandri was virtually defenceless in the face of Nagash's attack. The few companies of the city watch that attempted to contest the landings were broken within an hour, and then Nagash's troops descended upon the helpless inhabitants of the city.

The sack of Zandri lasted for three horrifying days. Nagash's forces systematically looted and burned their way from one end of the city to the other. The great slave markets were emptied and their human chattel loaded onto the Khemri ships. The city's noble houses were pillaged and the families enslaved. Warehouses were emptied of valuable goods until the army's ships could hold no more. The rest were put to the torch, along with two-thirds of the ships tied up in the harbour. Through it all, the embassies of the other great cities took refuge in the city temples and looked on with abject terror as Nagash took his revenge for all the humiliations that King Nekumet had heaped upon Khemri.

On the morning of the fourth day, the traumatised survivors of the city crept furtively out into the streets to find their tormentors gone. The cargo haulers, packed with loot and thousands of slaves, had slipped their moorings and departed during the night. Nagash's army, meanwhile, had passed through Zandri's eastern gate and set out upon the Great Trade Road after King Nekumet and his warriors.

* * *

NAGASH SET A brutal pace for his army, marching them all day and halfway through the night in an effort to catch up with the Zandri forces. They camped by the side of the road and ate whatever they had to hand before catching a few hours' rest. Then, they rose at dawn and started the process again. Along the way they overtook a number of merchant caravans heading east with supplies for the Zandrians and relieved them of their burdens.

Two gruelling weeks passed before the Khemri army's scouts located the fires of the Zandri camp. The enemy's march had been slowed nearly to a crawl by relentless attacks from Arkhan's cavalry troops, and there were signs that their supplies were running low. With all of the Zandri scouts drawn eastwards, searching in the wrong direction for Nagash's army, King Nekumet had no inkling that the bulk of Khemri's forces were camped just a few miles along the road behind his troops.

As the Khemri army settled wearily onto the sands to either side of the road, Nagash ordered his men to erect a tent for him a few hundred yards further west, away from the bulk of the army. Sukhet, the young prince, was left in the care of Raamket, and the king sent Khefru to go and fetch one of the scores of slaves that the army had brought with them from Zandri. The battle would begin in earnest after first light, but Nagash intended for the opening moves to take place in the cold hours of darkness.

Creating the ritual circle was difficult on the uneven ground in the centre of the tent, and reminded Nagash of the near-insurmountable problem he would face on the morrow. His army was still outnumbered two to one, and his men were nearly exhausted by the long march. The use of sorcery would be vital in the coming battle, but how could he draw upon the necessary life force to cast his spells? He would be too far from the battle-line to make use of the deaths of his and Nekumet's men, and an elaborate ritual circle would be difficult to create and maintain on the open ground. It was a problem he had yet to find a solution for.

Nagash had just completed the circle when Khefru returned, dragging a young slave along with him. The young man, a long-limbed northern barbarian, was near catatonic with exhaustion, hunger and fear. He stumbled into the tent like a sacrificial bull, dull-witted and uncomprehending of his fate. The king pictured Khefru slitting the barbarian's throat and emptying his blood into a copper bowl, just like those simpering fools in the Zandri camp.

The king paused, suddenly frowning in thought. Khefru caught the change in his master's demeanour and gave the barbarian a worried glance.

'Is he not suitable?' the priest asked. 'He's strong and healthy, I assure you.'

Nagash waved Khefru to silence. His mind raced, considering the possibilities. The king nodded to himself and dragged his foot through the ritual circle, obliterating its carefully formed lines.

'What are you doing?' Khefru asked, his brow furrowing in confusion.

'Get that tunic off of him,' Nagash ordered. He went to a cedar chest by the tent flap and drew out a brush and a bottle of ink. 'Then go find me a copper bowl. I want to try an experiment.'

The priest shook his head in bemusement, but did as he was commanded. Nagash used a pair of copper needles to freeze the slave in place, and then began to paint the ritual symbols of the Incantation of Reaping directly onto the barbarian's pale skin. By the time Khefru returned with a suitable bowl, the slave's body was covered in hieroglyphic patterns.

'What in the name of all the gods?' Khefru asked, staring at the slave's body.

'The name of the gods, indeed,' Nagash said. During the process he'd made refinements to the ritual markings, tailoring the incantation to the new process he'd envisioned. 'The answer was right in front of me all along, Khefru. The priests drain the blood of the sacrificial bull and share it with the king and his men before battle. Why?' Khefru frowned thoughtfully.

'So that they can receive the benefits of the ritual,' he said.

'Exactly,' Nagash said. 'And why the blood? Because it contains the animal's life essence. Do you see? The power lies in the blood!' The necromancer straightened and drew his curved dagger. 'Come here and ready the bowl.'

The king reached up and grabbed a handful of the slave's hair, bending the head forwards and placing the blade of the knife under his chin. Khefru had just enough time to get the bowl in position before Nagash slit the barbarian's throat from ear to ear. As the steaming blood poured into the bowl he began to chant the Incantation of Reaping.

Moments later the slave's lifeless body toppled onto the ground. Nagash wiped the dagger clean using the slave's hair, and then held a trembling hand over the bowl. His eyes lit with avarice.

'I can feel it,' he whispered. 'The power is there, in the blood!' He held out his hands. 'Give it to me! Quickly!'

Khefru offered up the bowl, and without hesitation Nagash brought it to his lips. It was hot and bitter, dribbling over his chin and staining his robes, but the taste set his nerves on fire. The slave's vigour flooded into him, filling the king with strength unlike any he'd known before. Greedily, he took deeper and deeper draughts, until the blood ran in thick streams down his chest.

Nagash let the empty bowl tumble from his fingers. Power radiated from his skin like heat from a forge.

'More,' he hissed. 'More!' The look he turned upon Khefru sent the young priest stumbling from the tent in terror.

Burning with stolen vitality, Nagash threw back his head and uttered a terrible, triumphant laugh. Then he began to weave the incantations that would seal Zandri's doom.

━━◄ TWENTY-TWO ►━━

Spirits of the Howling Wastes

The Great Desert, in the 63rd year of Ptra the Glorious
(-1744 Imperial Reckoning)

THE SKELETAL HORSEMEN attacked the army's makeshift
camp many times over the course of their first night in the
desert, and did so every night thereafter.

They would ride out of the darkness, dry hoofbeats
near-silent on the shifting sands, and fire a volley or
two of arrows into the press of men before whirling
around and vanishing back into the night. Warriors
would jerk awake at the screams of wounded men and
scramble to their feet, believing that the undead hordes
of Bel Aliad had caught up with them at last. Reeling
with exhaustion, shivering with fear, they would clutch
their weapons in white-knuckled hands and search
frantically for the source of the attack, but by then the
enemy was long gone. Cold and frustrated, the men of
the Bronze Host eventually wrapped themselves back in
their short cloaks and tried to calm down enough to

sleep once more. Then, an hour or two later, the horse-men would attack once again.

Sometimes the riders fired at random into the camp. Other times they sought out specific targets. They shot at any priest they could see, especially the handful of Neru's acolytes who had survived the attack outside Bel Aliad. The ward they laid around the camp kept the undead riders at a distance, but the magical invocation had to be maintained in a constant, nightly vigil. Akhmen-hotep was forced to send a heavily armoured escort with the acolytes to shield them from enemy arrows as they walked the perimeter beneath the gleaming moon.

It was a hazardous duty, and one or more of the acolytes' bodyguards were wounded each night, but without the protective ward the army was vulnerable to more than just Nagash's horsemen. The Great Desert was home to a multitude of hungry and malevolent spirits that preyed upon the living, and their howls could be heard among the dunes when the moon's light was dim.

Each dawn, the army would find itself a little diminished from the day before. Wounded men died in the night, overcome by their wounds or sickened by the chill air. Khalifra's fever worsened as an infection set in around the barbed arrow in her shoulder. She lingered, raving, for four more days, but despite Memnet's constant ministrations the high priestess finally succumbed. Her body was prepared as best as her acolytes could manage and wrapped in scavenged linen for the long journey home.

The bodies of the common warriors were removed from the camp by a special detail overseen by Hashepra, the Hierophant of Geheb. Out of sight of their comrades, the men methodically dismembered the corpses and removed their organs, so that Nagash could not add them to his blasphemous ranks. Hashepra commended their spirits to Djaf and Usirian, and their mutilated bodies were buried beneath the sands.

There was little water and even less food to keep the army going. Within three days they had to begin butchering the wounded horses and ration the meat carefully so that every warrior had at least something to eat. Nothing was wasted. Even the blood was collected carefully in Geheb's great sacrificial bowls and given to the men a swallow at a time. The constant night attacks nevertheless took their toll, sapping the men's strength and slowing their pace.

It was eight days before the Bronze Host reached the first of the Bhagarite supply caches. The surviving desert raiders had turned sullen and belligerent since the retreat from Bel Aliad. They were furious with the king for taking their swords and leaving them to the mercy of the city's undead citizens, and yet paradoxically resentful that they had not yet been allowed to die and join their kin, as they'd expected. The warriors of the host regarded them with naked hostility, blaming the Bhagarites more than Nagash for their present misery. After one of the guides was set upon by a gang of warrior-aspirants and nearly beaten to death, the king was forced to use his Ushabti to guard the Bhagarites from his warriors.

After more than a week in the desert, hungry and fleeing from an implacable army of the dead, Akhmen-hotep's men were becoming their own worst enemies.

'How much?' the king asked, sitting in the cool shade cast by the gully wall. His voice was a dry, rasping croak, and his lips were cracked by thirst. Like the rest of the army, he drank only three cups of water per day, and the last drink had been more than four hours ago.

The army had reached the third of the Bhagarite supply caches: a series of hidden caves among the narrow defiles of a range of sheer sandstone cliffs that rose like weathered monuments from the desert sands. When they'd arrived the warriors had scrambled like lizards into the shade of the twisting gullies, heedless of the serpents and scorpions that no doubt sheltered beneath the rubble at the base of the cliffs. Many of the warriors had cast aside their heavy bronze armour days ago, next went the shields, and even their polished helmets. Some didn't even carry weapons any longer, having divested themselves of every bit of unnecessary weight that they could manage. They were ragged, filthy and dull-eyed, little more than animals preoccupied with survival in a hostile land. Only the king's Ushabti maintained their weapons and harness, still true to their sacred oaths of service to their god and their king. The leonine devoted seemed untouched by the privations of the brutal retreat, sustained in body if not in spirit by the gifts of mighty Geheb. They were the king's strong right hand, and perhaps the only thing that held the army together after all that it had suffered.

Hashepra sighed, wiping dirt from his hands, and glanced over his shoulder at the low cave gaping on the far side of the gully wall.

'There's a spring inside, thank the gods, but only eight jars of grain,' he said.

Akhmen-hotep fought to hide his disappointment. Beside him, Memnet shifted silently on his haunches. The Grand Hierophant had lost a great deal of weight over the course of the campaign. His once-round face was sunken-cheeked, and his wide girth had shrunk so quickly that the skin hung from his waist like a half-empty sack. Though he could have claimed a greater share of the food as his proper due, the high priest had taken even less than the king. If anything, the nightmarish journey across the sands seemed to have made the Grand Hierophant stronger and more assured than ever before, and Akhmen-hotep had found himself depending heavily on his brother as the situation worsened.

'The caches are getting smaller,' the king said wearily. Hashepra nodded.

'Honestly, I don't think the Bhagarites expected to live long enough to worry about a return trip,' he said. 'I expect we exhausted the major caches on the way to Bel Aliad. All that's left are bandit hideouts like this one.'

Akhmen-hotep ran a wrinkled hand over his face, wincing as he brushed the sores on his forehead and cheeks.

'Eight jars won't last us more than a couple of days. How far to the next cache?'

The Hierophant of Geheb grimaced, and said, 'Three days, more or less, but the Bhagarites say it lies north of here, not east.'

'And the closest one further eastward?'

'A week at least, they said.'

The king shook his head.

'We'll have to kill more of the horses. How many are left?' he asked. Hashepra paused, trying to think. Memnet raised his head and cleared his throat with a hoarse cough.

'Twelve,' he said.

'Twelve horses, out of a thousand,' Akhmen-hotep murmured, musing bitterly on so much lost wealth. The retreat had been more ruinous than any battlefield defeat. The king couldn't imagine how his city would recover.

'The Bhagarites still have twenty,' Memnet replied. 'We could start with them instead.'

'The horsemen would sooner give up their right arms,' the king said, 'and the horses are the only thing we have that ensures their cooperation.'

Hashepra sank down onto his haunches beside the king.

'The men won't see it that way,' he said quietly. 'They already grumble that the Bhagarite horses are being fed while the army goes hungry. Soon you might be forced to put a guard upon them as well.'

Akhmen-hotep glanced worriedly at the priest, and asked, 'Have things got as bad as that?' Hashepra shrugged his powerful shoulders.

'It's hard to tell,' he said. 'My acolytes have heard some talk here and there. The men are hungry and afraid. They don't trust the Bhagarites, and they resent your protection of them.'

'But that's madness,' the king hissed. 'I don't like it any better than anyone else, but without the Bhagarites we won't make it out of the desert alive.'

'This doesn't have anything to do with logic, great one,' Hashepra said, shaking his head. 'The men are barely rational at this point.'

'No.' Memnet interjected. 'It's not the men who are the problem. It's Pakh-amn. He's turning them against you, brother, and you're letting him do it.'

Akhmen-hotep scowled at the ground between his feet. He hadn't seen very much of the Master of Horse since their first night in the desert. The young nobleman kept to the back of the army, claiming that he maintained a rearguard in case Nagash attacked the column in force, but it had been weeks, and such a threat had yet to materialise.

Hashepra eyed Memnet dubiously, and said, 'Pakh-amn is an arrogant rogue, perhaps, but no traitor. He's served the king ably since we left Ka-Sabar.'

'Has he? I wonder,' the Grand Hierophant said. 'He enjoys the admiration of the warriors, without being forced to make the difficult decisions to keep the army alive. Has he made any effort at all to curtail the men's resentments?'

Hashepra had no answer to the priest's question. Akhmen-hotep set his jaw stubbornly. 'A mutiny wouldn't improve our odds of survival,' he protested.

'Pakh-amn doesn't want an army; he wants a throne,' Memnet said. 'He wouldn't care if he walked out of the desert alone, so long as Ka-Sabar was his.'

'Enough!' the king snapped, cutting off his brother with a curt wave of his hand. 'I've heard this all before. If Pakh-amn means to move against me, let him come. In the meantime, let's clean out this cache and move on. We're wasting precious time.'

The king climbed unsteadily to his feet. As one, his Ushabti rose gracefully from the shadows and followed along in Akhmen-hotep's wake as he made his way back to the army's remaining chariots. Hashepra watched the king go, his expression thoughtful.

'There is something sinister at work here,' he mused. 'The acolytes of Neru have found places where their nightly wards have been tampered with. Someone is stealing out of the camp late at night, but so far the sentries have been unable to catch who it is.'

Memnet glanced up at Hashepra, his expression intent.

'Have you told the king?' he asked.

'Not yet,' the hierophant said. 'I have no interest in starting a witch hunt. The army's morale is fragile enough as it is. My acolytes and I are investigating the matter quietly. Tell me, do you have any evidence of Pakh-amn's intentions?'

'No,' Memnet said, shaking his head. 'The Master of Horse is too clever for that. All we can do is watch for signs that he is about to make his move. I fear that we will have little warning, which is why I have begged my brother to take action before it is too late.'

Hashepra nodded.

'Well, now at least I have a direction to look in,' he said, rising to his feet. 'I'll keep a close eye on Pakh-amn and see what the man is up to. Perhaps I can uncover enough evidence to expose him.'

'I will pray to the gods for your success, holy one,' Memnet said, nodding, but the Grand Hierophant did not sound too hopeful.

THREE DAYS LATER, Hashepra was dead. His acolytes found him in the early hours of the morning, wrapped tightly in his cloak. When they unwound the tattered fabric they discovered a giant black scorpion nestled in the hollow between the hierophant's shoulder and neck. He had not been the first man to perish in such a way since the retreat began, for Sokth's children were fond of taking refuge among the living and tormenting them with their terrible stings. The venom of the black scorpion turned the body as rigid as stone, and Hashepra had died in agonising silence, unable to make a single sound as the poison worked its way to his heart.

The news of Hashepra's death filled the rest of the army with superstitious dread, and men took to giving offerings to Sokth from their already meagre rations, in the hope that the God of Poisoners would spare them. Akhmen-hotep tried to prevent the practice, arguing that fear was a poison all its own, but the men would not listen, and thus grew weaker still.

In the end, the king was forced to slaughter four more of the precious horses and ration the meat and blood carefully to get the army to the next bandit cache, only to find that the caves had been emptied a long time before. The anger and despair among the men had been palpable, and resentment against the Bhagarites nearly led to a riot. Only the king's Ushabti managed to keep the desert guides alive. That night, however, two of their horses were killed and butchered, evincing wails of horror and bitter curses from the desert horsemen when the bones were discovered the following morning. The perpetrators of the deed remained a mystery.

On the night of their fifteenth day in the desert, the acolytes of Neru and their exhausted bodyguards were slain in a brutal ambush just before dawn. The men, well-practised in watching for signs of mounted attackers, were caught unawares when a dozen skeletal archers rose from the sands on the other side of the camp's protective ward and fired into their midst. The heavy infantry were the first to die, shot through the throat or pierced in the back at nearly point-blank range. Then the ambushers turned their bows on the fleeing acolytes. By the time reinforcements arrived the skeletons had disappeared, and the army had lost what little protection it had against the hungry night.

From that point forward, Akhmen-hotep was forced to keep half the army awake while the other half snatched a few hours' sleep, rotating the groups every four hours. Attacks from the skeletal horsemen continued, and casualties mounted. Warriors who were caught sleeping on watch forfeited their food ration for the next day, which was tantamount to a death sentence. With so few chariots remaining, men who could no longer march had to be left behind.

Slowly but surely, the spirits of the desert closed in. Nightmares plagued the sleeping men, and strange figures stalked the edges of the camp beneath the moonlight. Men sometimes rose from sleep and tried to walk off into the sands, swearing they heard the voices of their wives or children. Those who succeeded were never seen again.

The Bhagarites led the army to one empty cache after another, and bore the king's recriminations with looks of sullen contempt. The number of horses dwindled, until by the twenty-fourth day the last of the chariot pullers was dead. According to the guides, the next cache was more than five days away. The Bhagarites would no longer say for certain how many more days it would take for them to reach the far side of the desert.

Days passed, and the rations dwindled. Groups of men began lurking around the picket line where the last Bhagarite horses were kept, despite the warning glares of the Ushabti who had been set to guard them. Desperate as they were, none of the warriors dared to try their luck against the devoted, but the same could not be said of the Bhagarites.

On the thirtieth night of the retreat, while strange, savage creatures paced and howled in the darkness beyond the edge of the camp, the desert raiders commended themselves to Khsar and slipped away from the handful of Ushabti that still guarded them. Though the devoted were more than capable of fending off the advances of their starving kinsmen, their powers were not equal to the guile and stealth of the Bhagarites, who were horse thieves of nearly supernatural skill. The raiders had reached the pickets and climbed bareback onto their mounts before the devoted knew what was happening.

Shouts of alarm rang out across the camp as the desert riders spurred their beloved horses past the surprised bodyguards out into the sands. A few of the men tried to chase after the riders, but none got very far. Khsar's divine animals were still as swift as the desert wind, and fled like smoke from the warriors' outstretched hands. Their riders, free at last, threw back their heads and stretched their arms up to the sky, feeling the pounding of the hooves and the whisper of the wind against their skin one last time.

Without food or water, the last men of Bhagar and their beloved horses rode into the trackless desert, commending themselves into the embrace of their faceless god.

AFTER THE MEN of Bhagar were gone, there was nothing left but to march eastwards and pray to the gods for deliverance.

The army dwindled swiftly, like grains of sand spilling from a broken glass. Men died in the night, taken by madness or hunger, or simply fell to the ground during the march and refused to get up again. The hostility of the warriors subsided, along with all other emotions. They had been emptied of thought and feeling by the desert, and now waited only to die.

Then, when the Bronze Host was at its weakest, Nagash's horsemen struck the deadliest blow of all. On the night of the thirty-second day they slipped easily past the unseeing sentries and left their handiwork to be discovered by the stunned warriors at the first light of dawn.

Ten jars of grain and fifteen jars of water were left in plain sight, distributed evenly around the ragged camp. The men fell upon them in a frenzy. When the jars were empty, they broke apart the thick vessels and licked the insides clean.

Then, with a little food in their bellies, the warriors of the Bronze Host sat down and thought about what the strange gift meant.

AKHMEN-HOTEP AWOKE with a start. Overhead, the night sky was bright and clear, scattered with a sweep of glittering stars.

He hadn't meant to sleep. The king sat up, blinking owlishly into the darkness. A handful of his Ushabti surrounded him, staring watchfully around the camp. The rest were walking the perimeter, alert for the enemy's next move. If the skeletons meant to repeat the tactic of the night before, the king meant to stop it.

His bodyguards were under strict orders to drive off the skeletons and destroy any food or water they left behind. Akhmen-hotep knew that it was the only way to deal with the danger. The rations were deadlier than any spear or knife. With them, Nagash could tear the Bronze Host asunder.

Suddenly, three of the Ushabti rose to their feet, blades at the ready. A figure was approaching, picking his way carefully past knots of sleeping men. As he drew near, the king saw that it was Memnet. Waving for the devoted to relax, the king rose to meet his brother.

Akhmen-hotep saw that the Grand Hierophant was upset. His haggard face was pale, and his eyes were wide with fear.

'The time has come,' he whispered. 'They are making their move even now!'

Fear, and worse, a terrible despair, swept through the king.

'Who?' he asked.

Memnet wrung his shaking hands, saying, 'A score of lesser nobles and their men, a hundred warriors, perhaps more. The water and food were the last straw. They believe that if they treat with Nagash they will be allowed to return to Ka-Sabar in peace.'

Akhmen-hotep nodded grimly. If he summoned all of his bodyguards, he could cut the heart out of the conspiracy. A dozen Ushabti had little to fear from a hundred starving warriors.

'Where is Pakh-amn?' he asked.

'Here I am,' the Master of Horse answered.

Pakh-amn and a dozen noblemen were approaching the king and his guards with weapons in their hands. The young nobleman's face was taut with anger.

'Your men have turned against you, great one,' he declared. 'The consequences of your folly have caught up with you at last.'

Akhmen-hotep heard the sounds of fighting and the screams of dying warriors echo from across the camp. His bodyguards were under attack by the men they had been trying to protect.

'Did you think to cut my throat while I slept?' he snarled at Pakh-amn. 'Or did you plan to give me as a gift to your new master in Khemri?' The accusation struck the young nobleman like a blow. He paused, his expression stricken. Seizing the opportunity, the king reached for his sword. 'Kill them!' he commanded his Ushabti, and the five bodyguards charged forwards without hesitation, their ritual blades flashing.

Shouts of alarm and the clash of blades filled the air as Pakh-amn and the noblemen recoiled from the Ushabti's fierce assault. Men fell like wheat before the blades of the devoted, cut down by blurring strokes that sliced effortlessly through their armour. Pakh-amn fought furiously, shouting curses as he turned aside one attack after another. A ritual blade landed a glancing blow against his sword-arm, and then another bit deep into his thigh. The nobleman staggered, but fought on, parrying furiously as blood poured over his knee and spattered onto the sands.

Within moments Pakh-amn's warriors had been cut down. The Master of Horse lasted a few seconds more, but it was clear that the wound in his leg had cut the artery and his life was draining away. He stumbled, and an Ushabti's sword cut deep into his chest. With a groan, Pakh-amn sank slowly to the ground.

Akhmen-hotep walked over to the fallen nobleman. His heart was heavy, but his face was a mask of rage.

'Go and aid your brothers,' he told the devoted. 'Return to me as swiftly as you can.' With a snarl he kicked the sword from Pakh-amn's hand. 'I'll deal with this one.'

The Ushabti raced silently into the darkness. Akhmen-hotep watched the pulse of blood streaming from Pakh-amn's leg steadily weaken. The Master of Horse stood on the threshold between this world and the next.

'You damned fool,' Akhmen-hotep said. 'I would have honoured you when we returned to Ka-Sabar. Why couldn't you have settled for that? Why did you have to try to claim my throne as well?' A strange expression came over Pakh-amn's bloodless face.

'You've gone…' the young nobleman whispered, blood leaking from the corner of his mouth, 'You've gone mad… great one. The gods have… abandoned you… at last. I came… to save you.'

The king's angry expression faltered.

'You're lying,' he said. 'I know what you've planned. Memnet warned me.' He turned to his brother. 'Tell him–'

The knife felt cold as it slid into his chest. The pain was breathtaking. Akhmen-hotep's mouth opened in shock as he stared into his brother's eyes.

Memnet, once the Grand Hierophant of Ptra, glared angrily at his brother.

'I tried to tell you,' he said. 'I tried. Back at Bel Aliad, do you remember? The old ways are gone, brother. Nagash has become the master of death. He has overthrown the gods! If we are to prosper, we must worship him. Why couldn't you see that?'

The king's knees buckled. He fell, dragging Memnet's knife from his trembling hands. Akhmen-hotep landed on his back, next to Pakh-amn's body. The Master of

Horse was staring skyward, the tracks of his tears drying at the corners of his dead eyes.

The Priest-King of Ka-Sabar turned his eyes to the stars, seeking the faces of his gods.

ARKHAN THE BLACK rode out of the desert with a hundred of his horsemen at his back. The fighting in the camp had ended. The Ushabti had wrought a fearsome vengeance for the death of their king before they too had succumbed. Bodies lay everywhere, providing bloody testament to the Bronze Host's last battle. The vizier bared his black teeth in a gruesome smile.

Men prostrated themselves as the immortal and his retinue approached, cowering and trembling with terror. Some clawed at their faces and moaned like children, their sanity having fled at last. Of the four thousand warriors that had followed Akhmen-hotep on his ill-fated expedition, less than five hundred still survived.

The immortal guided his undead mount down a long, corpse-choked lane that ran all the way to the centre of the camp. Memnet the traitor awaited him there, standing over the body of his brother. Blood still stained the fallen priest's hands.

Arkhan reined in his decaying horse before Memnet and gave the wretch a haughty stare.

'Kneel before the Undying King of Khemri,' he commanded.

Memnet flinched at Arkhan's voice, but he raised his head in a gesture of defiance.

'I kneel only before my master,' the traitor said, 'and you are not him, Arkhan the Black.'

The immortal chuckled. Suddenly, a harsh, rasping wind rose among the company of skeletons at his back. Memnet first took the sound to be a kind of laughter, and perhaps it was, but the sound came not from desiccated throats, but from the stirring of insects that poured from empty eye sockets and gaping mouths, or crawled from the depths of ragged wounds. The swarm took flight, swirling into a column of seething life that descended before Memnet and assumed the image of Nagash.

'Bow before your master,' rasped the voice of the necromancer.

Memnet fell to his knees with a cry of fear, saying, 'I hear you, mighty one! I hear and obey! All has been done as you commanded,' he said, gesturing to the body of the king. 'See? Akhmen-hotep, your hated foe, is no more!' The head of the construct seemed to regard the dead king, and then turned to face Memnet once more.

'You have done well. Now rise, and claim your reward,' he said. Wringing his hands, Memnet struggled to his feet. Arkhan dismounted and stepped forwards with a sneer of contempt. Reluctantly he held out a vial of red liquid.

'Immortality is yours,' the king said. 'Take it, and go forth to rule Ka-Sabar in my name.'

Memnet took the vial and gazed at its contents with a mixture of awe and revulsion. 'As you command, Undying One,' he replied. 'My men will require food and water to complete our march.' Arkhan threw back his head and laughed. Memnet cringed at the awful sound.

'We have given you all the food we had,' he said coldly. 'Fear not. Your warriors will soon have no need for it.'

'Do you remember all I taught you?' the necromancer asked.

'I remember,' Memnet replied. 'All the dreams... they are still locked in my head. I know the incantations, master, every line, every syllable.'

'Then drink the elixir, and power over the dead will be yours,' Nagash declared. 'Drink. Your army awaits.'

Memnet stared at the vial for a moment longer, and then pulled off the stopper and drank the elixir in one swallow. A shudder wracked his wasted frame, and with a cry he fell to the ground, writhing and convulsing as the elixir burned through his veins.

Arkhan turned away from the spectacle with an expression of disgust. He looked westwards, where the rest of Memnet's army was slowly approaching over the dunes. All the corpses of Bel Aliad, men, women and children, plus the city's slaughtered mercenaries and the Bronze Host's battlefield dead, shuffled silently across the sands. The desert sun had rendered them down to nothing more than scraps of leathery flesh and bleached bone, and they numbered in the thousands.

The image of Nagash wavered and broke apart, transforming once again into a column of rasping, whirling insect life. It sped across the sands, engulfing Arkhan's form, and then like a desert cyclone it recoiled into the night sky, taking the immortal with it.

When Memnet's senses finally returned he was alone except for the broken souls of his brother's army and the raw, grinning faces of his own.

◄ TWENTY-THREE ►

The White Gates

The Western Trade Road, near Quatar, the City of the Dead, in the 63rd year of Ptra the Glorious (-1744 Imperial Reckoning)

LIKE A WOUNDED giant, the allied army stumbled and lurched its way along the winding road back to Quatar, leaving a trail of flesh and blood with each ponderous step.

Rakh-amn-hotep kept the army in camp during the worst heat of the day and on the march at night, believing that the Usurper's pursuing army couldn't manage a major attack beneath Ptra's blazing sun. There had been probing attacks by Numasi cavalry at dawn and dusk, but each time they were rebuffed with little loss. Nagash's main force, as far as the Rasetran king could gather, was at least half a day's march to their west, following them doggedly along the trade road.

Rakh-amn-hotep believed that Nagash was biding his time, like a jackal waits for its prey to weaken in the desert heat before closing in for the kill.

The defeat at the Fountains of Eternal Life haunted the Rasetran king, a man who had spent his entire adult life on the battlefield. He had plotted and planned the western march for more than two years, and in the end Rakh-amn-hotep had discovered that he wasn't even fighting the same sort of battle that his enemy was. He had read all the accounts of the battle at Zedri and believed himself a better general than either Nagash or Akhmenhotep, but he had still made the fatal error of fighting the Usurper as though he were a mortal king in command of a civilised army.

Nagash, however, was not swayed by furious assaults or swift cavalry movements. The thought of seeing thousands of his citizens, the lifeblood of his city, cut down on the battlefield was little more than an irritation to him. He could suffer blows that would have crushed a mortal king, only to rise once more.

Rakh-amn-hotep had begun to despair that they would ever be rid of Nagash.

More than three weeks after the battle outside the Fountains, the king could only think of keeping the army alive for one more day. The retreat had been a bitter, gruelling ordeal, without a doubt the hardest march of Rakh-amn-hotep's long life. Surviving those first days after the battle had been the hardest. With the water casks empty, the king had ordered his Ushabti to comb the army for every drop of liquid they could find. They confiscated all the remaining wine carried by the army's noblemen, and all the sacrificial libations brought by their multitude of priests.

The cavalrymen kept themselves alive by turning to the old bandit trick of drinking a cupful of their horses' blood each day. Even so, the warriors and animals of the host weakened quickly, and many of the wounded succumbed within days. It was only by the constant efforts of the Lybaran priests that their king, Hekhmenukep, still clung to life.

With the Lybaran sky-boats destroyed by Nagash's sorcery, the allied army paid the price of travelling without a proper baggage train. There were few wagons to draw upon, forcing Rakh-amn-hotep to send detachments of light cavalry on a long, dangerous march off to the north to try to draw water from the River Vitae, many leagues away. The cavalrymen were harassed by Numasi horsemen the entire way, but their courage and determination kept the army going long past the point of collapse.

Still, both armies had suffered greatly in men, animals and materiel. The Lybarans had seen every one of their war machines destroyed, for those that had survived the battle had exhausted their energies and couldn't keep pace with the army's swift retreat. Rather than allow the constructs to fall into the Usurper's hands, the army's engineers had breached the binding wards that kept the machines' fire-spirits in place. The resulting eruptions blew the engines apart in thunderous blasts of wood, metal and steam. Some of the senior Lybaran engineers, men who had devoted much of their lives to creating these wondrous machines, gave themselves up to the fires.

The Rasetrans suffered as well, particularly their jungle auxiliaries. The rationing of water amounted to a virtual death sentence for the giant thunder lizards, whose bodies were already taxed near to breaking point by the dry climate. The last of the great beasts died within a week after the battle, and the numbers of lizardmen dwindled swiftly thereafter. During the long night marches the chill desert air carried the eerie, keening sounds of the barbarians' death songs as they mourned the loss of their kin. The song died away a bit at a time, each and every night, until finally it was heard no more.

All that remained of the once-proud allied army was a bedraggled horde of wasted men and horses, and Rakh-amn-hotep had to concern himself with keeping his warriors from casting away their heavy weapons and armour to lighten their load on the march. He had already instituted severe punishments for warriors who were found to have abandoned their wargear, and still, each night the rearguard came upon bundles of leather armour and helmets, bronze swords and spears. The king would have begun ordering the offenders impaled if he'd had any wood to spare. He would be damned if he got the army back to Quatar only to find that they'd thrown away all the tools they would need to keep the city out of Nagash's hands.

The army was close to the White City, thank the gods, and the Brittle Peaks dominated the eastern horizon, their jagged flanks a dull black against the deep blue vault of the heavens.

Rakh-amn-hotep's chariot was heading westwards, back along the army's long, sinuous line of march. The king spent most every night ranging back and forth along the length of the allied host, checking the state of the companies and reminding the nobles of their responsibilities. It was a routine born of long habit, forged in the jungle campaigns south of Rasetra, and it had served the king well in the past.

They were nearly at the centre of the slowly marching column, passing alongside what was left of the baggage train and the huge wagons of the Lybaran court. Priests paced alongside the creaking wagon that held Hekhmenukep, their heads bowed as they prayed for the king's survival. As Rakh-amn-hotep's chariot rumbled past, one of the holy men straightened and beckoned to the king, nearly stepping out into the chariot's path.

Rakh-amn-hotep stifled a disapproving frown and touched the chariot driver on the shoulder, signalling him to stop. The weary horses needed little encouragement, their heads drooping as they snuffled about in the dust in search of something that might contain a few drops of moisture.

The Rasetran king squinted in the darkness at the approaching priest.

'Nebunefer?' he said, recognising the envoy from Mahrak. 'Since when did you become a healer?'

'One doesn't need the gift of healing to pray for the health of a great king,' the old priest said stiffly. His voice was rough and leathery, and his haggard face seemed even more careworn and stern after the privations of the long retreat, but the gleam in his dark eyes was as indomitable as ever.

The Rasetran king nodded grudgingly and kept his doubts to himself. Nebunefer had kept to the army's contingent of priests since their departure from Quatar, but Rakh-amn-hotep had little doubt that the old schemer was still somehow in close contact with the members of the Hieratic Council back in Mahrak and his spies scattered across Nehekhara.

'How is Hekhmenukep doing?' he asked.

'His condition is grave,' the old priest replied. 'His servants fear that an infection has settled into his lungs.' Nebunefer folded his arms and stared up at the king. 'The king needs the services of a temple, and very soon, or I fear he will not survive.' Rakh-amn-hotep gestured to the east.

'Quatar is almost in sight,' he replied. 'We should reach its gates early tomorrow night.' Nebunefer was unmoved.

'Tomorrow night may well be too late, great one. If the city is so close, we should press on. We could be in Quatar before noon.' The Rasetran king bristled at the note of command in the priest's voice.

'The men are exhausted,' he growled. 'If we keep them going past dawn, into the full heat of the day, we could lose many of them. Are the lives of a few hundred warriors worth the life of a king?' Nebunefer raised a thin eyebrow.

'I'm surprised you would ask such a question, great one.' Rakh-amn-hotep let out a snort.

'Right now I need spearmen and cavalrymen, not kings,' he said.

'But the king isn't just one man, as you well know,' Nebunefer countered. 'He represents his fighting men as well.

If Hekhmenukep dies, there is no guarantee that the Lybaran host won't take his body home and leave you to fight Nagash alone.'

The old schemer had a point, Rakh-amn-hotep admitted sourly. He turned and stared off to the east for a moment, trying to gauge the remaining distance to Quatar. He knew that another contingent of horsemen was due back from the river sometime near dawn. It might be enough.

'We'll see how things stand as we get closer to dawn,' the king said at last. 'If the men are able, we'll move on. Otherwise, you may have another day of praying to do.'

For a moment it seemed that Nebunefer would continue the argument, but after catching the hard look in the Rasetran's eye, he merely bowed to the king and went off to catch up with Hekhmenukep's wagon.

Rakh-amn-hotep watched him go, and then tapped his driver's shoulder.

'Turn us around,' he growled. 'Let's get back to the head of the column.'

The driver nodded and popped the reins, chiding the horses back into motion. They turned in a bouncing arc eastwards and rejoined the trade road once more. Rakh-amn-hotep paid little attention to the trudging men as the chariot rumbled down the column, his mind preoccupied with weighing the risk of a forced march against the very real possibility of losing Hekhmenukep and the Lybarans in the process.

He hoped the night didn't have any other surprises in store.

WHEN ARKHAN RECEIVED the summons he was more than three miles to the east, prowling along the trade road with a squadron of Numasi horsemen and nipping at the heels of the retreating enemy army. The cloud of locusts that swept down upon the immortal out of the darkness had spooked the still-living Numasi and their horses. Arkhan glared contemptuously at his erstwhile allies as the insects hissed and spun round his head.

'Return to my tent, favoured servant,' Arkhan heard in the rustle of chitin and the buzz of papery wings. 'The time of retribution is nigh.'

Arkhan turned command of the squadron over to its Numasi captain, ordering them to close and engage the enemy rearguard throughout the night. Then he turned, wheeled his undead horse around and raced off into the darkness.

The army of the Undying King was arrayed in a crescent formation that stretched for more than three miles from tip to tip, its outstretched arms reaching hungrily for the fleeing enemy host. Most of the warriors in the front lines were long dead, their flesh turned leathery by the desert air and their corpses home to burrowing scarabs and black desert scorpions. They advanced slowly and stolidly after their foes. When the king and his immortals halted the army at dawn they stood in ordered ranks, baking in the heat, until the time to march came once again.

By contrast, the remainder of the host, less than a third of Khemri's city levies and what was left of the allied armies of Numas and Zandri, followed a few miles behind the vanguard along the trade road, their heads bowed with hunger and fear. The living trembled at the sight of the walking dead, furtively making signs to ward off evil when they believed none of Nagash's immortals were looking. The Undying King drove them without mercy. Wounds were not tended, nor were they fed more than a meagre ration of water and grain each day. Nagash cared little about the condition of their flesh, for when the time came his warriors would fight, one way or the other.

The companies of living warriors averted their eyes and clutched their spears with trembling hands as Arkhan raced past. He came upon his master's pavilion near the rear of the column, arrayed on a level patch of sand a few hundred yards from the road. Other tents had been pitched nearby, and Arkhan saw many of the army's engineers labouring at a frantic pace under the stern gaze of several of the king's immortals. He had heard rumours of Nagash's new battlefield innovations, and presumed that they were being made in anticipation of the coming fight at Quatar.

More than a score of undead mounts waited outside the master's tent as Arkhan approached, and he carefully concealed a frown of disapproval. Since rejoining the army a few weeks past, he'd taken pains to avoid his fellow immortals. The years of solitude in his black tower had left him impatient and mistrustful of the company of others, particularly of his own kind. Steeling himself, he slid from the saddle and entered his master's tent without a passing glance at the slaves cowering outside.

The tent's main chamber was crowded with kneeling figures, all waiting upon the king. Arkhan spied Raamket, garbed in a fresh cloak of flayed human hide, and the bandaged figure of Shepsu-hur. The immortals studied Arkhan with the flat, hungry stare of a pack of jackals, and he bared his broken teeth in return.

Nagash, the Undying King, sat upon Khemri's ancient throne at the rear of the chamber, flanked by his uneasy allies. Arkhan could see at once that the campaign had left its mark on the three kings. Amn-nasir, the Priest King of Zandri, was nearly catatonic, his eyes glazed and his expression slack under the effects of the black lotus. Seheb and Nuneb, the twin Kings of Numas, had kept their wits so far, but both of the young men were anxious and uncharacteristically withdrawn. One of them, Arkhan couldn't tell which, kept biting at his nails when he thought no one was looking. The immortal could smell the blood on the king's fingertips from across the chamber.

The vizier marched past the kneeling immortals and sank to his knees directly at Nagash's feet. He could hear the faint moans of the necromancer's ghostly retinue swirling above his head.

'What is your command, master?' he asked.

Nagash straightened upon the throne.

'We draw close to Quatar,' the Undying King declared, 'and the time has come for the craven King of the White City to pay for his surrender at the Gates of the Dawn.' The necromancer stretched out his hand. 'I shall send you forth with these immortals to Quatar's great necropolis, and there you will raise up an army of vengeance to take the city from our foes. When the rebel kings of the east reach Quatar's walls, you will be there to bar their path and seal their doom.'

Now, Arkhan understood the strategy behind the necromancer's slow pursuit of the enemy army. He had been herding them onwards to Quatar, where he planned to trap them against the walls of the city and crush them without mercy. The vizier glanced back at the kneeling immortals. With so many together, they could raise a considerable army among the houses of the dead, easily enough to overwhelm Quatar's meagre garrison, and afterwards, who knew? The White City would be in need of a new king.

The vizier smiled and bowed his head to Nagash. 'It shall be as you command, master,' he said. 'We are your arrow of vengeance. Release us, and we will fly straight to your enemy's heart.'

The Undying King gave the vizier a grim smile.

'I count upon it, loyal servant,' he said. Then he beckoned, and slaves appeared from the shadows bearing goblets brimming with crimson liquid. 'Drink,' Nagash commanded. 'Fill your limbs with vigour for the battle to come.'

Arkhan was on his feet in an instant, feeling the sudden tension in the air as the immortals reacted to the presence of the elixir. A slave stepped before the vizier and offered him the first taste. Arkhan found himself staring into Ghazid's blue eyes as he took the vessel in both hands and drank deeply, his body shuddering with the taste of power.

The rest of the immortals surged forwards like jackals around a corpse. Ghazid watched them drink and cackled with glee, his eyes glittering with madness.

THE HOWLING SWARM sped across the face of the moon in the early hours of the morning, passing undetected over the heads of the enemy army retreating to the east. Faster than the flight of a night hawk, they sped to the great plain at the foot of the Brittle Peaks, where the towers of Quatar rose like white sepulchres beneath the stars. Ribbons of smoke curled into the night sky from the poorer districts of the city, where victims of the plague were still being found and given to the flames.

The swirling, seething swarm passed over the near-deserted city and its furtive sentries, seeking the vast complex of tombs that spread along the foot of the mountains east of Quatar. The huge swarm seemed to hover over the necropolis for a moment, billowing this way and that as though searching among the maze of crypts. Then the living cloud gathered itself and hurtled southwards, crossing the road leading from Quatar to the Gates of the Dawn and settling among the shabby, crumbling tombs of the city's poorer citizens.

Smoking husks of dead insects showered down among the tombs as the immortals came to rest after their long flight from Nagash's pavilion. Arkhan paused for a moment to check his bearings and gauge the height of the moon. It was less than three hours until dawn, he reckoned. There was little time to lose.

Hissed commands passed among the immortals. They fanned out quickly among the tombs, spacing out in an arcane pattern that they had been taught centuries past. Arkhan stood in the centre of this sorcerous web, his veins brimming with inhuman power. He reached out with his senses and felt the currents of magic rippling through the air. Even hundreds of leagues distant he could feel the pulse of the Black Pyramid like the thundering heart of a god.

Arkhan raised his hands to the black sky and began the great invocation, and one by one his fellow immortals joined in, until the air shook with their dreadful voices. Dark magic spread like a stain among the tombs, seeping irresistibly past the cracked facades and flowing over the shrouded bodies within. The vizier knew that the poor could not afford the elaborate protective wards that were typically worked into the tombs of the nobility, making his task that much easier.

The ritual continued for more than an hour, growing in complexity and power until Arkhan thought that he could feel the energy humming along his skin. Faint curtains of dust rose above the countless tombs as their contents began to shift and press at the thin stone walls. Portals cracked apart and collapsed in a shower of rubble as the first warriors of Arkhan's new army shambled out into the darkness.

Hundreds upon hundreds of skeletal figures clawed their way from their tombs, their eye sockets lit with tiny sparks of grave-light. Tattered, filthy wrappings fluttered from their limbs as they shuffled silently westwards in response to Arkhan's will. In the broken ground outside the necropolis they formed into rough companies, directed by the subordinate efforts of the remaining immortals. Within two hours the army of the dead numbered thirty thousand strong, testing Arkhan's necromantic powers to the very limit.

The sky was paling to the east. Arkhan knew that at dawn his control would weaken, as he was forced to take shelter from the sun's rays. Soon the people of Quatar would look pleadingly to the east, begging for deliverance from the ghastly horde that swept over their walls.

Not one would live to see the dawn.

◄ TWENTY-FOUR ►

The Blood of Princes

Khemri, the Living City, in the 46th year of Ualatp the Patient (-1950 Imperial Reckoning)

THE PRIEST KING of Khemri stood beneath the blazing noonday sun and tried not to think of blood.

He stood upon an overseer's platform at the edge of the Plain of Kings, watching the labourers at work on the foundations of the Black Pyramid. At Nagash's command, the great plain at the heart of Khemri's necropolis had been transformed. His plan for the pyramid made use of every last hectare of available space set aside for future kings, and demanded still more besides. Scores of smaller crypts had been disassembled and relocated to other parts of the necropolis in order to make room for stone-carving yards, staging areas and rubbish piles. A wide avenue had been built running north from the great plain, requiring the demolition of still more crypts so that huge blocks of marble could be brought from the barges tied up along the river. At the moment it was being used to remove hundreds of cart-loads of sandy soil as Nagash's army of slaves excavated the pyramid's subterranean chambers. When it was complete, the Black Pyramid would dwarf every other structure in the necropolis. Indeed, it would be the largest single structure anywhere in Nehekhara. The king's ambitions required nothing less.

Nagash folded his arms tightly around his chest. Despite the heat of the day, his bones felt brittle and cold, and an aching weariness began to sap the strength from his limbs. He would need to feed again soon. Months of experimentation had allowed Nagash to refine the process of leeching vitality from living blood, but its effects were all too fleeting. Depending on the quality of the source, the king could enjoy a few days of youthful vigour, or a week at most.

The benefits were astonishing. Nagash could not remember possessing such strength or clarity of thought in his entire life, but each time the tide of blood receded he was left feeling weaker and more wretched than ever before. No amount of food or rest could take away the awful chill that settled into his bones, or the alarming weakness that left him as helpless as a child. The only answer was to find another source of blood.

Fortunately, the king had those in plentiful supply.

There were half a dozen slave camps situated around the edges of the city's necropolis, enclosed by perimeters of trenches and spiked wooden barricades and patrolled by horsemen from the king's army. Since the sack of Zandri, more than thirty thousand labourers had been assembled for Nagash's grand scheme, including the bulk of King Nekumet's army and two-thirds of his citizens. Still more were arriving each day, as Nehekhara's other great cities sent tribute to ensure that they didn't suffer the same fate as Nekumet and his people.

The battle on the road to Khemri had been swift and decisive, thanks in no small part to Zandri's large force of mercenary troops. The superstitious northern barbarians had no faith in the gods of the Blessed Land, and as such they enjoyed no protection from the incantations of Neru's priestesses. That left them vulnerable to Nagash's sorceries, and over the course of the night he had tormented the warriors with all manner of ghostly visions and portents of doom. By midnight the barbarians were panicked and on the verge of riot, and when Nekumet and his noblemen attempted to restore order, the mercenaries rose up in revolt.

Chaos tore through the enemy camp as the Zandri army turned upon itself in hours of confused, brutal fighting. By dawn, the surviving mercenaries had managed to escape the Zandri camp and blundered southwards, deeper into the desert. Nekumet's remaining troops were exhausted, hungry and dispirited, and their camp all but destroyed. At dawn, the dazed survivors began to salvage what they could from the wreckage, and then Nagash's army appeared in full battle order on the road behind them.

Despite everything they had endured the night before, Nekumet's troops still managed to form up and offer battle, but before long they found themselves under attack from Arkhan's cavalry as well, and the Zandrian battleline quickly disintegrated under the pressure. By mid-morning King Nekumet offered his terms of surrender to Nagash, but the King of Khemri refused. There would be no terms. Zandri would surrender unconditionally, or they would be slaughtered to a man. Dismayed, Nekumet had no choice but to comply.

By the end of the day, the survivors of Zandri's army had been disarmed and bound into slave coffles for the long march to Khemri. Nekumet, stripped of his crown and royal robes, was dressed in sackcloth and sent home on the back of a flea-bitten mule. It was only when he'd arrived at Zandri's broken gate that he learned what Nagash had done to his city.

News of the battle raced across Nehekhara like a storm wind, borne by the shocked ambassadors fleeing the ruin of Zandri. In Khemri, crowds of citizens turned out along the great avenues to cheer the return of their conquering king. The Living City's pre-eminence had been restored in a single, brutal stroke, and Nagash's great work could begin in earnest.

The king surveyed the scope of the excavations once more and nodded thoughtfully. A small retinue of scholars and slaves stood next to him, bearing copies of the pyramid's plans for Nagash's reference. To the king's right stood Arkhan the Black, clad in fine robes and wearing gold rings stolen from the defeated Zandrian nobles. He had been rewarded well for his efforts against Nekumet's army, and was the king's chief vizier, charged with overseeing the construction of the Black Pyramid. Also, he had been the first of Nagash's vassals to taste the king's life-giving elixir and enjoy the vigour of youth once more.

Nagash gauged the progress of the excavations and judged that they were proceeding well.

'Continue as planned,' he told his vizier. 'The excavation will proceed night and day until completed.'

'Does that include our citizens, or just the slaves?' the vizier inquired carefully. To speed construction further, Nagash had ordered the city's criminals put in the slave camps, and every citizen due to perform his annual civil service was sent to the construction site. Until the massive structure was finished, Khemri's roads and infrastructure would go untended.

Nagash considered the question and waved his hand expansively.

'Save the most difficult and dangerous tasks for the slaves,' he said, 'but everyone must still do their part.' Arkhan bowed.

'It shall be as you say,' he replied, 'but deaths among the slaves will increase. We have lost a sizeable number already due to hunger and disease.'

'Disease?' the king frowned. 'How is that possible?' The vizier shifted uncomfortably on his feet. He, too, was showing the first pangs of hunger; his eyes were sunken and his hands trembled slightly with cold.

'The priests of Asaph and Geheb have not been especially diligent in cleansing the camps of sickness,' he said. 'I have complained to the hierophants, but they claim that their priests are occupied with other matters.'

'Such as trying to undermine my rule,' Nagash growled. The temples of the city had been a constant nuisance since his ascension. They sent elders to the Grand Assemblies, calling on him to relinquish Neferem and agree to step aside as soon as Sukhet reached adulthood. Their acolytes spread rumours among the populace that the gods were displeased with his rule, and would punish Khemri unless he was forced out. No doubt they were taking their orders from the Hieratic Council at Mahrak, which had a vested interest in maintaining its authority over Nehekharan affairs. If he thought he could get away with it, Nagash would have gladly sent his warriors to clean out the temples and put the damned priests to work in the slave camp, but unfortunately the council still held too much power and influence over the other great cities, and so for the moment he had to endure their interference.

A chill wracked the king's powerful frame. He folded his arms tighter and scowled down at the pyramid's foundations.

'Any workers who perish, especially those who die at the excavation site, are to be added to the pyramid's inner structure. Bury them in the substrate. Mortar the walls with their blood and bones. Exactly how you do it isn't important, so long as their deaths are part of the pyramid's construction. Do you understand?'

The vizier nodded. Of all the king's vassals, Arkhan had the strongest grasp of the principles of necromancy. The death energies contained within the pyramid would help attune the structure to Nagash's invocations, and make it more receptive to the faint winds of dark magic.

'It will be done,' he said, bowing once more.

Satisfied, Nagash was about to take his leave and return to his studies at the palace when he caught sight of Khefru hurrying up the steps to the overseer's platform. Like Arkhan, the young priest had also been the recipient of the king's sorcerous elixir, though in Khefru's case he participated only at the king's express command. The servant's reluctance baffled Nagash, but it was clear that Khefru's ravaged health had benefited as much as the rest from the infusion of sorcerous vigour.

The young priest approached the king and bowed. Nagash studied the man intently.

'Why aren't you at the palace?' he asked. Among other things, Khefru was responsible for keeping watch over Neferem and her son, who were isolated from one another in different parts of the palace. Khefru paused for a moment to catch his breath. Under the harsh light of the sun, his skin was a pale, unhealthy yellow.

'An advance party arrived in the city an hour ago, with word that a royal delegation from Lahmia was on the way. King Lamasheptra is expected to arrive by late afternoon, and will request an audience at this evening's Grand Assembly,' he said.

The king's expression darkened.

'Where, no doubt, Lamasheptra will insist upon seeing his sister Neferem, and her son.'

'The advance party didn't specifically mention such a request,' the young priest said carefully. Nagash glared at the man.

'Don't be an idiot,' he snarled. 'Why else would the Lahmian king leave his flesh-pots and travel halfway across the country?' A faint shiver gripped Nagash's frame, which he quelled with gritted teeth. For a moment he wondered if perhaps there was time to feed before meeting with Lamasheptra, but the notion smacked too much of weakness, and he forced it aside. 'Frankly, this comes as no surprise,' he continued. 'It was only a matter of time before Lamasheptra managed to gather his courage and come here to test the strength of the old alliances.' He glowered at Khefru. 'How many warriors has he brought?'

'A handful of Ushabti and a squadron of horsemen. No more,' the priest said with a shrug.

Nagash nodded. 'Then he won't be planning on doing anything reckless. Very well,' he said, waving impatiently at Khefru. 'Inform Neferem and Sukhet that they will be attending the Grand Assembly this evening. Who knows, perhaps the sight of her son after so many years will break Neferem's resolve at long last. That would almost make the evening's farce worthwhile.'

THE LAHMIAN DELEGATION arrived at Settra's Court with a fanfare of trumpets and the rhythmic tinkle of ankle bells, accompanied by the whisper of silk and the patter of soft flesh on polished marble. Conversations stopped and heads turned as half a dozen dancing girls wove their way down the gleaming aisle, swirling through twisting ribbons of orange, yellow and red like beguiling sun-spirits. Jaded noblemen from all over Nehekhara forgot what they'd been saying a moment before as they caught tantalising glimpses of bared shoulders, rounded hips and dark, flashing eyes.

Behind the dancers came the Lahmian king, striding along the aisle in a blissful cloud of narcotic incense. Lamasheptra was lean and graceful, his steps as light and swift as the dancers that preceded him. He was a young, handsome man, little more than a child. The Kings of Lahmia married very late in life, claiming that they served their goddess best by drinking deep of all the decadence their city had to offer. Lamasheptra still had many decades of worship left in him, with a smooth, unlined face the colour of dark honey and limpid brown eyes. He had a sharp nose and a full, sensuous mouth framed by a close-cropped beard, and tightly curled black hair that hung well past his shoulders. Unlike the custom of most young nobles, Lamasheptra wore soft, flowing yellow silk robes that hung open at the chest, and patterned silk trousers.

Gold rings glittered on his soft fingers, and an earring set with a gleaming ruby hung from his left earlobe. The assembled nobility stared at the Lahmian king as though he were some kind of exotic animal, and Lamasheptra revelled in the attention.

Not too long ago the king's court was an echoing, empty space, even during King Thutep's Grand Assemblies. Now, the space was as full as it had ever been. Throngs of newly raised nobility, bedecked in gaudy kilts and half-capes, stood and gaped at the Lahmian procession, while the ambassadors of Numas, Rasetra, Lybaras and Ka-Sabar stood in tight, apprehensive groups and whispered amongst themselves. The first emissaries had begun arriving within a month after the king's victory over Zandri, and they had listened fearfully as Nagash instructed them on the new state of affairs in Nehekhara. After what had happened to Zandri, none dared gainsay the man some called the Usurper.

At the far end of the great hall, gathered like a pack of baleful jackals, stood the king's chosen, his viziers and captains, those who served him first and best. They watched Lamasheptra and his retinue approach with the sharp stares of predators. In their midst, perched upon the dark throne of Settra the Great, sat Nagash the king. His eyes were intent upon the approaching Lahmians, but his face was coldly neutral.

A dozen steps from the dais the swirling dancers stopped and bowed, their silken ribbons rippling sinuously around them like tongues of flame. Lamasheptra passed among them and approached to the foot of the stone steps, so close that Arkhan and Shepsu-hur had to bow and give way for the king to pass.

Lamasheptra spread his hands in greeting and gave Nagash a dazzling, practised smile.

'Greetings, cousin,' he said to the Usurper. 'I am Lamasheptra, fourth of the name, son of the great Lamasharazz. It is an honour to meet you at long last.'

'Then I am pleased for you,' Nagash said coolly. His smile did not reach the depths of his dark eyes. 'It has been some time since the sons of Lahmia attended upon the King of the Living City. I had begun to believe that you and your father meant to offer me insult.' Looks of shock flitted across the faces of the dancers, but Lamasheptra would not be baited.

'It is a long journey to the Living City, cousin,' the Lahmian king said smoothly. 'You may as well say the slow-moving river or the sandy road means to mock you.' Nervous laughter rose from the crowd, earning warning stares from the king's chosen. Lamasheptra pretended not to notice. 'I would not dream of offending a cousin of mine, especially one who has earned for himself such a fearsome throne.'

'Well said,' Nagash replied, his voice full of soft menace. 'What, then, is the reason for this timely visit?'

'What else, cousin? Duty and loyalty,' Lamasheptra said, 'and love of family. Before my blessed father died, he made me swear before the goddess to offer his blessings to his nephew Sukhet, whom he never knew. He also bade me give his farewells to his sister, Neferem. And so, to honour my father, I have made this long journey.'

'For Neferem, and for Sukhet, but not for me, your cousin?' Nagash asked.

Lamasheptra laughed, as though Nagash were the soul of wit. 'As though I could ignore the great Priest King of Khemri! Naturally, I have come to honour you, and assure you of Lahmia's continued esteem.'

'Nothing would please me more,' Nagash replied. 'For centuries, Khemri has treasured Lahmia's esteem greater than any other city's. I assume, then, that Lahmia will join the other cities of Nehekhara in providing a small token of this esteem.' The Lahmian's smile did not waver.

'One cannot put a price on esteem, cousin,' he said. 'What sort of token would satisfy you?'

'A thousand slaves,' Nagash said with a shrug. 'Surely a modest gift for such a wealthy city.'

'A thousand slaves a year?' Lamasheptra asked with a frown.

'Certainly not,' Nagash replied with a chuckle. 'A thousand slaves a month, to help with the great work I am building in Khemri's necropolis, and in the interests of peace, of course.'

'Peace. Of course,' the Lahmian replied, 'and a smaller price than Zandri was required to pay, I'm sure.'

'Indeed so,' Nagash said. 'I'm pleased to see you understand.' The Lahmian nodded.

'Never fear, cousin. I understand a great many things,' he said. Then he nodded to the lesser throne at Nagash's right. 'What I do not see is my noble aunt and her son. I have heard so many stories of Neferem's legendary beauty, and I have longed to witness it for myself.' He bowed slightly in the direction of the throne. 'I have a gift for her from the people of Lahmia, to show their continued love and devotion for the Daughter of the Sun. I trust you will permit me to present it to her?'

'We are always pleased to receive gifts from the great cities,' Nagash said dismissively. 'Bring it forth, and let us see it.'

Lamasheptra smiled broadly and beckoned to his retinue. A small figure slipped from the midst of the bodyguards, courtiers and slaves and hurried to the base of the dais. Nagash saw that it was a young boy, scarcely more than fifteen years of age, but he wore the bright yellow robes of a priest of Ptra. The boy stood at Lamasheptra's side and bowed deeply to Nagash.

The King of Khemri glowered at the boy. 'Is this some kind of jest?' he asked.

'An understandable reaction, cousin,' Lamasheptra said with a chuckle, 'but I assure you, Nebunefer here is a fully sanctified priest. The priests at Mahrak proclaim him to be the most gifted young man of his generation, and that the Great Father has a special destiny in mind for him. For now, though, he will wait upon the queen and see to her spiritual needs, since she is unable to attend the rites at the city temple.'

Nagash fought to conceal his irritation. The Lahmian fop was a clever one, he had to admit, but what were his motives? Had the Hieratic Council bribed him to send their little spy into the palace, or was Lamasheptra a willing ally of the damned priests?

He could refuse the gift, of course, but doing so would suggest weakness, and Mahrak would simply send one after another until they forced his hand. Nagash eyed the boy suspiciously. Nebunefer's face was open and confident, full of the self-assurance of youth. The king wondered what the boy's blood would taste like, and smiled.

'Welcome, boy,' Nagash said to Nebunefer. 'Serve the queen well, and in time, you will be rewarded.'

Nebunefer bowed once more. Lamasheptra's eyes glittered with triumph.

'Where is my beloved sister and her son?' he asked. 'I had thought to find her here, presiding over her guests and loyal subjects, as good rulers ought.'

Nagash considered Lamasheptra for a long, silent moment. Then he raised his right hand and beckoned to the shadows behind the throne.

Whispers rose from the darkness, followed by the sound of shuffling feet. The first person to appear was not Neferem, nor even Sukhet, but an old man, limping and broken, as though his bones filled his skin like shards of clay. His head was bald and scarred, his lips slack and twitching, but his blue eyes were sharp and fever-bright. Ghazid, the last Grand Vizier of Khemri, turned and beckoned to the shadows like a child calling for his playmates. He was ignorant of the staring faces in the crowd. The looks of horror and pity had no meaning for him any more. Nagash had spared his life on the night that he had buried his brother alive, but not out of mercy. He had given the old man into the hands of his vassals, who had tortured him inventively for many years. Age and great pain had worn away his once-sharp mind, until he was little more than a child in an old man's body. Then Nagash had returned him to Neferem and Sukhet as a gift.

Ghazid beckoned a tall, noble-looking young man out into the light. He was clad in noble finery, with a kilt and cape of purest samite and a prince's golden headdress on his brow. Sukhet had the handsome features of his father and the fierce demeanour of his illustrious grandfather, with piercing eyes and a strong, square chin. Gasps rose from the assembled crowd at the sight of him. Even Lamasheptra seemed struck by the young man's regal bearing.

Sukhet, son of Thutep, carried himself with great dignity and poise. He stepped past the great throne as though it were empty and descended the stone steps until he stood before the Lahmian king. A ripple of unease passed through the king's chosen at the sight of the young prince. Arkhan in particular eyed Sukhet as though he were a form of especially venomous snake.

Lamasheptra smiled warmly at Sukhet, apparently ignorant of the apprehensive stares of the noblemen around him. He started to speak, but the words dried up in his throat as he saw the Daughter of the Sun emerge from the darkness behind Nagash's throne.

She wore a simple gown of purest white, cinched by a girdle of leather and burnished copper that hung lightly upon her hips. Her long, black hair had been washed with scented oils and pulled back in a thick braid that hung nearly to her waist. The queen's green eyes were vivid in their kohl-darkened orbits, but no other balms or tinctures had been added to her face. Her feet were bare, as was her brow: the heavy golden cape and wondrous headdress of the queen had been left behind, along with the gold bracelets and rings that she had brought with her from far-off Lahmia. Neferem, Queen of the Living City and Daughter of the Sun, cloaked herself in anguish and loss. Her face was a pale mask, beautiful but still, like the image carved upon a sarcophagus.

The queen was not the young maiden she once had been. Life and loss had left their mark upon her features, ageing her well beyond her years. Gasps filled the echoing court at the sight of her, and even Lamasheptra was taken aback. The king staggered a half-step back, as though the sight of her were a physical blow. For the briefest instant, his brown eyes glanced at the man upon Khemri's throne, and then slowly, reverently, the King of Lahmia sank to his knees before Neferem.

In a rippling whisper of cloth, the rest of the court followed suit. Some knelt gracefully, while others simply fell to their knees in wonder. Within moments the only men standing were the king's chosen, who looked to one another with shifting, apprehensive stares, and the queen's son, Sukhet.

The prince turned, and saw his mother for the first time in nearly a decade.

Nagash studied the pair over steepled fingers and fought to stifle his anger. This had been a mistake. He should have arranged a private meeting between Lamasheptra and Sukhet instead of permitting this spectacle. He'd thought to demonstrate his control over Thutep's wife and heir by allowing them a brief moment at court, but he hadn't counted on the enduring superstition and sentimentality of the populace.

Sukhet stared into his mother's eyes, and in that moment he forgot himself. All dignity fled as he rushed to his mother and reached for her hands. Neferem reached for him as though in a dream, a slight frown of bemusement penetrating her shock. The prince took her hands in his and touched his forehead to them in a sign of reverence.

The King of Khemri paid no mind to the maudlin scene. His eyes were on Lamasheptra alone. The Lahmian was watching mother and son with an awestruck expression that could not quite hide the calculating look in his dark eyes.

At that moment Nagash realised that Sukhet had to die.

They came for him in the dead of night, when the rest of the palace was sleeping. Sukhet's cell was two levels beneath the sprawling palace, in a cramped chamber formerly reserved for storing expensive spices and wines. The entire section had been abandoned decades ago, back in Khetep's time. Only Khefru and Ghazid came and went through its darkened corridors these days, and Nagash's servant alone had the key to Sukhet's chamber.

Khefru led the way, holding an oil lamp in one trembling hand. The priest moved unerringly through the labyrinthine hallways, until he finally came upon an unmarked door of heavy, scarred teak. Khefru fumbled in his robes for several long moments before producing a long rod of tarnished bronze that he fit into the door's massive wood and bronze lock.

The mechanism turned with a loud clatter. As Khefru started to pull the door open, Arkhan the Black stepped forward and shoved the servant roughly aside, sending the oil lamp crashing to the floor. Behind the vizier, Raamket and Shepsu-hur rushed silently into the cell.

The chamber was small, barely twelve paces by six. A narrow bed was set against one long wall, with a cedar chest at the end for the prince's clothes. Opposite the bed stood a narrow table with a single chair and a small oil lamp, where the prince would take his meals or read books brought to him from the library. Though he was allowed to walk the grounds of the palace within carefully proscribed limits, the small room had been Sukhet's home for nearly ten years.

Ghazid rose from his pallet just inside the door, his battered face gaping in terror. He let out a wordless, childlike cry of fear as Raamket seized his arms and hurled him out of the way. The servant hit the stone wall beside the table and crumpled into a senseless heap.

Sukhet bolted from the narrow bed as the two noble-men closed in on him. Raamket reached him first, closing a powerful hand around the prince's left arm. Sukhet's right arm flashed downwards in a blurring arc, and Raamket let out a roar of pain. The handle of a small eating knife jutted from the man's collarbone, just a few inches to the right of his neck.

Shepsu-hur stepped forwards and smashed his fist into the prince's face, breaking his aquiline nose and splitting his lip. Sukhet's head jerked back and hit the wall over the bed, and the young man collapsed.

Raamket and Shepsu-hur grabbed the prince's legs and dragged him roughly onto the floor. Ghazid, regaining his senses, cowered against the wall and began to wail in terror. Sukhet spat blood and tried to tear himself free from the grip of his assailants, but then a shadow fell over him from the doorway of the cell.

Nagash loomed over the young prince with a pair of long, copper needles clutched in his hands.

'Hold him still!' he snapped. The coppery smell of spilled blood hung in the close air of the chamber, making the king almost dizzy with hunger.

Shepsu-hur and Raamket tightened their grip on the prince's arms, their faces contorted with effort. Nagash lunged forwards like a striking snake and drove the needles home. Sukhet's body went rigid with agony, the sight of which made Ghazid wail all the louder.

'Shut him up!' Nagash snarled, and Raamket began to beat the old man. At a nod from the king, Shepsu-hur stripped away the prince's tunic and threw it aside.

'The ink!' Nagash commanded, turning and stretching his hand to Khefru, who still stood in the corridor beyond.

The young priest hesitated, clutching the brush and ink pot in his hands. A look of dread marked his sallow, puffy features, but he had been given a taste of the king's elixir more than once, and a faint gleam of hunger shone in his eyes.

'Surely there is another way,' Khefru stammered. 'We can't do this, master. Not to him.'

'You dare to question me?' the king hissed. 'You, of all people? He is flesh and blood, just like all the others you stole off the city streets. He is no different from the slaves whose blood you drained, and then sipped from a golden cup!'

'He is a prince!' Khefru cried. 'The son of Thutep and the Daughter of the Sun. The gods will not forgive us!'

'The gods?' Nagash said incredulously. 'You little fool. We are gods now. The secret of immortality is ours.' He gestured to the stricken prince. 'His body is charged with divine power. Imagine how much sweeter, how much more potent it will be. We might not need another taste for a hundred years!'

Anguish wracked Khefru's face. 'If it's divine blood you want, then kill a priest!' he cried. 'If he dies, you lose your hold on Neferem, and Lahmia may well declare war against us. Is that what you want?'

'Neferem will not hear of this,' Nagash said coldly, 'until such time as I choose to tell her. Neither will Lahmia be told.' He took a threatening step towards Khefru. 'Sukhet has to die. He is too dangerous to be allowed to live. Did you not see how the people reacted to him at court?'

'But the queen–' Khefru stammered.

'The queen does not rule here!' Nagash roared. 'Don't tell me you have fallen under that witch's spell, have you? Have you? Because if you would rather I took the blood of a priest, I will open your veins here and now.'

Khefru recoiled from the king's malevolent voice, straight into the arms of Arkhan, who held him in an iron grip. The priest glanced up into the vizier's ghoulish face, and the courage went out of him. With trembling hands, he held out the ink and brush to the king.

Nagash took the instruments and turned back to the prince's rigid body. His eyes shone with avarice.

'Have a bowl ready once I've finished with the glyphs,' he said as he knelt beside Sukhet. 'I don't want to waste a single drop.'

HOURS LATER, NAGASH swept down the darkened corridor outside the queen's chambers, his robes billowing behind him like the wings of a desert eagle. Blood roared in his temples and burned along his veins: stolen blood, hot with the vitality of youth and the divinity of royal birth.

The guards standing outside the queen's door were hard-bitten men, cruel and incorruptible. As the queen's jailers they were prepared to die at a moment's notice to keep the queen's chambers sacrosanct, but they all quailed like frightened children at the sudden appearance of the king. They looked into Nagash's eyes and glimpsed the terrible power burning in their depths, like the fiery gaze of Usirian. As one, the guards sank to their knees and pressed their foreheads to the stone, their bodies trembling in fear. The king paid them no mind, sweeping past them like a storm wind and knocking the heavy door open with a brush of his left hand.

At once, a chorus of frightened shouts arose from the maids sleeping in the great antechamber beyond. They rose from their couches in terror, crying out the name of their mistress and begging the gods for aid.

'Silence!' Nagash cried, clenching his left hand into a fist and reciting an incantation in his mind. At once, the shadows of the great room thickened like ink and swallowed the women up in an icy embrace. He glided across the piled rugs, past their silent and quaking bodies, and burst into Neferem's bedroom.

The chamber was luxuriously appointed, with a gleaming marble floor and a high terrace that looked northwards towards the great river. Neferem had risen swiftly from her bed and covered her naked body with a silk sheet. Her black hair was unbound and spilled across her bare shoulders, and her eyes gleamed like a cat's in the moonlight. For the first time, a look of real fear shone upon Neferem's face.

Once more, Nagash looked upon her and was gripped with desire. With the power seething in his body, power drained from her son's veins he knew that he could take whatever he wished from her. He smiled a jackal's smile.

'I've been thinking,' he said slowly.

Neferem said nothing. Her body was taut with tension. All at once, Nagash realised that she had positioned herself with her back almost to the terrace across the room. If he took one step closer, he was certain she would throw herself from the balcony. The thought only made him want her even more.

'When I saw you at the assembly today, alongside your son, I realised that what I had done to you was wrong,' Nagash said. He indicated the bedroom with a wave of his arm. 'It isn't right to keep you locked up here, like a caged bird. I cannot possess you in such a way. Your will is strong, nearly as strong as mine, and you have already said that you would sooner die than submit to me. Every year that passes only draws you further from my grasp, until one day you will shed your mortal flesh and join your husband in the afterlife.'

A wary look came over Neferem's face. Her body relaxed very slightly.

'What you say is true,' she replied. 'If you thought to break my will by reuniting me with Sukhet this afternoon, it did just the opposite.'

'Oh, I know,' the king said. 'Your will is very strong, nearly as strong as mine. I see that now. And so, I'm here to set you free.'

The Daughter of the Sun gave Nagash a bewildered look.

'What do you mean?' she asked.

'I mean you have a choice,' the king said with a smile. 'Here and now, I swear an oath before the gods not to harm Sukhet from this moment forward. I will not use him to compel you ever again.' He took a slow step forwards. 'You are free to choose your own fate. Either remain here as you are and rule alongside me, or drink this, and life as you know it will end.'

Nagash raised his right hand. In it he held a small golden cup, half-full with dark liquid. The elixir was still warm, fresh from Sukhet's young heart. The queen considered the cup. Her face became very still and calm.

'You swear that Sukhet will be safe?'

'From this moment forward he may do as he wishes,' Nagash said. 'I swear it, by all the gods.'

The Daughter of the Sun nodded, and came to a swift decision. 'Give me the cup, then,' she said.

'Are you certain?' Nagash asked. 'Once you have drunk from the cup, there will be no turning back.' Neferem raised her chin and gave Nagash a haughty look.

'I have never been more certain of anything in my life,' she replied. 'Let the darkness come. I weary of this sad and terrible life.' The necromancer smiled.

'As you wish, o queen,' he said, and handed the cup to her. 'Drink deep, loyal wife. The effect will be swift and painless.'

⫷ TWENTY-FIVE ⫸

The Road of Bones

Quatar, The City of the Dead, in the 63rd year of Ptra the Glorious (-1744 Imperial Reckoning)

THE ARMY OF the east had marched through the night and on into the sunrise, hastening their steps towards the City of the Dead.

The first companies crested the high dunes at the western edge of the Plain of Usirian just before midday, and when they saw the white city shimmering in the searing light they raised their hands to the sky and thanked the Great Father for their deliverance. They lurched and stumbled down the sandy slope, breaking ranks as they succumbed to the promise of cool water, fresh food and a pallet in the shade where they could sleep without fear. The noblemen in command of the companies made a half-hearted effort to restore discipline, but their throats were caked in dust and after weeks of strict rations they were hungrier than they had ever been in their lives. When the subsequent formations reached the edge of the plain and saw the headlong rush for the city they joined in, until by the time Rakh-amn-hotep reached the dunes with the army's centre he saw a veritable flood of tanned bodies pouring across the rocky ground towards Quatar's stained walls.

The king reined in his chariot with a stream of bitter curses. The leading edge of the mob was more than a mile away. There was no stopping them, but Rakh-amn-hotep vowed that he would have their commanders whipped before the day was out. His presence at the dune crest kept the rest of the army in line. He could see temptation in the eyes of the men, but one look at the king's furious expression was enough to remind them of their training, and their discipline held as they continued on to Quatar.

Rakh-amn-hotep waited there as the rest of the host filed past, baking in the still, dusty air as he watched for the leading elements of the army's rearguard. The long, terrible retreat would not be done until the last man of the last company passed through the city gates.

The king's chariot driver wiped his gleaming brow and pulled a thin leather flask from his belt. He offered it first to the king, but Rakh-amn-hotep stoically declined.

'Drink your fill,' he told the man. 'I can wait.'

When the creak and rumble of chariot wheels reached the king's ears several minutes later it took Rakh-amn-hotep by surprise. He found himself blinking dazedly to the west.

'So soon?' he murmured. 'By the gods, is this all we have left?'

The army's remaining chariots and its squadrons of heavy horsemen rode past the king in good order, tired but proud of their hard duty covering the army's retreat. The Rasetran chariots were pulled by horses, taken from the supply train when their swift jungle lizards had perished in the heat. The charioteers raised their weapons in weary salute to the king.

Ekhreb, the king's champion, appeared with the last of the rearguard squadrons, riding in the saddle of a dust-stained mare.

'What did you do with your chariot, you damned fool?' the king asked.

'Traded it to a bandit princess for a cup of cool water,' the champion replied in a deadpan voice.

'She didn't try to entice you with her other charms?'

'She may have tried. I was too busy drinking.'

The king managed a weary chuckle, and asked, 'What did happen to your chariot?' Ekhreb sighed.

'We hit one too many rocks cutting back and forth across the road. The left wheel was cracked through. Fortunately, the cavalry has plenty of spare horses.'

'Any signs of pursuit?' the king asked, but the champion shook his head.

'Not since dawn,' he said. 'We were probed by some Numasi horsemen just before the moons set, but they withdrew off to the west just before daybreak.' Rakh-amn-hotep nodded thoughtfully.

'They assumed we'd make camp at daybreak, like normal,' he said. 'Now they're more than half a day's march behind us. That's the first good news we've had in weeks.'

'And not a moment too soon,' Ekhreb agreed. He gestured at the distant mob streaming across the plain. 'The men are at their breaking point.'

'Only half of them,' the king replied testily. 'It's a disgrace, but the officers are to blame. After we've had a day's rest I intend to sort things out, believe me.'

'And there will be much wailing and gnashing of teeth in the city of Quatar,' the champion said with a rueful grin. He watched the running figures for a moment, and then his brow furrowed in bemusement.

Rakh-amn-hotep was just about to order his chariot forwards again when he caught the look on his champion's face.

'What is it?' he asked.

'I'm not sure,' Ekhreb said. 'Does the city look strange to you?'

AT THE FAR end of the Plain of Usirian the city of Quatar shimmered like a desert mirage. Its white walls, once stained with the red rain of Nagash's terrible plague, had been bleached by years of relentless sunlight, and they shimmered with heat like clay fresh from the kiln. The City of the Dead gleamed like a new sepulchre, and the men of the allied army rushed towards it with open arms and hoarse shouts of joy.

None of the exhausted warriors noticed that Quatar's gates were still shut, at a time when there ought to have been a meagre but steady flow of traffic into and out of the city. Nor did they wonder at the lack of smoke hanging over the rooftops. The hearths and clay ovens had all gone cold during the night.

The warriors made it to the cool shadow of the city walls and fell to their knees, gasping, and in some cases weeping in relief. Red-faced noblemen shouted up at the battlements, calling for a guard to throw open the gates. After a moment, the rest of the men took up the shout, calling loudly enough to wake the dead.

In the darkness of the city's eastern gatehouse half a dozen pallid figures were startled awake by the clamour. They cursed in surprise at the sound of hundreds of shouting voices, and in their fear and confusion they commanded their warriors to awaken.

All along the broad walkway running atop the western wall, thousands of skeletal warriors began to stir. Bleached skulls rose from the stone walkway, turning this way and that in search of their foes. Bones clattered and scraped as they reached for bows and arrows or bundles of bronze-headed javelins. There were no shouted commands, nor the strident call of war-horns. Silent and purposeful, the undead warriors climbed to their feet and took aim at the helpless men below.

The first hissing flight of arrows went almost unnoticed by the warriors on the plain. Men toppled over dead with scarcely a sound, or collapsed in shock as the pain of their wounds took hold. The groans of the dying were drowned by the cheers and desperate pleas of their comrades for several seconds more, until a ragged volley of javelins darkened the sky overhead and fell in a deadly rain among the reeling mob. Shouts of relief turned to frightened screams as scores of men were wounded or slain. Warriors shouted in panic and confusion. Some waved their arms wildly at the gaunt silhouettes atop the wall, believing that the city's defenders were firing on them by mistake. Officers shouted conflicting orders, some acting on instinct and trying to form the men into companies, while others screamed for a full retreat and fled back towards the rest of the army. The men caught in between, dazed with exhaustion and hunger, were cut down where they stood.

WHEN THE FIRST arrows started to fly, Rakh-amn-hotep could not believe his eyes. He rubbed his hand across his face and squinted into the harsh light, convinced that he'd been mistaken. Then he heard the faint sound of screams and the strident call of horns from the centre of the army and the awful truth struck home.

'Gods above,' the king said softly, his voice numb with despair. 'Nagash has taken Quatar. How in the name of all that is holy…'

Ekhreb cursed, reaching for his sword.

'What do we do, great one?' he asked.

The world seemed to spin around the king. He swayed on his feet, clutching the side of the chariot to steady himself.

'Do?' he echoed, his voice filled with dismay. 'What can we do? That monster is always one step ahead of us! It's as though he knows our every thought–'

'If that were true his men would be right on our heels, herding us to slaughter,' the champion snapped, his tone so sharp that it struck the king like a blow. 'Get a hold of yourself. Nagash is no all-seeing god. He's taken Quatar, but we're not encircled yet. We still have room to manoeuvre, but the men need direction. What are your orders?'

Rakh-amn-hotep recoiled from the champion's stern tone, but Ekhreb's words had their desired effect. Anger replaced shock and despair, and the king began to think.

'All right,' the king growled. 'Let's get ourselves out of this mess.' He stared at the distant city and shook his head bitterly. 'We can't retake the city, not in the shape we're in.' Once more, despair threatened to overwhelm him, but the Rakh-amn-hotep pushed the feelings aside. 'We'll have to continue the retreat.'

The champion nodded. 'South, down the trade road to Ka-Sabar, or north, towards the River Vitae?' he asked.

'Neither,' Rakh-amn-hotep growled. 'If we go north, Nagash can trap us against the river and destroy us. And Ka-Sabar lies too far to the south. Without supplies we'd lose more than half the army on the march.' With a bleak look on his face, he pointed further eastwards, beyond the City of the Dead. 'No, we'll have to circle around Quatar and risk the Valley of Kings. It's more defensible, and Mahrak lies at the far end. We know we can find safe haven there.'

The king did not point out that such a retreat would spell the doom of the great crusade against the Usurper. Nagash would pursue them eastwards, and from this day forward the armies of the east would be fighting, not for the sake of Nehekhara, but for the survival of their people. The alliance would very likely end, as each king sought to make his own peace with Khemri.

Rakh-amn-hotep looked out across the Plain of Usirian and felt the tides of war turning, flowing inexorably from his grasp.

'Form up your horsemen and chariots,' he told Ekhreb, and pointed off to the south-east. 'You'll lead the advance around the southern edge of the city in case the enemy tries to block our path to the valley. If no one challenges you, ride on to the Gates of the Dawn and seize the fortifications. There are cisterns and storehouses within the walls. We'll take all we can carry and see if the Lybarans can find a way to collapse the gates behind us. That might buy us another day or two.'

Ekhreb accepted Rakh-amn-hotep's orders with a curt nod. After all he had seen during the battle at the fountains and the grim retreat afterwards, the thought of destroying the ancient Gates made no impression on him at all.

'What about you?' he asked the king. The Rasetran nodded at the chaos spreading across the plain.

'I'm going down there to rally those damned fools and get them moving,' he said. He held out his hand. 'Get going, old friend,' he told his champion. 'I'll see you in the valley beyond the Gates of the Dawn. By then I'll have figured out a proper punishment for giving me the sharp side of your tongue.' Ekhreb gathered up his reins.

'You could relieve me of command and send me home,' he offered. 'It would be a terrible disappointment, but I imagine I could live with it.'

'Couldn't we all,' the king retorted, and the two warriors parted ways, racing to pull their army back from the brink of destruction once again.

ARKHAN AWOKE IN darkness, feeling the stirring of his skeletal warriors like the buzzing of wasps within his brain.

He was sitting upon the Ivory Throne of Quatar, his pale face and hands stained black with drying blood from the entertainments of the night before. A handful of immortals slept upon the blood-spattered floor around the throne, surrounded by the detritus of their revels. Most of the vizier's undead brethren had scattered across the city with the coming of the dawn, seeking their own solitary havens to wait out the light of day. It appeared that he was not the only immortal growing ever more solitary and mistrustful as the years went by.

The vizier experienced a moment of disorientation, like a man wakened suddenly from a dream. He could sense a portion of his makeshift army in action off to the west, probably the bowmen he'd situated along the city wall. Though the undead were extensions of his will, his ability to sense their activities was vague at best despite his growing skill. At the moment the connection was more tenuous still, and with a start he realised that it was midday, and the hateful sun was almost directly overhead.

The other immortals were beginning to stir, peering warily into the darkness of the throne room. Raamket rose swiftly to his feet, swathed in a fresh kilt and a knee-length coat of soft flesh. Nagash had been very specific as to the fate of Nemuhareb, the Priest King of Quatar, but less so with the rest of the king's family. The immortal had stripped away the skin of Nemuhareb's children with care.

'What is happening?' Raamket hissed. Clothed in human skin and dappled with dried gore, the noble's voice was thin and fearful as a child's.

'The enemy is here,' Arkhan snarled, leaping from the throne. Behind him came a rustle of flesh and the faint drip of blood as the wind of his passing stirred what was left of the Lord of Tombs. At the command of the Undying King, Nemuhareb had been skinned alive, and his hide, with its nerves carefully and magically preserved, had been stretched across a standard pole and painted with necromantic runes using the king's heart blood. When Nagash's army eventually marched from Quatar they would carry the flayed skin and tormented soul of Nemuhareb before them as a warning to those who would defy the will of Khemri.

'The damned eastern kings force-marched their armies the rest of the way to Quatar instead of waiting one more day as Nagash expected,' Arkhan continued, his anger growing by the moment. He cursed himself for a fool.

After weeks of hounding Akhmen-hotep and the Bronze Host across the Great Desert he'd allowed himself to indulge in too much celebration after his easy conquest of Quatar. Now, instead of Nagash's army pinning their foes against the city walls and slaughtering them, Arkhan was faced with stopping the eastern armies with the scrapings taken from the city necropolis. The archers and javelin throwers on the walls were the best-armed troops he had, and his immortals were imprisoned inside their own havens for as long as the sun burned overhead.

The vizier's blood-smeared hands clenched into impotent fists. Furious, he sent a single, burning command to his undead army.

At this point there was nothing left for Arkhan to do but kill as many of the easterners as he could.

THE EASTERN END of the Plain of Usirian had been transformed into a killing ground. Hundreds of dead and dying men littered the rocky field beneath the walls of Quatar, and still the arrows arced through the blazing sky. The survivors of the allied armies' ill-fated lead companies were in full flight, trampling one another in their haste to escape the rain of death. As they ran, bony hands burst from the loose soil and clutched at their ankles. Men fell screaming as the earth heaved and countless skeletons burst from the ground among the panicked troops and set upon them with jagged teeth and claw-like fingers.

Those few that survived the jaws of Arkhan's fearsome trap retreated back to the main body of the eastern host and sent tremors of terror and despair through the ranks. Men wavered, already pushed to the limits of their resolve by the hardships of the long retreat. Officers shouted encouragement and uttered blistering oaths to try to keep their warriors in line, but for a few, desperate moments the allied army teetered on the brink of collapse.

Then, just as all seemed lost, the sound of war-horns carried through the din and the earth rumbled like a drum under the beat of thousands of hooves as the army's weary cavalry swept down the column's right flank and charged once more into the fray. They smashed through part of the shambling horde of skeletons, smashing their bodies to pieces and grinding them under their hooves before swinging to the south and circling around the enemy-held city.

Though the charge had only stopped part of the enemy attack, it restored some of the army's lost courage and halted the mindless spread of panic. Moments later Rakh-amn-hotep reached the centre of the army, riding past the frightened companies and galvanising them with his presence. He roared imprecations at the retreating warriors, halting them in their tracks through the sheer, indomitable force of his presence. Oblivious to the arrows hissing through the air around him, he sent the shattered companies marching to the rear of the column and formed a battleline to receive the advancing horde.

The skeletons attacked in waves, clawing mindlessly at the shields and helms of the exhausted spearmen, but with the king at their back the companies stood their ground and they hurled back one assault after the next. Men in the rear ranks picked up rocks and hurled them at the shambling skeletons, smashing skulls and splitting ribcages.

After weathering five separate attacks, Rakh-amn-hotep passed a command to his signallers, and the army began to advance. The companies pressed forwards, a step at a time, carving a path through the skeletal horrors and slowly working their way around the perimeter of the city towards the Gates of the Dawn.

Arrows continued to rain down on the warriors from the walls of Quatar, but the range was great, and few found their mark. Rakh-amn-hotep rolled up and down the length of the advancing army, encouraging them to keep pushing forwards against the tide of bones.

One hour passed, and then another. Weary beyond reason, the army fought on, passing south of Quatar and then forcing their way eastwards. The Rasetran king turned his attention to forming a rearguard from the mauled companies at the back of the column, standing with them and holding off what remained of the undead attackers while the rest of the host retreated safely beyond their reach.

The fire of the archers dwindled steadily as their supply of arrows ran low, and less than two hundred skeletons remained on the sun-baked plain to challenge the retreating host. The ghastly mob made one last attempt against the rearguard, and this time the eastern warriors responded with such fury that not one of the grisly warriors survived.

Alone and unchallenged upon the field, the rearguard raised their spears and offered praise to the gods and to Rakh-amn-hotep for their victory, but when the warriors turned to salute their king they found his chariot empty. Rakh-amn-hotep lay upon the ground just a few yards away, his chariot driver kneeling at his side. An arrow, one of the very last fired from the city walls, had taken the bold king in the throat.

◄ TWENTY-SIX ►

The City of the Gods

*Quatar, the City of the Dead, in the 63rd year of Ptra
the Glorious (-1744 Imperial Reckoning)*

So LONG AS he drank his master's elixir, Arkhan the Black
was immortal. Thus, pain applied in just the right way
could be made to last a very, very long time.

The vizier writhed and gurgled in a sticky pool of his
own fluids, smothered by a wet, chitinous blanket of
tomb beetles. His clothes and most of his skin had long
since been eaten away, and the flesh beneath chewed to a
pulp as the scarabs worked their way into the tender
organs beneath. When he tried to keep screaming, the air
whistled tunelessly through the gaping holes in his throat,
and all that emerged from his gaping mouth was the
rustling, tearing sound of hundreds of pairs of mandibles.

Nagash sat straight-backed upon the throne of Quatar
with the hide of its former ruler stirring at his back. His
immortals, as well as the vassal Kings of Numas and Zandri, all waited upon the king as he meted out his

displeasure on the vizier. Nagash's undead champions watched Arkhan's suffering with wary, subdued expressions. Never before had they been shown the agonies that one of their own kind could be made to endure, and, to a man, they all feared that they could be next. For the kings, however, the horror was even worse. Seheb and Nuneb had collapsed early on, their eyes wide and feverish with shock. Their Ushabti had little choice but to take the twin kings by the arms and hold them bodily upright until Nagash declared the audience to be at an end. Amn-nasir drank and drank from the goblet clutched in his trembling hand, but no amount of wine and crushed lotus could banish the scene unfolding at his feet.

The beetles had been at work for more than an hour, and yellowed bones could be seen amid the tattered scraps of red meat still clinging to Arkhan's frame. With a rustle and a swirl of the necromancer's ghostly retinue, Nagash stretched forth his hand and the swarm of beetles fled the vizier's ruined body in a chittering tide, racing across the marble floor and over the sandalled feet of the immortals.

'You failed me,' the Undying King said. He rose to his feet and approached Arkhan's ravaged form. 'I delivered our enemies into your hands, and you let them slip away.'

Arkhan's body shivered and twitched. He turned his shredded face to his master. Blood and other fluids pooled in the empty eye sockets. His jaw worked clumsily, driven by just a few remaining shreds of muscle, but the only sound he could manage was a thin, tortured wheeze.

The Undying King held out his hand, and Ghazid, his servant, appeared from the shadows behind the throne. The blind wretch carried a wide copper bowl brimming with a thick, steaming crimson fluid, and he walked with exaggerated care, as though fearful of spilling a single drop. A shiver went through the immortals as they smelled the elixir. One or two even forgot themselves and took a step or two towards the bowl, their blue lips drawn back in a rictus of thirst. Nagash stilled them with a single look.

For several long minutes there was only the swish of the servant's feet upon the stones and Arkhan's jagged, whistling breaths.

It had been barely seven hours since the ambush outside the city walls. The main body of Nagash's host had arrived within two hours after sunset. As soon as the king realised he'd been deceived he'd driven his troops forwards with merciless zeal, but by then it was already too late. The armies of the east had withdrawn far up into the Valley of Kings, and the Lybarans had managed to collapse the Gates of the Dawn behind them. The king's skeletal horde was digging its way through the rubble with the untiring energy of the living dead, but it would be hours, perhaps days, before a path could be cleared to allow the army through.

The plain outside the City of the Dead was carpeted with the bodies of the fallen. Perhaps five thousand enemy troops had been killed in the battle, but many more had managed to escape. The Undying King had not been pleased by the news.

Ghazid came to a halt beside his master. Nagash glanced down into the bowl's depths, and placed his palm against the red, turgid surface.

The necromancer's gaze fell to the vizier's ruined body. His ghostly servants reached out to Arkhan, winding ethereal tendrils around his arms and legs, and then picking him up off the floor. He hung upright before his master, dangling awkwardly like a smashed puppet. Blood ran from the chewed flesh in long, ropy strands.

Nagash stepped forwards and pressed his bloody hand to Arkhan's raw face. The immortal stiffened, bones and cartilage crackling wetly as the sorcerous mixture went to work restoring the vizier's body. Limbs twisted and popped, pulled back into place by knitting muscle and tendons. Blood poured in a rush from split arteries and veins as Arkhan's heart gained strength, pouring onto the marble, and then slowing steadily as the vessels closed and were covered by a pale film of skin.

More cartilage popped in Arkhan's throat. The vizier's chest swelled with an agonised breath, and he let out a single, tortured scream.

The Undying King took his hand away from Arkhan's face. The red print of his palm and fingertips vanished in moments, like water soaked into parched earth. Arkhan shuddered convulsively, and then spoke. His words came haltingly as his lips grew back to cover his teeth.

'We... did... all,' he stammered. 'All that... could... be done.' Arkhan shuddered again. Newly formed eyes rolled in their sockets. 'They... came in daylight.'

'Better you had burned and done my bidding!' Nagash cried, and the braziers guttered as though caught in a desert wind.

'Slay me then!' Arkhan said. 'Cast me to the flames if it please you, master.'

Nagash gave his vizier a calculating stare.

'In time, perhaps,' he said. 'For now, you will continue to serve me. We march upon Mahrak as soon as a path to the valley has been cleared.'

A stir went through the assembly, and Amn-nasir's face rose from the depths of his goblet.

'Mahrak?' he asked hoarsely, as though the name made little sense to him. Seheb let out a groan. Nuneb stiffened.

'We cannot,' Seheb said, his lips trembling with fear. 'We dare not march upon the City of the Gods! You go too far–'

'No city in Nehekhara has need of two rulers,' Nagash said coldly, turning and fixing Seheb with a contemptuous stare. The necromancer pointed to Nuneb. 'Bring him here.'

At once, half a dozen immortals moved towards the twin kings. Their Ushabti moved to shield the kings, their hands darting to the swords slung across their backs.

'No!' Seheb cried. The young king fell to his knees. 'Forgive me, great one! I… I misspoke. I merely meant to say that we have thrown back the invaders. The west is secure, and our cities have been neglected for many years.' He cast about fearfully, looking to Amn-nasir for support and receiving only a hooded stare in return. 'If you would complete the destruction of Rasetra and Lybaras, so be it, but what purpose would it serve to attack Mahrak?'

'Who do you imagine we do battle with, you little fool?' Nagash snarled. 'Do you think these petty kings would dare defy Khemri alone? No, Mahrak is the heart of this rebellion. The Hieratic Council fears me, for I have learned the truth about them and their feckless gods.' The necromancer raised his bloodstained hand and clenched it into a fist. 'When Mahrak falls, the kings of the east will bow to me, and a new empire will be born.'

Seheb stared up at the Undying King, his eyes bright with fear. The immortals were only a few steps away, waiting on Nagash's command. Steeling himself, he pressed his forehead to the marble floor, as a slave would before his master.

'As you command, great one, so shall it be,' he said. 'Let Mahrak be brought to its knees before your might.'

Nagash considered the twin kings for a moment more, and then waved the immortals away.

'The last battle is almost at hand,' he said, as the pale figures returned to their places. 'Serve me well, and you will prosper. Immortality itself will be yours.'

Another wave of the necromancer's hand, and his spirits released Arkhan. The vizier landed in a heap, still too weak to stand, but his skin was whole once more. Nagash studied the fallen vizier and nodded thoughtfully.

'Great shall be the wonders of the coming age,' he said.

THE GODS ALONE saved the armies of the east, or so its warriors believed.

They had found the Gates of the Dawn abandoned, a thing unheard of since Settra's time, hundreds of years past. Ekhreb and his riders took the fortifications without incident, and found its storehouses well stocked with food, water and supplies, enough to sustain the army on the long march to Mahrak. The companies each drew their own stores as they passed through the gates into the Valley of Kings, and were even able to steal a few hours' rest while the Lybaran engineers searched for a way to bring the fortifications down.

While they waited, the rumour spread that Rakh-amn-hotep, the Rasetran king, had been killed by an arrow, fighting alongside the rearguard outside Quatar. Hekhmenukep, the Priest King of Lybaras, still clung to life, but none knew for how long. The host's surviving nobles began to talk of returning to their homes. For the space of a few hours that afternoon, the army once again teetered on the brink of destruction.

Then the news spread through the ranks: Rakh-amn-hotep still lived! The enemy's arrow had wounded him gravely, but by luck alone the shaft had missed the major arteries. The rearguard brought him into the fortifications, where the army's priests took him under their care.

Then, when the Lybaran engineers had done their work, trumpets blared from atop the fortifications, and the army was assembled in ranks on the western side of the wall. Amid a fanfare of horns, a column of chariots rode through the gates and passed slowly down the length of the column. Cheers went up from the weary Lybarans as they saw their king riding in the lead chariot. Hekhmenukep's fever had broken over the course of the afternoon, and he had ordered his Ushabti to prepare his chariot so that the men could see that he was well. He managed little more than to stay upright as he rode all the way to the front of the army, but the gesture had the desired effect. Their morale restored, the army resumed their long retreat eastwards, towards Mahrak. Behind them, the ancient fortifications built by the first king of Quatar collapsed in a rumble of grinding stone and a rising pall of chalk-white dust.

The destruction of the gates bought the army two full days. The allied host made good use of the time, racing all night and half the next day along the broad, dusty road that ran the length of the sacred valley. They camped in the shadows of the oldest tombs in Nehekhara, where the tribes laid their chiefs to rest before the creation of the great cities. There was great power invested in the ancient tombs, and the priests of the allied armies drew on that power with a willingness they'd never demonstrated in the march to the west. They summoned desert spirits and wove cunning illusions to trap and confound their pursuers, while mounted raiders laid bloody ambushes for any enemy horsemen that pressed too closely to the retreating column.

Two days after the battle at Quatar the sky to the west turned dark as pitch, like the heart of a raging sandstorm, and the allied army knew that Nagash and his forces had entered the Valley of Kings. Cloaked in howling blackness, the immortals and the companies of the dead pursued the allied armies without pause. As the undead horde stumbled onto the traps laid by the priests the valley shook with peals of thunder and strange, unearthly roars, and lurid flashes of lightning lit the edges of the dust clouds as the armies marched at night.

Slowly but surely, the gap between the two armies closed. The immortals learned to defeat the priests' illusions, and their necromantic powers allowed them to banish or destroy the spirits sent against them. They ransacked the ancient tombs to find more bodies to replenish their ranks, leaving nothing but rubble and ruin in their wake. With each passing night, they drew closer to their quarry, until the army's rearguard was locked in constant skirmishes with Numasi scouts and light infantry.

The terrain in the Valley of Kings was, however, favourable to defensive fighting. Clusters of stone crypts prevented massed cavalry charges and provided defensible positions for infantry and archers. There was no room to outflank the allied rearguard, and the defenders could fall back from one line of improvised fortifications to the next. The undead attackers pressed hard against the rearguard, and losses mounted, but the stubborn defenders succeeded in keeping Nagash's troops away from the main body of the retreating host.

Two weeks later, with roiling dust clouds looming at their backs, the vanguard of the eastern armies reached the Gates of the Dusk, and the warriors of the east fell to their knees and thanked the gods for their deliverance.

THE GATES OF the Dusk were older by far than their distant cousins to the west, some scholars even claiming that the great stone obelisks marking the entrance to the valley predated the Great Migration, though none would speculate on who could have raised such towering structures, or why. The massive stone pillars, eight in all, rose more than a hundred feet above the valley floor, and were arrayed side-by-side along the ancient road that wound along the base of the valley. During Settra's time, low walls had been built from the sides of the valley up to the base of the obelisks, but construction was halted shortly thereafter when a terrible plague swept through the work parties. The architects took this to be a sign of the gods' displeasure, and no further attempts were made to fortify the eastern end of the valley. A sprawling village of stone and mud-brick buildings that once supported the labourers still stood a quarter of a mile to the east of the great gates. Over time, it had been taken over by the temples of Djaf and Usirian as a stopping place for pilgrims who sought to visit the tombs of their ancestors within the valley. The village bustled with activity as the armies of the east filled the narrow streets and looked for places to make camp.

Rakh-amn-hotep had been carried into the centre of the village and placed in an abandoned manor that had once belonged to a Lybaran royal architect. He was brought aboard an improvised palanquin layered with cloaks and cushions, and his Ushabti carried him with the utmost care. Ekhreb and a squadron of horsemen kept onlookers and well-wishers at a distance as the king was brought into the manor.

While his miraculous survival was well known among the rank and file of the army, and, indeed, served to inspire the warriors many times during the hard march down the valley, what was not commonly known was that the bronze arrowhead had lodged deep in the king's spine. Rakh-amn-hotep could move his eyes and manage a weak grunt if asked a simple question, but that was all. For all intents and purposes he was a living man trapped in a lifeless body.

The king's servants made Rakh-amn-hotep as comfortable as they could in a secluded part of the house, while Ekhreb and the army's captains gathered and began making plans to defend the Gates of the Dusk from Nagash's horde. Rakh-amn-hotep lay in the dim light of half a dozen oil lamps and listened to the murmuring voices in the manor's common room, while a dozen priests dressed his wound and washed his body in warm water and scented oils.

It was almost dawn. The army was almost fully encamped at the gates, with only the last squadrons of the rearguard still arriving from the night's skirmishes. Suddenly, the king heard a commotion in the street outside the manor, and surprised shouts at the manor door. Conversation in the common room abruptly ceased, and the priests attending the king shared worried glances as the commotion near the front of the old house increased.

Rakh-amn-hotep's hearing had grown as sharp as a bat's since his injury. He could tell that the voices were moving, heading deeper into the house. After a few moments it became clear that they were, in fact, coming his way. His gaze fell upon the room's single wooden door.

The assembled priests climbed nervously to their feet as footfalls sounded in the corridor beyond. The door latch rattled, and Ekhreb stepped swiftly inside. The champion was still covered in white dust from the road, and there was an agitated expression on his handsome face. Ignoring the startled looks from the priests, he approached the king and bowed.

'Nebunefer is here, with a delegation from the Hieratic Council at Mahrak,' he said gravely. 'They wish to see you.'

The two men locked eyes. It was a shameful thing for a man to be seen in such a crippled state, much less a king. Ekhreb looked willing and ready to send the delegates back to Mahrak if the king so wished.

After a moment, Rakh-amn-hotep drew a deep breath, and let out a single grunt: *Yes.*

Ekhreb bowed his head once more, and returned to the doorway.

'The Priest King of Rasetra welcomes you,' he said into the darkness.

The priests in the room bowed their heads and withdrew quickly to the edges of the room, and then sank to their knees as Nebunefer strode through the doorway. The aged priest had dispensed with his dust-stained robes, and wore the golden vestments of a high priest of Ptra. Behind him came four cloaked and hooded figures, their features completely hidden in layers of gauzy cotton.

The delegation approached the king's side and bowed deeply. Nebunefer raised his hands.

'The blessings of Ptra the Glorious be upon you, great one,' the priest intoned. 'Your name is spoken with reverence in the temples of the great city, where it rises like pleasing music to fill the ears of the gods.' Nebunefer turned and indicated the hooded figures with a sweep of his hand. 'The Hieratic Council has been informed of your heroic deeds, great king,' the priest said gravely, 'and they wish to give you this gift as a token of their gratitude.'

Nebunefer bowed once more and stepped aside. As one, the figures reached up and drew back their hoods. Several of the priests in the room gasped in surprise.

Rakh-amn-hotep found himself staring up at four identical golden masks, each one shaped by a master craftsman to capture the essence of a goddess. They were breathtaking in their perfection, from their almond-shaped eyes to the sleek curves of their cheeks and the promise of their full lips. The hammered gold glowed under the lamplight, and in the shifting shadows it seemed as though the masks smiled lovingly down upon the king. Black shadows pooled at the base of the priestesses' long, pale throats. Each young woman wore a necklace of black asps to guard her virtue and show her devotion to the goddess Asaph.

The priestesses gathered around the king's head and stretched forth pale hands decorated in sinuous henna tattoos. Rakh-amn-hotep felt their cool touch as they peeled away his bandages and brushed lightly at his face. Then they laid their hands upon his wound and in a single voice they began to chant.

The incantation was a long and arduous one, requiring a combination of timing, finesse and power. The priestesses' hands wove a delicate web around the king's wound, teasing the bronze arrowhead away from Rakh-amn-hotep's spine and knitting the flesh together in its wake. By the time they were done the oil lamps had burnt out and bright morning sunlight was slanting into the room from the corridor beyond.

Three of the priestesses drew up their hoods and withdrew to the doorway. The fourth studied the king in silence for a moment, and then bent towards him until her perfect golden mask was scant inches from his face. The flickering tongues of asps tickled the king's chin.

Large, dark eyes looked into the king's. The priestess exhaled, and Rakh-amn-hotep could somehow feel it through the mask, as though it had slipped past the goddess's rounded lips. Her breath was warm and soft, and smelled of vanilla.

'Rise,' the priestess whispered. 'Rise, and give glory to Asaph.'

With that, the priestess withdrew, drawing her hood up over her head and slipping silently from the room with her retinue at her back.

Rakh-amn hotep watched them go. He breathed deeply. A faint tremor passed through his body. His fingers twitched. Then slowly, painfully, the king pushed himself upright. He swung his legs over the edge of the palanquin and took another deep, racking breath. Then he pressed his hands to his face.

'Glory be to Asaph,' he said in a ragged voice.

'Glory be to Asaph,' Ekhreb echoed solemnly. Nebunefer smiled.

'I am glad to see you well, great king. Given all you and your people have done in the long war against the Usurper, this was the least that we could do.' The Rasetran king lowered his hands and gave the priest a forbidding stare.

'About damn time,' he growled. Nebunefer's smile faded. 'Excuse me?'

'There are perhaps a thousand men between here and the Fountains of Life whose bones are bleaching in the sun because our healers could not save them,' the king said. 'Where were the priestesses of Asaph then?' With a grunt, the king levered himself to his feet. 'Where were the priests of Mahrak when a plague of madness was raging through Quatar? We have marched and fought and bled for your sake, Nebunefer. Nagash is nearly upon your doorstep, and it's past time for you and your holy men to join the fight.'

The old priest bristled at the king's tone.

'We have opened our coffers to you and Hekhmenukep,' he snapped. 'We paid for your armies twice over!'

'You can keep your damned gold!' Rakh-amn-hotep shot back. 'We would have fought that monster even had it beggared us!' The king took a step towards the old man, his anger rising. Then he caught himself. With an effort, he took a deep breath and continued. 'You marched with us, Nebunefer. You were at Quatar. You've seen the bodies. Tens of thousands of dead men... Even if we win, our cities may never be the same again. If the Hieratic Council had been with us in the west–'

'It isn't as simple as that, great one,' Nebunefer said.

'I've heard the stories of the battle at Zedri,' Rakh-amn-hotep said. 'I know that Nagash's defilement of Neferem has given him the power to negate your invocations, but by the gods! The things that your priests might have done to sustain us, far from the battle line...'

'You know far less than you imagine,' Nebunefer hissed. He started to say more, and then paused. The old priest stared hard at the holy men ringing the room. 'Leave us,' he commanded.

When the priests were gone, Nebunefer glanced warily at Ekhreb, but Rakh-amn-hotep folded his arms stubbornly, and said, 'He deserves to hear this as much as I do, perhaps more so.' Nebunefer frowned, but finally he shrugged his bony shoulders.

'Very well,' he said with a sigh. 'Do you know why Neferem renders our invocations powerless?'

The Rasetran king considered the question, and then answered, 'Because she represents the covenant between the gods and men, which is why Settra coerced the Hieratic Council into allowing his marriage to the Daughter of the Sun, hundreds of years ago. He sought to bind the sacred covenant governing all of Nehekhara with his household, and to prevent the council at Mahrak from ever turning their powers against him.'

'But,' Nebunefer said with a raised finger, 'the great king didn't fully appreciate the significance of his marriage.

The Daughter of the Sun does not represent the sacred covenant, she is the covenant made flesh.'

Rakh-amn-hotep scowled at the priest, and asked, 'Why would the gods do such a thing?' Nebunefer smiled faintly.

'As a sign of faith,' he replied. 'Faith that our ancestors would honour their promise to give offerings and worship to the gods.' The king nodded thoughtfully.

'And Nagash has claimed this covenant for his own. Gods above, he's a usurper in more ways than one.'

Nebunefer shook his head ruefully, and said, 'For all his vaunted intelligence, Nagash doesn't seem to fully appreciate what he's done. If he wished, he could command the powers of the gods, in exchange for sacrifice and worship. As terrible as things have been, but for the Usurper's arrogance it could have been far worse.'

'That remains to be seen,' Rakh-amn-hotep growled. 'Since Neferem represents the covenant, she is the conduit for the gods' power. But such things work both ways.'

The old priest nodded. 'Our offerings do not reach the gods, nor do their gifts bless us in return,' he said. 'Nagash has cut us off from our power, great one. We have not acted until now because we cannot.'

The king's hand strayed to his throat. 'But what the priestesses just did...' he began.

Nebunefer sighed. 'A lifetime's devotion to the gods transforms us. Our souls become charged with the power of the divine. Now, that is all we have left.' He nodded towards the door. 'Those four priestesses gave up part of their souls so that you could walk again.'

'Great gods,' Rakh-amn-hotep whispered. 'How are we to stop this monster? His army will be here an hour after sunset. We must hold him at the Gates of the Dusk.'

'We cannot hold Nagash here,' Nebunefer said. 'The gates are poorly fortified, and your armies have been badly mauled already.'

'My men don't lack for courage,' the Rasetran king growled, 'especially now that the beast is breathing at their door.'

Nebunefer chuckled.

'After all that your warriors have done, no one will ever question their courage,' he said, 'but if they remain here they will be overrun by dawn. Ask your man here if you don't believe me.'

The king looked to his champion. Ekhreb scowled, but nodded reluctantly.

'He's right, great one,' he said, 'Those walls weren't built high enough or broad enough to stop a determined army, and the men have nothing left to give. They will fight if you give the order, but they won't last for long.'

'What would you have us do, then?' Rakh-amn-hotep asked the priest with a sigh.

'Withdraw,' Nebunefer replied. 'Return to your cities and rebuild your armies.'

'And what about Nagash?'

'Nagash means to conquer Mahrak,' the old priest said. 'He has dreamt of humbling us for a very long time, and now he has the chance.' He faced the king. 'You are right, great one. The time has come for us to pay our tithe of blood. We will fight the Usurper at the City of Hope until you and Hekhmenukep can return and break the siege.'

'That could take years, Nebunefer,' the king replied. 'You just said yourself that the Hieratic Council is powerless.' Another faint smile crossed Nebunefer's face.

'I never said the word powerless, great one. We still have our Ushabti, and the city is protected by wards that even Nagash would be hard-pressed to break. Fear not. We will hold out for as long as we must.'

Rakh-amn-hotep began to pace around the dimly lit chamber. His knees felt weak, but after he'd learned what had been done to restore his limbs, he didn't think he'd ever sit down again.

'What of Lahmia?' he said. 'Those libertines have done nothing, even when Nagash took their royal daughter and slew her son. How long do they think they can sit by and watch Nehekhara burn?'

'We have sent emissaries to Lahmia many times,' Nebunefer said. 'So long as Neferem is tied to the Usurper, they refuse to act.' The king chuckled bitterly.

'For me, that would be more than enough reason to act.' He glanced at Ekhreb. 'What is the hour?'

'An hour before noon, great one.'

Rakh-amn-hotep sighed. There was much to do, and little time.

'I want our forces on the march by mid-afternoon,' he told his champion. Ekhreb managed a grin.

'Another long march,' he said. 'The men will start to regret all those prayers for your swift recovery.'

'No doubt,' the king said, 'but at least this time they'll be heading home.' Rakh-amn-hotep turned to Nebunefer. 'Any supplies you could give us–'

'They are on the way here even now,' the priest interrupted. 'You can take the wagons, as well. We'll expect you to return them in due time.'

The king nodded to Ekhreb, who bowed low and hastened from the room. Moments later he could be heard barking orders to the captains waiting in the common room.

Nebunefer bowed low to Rakh-amn-hotep.

'With your permission, great one, I must depart,' he said. 'There is much to be done in Mahrak before the Usurper's army arrives.' The king nodded, but his expression turned grave.

'I cannot speak for Lybaras, but I and my people will not abandon you. That said, I can't guarantee when we will return. You may have to endure for a very long time.'

Nebunefer smiled, and said, 'With the gods, all things are possible. Until we meet again, Rakh-amn-hotep. In this life, or the next.'

━◄ TWENTY-SEVEN ►━

The Undying King

*Khemri, the Living City, in the 62nd year of Qu'aph
the Cunning (-1750 Imperial Reckoning)*

THE EVENING AIR blowing through the open entryway of Settra's Court was pungent with the reek of cinders and scorched flesh. Faint shouts and terrified screams sounded in the distance. Khemri, the Living City, was on fire.

'Explain this,' Nagash said to his immortals. His cold voice echoed faintly in the cavernous space. 'This is the third night in a row that there have been riots in the Merchant Quarter.'

The black-robed noblemen, a hundred in all, shifted uneasily around the darkened court and stole wary glances at one another. Finally, Raamket stepped forwards and ventured a reply.

'It's the same as always,' he grunted. 'The harvest was poor. Trade has suffered. They crowd together in the marketplace like sheep and bleat the same things, over and over again. When darkness falls, they grow bold enough to cause trouble.' The nobleman shrugged. 'We kill the rabble-rousers when we catch them, but the rest of the herd never seems to get the message.'

'Then perhaps you're being too selective,' the king snapped. He leaned forwards on his throne and glared down at Raamket. 'Send your men through the quarter and kill every man, woman and child you find. Better yet, impale them on spikes around the city wells, so that every matron who has to come to draw water can listen to their cries of agony. Order must be restored. Do you understand? Kill however many you must to put an end to this disgraceful unrest.'

Arkhan the Black stood at Nagash's right hand, close by the dais. He took a long drink from the goblet in his hand and stared into its depths.

'Killing that many people will be counterproductive,' he said grimly. 'Our labour pool is small enough as it is, to say nothing of the city watch or the army. Every citizen we put to death only places more strain on those who survive.'

The emptiness of Settra's Court attested to the vizier's observation. Where the hall was once packed with obsequious nobles and scheming ambassadors, now only the king and his immortals remained, along with a handful of slaves and Nagash's silent queen. One way or another, the Black Pyramid had consumed everyone else.

It had been an epic labour, far in excess of the king's worst predictions. Quarrying the marble and transporting it alone had occupied tens of thousands of workers and required expert stonesmiths to properly select and shape the massive ebon blocks. Accidents and misfortune took their toll, both at the quarry and at the construction site: a cable snapped, or tired labourers grew inattentive, and men died in shrieking agony beneath tons of black marble. In the first ten years, Nagash had used up half the slaves he'd taken from Zandri, and more continued to die every day.

Nevertheless, the work went on. When setbacks occurred, Nagash ordered his taskmasters to work deep into the night. The city watch sent a steady stream of gamblers, drunkards and thieves to the slave camps outside the necropolis to try to stem the growing tide of casualties. When the criminals ran out, they sent anyone they caught on the streets after dark. The great cities also continued to send their monthly tithes to Khemri, buying peace with the Usurper with a steady flow of blood and coin.

Still, it wasn't enough. Construction fell behind schedule, year upon year. No one in Khemri believed that the structure would be completed in Nagash's lifetime. Years passed, but the King of the Living City did not seem to feel the passage of time, and neither did the king's chosen vassals, whose power and wealth in the city increased with each succeeding decade. Rumours were whispered among the lesser nobles of the court: had Nagash unravelled the deepest mysteries of the Mortuary Cult? Had he been blessed by the gods to lead Nehekhara to a new golden age?

Then Neferem began appearing at the king's side during his Grand Assemblies, seated upon the lesser throne and assuming the duties of a queen, and the rumours took a much darker turn.

As the years passed and the number of deaths continued to mount, the annual civil service for Khemri's citizens was extended from a month to six months, and then up to eight. Fields outside the city grew fallow for want of farmers, and Khemri began to spend a great deal of gold importing more grain from the north. Trade suffered for want of craftsmen and artisans, and prices increased. Khemri's new golden age lost its lustre quickly.

Lahmia was the first of the great cities to withdraw its ambassadors and renege on its monthly tithe. Others followed quickly: Lybaras, then Rasetra, Quatar and Ka-Sabar. They had calculated that Khemri didn't have enough population left to raise a proper army to enforce their claims, and they were right. The king vowed that work on the pyramid would continue, regardless of the cost. Nagash modified the civil service decree once more, so that every father and eldest son in every household in the city, common or noble, would serve continuously until the massive edifice was complete.

The court emptied quickly. A few noble families tried to flee the city entirely, making for the dubious safety of the east. Nagash ordered a squadron of light horsemen sent after them, offering a hundred gold coins for the head of every man, woman and child they caught. It was a gamble, of sorts, for there was no way to be certain that the horsemen would follow orders once they had left Khemri behind, and Nagash could not send an immortal to command them. For as much as the king and his chosen vassals had become ageless and powerful beyond mortal ken, they nevertheless paid a steep price for their gifts. The light of Nehekhara's sun burned their skin like a firebrand and sapped their terrible strength, forcing them to seek refuge in the deepest cellars or crypts during the day. The problem had confounded the king for decades, and the answer continued to elude him. It was as though Ptra himself opposed Nagash's will, scourging him and his immortals with fire.

'The priests,' Nagash muttered darkly. 'They are the ones to blame for this.'

He knew it to be true. The priests were immune from conscription or civil service, and they spent their days skulking in their temples and looking for ways to undermine him. They asked after Sukhet continually, and Nagash suspected that they had spies in the palace searching for where he was kept.

Arkhan shifted uncomfortably.

'No doubt you are right, master, but what can we do? Attacking them is tantamount to attacking Mahrak, and if we did that, then the whole country would rise up against us.'

Nagash nodded absently, but his gaze drifted to Neferem. The queen sat straight-backed in her chair, showing no reaction to what was being said. He wondered if perhaps she was in league with the priests as well.

The gift of the elixir to Neferem had been a necessary one. He was determined to possess her beauty, if he had to take a thousand years to wear her down. Nagash had seen how the elixir had affected the will of his vassals, who were helpless to resist its seductive pull, and he hoped that she would succumb as well. Though it made her more agreeable in general, the queen's will was entirely unaffected.

She had, however, stopped pestering him with questions about her son. That at least was a blessing.

The problem, the king suspected, was that duplicitous priest Nebunefer. Nagash was certain that he was a spy sent by Mahrak, and he could come and go freely from the palace now that the king and his immortals had to sleep through the day. Something was going to have to be done about that man, the king decided, something quick and fatal, and it was going to have to happen soon. Mahrak could protest all it liked.

Then, shadows passed across the open entryway to the court. The immortals were immediately on their guard, their hands straying to the swords at their belts. Nagash frowned curiously. When was the last time a citizen had appeared at one of the Grand Assemblies? Twenty years? More?

'Come forward,' the king called out. His voice rang sharply through the stillness. 'What do you have to say?'

There was a few moments' hesitation, before a solitary figure appeared in the entryway. He approached the dais with slow, faltering steps, silhouetted by the moonlit entryway behind him. Nagash could tell at once that it was an old man, bent and nearly broken by the weight of years. When he was three-quarters of the way down the long, echoing aisle, the king recognised who it was, and felt a surge of anger.

'Sumesh? Why aren't you at the pyramid? What's happened?'

A stir went through the immortals as the pyramid's last surviving architect shuffled painfully into the king's presence. Sumesh was more than two hundred and thirty years old, positively ancient by Nehekharan standards. Though Nagash had ensured that he was a very wealthy man, Sumesh was haggard and his body twisted with age. His gnarled hands trembled and his shoulders were bent.

Sumesh did not answer at first. The architect strode up to the foot of the dais and carefully knelt upon the stone before turning his face up to the king.

'Great one,' he said in a quavering voice, 'I have the honour to inform you that the last stone was fitted into place an hour past. The Black Pyramid is complete.'

For a moment, Nagash could not believe his ears. A glimmer of triumph shone in his dark eyes.

'You have done very well, master architect,' he said. 'I am indebted to you, and will ensure that you are well rewarded.'

No sooner had the words escaped his lips than Arkhan stepped behind Sumesh and cut his throat from ear to ear. The immortals growled hungrily as the old man's blood poured out onto the marble steps, and his corpse collapsed face-first onto the stones. Nagash studied the spreading pool of crimson at his feet and smiled.

'It appears that a solution has presented itself,' he said.

THE KING DISPATCHED his orders at once. The slaves were ordered back to their camps and given an extra ration of food and wine. Arkhan, Raamket and the rest of the immortals were sent out into the city streets to put an end to the rioting by any means necessary. Then Nagash left the queen in the care of Ghazid, and had Khefru lead him through the fire-lit streets to the necropolis, where the new pyramid waited.

It could be seen for miles along the road to the necropolis, towering high above the petty crypts and seeming to swallow the light of the moon. The Black Pyramid was darker than the night, its edges knife-sharp against the indigo sky. Arcs of pale lightning would occasionally crawl across its polished surface, sending pulses of invisible power washing over Nagash's skin.

The pyramid was a collector and an attractor of dark magic, and for two hundred years it had glutted itself on the spirits of tens of thousands of slaves. That energy coursed through its glossy stones, stored for a single purpose: a ritual unlike anything Nagash had ever performed.

The palanquin crossed a vast plaza made of close-set marble flagstones and stopped before a featureless, unadorned opening at the base of the pyramid. It was no more than a square opening in the side of the great structure, just wide enough for two people to enter side-by-side. Nagash and Khefru passed through the opening and were swallowed by the darkness beyond.

At a gesture from the king, the corridor beyond was suffused with a pale green grave-light that seeped from the very stones. The floor, walls and ceiling of the passageway were intricately carved with thousands of hieroglyphics, placed with exacting care by expert stonemasons. Nagash ran his fingers along the carvings as he climbed the sloping corridor, tasting the enormous power roiling within the structure.

'Yes,' he whispered. 'The alignment is complete. I can feel the energies building.'

Khefru strode along six paces behind the king. His face was a mask of dread.

'Sumesh outdid himself,' he said quietly. 'He finished months ahead of schedule.'

'So he did,' Nagash said, and chuckled at the realisation. The power coursing through him was far sweeter and more potent than any wine, and he drank deeply of it.

He led Khefru upwards through the nacreous light, through a twisting maze of corridors and stark, empty chambers that pulsed with necromantic energies. Both master and servant navigated the labyrinth with the ease born of familiarity. Nagash had moved his arcane researches, and later, his abode, into the pyramid five years before, as the work parties laboured to complete the upper quarter of the structure. The labourers knew full well the extent of the deadly traps sown throughout the pyramid, and knew better than to trespass beyond the unfinished areas of the construction site.

Finally, the king reached the heart of the vast pyramid: the ritual chamber. It was a large, octagonal room whose walls curved upwards to form a faceted dome above a complex ritual circle some fifteen paces across, carved directly into the marble floor and inlaid with crushed onyx and silver. Thousands of complex hieroglyphs had been carved into the gleaming walls, each one painstakingly designed to focus the death energies stored within the pyramid and channel them into the ritual circle. Nagash stood in the doorway for a moment, studying the interplay of energies that flowed across the graven walls and the circle-inscribed floor. Finally, he nodded in grim satisfaction.

'It is perfect,' he said with a jackal's smile. Nagash walked reverently across the room and took his place in the centre of the ritual circle. 'Go to the sanctum and gather my books,' he ordered his servant. 'There is much work to be done, and not much time before the dawn.'

Khefru still lingered at the chamber's entryway, his expression troubled.

'What ritual, master?' he asked in a dull voice.

'The one that will usher in a new age,' the king said, fully intoxicated by the power at his command. 'The false gods must perish to make way for mankind's true master.'

With his back to Khefru, Nagash could not see the look of horror etched into the servant's ravaged features.

'You… you cannot think to slay the gods, master. It's not possible.'

Even as he said it, Khefru cringed, expecting a furious tirade from his master, but it appeared that Nagash was in a magnanimous mood.

'Kill them? No. At least, not at first,' he said calmly. 'First we must starve them of the power they have stolen from our people. When the priests of Nehekhara are dead, the temples will empty and the gods will no longer receive the worship that sustains them.'

Khefru said, aghast, 'That would break the covenant! Without that, the land will die!'

Nagash turned to his servant.

'After all this time, you still don't understand, do you?' he said, as though speaking to a child. 'Life and death will have no meaning once I am master of Nehekhara. There will be no fear of hunger or disease. Think of that! My empire will be eternal, and one day it will spread across the entire world!'

Khefru could only stare in shock at the king's pronouncement. After a moment, the triumphant glow waned from Nagash's face.

'Now go,' he said coldly. 'It is well past the hour of the dead, and there are many preparations to be made.'

THE KING LABOURED for several hours in the ritual chamber, laying the groundwork for his incantation. Khefru stood at the margins, taking precise notes as ordered and fetching arcane powders and paints from the sanctum many levels below. His face, backlit by the flickering energies that surrounded his master, was thoughtful and deeply troubled.

Finally, when dawn broke above the distant mountains, Nagash called a halt.

'It is almost complete,' he said. 'By tomorrow at midnight, the incantation will be ready.'

As the sun rose into the sky overhead, Nagash left the ritual chamber and followed a twisting passageway down one level to his crypt. Many of his immortals had taken up residence in the lower levels of the pyramid, at the king's command, and were probably already secured in their stone sarcophagi.

The crypt was a pyramid in miniature, with four slanting walls that came to a point over the king's resting place. Powerful incantations were carved into each of the walls and the symbols filled with powdered gemstone to enhance their longevity and potency. They glowed with an inner light as Nagash entered the chamber.

At the centre of the room stood a low stone dais, and upon it rested a marble sarcophagus fit for a king.

Khefru rushed forwards as Nagash strode to the dais, stepping up to the sarcophagus and gripping the stone lid. With supernatural strength he lifted the covering clear with a smooth, practiced motion and set it aside.

Inside the stone coffin were perfumed cushions and sprigs of aromatic herbs, laid aside for the comfort of the king. Nagash climbed inside without hesitation and lay down. The marble enclosure channelled the energies of the pyramid and helped restore his mind and body while he drifted in a kind of cataleptic trance.

As soon as he was settled, Khefru lifted the lid once more and prepared to set it into place. At the last moment, he hesitated. Nagash glanced impatiently at his servant.

'What is it?' he snapped. 'I can see the questioning look in your eyes. Out with it.'

'I…' he began. 'I beg you to reconsider this, master. Your pyramid is finished, but Khemri as a whole is weak. If you strike out at the priests, there will be no turning back.' The king's face hardened into a mask of rage.

'With the power at my command, I can take a thousand men and defeat every city in Nehekhara. They would not tire, would not fear, would not falter, for they would not die. You're a fool, Khefru. Once I thought you an ambitious man, but the truth is that you have always been a coward. You don't have the strength to stand up to the fates and choose your own destiny.'

Khefru stared down at the king for a moment longer, and his expression fell.

'Perhaps you're right, master,' he said, as he slid the stone lid back into place. 'Sleep well.'

NAGASH AWOKE TO a strange, scratching sound above him. For a moment, he did not understand what he was hearing. His mind was still immersed in heady dreams of vengeance and conquest. Had he imagined the sound? Was it borne from dreamlike vistas of burning cities and plains of bleached bone?

Then a thin trickle of stone landed upon his chest and he knew that this was no dream, but something altogether worse. Someone was drilling a hole in his sarcophagus.

There was a scrape of metal as a tool was removed from the breach. His mind raced as he tried to understand what was happening, and then something thick and cool fell in a steady trickle onto his chest.

Lamp oil, he realised with a growing sense of horror. Someone meant to burn him alive inside his coffin.

With a wordless snarl, he shoved hard against the stone lid, but the covering was held fast. More heated shouts occurred above him, and the pouring oil abruptly ceased. The next thing to come through the bore-hole would be a red-hot coal.

Seething with anger, Nagash put his hands against the lid of the sarcophagus and roared a furious incantation. The power of the pyramid flowed into him like a torrent and the stone lid exploded with a flash of heat and a thunderous detonation.

The blast, in such a confined space, stunned and blinded the king. For a fleeting instant there was a flare of searing agony, and then a rush of air and the hissing of flames. The blast had ignited the oil soaking into his robes! Nagash screamed in anger and pain, breathing in a gust of flame that raked red-hot talons down his throat and into his lungs.

Deaf and blind, Nagash could do nothing but call upon the pyramid's power once more. A cold gust of wind erupted from the sarcophagus, snuffing the flames and tearing the oil-soaked robes from his torso. The king croaked another incantation and he burst from the smoking coffin like a bat, his arms spread wide as he leapt straight up into the air.

Men were screaming in the small chamber, a confusing babble of orders, sacred oaths and bitter curses. Nagash fetched up hard against the ceiling and tried to force his eyes to function. Power boiled into his eye sockets, causing still more pain but clearing the spots of colour from his vision.

The smouldering corpses of young men lay scattered around the king's chamber, their bodies torn by shrapnel from the exploding stone lid. Four men, who had been standing close to the entrance and had escaped the worst of the blast, were fanning out into the room and raising their hands as though to abjure the king. Nagash felt their power at once, and then recognised the robes they wore. Priests!

One of the men, a young priest of Ptra, raised his hands and uttered a sharp invocation. There was a flare of golden light, and a spear of flame jetted from the man's open hands.

With a curse, Nagash dodged to the right, croaking out a banishment spell even as he tumbled through the air. The holy flame struck the ceiling and seared his face and hands before it collapsed under the weight of his counter-spell. Without hesitation, Nagash flung out his hand and sent a flurry of ebon darts from his fingertips. They pierced the young priest like arrows, catching him in the right arm, chest and neck. He collapsed, writhing and choking on his own blood.

A booming voice roared out words of power, and Nagash felt the air tremble around him. Stone shards on the floor quivered, and then streaked through the air towards him. Once again, the king used his power of flight to dive across the room and escape the lethal hail. Pellets dug painfully into his legs, but the worst of the blast passed him by.

The surviving priests were all focusing on him. Abruptly, the wind supporting him rebelled, as though gripped by another man's will. Nagash was caught unawares and sent plunging to the ground, just as another bolt of flame tore through the spot where he had been, He landed painfully on his side, listening to the angry shouts of the priests as they tried to coordinate their attacks.

Lying on the stone floor, Nagash was partially hidden behind his smouldering sarcophagus. He glimpsed the legs of one of his attackers and snapped out a fierce incantation. At once, the floor beneath the attacker turned into a pit of darkness, and the priest had time for one terrified scream before he disappeared from sight.

The king heard the startled shouts of the two surviving attackers on the opposite side of the sarcophagus. Their voices dropped to a whisper as they discussed what to do next. Nagash cast around quickly, looking for some means to turn the tables on the two priests. His gaze fell upon a trio of bodies to his left, and he was suddenly reminded of his last conversation with Khefru, only a few hours before. On impulse, he stretched out his hand towards the bodies and began to improvise.

The power of the pyramid flowed through his fingertips towards the corpses. For a moment, nothing happened. Then, one of the dead men stirred. Slowly, clumsily, the corpse rolled onto its stomach and tried to clamber to its feet.

There were more nervous whispers on the other side of the coffin, and then silence. Nagash gathered himself, watching the shambling corpse intently. As it swayed unsteadily to its feet, the priests saw it and attacked. A gust of wind seized the corpse and pulled it up into the air above the sarcophagus, where a spear of flame pierced its chest and set it alight.

The two priests cried out in triumph just as Nagash rose quietly on the right side of the coffin and raked the attackers with a storm of necromantic bolts.

As the dead men collapsed to the ground, Nagash lurched towards the entryway. With the rush of battle fading, a flood of agony threatened to overwhelm him. Cursing, he drew upon the pyramid still more, silencing the pain and trying to heal his wounds.

A figure stood just outside the entrance. Nagash came up short, his right hand rising with a hiss.

'It's me, master,' Khefru said. The servant stepped into the room, a look of shock and surprise on his face. 'I... I tried to get to you in time,' he stammered. 'They got here just ahead of me.'

'Indeed,' the king growled. His voice, issuing from a flame-scarred throat, sounded almost bestial.

Khefru stared at the king's burned body, momentarily transfixed by the enormity of what had happened.

'You're hurt,' he said shakily. 'Please. Let me tend to your throat.'

He stepped closer, tentatively touching the king's burned neck with his fingertips. The gesture covered the movement of his right hand, which thrust a needle-pointed dagger straight into the king's heart.

The two men froze, locked in a grim tableau. Khefru grunted, trying to force the knife deeper, but Nagash had seized his wrist. The point of the knife had penetrated little more than an inch into the king's chest.

'Did you think I would not guess?' Nagash said to him, the growl in his voice nothing to do with his injuries. 'How else could the priests have reached my chambers?'

A flicker of fear played across Khefru's face, and then his expression hardened as he surrendered to the inevitable.

'You went too far,' he snarled. 'You were the most powerful priest in Khemri! You could have lived a rich, indolent life. Instead you threw it all away for this... this nightmare! It's obscene!' he cried. 'Can't you see what you've become? You're a monster!'

Khefru heaved on the dagger with the last reserves of his strength, trying to finish what he'd begun, but the weapon did not budge an inch.

Nagash reached up with his left hand and placed it on Khefru's chest.

'Not a monster,' he said. 'A god, a living god. I am the master of life and death, Khefru. Alas, you were too faithless to believe me. So now I must show you.'

The king clenched his left hand and drew upon the power of the pyramid. Khefru stiffened, his eyes widening and his mouth gaping in a silent scream. Nagash began an incantation, shaping the words as he went along and focusing his will with singular intent. The servant's body began to convulse.

Nagash drew his left hand away from Khefru's chest, and as he did so, he drew a glowing filament of energy along with it. The king's eyes never left Khefru's as he slowly and remorselessly drew his servant's soul from his body. As he did so, Khefru's stolen youth fled with it, causing his body to shrivel and decay before Nagash's eyes. When he was done, nothing but a stream of dust trickled from his clenched right hand.

Khefru's ghost floated before the king, moaning softly in terror and pain.

'Now you will serve me forever more,' Nagash said to the spirit. 'You are bound to me. My fate is now yours.'

The king turned and found Arkhan and the other immortals standing outside the doorway to the chamber. They were weak and disoriented, having been roused rudely from their slumber.

'What has happened?' Arkhan gasped. Nagash eyed his men coldly.

'We have been betrayed,' he said.

* * *

FILLED WITH ICY rage, Nagash climbed the twisting ramps to the pyramid's ritual chamber. His mind worked swiftly, creating a picture of what his enemies intended. Khefru's betrayal was no isolated thing. He had approached the priesthood and offered to lead them to the crypt chamber, but Nagash had no doubt that the priests had bigger plans of their own. Even now they would be in the palace, searching for Neferem and persuading her to take control of the city. It was not an assassination, but a coup.

His enemies had acted prematurely, no doubt surprised by the early completion of the pyramid. With more time to plan and gather their resources, the priests might have succeeded. Instead, they had failed, and their doom was sealed.

The king hastened into the ritual chamber and gathered his concentration. All the elements were in place. He had but to utter the incantation, and the age of gods and priests would come to a terrible end.

POWER BUILT WITHIN the Black Pyramid as Nagash's incantation began. Every slave who died during its construction, more than sixty thousand souls, was focused by the king's fury into a single, terrible spell.

Above the pyramid, the sky began to warp, and then darken. Black clouds boiled into existence where none had been before, lit from within by savage bursts of lightning. The density and power of the unnatural storm grew more and more intense, casting its shadow in a spreading pool across Khemri's necropolis. Where it fell, the dead trembled uneasily in their graves.

For more than half an hour the energy grew in power, until it seemed that the sky would split beneath its awful weight. Then, with a hideous, piercing scream the storm burst in an irresistible wave, racing in a series of ebon ripples across the sky.

The shadow of Nagash's fury spread to every corner of Nehekhara in the space of just a few minutes. Darkness fell across the great cities, and every priest or acolyte touched by the shadow died in a single, agonising instant. Only those who by sheer fortune were shielded by stone survived the lash of the necromancer's power.

NAGASH KNEW AT once that his ritual had only partially succeeded. He'd moved too quickly, and his focus had been tainted by his anger and his lust for revenge. Thousands had died, to be sure, but it was not yet enough.

The reserves of necromantic power inside the temple were weakened, but enough remained for a single invocation. Nagash uttered the words of power, and a pall of dust and shadow spread from the necropolis and fell upon Khemri, cloaking the Living City in artificial night.

The king turned to his immortals. To Raamket he said, 'Take two-thirds of the chosen and drown the temples in blood! Slay every holy man or woman you find!'

To Arkhan, Shepsu-hur and the rest, Nagash simply said, 'Follow me.'

DOZENS OF ROBED bodies littered the plaza outside the royal palace. Nagash led his twenty-five men straight to Settra's Court, where he found the queen and the high priests of the city. They were bickering like children, each one with a differing idea of what to do next. Most were ashen-faced, on the verge of panic after the king's shadow had fallen across the city.

Nagash and Neferem's eyes met across the length of the vast, shadowy court. The queen's face lit with an expression of pure hatred, and the priests turned to face the king with mingled expressions of anger and dread.

'Kill them,' Nagash commanded his men, 'all but Neferem. She belongs to me.'

The immortals did not hesitate. Swords and knives leapt from their scabbards as they raced down the length of the court. The high priests all began to talk at once, throwing up their hands and uttering a bewildering array of invocations, but Nagash was prepared for them. Shadows raced across the marble tiles, and sped from the darkness beyond the tall pillars flanking the centre aisle. They swept down on the priests like vultures, freezing their hearts just as they had stolen the will of Thutep, the former king.

The high priests of the living city were made of sterner stuff than Nagash's late brother. Amamurti, the aged high priest of Ptra, threw off the king's fist of shadow and hurled a spear of flame the length of the hall. It struck Shepsu-hur full in the chest, setting him ablaze in an instant. The immortal screamed in terror and pain, his skin melting like tallow in the heat. He staggered, pawing desperately at his chest and face, and then with an effort of will he collected himself and continued to run, closing the distance with the man who had wounded him.

Another immortal toppled to the floor with his legs nearly cut out from under him by a handful of stone projectiles. Wind buffeted the warriors, threatening to pull them off their feet. Arkhan caught sight of the Hierophant of Phakth and stopped his invocation with a hurled dagger. The high priest fell to his knees, clutching at the knife that had sprouted from his throat.

Before the hierophants could ready another wave of spells the immortals were upon them. Swords flashed, and men were torn asunder. The Hierophant of Djaf met the charge head-on, cutting one immortal down with a single stroke of his sword before another buried his knife in the high priest's eye. Arkhan reached the fallen Hierophant of Phakth and despatched him with a swift stroke of his blade.

Nagash paced along the aisle in the wake of his warriors, already casting a new incantation. As the priests fell he tore their life essences from their bodies and bound them as he had done to Khefru. One by one their moaning forms were drawn through the air towards the king and formed an unnatural retinue around his body.

The High Priestesses of Asaph and Basth fell next, their heads severed as they tried to fight back-to-back against the immortals. The Hierophant of Tahoth fell next, pleading for mercy as Arkhan slit his throat. The rest fell back, climbing the dais and forming a barrier between the queen and Nagash's men. As they did, the High Priest of Sokth took a dagger in his leg and fell onto the steps. An immortal leapt on him like a desert lion and sank his teeth into the man's face.

That left only Amamurti and the Hierophant of Geheb. The high priest of the earth god was already bleeding from half a dozen wounds, but he continued to fend off his attackers with brutal sweeps of his bloodstained hammer. One immortal grew too bold and tried to cut at the hierophant's knees. The high priest smashed the warrior aside with a blow from his hammer, but that created the opening Arkhan was looking for. Swift as a viper, he leapt forwards and brought down his gleaming khopesh, and the hierophant's hammer, along with his arm, bounced wetly across the stone steps.

The Hierophant of Ptra called out the name of his god and hurled a gout of hissing flame down the steps at the advancing immortals. Three of them were struck full-force and collapsed in heaps of blackened bones and bubbling flesh. Before Amamurti could cast another invocation he was struck by three flung daggers, one of which pierced his heart. The high priest sank slowly to the dais beside Neferem's paralysed form, his life essence bleeding from his eyes and gaping mouth.

Nagash stepped slowly through the carnage. With a wave of his hand he snuffed the flames that were scourging Shepsu-hur's body, and then climbed the steps until he stood eye-to-eye with the queen. For the first time Nagash noticed the terrified form of Ghazid, crouched fearfully in the shadow of Settra's throne.

The king's gaze returned to Neferem. The Daughter of the Sun was quivering with rage, struggling to break the hold that Nagash had over her. Once upon a time she might have succeeded, but decades of drinking Nagash's elixir had taken its toll on her will.

'Where is that snake, Nebunefer?' the king growled. 'I know he had a hand in this treachery.'

'He is not here,' the queen answered defiantly. 'I sent him away, in case the priests failed to kill you.' She tried to move, to advance upon him with clenched fists, but Nagash's will held her fast. 'Whatever happens here, at least he will survive to raise the other great cities against you!'

'You dare defy me, your rightful king?' Nagash roared.

'You killed my son!' Neferem said through clenched teeth. Her voice seethed with hatred. 'Khefru told me everything.'

'Did he tell you that you drank Sukhet's blood an hour later?' Nagash replied. 'Yes. You owe your continued youth to his murder.'

Tears leaked from the corners of Neferem's eyes, but the hatred on her face remained.

'Kill me and be done with it,' she hissed. 'It doesn't matter now. You've spilled the blood of holy men, Nagash. The gods will engineer your ruin far better than I.'

'You think this is terrible?' Nagash said, indicating the pile of torn and bleeding bodies. The ghosts shifted around him, wailing piteously. 'This is but the prologue, my foolish little queen. I have not yet begun to sow the seeds of slaughter across Nehekhara. When I am done, Mahrak will lie in ruins, and the old gods will be cast down forever. And you will stand by my side and watch me do it.'

Nagash's left hand shot forwards and closed around Neferem's throat.

'From the moment I saw you, I knew that I had to possess you,' he said. 'That time has now come.'

Neferem started to speak, but suddenly her body stiffened as Nagash began to chant. Power coursed through the queen's body, bursting from her eyes and mouth in a torrent of glowing green light. Her lifeforce was torn from her, flowing to Nagash in a slow, inexorable stream. A faint, tortured scream rose from the queen's throat: a sound of terrible anguish and pain that seemed to go on and on.

Tendrils of smoke rose from Neferem's skin. Her flesh shrank and her skin wrinkled like dried leather. The flow of energy from her body began to dwindle. Her shoulders drooped and her head bobbed on her almost-skeletal neck, but somehow the queen continued to survive.

Nagash drew the life from her until he could take no more. In the space of a minute, the Daughter of the Sun had been transformed into a living horror, her body somehow sustained by the bindings of the sacred covenant. Her withered legs gave out beneath her, and Neferem sank painfully to the dais, right beside Settra's throne.

The king studied Neferem in silence. His immortals stared at the king and his queen with horror and awe. Behind the king's throne, concealed in darkness, Ghazid held his head in his hands and wept.

◄ TWENTY-EIGHT ►

The City of the Gods

*Mahrak, the City of Hope, in the 63rd year of Ptra
the Glorious (-1744 Imperial Reckoning)*

BLUE-GREY SMOKE wreathed the thousand temples of the
city of Mahrak, filling the air with the fragrances of sandalwood, frankincense and myrrh. A riot of horns,
cymbals and silver bells echoed and re-echoed down the
narrow streets and across the great plazas where the faithful gathered for prayer and sacrifice. Priests slaughtered
herds of oxen, goats and lambs, casting their flesh and
blood into the flames. In some households, young slaves
were fed cups of wine laced with the black lotus, and then
were led to the sacrificial bonfires that burned before the
great Palace of the Gods. Across the City of Hope, beseeching hands were cast skywards, imploring the heavens for
deliverance from the terrible darkness approaching from
the west.

The people of the city had good reason to believe that
the gods would intervene. At the centre of the city,

surrounded by a walled plaza in the heart of the Palace of the Gods, lay the Khept-am-shepret, the miraculous Sundered Stone that saved the seven tribes from extinction during the darkest days of the Great Migration.

Bereft of their ancient homes, bereft of their gods, weakened unto death by the sun and the endless, scorching sands, the tribes had come to this great plain and found that they could walk no more. In ages past their gods had been the spirits of the trees and the jungle springs, of the panther, the monkey and the python.

Here, in this great, empty wasteland, the tribes in their desperation prayed to the sun and the blue sky for salvation, and Ptra, the Great Father, was moved by their pleas. He stretched forth his hand, and a great boulder in the tribes' midst split apart with a sound like a thunderbolt.

Stunned, the tribes gathered around the sundered stone, and saw fresh, sweet water come welling up through the sharp-edged cracks. The tribes drank, cutting their hands on the knife-edged stones and thus offering their first sacrifices to the gods of the desert. In the days that followed the great covenant was pledged and the Blessed Land was born.

Mahrak began as a collection of temples, one for each of the twelve great gods, and a glorious palace where the tribes could come together and offer worship on the high holy days of the year. Slowly but surely, the city grew up around these great structures, as cities are wont to do, first with districts of modest dwellings to house the workers building the temples, and then with marketplaces and bazaars where traders could come and ply their wares. Then, as centuries passed and the tribes spread across Nehekhara to found other great cities, Mahrak increased in wealth and influence as distant rulers sought the wise counsel and prayers of the temples.

The temples were gargantuan affairs, having grown along with their burgeoning fortunes: Geheb's temple was a mighty ziggurat that dominated the horizon to the east, lit at its summit by a roaring flame that had not been extinguished in four hundred years. Nearby, Djaf's temple was a sprawling complex of low, massive buildings built from slabs of black marble, while to the west, beyond the perfumed gardens of Asaph, the ivory tower of Usirian rose from the midst of a sprawling, intricate labyrinth formed by walls of polished sandstone.

The Palace of the Gods, the seat of power of Nehekhara's Hieratic Council, sat at the feet of a massive pyramid that rose more than two hundred feet into the sky. At its summit sat an enormous disk of polished gold that caught the sun's rays and reflected Ptra's glory in a shimmering beacon that could be seen for leagues across the eastern plains. All of the temples, even the broad field of black obelisks erected in obeisance to dreadful Khsar, the Howling One, glittered with ornaments of gold, silver and polished bronze, surrounded by crowded neighbourhoods of mud-brick buildings whose narrow streets only saw sunlight when Ptra's light hung directly overhead.

Mahrak was the oldest, largest and most splendid of Nehekhara's great cities, home to thousands of priests, priestesses and scholars and the tens of thousands of traders, craftsmen, labourers and pilgrims who served them. Many of Nehekhara's wealthiest families maintained residences in the city, and in centuries past a constant stream of noble visitors made their way to the city in search of blessings or advice. That had been before the rise of the Usurper in Khemri.

To the west, the swirling, blue-black clouds were already past the Gates of the Dusk and bearing swiftly down upon the City of the Gods. Standing upon the battlements near Mahrak's western gate, Nebunefer tucked his thin arms into the folds of his robes and nodded in grim satisfaction. The armies of Rasetra and Lybaras were withdrawing to the south-east, the dust of their passing still hanging in the late afternoon air along the southern horizon, but the Usurper's army showed no signs of pursuing them.

Nagash wanted a final reckoning with the council and he would have it, regardless of the cost. Nebunefer hoped the price would be more than the Usurper could afford to pay, not that such a thing would stop him.

A hot wind gusted over the battlements, full of grit and the musty smell of the grave. A thin line of warriors stood along the walls, awaiting the arrival of the foe. Mahrak had never needed an army before, and even as the Usurper grew in power at Khemri, the Hieratic Council refused to consider raising one. That would have been tantamount to admitting that Nagash's power exceeded that of the gods. Each temple did have its own corps of Ushabti, however, and there were no finer warriors in all of the Blessed Land.

The devoted were the paladins of the gods, men who dedicated their lives to serving their deity and protecting the faithful from harm. In return for their devotion the gods gave them wondrous and terrible gifts, in proportion to the strength of each Ushabti's faith and the worthiness of his deeds. In other Nehekharan cities the Ushabti guarded the priest king, who was a living embodiment of their god's will, but in Mahrak the devoted guarded the temples and the persons of the Hieratic Council, who by virtue of their station were second only to the gods.

In distant Ka-Sabar the Ushabti of Geheb were tawny-skinned giants with leonine fangs and lambent eyes; in Mahrak, however, Geheb's devoted were transformed into towering, manlike lions, with a desert cat's fearsome strength and speed and hands tipped in deadly claws. The devoted of Djaf had the heads of ebon jackals and the cold touch of death in their fingertips. Ptra's Ushabti were golden-skinned titans too beautiful and terrible to look upon. Their voices had the pure tone of trumpets, and their hands could shatter swords.

By ancient tradition each temple mustered no more than two score and ten of these holy warriors, and they gathered along the wall in all their glory: six hundred holy warriors against Nagash's thousands.

As mighty as Mahrak's Ushabti were, they were not the city's only defences. Vast and ageless powers had been woven into the city's walls and foundations: spirits of the desert and divine servants of the gods, who stirred awake at the approach of Nagash's horde. These guardians were not bound by the covenant, at least not in any direct sense, and thus they could not be turned aside by the will of the Daughter of the Sun. The Usurper was about to learn that the gods, though bound, were still far from helpless.

A stir went through the ranks of the devoted along the battlements to Nebunefer's right. The old priest turned and caught sight of three imperious figures clothed in vestments of yellow, brown and black advancing down the length of the wall towards him. Nebunefer bowed deeply at the approach of his master, Nekh-amn-aten, Hierophant of the great Ptra. Flanking the high priest were Atep-neru, the inscrutable Hierophant of Djaf, and the scowling, belligerent Khansu, Hierophant of Khsar the Faceless.

'This is an unexpected honour, holy ones,' Nebunefer said. 'No doubt the devoted will draw inspiration and courage from your presence.'

Nekh-amn-aten waved the priest to silence with an irritable hand gesture.

'Spare us the platitudes,' the hierophant growled. 'All that time spent among kings has thoroughly corrupted you, Nebunefer. I've never heard such simpering drivel in my life.'

Nebunefer spread his wrinkled hands and smiled ruefully. The hierophant had been born in Mahrak, and had never once gone abroad. As far as the old priest knew, this was the first time Nekh-amn-aten had set foot on the city wall.

'No doubt you are right, holy one,' he said diplomatically. 'The courts of our allies are rife with all manner of ease and comfort, certainly nothing like the stern life we enjoy here.'

Khansu glowered at Nebunefer's impertinent tone, but Nekh-amn-aten seemed not to hear. Tucking his hands in the sleeves of his heavy cotton vestments, the hierophant stepped to the edge of the battlements and stared out at the roiling clouds that bruised the western horizon.

'I never should have let you talk me into this,' he said sourly. 'We ought to have kept our allies close by and let Nagash focus his attentions on them.'

'To what end, holy one?' the old priest asked with a sigh. 'The armies of Rasetra and Lybaras have fought like lions, but their strength is spent. If they had remained, as Rakh-amn-hotep was determined to do, we would be standing here witnessing their slaughter.'

Nekh-amn-aten grunted irritably, and said, 'And Nagash would have spent much of his army's strength destroying them, perhaps leaving him too weak to challenge us.'

The anger Nebunefer felt at the hierophant's callousness, surprised him. Perhaps he had spent too much time among the priest kings after all.

'The advantage is ours, holy one,' he said forcefully. 'We will let the Usurper break his teeth against our walls, while our allies rebuild their armies and return to finish what they have begun.' Atep-neru turned to Nebunefer.

'How long will that be, priest?' he asked in a sepulchral voice. 'Two months? Ten? A year, perhaps?'

Khansu growled irritably, and said, 'A year? What foolishness. The campaigning season is nearly done. Once Nagash sees he cannot breach our defences he will make for Lybaras, or perhaps withdraw to Quatar.'

Nebunefer took a deep breath and fought to conceal his irritation. How many times must he repeat himself?

'What does Nagash care for seasons of war?' he asked. 'His warriors are not needed back in Khemri to gather in the harvest.' The old priest shrugged. 'His miserable subjects can all starve to death for all he cares. Indeed, in death they would become more useful to him still. No, he will remain here, on this side of the Valley of Kings, until all the eastern cities have burnt or bowed before him. And make no mistake, he will start his campaign here. He knows we have sent Rasetra and Lybaras against him, and may even suspect that we were behind the attack on Bel Aliad. If he conquers Mahrak, the war could end in a single stroke. Mark my words, he will attack us with everything he possesses, and if he cannot overcome our defences we could be facing a long and protracted siege.'

Nekh-amn-aten clasped his hands behind his back, still staring out at the spreading clouds.

'How long can the city withstand such a siege?' he asked. Atep-neru tapped a long finger against his chin.

'We will not lack for water,' he said. 'Our cisterns are full, and the Sundered Stone remains a wellspring for the faithful. If we ration the supplies in the storehouses, we could last for three years if we had to.'

Nekh-amn-aten turned to Nebunefer. 'Three years,' he echoed, his expression darkening. 'Do you think it will come to that?' The old priest thought back to the last time he spoke to the Rasetran king. *You may have to endure a very long time.* Nebunefer met his master's worried gaze.

'Only the gods can say,' he replied.

THE ARMIES OF the Undying King reached the holy city just a few hours past nightfall, pouring over the dunes in a hissing tide of dry leather and dusty bones. The ranks of the undead had swelled dramatically over the course of the relentless march through the valley. Skeletal archers from Zandri formed skirmish lines ahead of the clattering spearmen, and bony Numasi horsemen paced silently behind the tireless battleline, escorting Nagash's immortal captains. Further back, towards the rear of the silent, rattling horde, other, more terrible creations lumbered across the sands, driven by the will of their implacable masters.

When Nagash's vast host had left Khemri for the Fountains of Eternal Life it had been comprised entirely of living, breathing men. Now, less than a quarter of that number remained. Packs of jackals loped in the army's wake by night, and great flocks of carrion birds wheeled silently above them by day. The pickings for the scavengers were scarce, but the presence of so much death and decay nevertheless proved too great for them to ignore.

A terrible, keening wind whistled through the undead ranks, plucking at frayed tatters of clothing and torn pieces of leather or parchment-like human skin. Its breath sucked veils of sand and dust into whirling patterns that rose above the bleached skulls of the warriors and fed the roiling mantle of darkness that shrouded the host from the burning touch of the sun.

The constant, howling dust storm forced the immortals and the living warriors of the army to march with their shoulders wrapped in capes with desert cowls drawn tightly around their faces. The men of Zandri and Numas were numbed and half-deafened by the constant roaring of the storm, and more than one horse had to be put down after the fine, swirling grit had put out their eyes. It had been the same for weeks on end as Nagash drove them along the dreadful valley in pursuit of the armies of the east.

They had expected to find their foes holding onto the Gates of the Dusk in a last, desperate attempt to keep the Undying King at bay. For the last few days the army had been at a forced march, hoping to reach the end of the valley and catch their enemies unawares, but when the vanguard of skeletal horsemen reached the gates they'd found the low walls abandoned and the village beyond eerily silent. The immortal commanding the vanguard had angrily sent a messenger in search of a living Numasi horseman with enough of a brain to make sense of the tracks they'd found on the other side of the town. From what the exhausted cavalryman could tell, they had missed their foes by only a few hours. When Nagash received the news he ordered the army forwards in full battle array, expecting to catch the allied armies at the gates of Mahrak.

At a silent command, the vast western host clattered to a halt just over a mile from the walls of the holy city. Nagash's immortal captains reined in their mouldering horses and raised their heads, sensing the currents of power coiling restlessly through the sands ahead. Halfway between Mahrak and the invading army ran a shifting, tenebrous line of demarcation where Nagash's veil of shadow pressed against the city's ancient wards. Beyond that restless line of darkness the plains before the city were pale and gleaming beneath Neru's silver light.

The sky above Mahrak was a cobalt tapestry, woven with threads of glittering diamond. Watch-fires burned from great braziers atop the city walls, bathing sections of the battlements in pools of molten orange light. There was no mob of panicked soldiers struggling to pass through Mahrak's western gate, which puzzled the immortals. But for the potent energies encircling the city, Mahrak seemed surprisingly quiet.

Hours passed while the rest of the army moved into position and messengers were sent from the vanguard to make their report to the Undying King. Once again, the weary Numasi riders were brought forwards, and still more hours passed before the riders established that the allied armies had circled around the city to the south and were withdrawing in the direction of their homes. As the news filtered down to the king's immortals, many assumed that they would continue the pursuit, and shifted their tireless horsemen further down the battle-line to the south.

Nagash's orders, when they were issued at around midnight, caught many of his captains by surprise. The Numasi horsemen were ordered to secure the army's flank to the south-east and keep a watch on the allied armies' retreat, and the reserve companies were brought forwards and arrayed behind the main battle-line. Quartermasters and their slaves went to work pitching tents and creating corrals for their wagon horses a quarter of a mile behind the army, while armourers unpacked their portable forges and siege engineers went to work hauling their ponderous engines in the direction of the waiting city. Groaning wagons rolled along in their wake, laden with baskets of grinning skulls and casks of reeking pitch.

The attack on the City of the Gods would begin in the hours just before dawn.

ARKHAN THE BLACK paced through the predawn darkness, wishing for a horse.

The hungry wind had eased considerably over the last half an hour, leaving his ears ringing and his nerves unsettled by the lack of sound and pressure. Much of the swirling dust had settled, and had he a mount he could have observed the army from one end of the battle-line to the other, which was entirely the point. The captains would need the visibility to command their companies, and the siege engineers would need to observe the fall of their artillery during the march to the walls.

More than eighty thousand corpses stood in tight ranks twenty deep, arrayed in a rough crescent formation that stretched for nearly three miles north to south. Another forty thousand spearmen waited in reserve, surrounding the firing positions of fifty heavy catapults. In between the main battleline and the reserves were squadrons of undead horsemen and their immortal captains, plus five thousand skeletal archers. The bowmen would march close behind the spear companies, raking the enemy battlements with a steady rain of arrows while the assault troops attacked the main gate. Only when the gate had fallen would the cavalry spring into action, charging through the gap to sow chaos and death across the City of Hope.

Arkhan noted that none of the Undying King's living allies would take part in the attack. The Numasi remained off to the south-east, ostensibly guarding the army's flank from the withdrawing eastern forces. Zandri's troops had been placed upon the northern flank and allowed to remain in camp until further orders.

It was clear that Nagash did not trust his vassals, particularly where Mahrak was concerned. The vizier understood his master's growing paranoia all too well.

Since the debacle at Quatar, Arkhan hadn't commanded so much as a scouting party. Indeed, the king had forbidden him to so much as wear his sword and armour during the long march. He was not even allowed to ride a horse. Short of ordering him to march naked behind the army's baggage train, Nagash had subjected Arkhan to every possible humiliation. The vizier had come to suspect that the only reason he hadn't been destroyed outright was so that he could serve as a constant reminder to the rest of Nagash's captains.

For a while, Arkhan had believed that the punishment would cease, eventually, and he would return to favour once again. Now, he wasn't so sure, and he wondered what, if anything, he was going to do about it.

The vizier strode down the length of the battle-line behind the waiting horsemen, seeking one immortal in particular. Most of the pale figures he spotted threw a mocking salute or sneered in contempt. Arkhan kept his face neutral, but made a note of each and every slight. *If I can fall, so can you,* he thought, and when that happens, I'll be waiting.

Finally, near the centre of the line, he caught sight of the one he was seeking. Shepsu-hur was sitting in the saddle of his skeletal warhorse, his bronze helmet resting on the saddle between his thighs and his hands busy running a whetstone along the edge of a sharply pointed knife. He stiffened slightly and turned in the saddle, as though sensing the weight of Arkhan's stare. Bits of dry linen flaked away from his burned limbs as he moved, and his ruined face cocked curiously to one side as he saw his former master. After a moment's consideration the maimed champion sheathed his knife, brought his horse about and approached the vizier. Like most of Nagash's immortals, Shepsu-hur no longer bothered using reins: a dead horse cared nothing for a bridle, being directed solely by the rider's will.

'Not long now,' Arkhan said by way of greeting as the immortal approached. Shepsu-hur nodded, his dry leather wrappings crackling and creaking as he moved.

'I'm surprised you won't be joining us,' he said in his ravaged voice. 'I expected Nagash to return you to command in time for the assault. It's foolish not to make use of your talents when so much is at stake.'

The words of rough praise would have heartened a mortal, but Arkhan felt only resentment at his master for the obvious slight.

'It's been weeks,' he growled. 'Nagash has forgotten me, I expect. I'm sure that Raamket or someone else began scheming to take my place the moment I fell out of favour.' Shepsu-hur nodded gravely.

'Raamket's the one, which I'm sure comes as no surprise. You did yourself no favours by keeping to that tower of yours for so many years.' The vizier nodded.

'True enough,' he said. He eyed Shepsu-hur and wondered if the immortal had ever chafed under Nagash's bond as he had. Was he the only one who had sought to free himself from the master's chains? Surely not.

'How many allies do you think Raamket has among the court?' he asked. The champion shrugged, sending another shower of brittle cloth tumbling to the ground.

'Not many, I expect. He was never that popular, especially in the beginning, but now that he has the master's ear that will no doubt change.' Shepsu-hur studied Arkhan thoughtfully. 'Why do you ask?'

'Just considering my options,' Arkhan said carefully.

Shepsu-hur nodded. As the immortal started to reply there was a shout from the rear of the army and a series of heavy *thuds* rumbled along the length of the battle-line as the catapults went into action. Streaks of livid green light arced over the waiting spearmen as bundles of enchanted skulls plunged towards Mahrak's walls.

Horns boomed hollowly nearby, and Arkhan saw a flare of sorcerous fire a few score yards to his right. A phalanx of withered corpses bearing white-faced shields and great swords had appeared along the slope of a high dune at the rear of the waiting horsemen: the corpses of Quatar's royal bodyguard, bound into Nagash's service and bearing the flayed standard of their former king. The Undying King stood behind the ranks of the Tomb Guard, surrounded by his spectral retinue and attended closely by Raamket and a handful of slaves. Beside Nagash walked the broken figure of Neferem, her withered face twisted into a mask of silent grief.

Arkhan felt the necromancer's unspoken command buzzing in his brain like a swarm of ravening locusts. A stir went through the waiting horsemen. Shepsu-hur straightened in his saddle.

'It begins,' he rasped, reaching for his helm. The immortal nodded to Arkhan before slipping the helmet onto his head.

'We'll speak of Raamket and his allies again once the battle is done,' he said.

The catapults fired again, hurling their screaming projectiles at the city. With a clatter of bone, wood and metal the first spear companies began to move, rolling in a silent, inexorable tide towards the city walls. Arkhan felt the earth tremble at the tread of eighty thousand pairs of feet.

'How long, do you reckon?' he asked the champion. Shepsu-hur looked towards the City of Hope.

'An hour. Perhaps less. Once the gate is breached, the city is doomed.' He shrugged. 'Perhaps they will surrender before it comes to that.'

'Is Nagash interested in surrender?'

The immortal looked down at Arkhan and gave him a fanged smile.

'The Undying King has said that every man who brings him a living priest will be paid his weight in gold. The rest are to be slain out of hand.' The vizier was surprised at the news.

'Slain? Not enslaved?' he asked. Shepsu-hur shook his head in reply.

'Today, the age of the old gods comes to an end,' he said. 'The temples will burn and the faithful will be put to the sword.'

'The men of Numas and Zandri will be outraged,' Arkhan declared, thinking back to the reaction of the kings in the palace at Quatar. 'They may well revolt.'

Shepsu-hur wheeled his horse around. The immortal glanced back over his shoulder.

'The men of Numas and Zandri may well be next,' he said, and went to rejoin his troops.

Arkhan watched the cavalry set off behind the implacable spearmen and looked beyond, to the silent walls of the City of the Gods. Invisible energies crackled through the air, swirling above the marching army like a building storm. A breeze plucked at the vizier's robes, kicking up tendrils of dust and grit. Arkhan couldn't say if it was Nagash's doing, or whether some other force was stirring as the army began to march.

ATOP THE NEARBY dune, Nagash the Undying King watched his army press forwards and contemplated Mahrak's doom.

Bale-fires were burning across the plain where bundles of screaming skulls had fallen short of the city walls. As the necromancer watched, the catapults launched another salvo, and this time many of the projectiles found the range. They burst against the walls in sickly green showers of bone and broken sandstone, or struck the battlements in blazing sprays of fire.

The spear companies were moving at a slow, measured pace, advancing in a broad line towards Mahrak's western wall. They had nearly reached the demarcation line where the necromancer's shroud met the city's defensive wards.

Nagash turned to his queen.

'Cast them down,' he told Neferem, pointing towards the starlit field. The Undying King was already gathering his power, drawing upon the energies of the Black Pyramid, hundreds of leagues distant. When the wards fell, his sorcerous shroud would rush in, and darkness would fall upon the City of Hope.

The first ranks of spearmen reached the city's wards. Neferem raised her withered arms and let out a long, despairing cry.

Down on the plain below, the breeze began to strengthen, pulling ribbons of sand into the air towards the waiting city. The spear companies continued forwards under the fire of the catapults, followed by thirty squadrons of light cavalry led by a third of his immortals. In their wake came thousands of skeletal archers, their tall bows held at the ready. They would do the majority of the fighting once the companies reached the walls, shooting at the city defenders as they fired down at the milling spearmen.

The march of the spearmen had sent a steady, rolling drumbeat across the sandy ground, but that tempo was punctuated by slow, heavy footfalls. *Thump… thump… thump…*

They crested the line of dunes just as the catapults fired another salvo at the city. Eight towering figures, each sixteen feet tall and crafted of fused bones and cable-like sinews, the bone giants wielded enormous clubs, fashioned from ships' masts cut down and banded together with thick strips of bronze. Fashioned after the complicated metal giants of Lybaras, they would assault the city's gate and hammer it down, paving the way for the cavalry to begin the slaughter.

The wind was continuing to strengthen, drawing more and more dust into the air above the plain. The necromancer's mantle of shadow was starting to unravel, drawn inexorably into the building vortex.

Thousands of skeletons marched forwards, their battered helmets and spear tips gleaming dully under the fading starlight. The city's wards had not fallen.

For a fleeting instant, the Undying King was stunned. He sharpened the force of his command, quickening the pace of his troops. The bone giants increased their stride, gaining swiftly on the advancing companies.

Overhead, the clouds of dust were boiling, their insides lit from within by a furnace-like glow. The wind had risen in power to an angry, lion-like roar. Then came a deafening *crack*, like a boulder splitting in the sun, and fire began to rain down upon the living dead.

Tumbling pieces of rock the size of wagon wheels arced from the clouds on trails of blazing crimson, landing among the tightly ranked spearmen and hurling their pieces skywards in plumes of dirt and flame. Each impact reverberated across the plain like a hammer blow, one falling atop another so quickly that they merged into a titanic, thunderous roar.

Huge holes were gouged in the spear companies, but the skeletal warriors did not feel hesitation or fear. Driven by the invisible lash of their king's will, the spearmen closed ranks and continued to press forwards. Bodies struggled onwards, their wrappings burning away as they walked. The catapults continued to fire, but as the skulls streaked through the clouds the bundles were burst apart and hurled earthwards, landing upon the skeletons below.

Furious, Nagash whirled upon his queen. He seized Neferem by her hair and wrenched her head around, cracking the desiccated skin of her neck.

'Break their power!' he commanded. 'Break it!'

Neferem raised her arms feebly, her face warped by pain and terror. She wailed like a lost soul, crying her torment to the heavens, but to no avail.

The immortals had penetrated into the wards, and as the fiery stones fell around them they quickened their pace, weaving their way past the struggling spearmen and racing for the gate. The giants followed suit, in some cases ploughing ruthlessly through any spearmen caught in their path. One giant was struck squarely in the forehead by a plunging stone, shattering its misshapen skull. The headless construct staggered for a moment, and then righted itself and continued on.

When the charging horsemen were less than a hundred yards from the city walls the sandy ground before them heaved and burst, throwing a curtain of dust high into the sky. The cavalry, going too fast to stop, plunged into the billowing wall and disappeared from view.

For a moment, Nagash could see nothing, and then a small shape came spinning out of the cloud like a flung potshard. By luck, it hit a bone giant in the chest and shattered in a spray of fragments. Belatedly, the necromancer realised that the shape had been one half of an undead horse.

The dust was starting to thin out, and large, dark shapes could be seen stirring within its depths. More bits and pieces were flung from the cloud, like fragments scattered by the sweep of heavy blows.

The giants had nearly reached the curtain of dust. They raised their clubs and swung them in broad, ponderous sweeps, cutting roiling wakes through the shroud and revealing massive, leonine shapes whose flanks were the colour of the desert sands. One of them rounded on the giants and leapt forwards, paws outstretched.

It struck the giant in the chest, talons shattering the fused ribcage and digging furrows in the construct's pelvis.

The monster was easily as large as the giant, with a lion-like body and a powerful, lashing tail, but the head of the beast was not a lion. It had a russet mane and slitted yellow eyes, but the face was that of a man.

The sphinx bared massive fangs and lunged at the giant's neck, snapping the knobbly vertebrae in a single, powerful bite. The construct toppled beneath the monster's weight and the sphinx tore it apart with sweeps of its sabre-like claws.

More sphinxes leapt from the settling dust cloud, their pelts covered in crushed pieces of bone and pale shreds of tissue. They dashed among the remaining giants, too fast for their clumsy weapons to touch, and tore at their legs with tooth and claw. One by one, the constructs crashed to the ground and were ripped to pieces.

Clouds of arrows arced across the plain and landed among the sphinxes as the surviving archers drew into range. The monsters raised their heads and snapped at the arrows as though they were no more than stinging flies, and then returned to their grisly work.

The spearmen were still pushing forwards under the hail of fire, but now they advanced singly, or in scattered knots of five or ten warriors. Their companies had been shattered, and the archers were suffering beneath the heavenly assault. The plain was carpeted in smouldering bones and broken bits of weapons and armour.

Baring his teeth in a silent snarl, Nagash raised his face to the heavens and roared in anger. Down on the field the surviving skeletons staggered at the sound, turned about and began to withdraw.

The sphinxes paced the broken ground at the foot of Mahrak's walls like hungry cats, staring balefully at the rest of the necromancer's forces. The remains of the cavalrymen and their immortal captains crunched beneath their paws. Not one of the riders had survived.

The huge beasts tossed their heads and roared defiantly at the retreating skeletons, their human-like faces both wrathful and triumphant as they stood among the broken bones of the horde.

Beyond the City of Hope, the first rays of dawn were breaking.

◄ TWENTY-NINE ►

The Lord of the Dead Lands

*Mahrak, the City of Hope, in the 63rd year of Djaf
the Terrible (-1740 Imperial reckoning)*

THE SLAVES BEGAN their work at dusk, edging warily across
the shadow line as soon as the sun disappeared behind
the sorcerous clouds to the west. They worked in groups
of fifty or sixty, with a third of their number dragging
hand carts while the rest scooped up armfuls of broken
bones or torn leather harness and loaded up the con-
veyances as quickly as they could. Companies of skeletal
archers watched over the bone gatherers from just behind
the demarcation line, ready to shoot any slave who lost
his nerve and tried to return before their cart had been
filled. The closer the scavengers got to Mahrak's walls the
more fearful they became.

Arkhan the Black stood atop the same low dune where
Nagash had unleashed his first attack on the city of
priests, and watched the progress of one particular band
of bone gatherers who were a few hundred yards farther

ahead than the rest. A scribe sat on the sands nearby with a portable writing desk balanced on his knees, ready to record the vizier's observations. Behind them the vast tent city of the besiegers was stirring, rising from the long day's slumber and making ready for another tedious night watching the shadow line and waiting for the city to fall.

Four years after the catastrophic opening of the siege, the western plain of Mahrak was carpeted in splintered bone, torn armour and broken weapons. Uncounted thousands of warriors had been hurled at the city, only to be smashed by fiery stones or shattered beneath the paws of the city's elemental guardians.

Company after company had been fed into the waiting maw of the city defences, using every conceivable tactic that Nagash and his captains could devise. They launched elaborate feints and flanking moves, hoping to over-whelm the defending wards. They supported the assaults with fierce bombardments and scores of lumbering bone giants. They even crafted burrowing constructs to try to tunnel across the killing field, all to no avail. The defences of Mahrak were as tireless and fierce as Nagash's undead attackers, and as the months turned into years the plain outside the city became a vast field of bones.

The carnage had grown so severe that the besiegers had to start using slaves to clear lanes through the debris to permit the movement of troops. Cart-loads of bones were dumped in huge liche-fields to the rear of the army, where the king's acolytes would pore through the wreckage for suitable parts to reassemble useful warriors or larger siege constructs. Further west, scavenging parties combed the necropoli of Khemri, Numas and Zandri, breaking into peasant crypts and raising new conscripts to restore Nagash's battered army.

The cost of maintaining the siege had grown so severe that the stored energies of the Black Pyramid had been dangerously depleted. Raamket had been sent back to Khemri after the first year of the siege to gather fresh souls for sacrifice. Rumour had it that barges of northern slaves were shipped downriver from Zandri every month to die in the depths of the pyramid.

The Undying King had made it clear to his vassals: if it took ten years, or ten thousand years, the siege of Mahrak would continue until the City of the Gods was no more.

Arkhan peered into the deepening gloom beyond the shadow line and gauged the progress of the scavenging party.

'Two hundred yards,' he said, and the scribe's brush whispered across the papyrus. 'Nothing yet.'

The party was well ahead of the other scavengers, wading through drifts of splintered bone that rose almost to their knees. The sky above the slaves remained clear, as expected. For the last year the besiegers had begun probing the city's wards in various ways, gathering information on how they operated in the hope of finding a way to unravel them. They had learned that groups of a hundred men or less could cross the shadow line without triggering the rain of fire and could move safely up to a quarter of a mile from the city. Once past that, however, they fell prey to the sphinxes.

There was some debate as to how many of those desert spirits protected Mahrak. Various observers claimed no more than half a dozen, while others insisted there was at least a score. The trouble was that the spirits came and went at will within the quarter-mile zone just outside the city walls. They could disappear into the sandy soil and emerge from a dust cloud hundreds of yards away, striking with terrible speed, before vanishing once again. Despite their best efforts, Nagash's troops had yet to injure a single sphinx, much less slay one.

The siege wasn't entirely one-sided, however. If Nagash's warriors couldn't enter Mahrak, they could at least make certain that nothing got out. Numasi patrols had intercepted numerous foraging parties over the last two years, and after sufficient torture, the prisoners had confessed to the desperate conditions inside the city. Mahrak's food stores had been exhausted long ago. The horses were gone, as were all the rats. Fighting had broken out around the temple of Basth when mobs of starving citizens went after the temple's sacred cats. Mahrak's fearsome Ushabti, the most terrible holy warriors in all of Nehekhara, found themselves turning their powers upon the city's faithful in a desperate effort to maintain order.

Initially, Nagash had been pleased by the news. It seemed as though the city might fall at any time, but the king's anticipation soon turned sour. Mahrak continued to endure, night after awful night, while to the south the Kings of Rasetra and Lybaras were no doubt rebuilding their broken armies to offer battle once more.

The sound of hooves on the far side of the dune caught Arkhan's attention. He stole a glance over his shoulder and saw a messenger wearing a hooded desert cape slide clumsily from the saddle of a sickly looking mare. Frowning, Arkhan turned his attention back to the slaves creeping towards the distant city. Whatever the rider had to say, he'd hear it soon enough. It was unlikely to be of much significance.

The messenger took his time climbing the rounded dune, his breath rattling noisily in his throat. Arkhan heard the man's laboured footfalls draw near, until he could smell the oily stink of sickness seeping from the wretch's pores. The vizier's pale lips curled in distaste. When the man spoke, his voice was a wheezing rattle.

'First we offer bones. Now we sacrifice flesh and blood to the lions of the desert,' he said. Arkhan felt a cold flash of irritation. Once upon a time he would have made the man suffer dearly for such impertinence.

'Have you a message for me?' he growled. 'Or have you chosen to risk your life by wasting my valuable time?' The messenger surprised him with a phlegmatic chuckle.

'The sands of time are running swiftly through our fingers, Arkhan the Black,' he said quietly. Irritation gave way to outrage. Arkhan rounded upon the messenger, his pale hands clenching into fists, and found himself staring into the sallow, haunted face of Amn-nasir, the Priest King of Zandri.

The immortal fought to keep the shock from his face. He stole a wary look at the nearby scribe, who was watching the exchange with dreadful fascination.

'Leave us,' Arkhan told the man. 'I'll relay my observations personally to the king.'

The scribe started to object, but thought better of it when he saw the look of menace in Arkhan's eyes. Without a word, he snatched up his materials and hastily withdrew down the far side of the dune. When the scribe was out of earshot, Arkhan turned back to the king.

'What is the meaning of this?' he hissed.

Amn-nasir's sunken eyes widened fractionally at the vizier's tone, although perhaps it was simply Arkhan's words making their way through the fog of wine and lotus root gripping the king's mind. Amn-nasir managed a fleeting smile, revealing a mouth full of stained, rotting teeth.

'I wished to see for myself how far the king's proud vizier has fallen,' he said softly. Some of Arkhan's former anger returned. He spread his arms wide.

'Then look,' he sneered. 'Drink deep, great one.'

The priest king's smile returned. A bright thread of drool slipped from the corner of his mouth, and he wiped at it absently with a trembling hand.

'Not even the mightiest among us are safe from Nagash's wrath,' he observed.

Arkhan bit back a sharp reply. What point was there in denying it? Amn-nasir had watched him writhe like a worm in the palace at Quatar. He thought back to Shepsu-hur's last words, before he'd ridden to his doom beneath the walls of Mahrak.

The men of Numas and Zandri may well be next.

A distant rumble sounded from the direction of Mahrak, followed by the faint sound of screams. With a curse, Arkhan turned back to the plain and saw that the carnage had already begun.

Three sphinxes reared above the panicked slaves, lashing out at the screaming men with huge, blood-slicked paws. Bodies spun through the air like straw dolls, split wide by the monsters' talons. It looked as though half the slaves were already dead, and the rest were fleeing in panic back towards the shadow line.

'Come on,' Arkhan murmured angrily. He studied the plain of bones around the fleeing slaves carefully. 'Rise up, damn you!'

One of the sphinxes seemed to leap lazily forwards among a knot of terrified slaves, crushing several beneath the weight of its paws and catching another in its fangs. The monster bit the slave in two, spat out the pieces, and then started to lunge for another victim, when suddenly the ground heaved around the struggling slaves and the sphinx jumped skywards like a startled cat.

Massive, low-slung figures erupted from the earth on either side of the sphinx. Jagged pincers the size of a grown man snapped at the monster's legs, and segmented tails made of gleaming bone stabbed at the creature's flanks with stingers as long as swords. Three bone constructs, wrought in the shape of huge tomb scorpions, surrounded the desert spirit and stabbed its flanks again and again, eliciting terrible, human-like roars of rage and pain.

The wounded sphinx retreated, dragging a paralysed hind leg and snapping defiantly at the scuttling constructs. The scorpions pressed forwards relentlessly, spreading out to attack the creature from three different directions at once. A sudden gust of wind across the plain kicked up a cloud of sand around the struggling figures and the sphinx's pack mates attacked. The leonine monsters coalesced out of the swirling sands and leapt onto the scorpions, snapping at the constructs' tails with their powerful jaws. Bone splintered and fragments were hurled into the air as the spirits savaged the constructs.

Within seconds, the ill-fated ambush was over. The six monsters paced around the shattered constructs for a few moments more, and then they turned their backs on the fleeing slaves and withdrew into the churning clouds of sand. Their dusky hides merged with the swirling dust, and then disappeared from view.

Arkhan studied the broken bodies of the scorpions and shook his head irritably. Six months of incantations and labour, all gone in moments. The vizier grimaced.

'Well, we managed to hurt one of the beasts this time,' he muttered bitterly. 'That's progress, I suppose.' Amn-nasir grunted scornfully, which in turn triggered a fit of painful coughing.

'Nagash has made a grave miscalculation,' the king finally said. 'He has kept us here for years, while our cities slide into ruin and our enemies grow in strength. If we had marched on Rasetra and Lybaras at once, we would have ended this war in a month. But now–'

'What?' Arkhan interrupted, his eyes narrowing suspiciously. The king hesitated.

'Every man has a limit to what he can endure,' he said, his voice almost too faint for the immortal to hear. The vizier studied the king's tormented face.

'We either endure, or we perish,' he replied.

'All men perish,' Amn-nasir said. 'Sometimes a good death is preferable to a wretched life.' Arkhan shook his head.

'You had your chance to rise up against Nagash many years ago, but you bowed your knee to him instead. Now it's too late,' he said.

'Perhaps,' the king said enigmatically, 'and perhaps not.'

'Stop playing children's games,' Arkhan snapped. 'Speak plainly, or not at all.'

'As you wish,' Amn-nasir said. 'The Priest King of Lahmia is on his way here, with an army at his back.' The vizier's eyes widened.

'Are you certain?' he asked, knowing how foolish he sounded even as the question passed his lips. Amn-nasir grinned again, enjoying Arkhan's surprise.

'My scouts spotted them yesterday. They will be here on the morrow,' he replied.

The failed ambush was forgotten. Arkhan's mind raced as he tried to grasp the implications of the Lahmians' impending arrival.

'An army,' he murmured. 'Why? Is Lamashizzar coming to side with Nagash, or with the people of Mahrak?' Amn-nasir shrugged.

'The Lahmians are famous opportunists. No doubt Lamashizzar senses that the balance of power is shifting, and seeks to exploit it for his own ends.'

Arkhan considered this, before asking, 'How large is the Lahmian army?'

'Perhaps fifty or sixty thousand troops,' the king replied, 'a mix of infantry and heavy cavalry, all clad in strange, outlandish armour.'

The vizier shook his head. Nagash had more than twice that number camped outside Mahrak.

'If Lamashizzar pits himself against the Undying King he will be destroyed,' he said.

'If he fights alone, yes,' Amn-nasir said, nodding slowly.

The immortal and the king stared at one another for a long, fraught moment.

'Are the men of Numas contemplating revolt as well?' Arkhan asked quietly.

'I do not speak for Numas,' Amn-nasir replied, his expression inscrutable. Arkhan stepped close to the king.

'You're a fool to tell me this,' he hissed. 'Nagash would reward me well for such information.' Amn-nasir was unmoved by the threat.

'Now who is playing children's games?' he said. 'Do you imagine that your master is capable of gratitude after all this time? Even if you whispered all I've said into Nagash's ear and he somehow trusted you enough to act upon it, do you truly think it would change anything?'

'Why talk to me at all?' the vizier snarled. 'You're right. I have no influence or power any more. The king sets me to menial tasks when it pleases him, and provides me only enough sustenance to eke out a weak, miserable existence.' He thought to say more, but shame held his tongue. For years he had been given little more than drops of the master's precious elixir, leaving him in constant torment. In desperation, he had taken to supplementing his meagre sustenance with the blood of animals. The bitter blood of horses, jackals, even vultures, partially lessened his terrible thirst, but did nothing to restore his vitality.

More than once over the last few years, Arkhan had contemplated disappearing into the desert and making his way back to Khemri. He knew where Nagash's arcane tomes were hidden, deep within the Black Pyramid, and somewhere in their pages were the formulas for creating the dreadful elixir. Those formulas would free him from Nagash's clutches forever, but the long, burning leagues between Mahrak and the Living City daunted him in his weakened state.

'You know more about Nagash and his powers than anyone,' Amn-nasir said, 'and you have every reason to desire his downfall. This is your chance, possibly your only chance, to be free of him. If you went to Lamashizzar and offered to share Nagash's secrets, it might be enough to sway him.' Arkhan frowned.

'Sway him?' The vizier felt his anger returning. 'All this bold talk of revolt is a fantasy, isn't it? You haven't spoken to Lamashizzar at all. For all you know, the Lahmians think Mahrak is on the verge of collapse and they're coming here to curry Nagash's favour. You want to use me as your stalking horse, stirring up the notion of rebellion and gauging Lamashizzar's reaction before you risk your own skin.'

For the first time, Amn-nasir's bleary eyes widened in anger.

'Think what you like, vizier,' he said coldly. 'I never claimed to know Lamashizzar's mind. But that doesn't change any part of what I've said to you.' The king reached up with his palsied hands and pulled up his desert hood.

'You and I know better than anyone what Nehekhara will become if Nagash triumphs,' Amn-nasir said. 'Mahrak cannot endure much longer, and no doubt Lamashizzar senses this. When that happens, darkness will spread across the east, and the Undying King will become the lord of a dead land. We stand upon the brink, Arkhan. This is our last chance to draw back from the brink of ruin.'

Arkhan did not reply at first. He stared out onto the bone-covered plain, and thought of Bel Aliad, and Bhagar, and even of Khemri.

'Lord of a dead land,' he murmured. He took a deep breath. 'I must think on this, great one. You say that Lamashizzar will arrive tomorrow?' The vizier glanced back at the king, but Amn-nasir was gone, already climbing back onto the saddle of his sickly mare. Arkhan watched the king go, and contemplated the future.

A DOZEN LEAGUES south-east of Mahrak ran a broken range of flat-topped hills, separated by narrow, steep-walled canyons and treacherous gullies. For centuries the terrain had been a haven for eastern bandits, until Nagash's father Khetep had ruthlessly cleansed it on his southern campaigns, more than two hundred years ago. Many of the steep hills were honeycombed with caves, some containing hidden wells and supply caches built by bandit gangs. A clever general could hide an army in that rugged landscape, which is exactly what Rakh-amn-hotep had done.

It had taken more than three months to move the companies of warriors into position. They moved by night to conceal the dust of their march and burned no fires save for a handful of meagre ovens set deep in the back of the hill caves. First the cavalry arrived, establishing a picket to keep Numasi scouts at bay and standing guard over the caches of supplies transferred by swift-moving wagon teams sent ahead of the infantry companies. By the time the Rasetran king arrived at the sprawling encampment, more than forty thousand warriors had been assembled, awaiting the call to battle. In the weeks that followed, another twenty thousand troops had arrived, bringing the army to nearly its full size.

The host was but a pale shadow of the proud force that had marched upon Khemri four and a half years ago. There were no lizardmen from the deep jungle and their massive beasts of war, nor were there squadrons of swift chariots drawn by hissing, saw-toothed reptiles. Every horse in Rasetra had been pressed into service, and every old veteran and callow youth had been armed and cased in heavy scales and fed into the crucible of war. This was the seed corn of his people. If this last campaign failed it would mean the end of his city. No one would be left to work the mills, or the smithies, or keep the market square going. Within a generation the jungle would claim Rasetra once more.

Rakh-amn-hotep reckoned that the same could be said of Lybaras. The warriors of the scholar-city had been arriving for the last month, and there was no mistaking the old men and clumsy young scribes filling the ranks of their spear companies. He imagined the huge libraries and schools of engineering and philosophy echoing and empty. The great war machines and wondrous sky-boats of Lybaras were no more, and would perhaps never be seen again.

A gentle wind was blowing off the mountains to the west and Neru was high and bright in the sky as the Rasetran king stood atop a low ridge and watched for the army's last expected arrivals. His Ushabti stood close by, wrapped in desert robes and hoods to conceal their divine gifts. A pair of scribes crouched at the base of a large boulder, comparing supply lists and making notations on wax tablets with dull copper styluses. Ekhreb stood to one side of the scribes, studying their notations carefully, and then went to the king's side. He nodded his head to Rakh-amn-hotep and the tall, slender figure standing at the king's right.

'All is in readiness,' the champion said quietly. 'The companies have drawn their supplies for the march, and will be ready to move at first light.' Rakh-amn-hotep nodded gravely.

'The picket is secure?' he asked. Ekhreb nodded.

'The Numasi haven't been patrolling as aggressively for the last few months. When they send out patrols at all, they rarely stray more than a few leagues from camp.' He sighed. 'Hopefully that doesn't mean that Mahrak has finally capitulated.'

There had been no word from the City of Hope for a very long time. Small scouting patrols had managed to steal close to Mahrak over the years and bring back news of the siege, but Rakh-amn-hotep had called off the missions just before he began sending his troops northwards. He didn't want to risk having one of his scouts taken prisoner and revealing the army's position.

After a moment the stout king shook his head.

'If Mahrak had fallen, Nagash's host would be bearing down on Lybaras right now,' he said. Secretly however, the king's instincts told him that the city was close to collapse. That they had endured as long as they had was a grim sort of miracle. He thought of Nebunefer, and wondered if the old priest still lived.

A stir went through the Ushabti. One of them pointed southwards, and the king peered into the gloom.

'Here they come,' Rakh-amn-hotep said portentously.

The plume of dust raised by the column was a faint smudge in the moonlit sky. Rakh-amn-hotep first spied a small squadron of chariots, no doubt the king's Ushabti, and then came a single, darkly painted wagon, drawn by a team of six horses. A final company of spearmen marched doggedly across the rough terrain behind the Lybaran court wagon.

As the king watched, a pair of Rasetran scouts broke cover from a shadowy defile further south and rode out to meet the column. There was a brief exchange, and one scout led the wagon and its bodyguards towards the ridge where Rakh-amn-hotep waited. The remaining scout wheeled his horse around and guided the spear company towards a nearby gully, where the troops could eat a decent meal and catch a few hours of sleep before the march began the next day.

Rakh-amn-hotep gestured to his companions and began walking down the ridge towards the oncoming wagon. The Lybaran Ushabti arrived first, dismounting from their chariots and bowing their heads respectfully to the Rasetran king as he approached.

The wagon, the last, battered remnant of Hekhmenukep's splendid mobile court, rattled to a halt a few moments later. Slaves raced around to the back of the conveyance, pulling its wooden doors open and placing a set of steps on the ground just as the Lybaran king emerged.

Hekhmenukep had healed well since the battle at the fountains. Deep wrinkles crowded the corners of the priest king's eyes, and he moved with greater care than he might have done years before, but otherwise he seemed in good health. He climbed down onto solid ground and approached Rakh-amn-hotep, trailed by an earnest-looking young man in royal robes.

'Well met, old friend,' Hekhmenukep said sombrely. He turned and gestured towards his companion. 'Allow me to present my son and heir, Prince Khepra.' Khepra stepped forwards and bowed to the Rasetran king.

'It is a great honour,' he said, his voice grave and his expression full of youthful seriousness. Rakh-amn-hotep nodded courteously to the young man.

'In return, let me introduce my own son,' he said, indicating the slender, robed young man standing nearby. 'This is Prince Shepret.'

At the sound of his name the robed figure stepped forwards and bowed. He drew back his desert facecloth, revealing sharp, aquiline features and startling green eyes.

'The honour is ours,' Shepret said. Though physically almost exactly the opposite of the stout, craggy-featured Rasetran king, Shepret's steely tone and brusque manner was just like his father's. Hekhmenukep smiled at Rakh-amn-hotep.

'It appears we think alike, you and I,' he said

'Indeed,' the Rasetran king replied. 'About time for the younger generation to make their mark in the world.' But Hekhmenukep could not mistake the look that went with Rakh-amn-hotep's words.

Both men understood that this was the last chance to save their homes. If they failed to break Nagash at Mahrak, the cities of the east were doomed. Better that their sons fight and die on the battlefield than bend their knees to the Usurper.

'I trust you've taken good care of my troops these last few months,' Hekhmenukep said, changing the subject.

The Rasetran king nodded. 'All is in readiness,' he said. 'Now that you've arrived we will march at first light tomorrow. There's no sense waiting any more than we must and risk a chance discovery by Nagash's scouts.'

Hekhmenukep nodded. 'And the Usurper suspects nothing?' he asked.

'As far as we can tell, he has no idea we're here,' Rakh-amn-hotep replied. 'His attention is focused entirely on Mahrak, and his Numasi allies are doing a poor job of securing his flank. We'll hit the Numasi encampment tomorrow like a thunderbolt, and drive through and into Nagash's positions before they know what is happening.'

'What of Zandri's army?' Hekhmenukep asked. 'Is there any sign of them?' Rakh-amn-hotep shook his head.

'We assume they are further north, guarding the Usurper's northern flank, too far away to make much difference once the attack begins. By the time they are able to join the battle the outcome will have already been decided.'

Hekhmenukep considered the plan and nodded. Both kings knew that their forces were badly outnumbered. Surprise was essential if they were to have a hope of defeating Nagash's horde.

'Let us pray that we can avoid notice for just a few hours more,' he said. 'The future of all Nehekhara depends upon it.'

THIRTY YARDS AWAY, two men lay behind another rocky ridge line, listening intently. The voices of the two kings carried easily through the cold night air. Eventually, the party climbed aboard the Lybaran court wagon and the procession made its way up into a hidden valley, where the bulk of the allied army waited.

The two Numasi scouts waited for more than half an hour, long after the last echoes of the wagon's passage had faded away. Slowly and carefully, they eased from their camouflaged holes and slipped like shadows down to the base of the ridge, where their horses waited. Without a word, the two men climbed into their saddles and parted ways, racing across the desert to carry the news to their master.

━━◀ THIRTY ▶━━

The End of all Things

*Mahrak, the City of Hope, in the 63rd year of Djaf
the Terrible (-1740 Imperial reckoning)*

THE LAHMIAN ARMY reached Mahrak by mid-morning of
the next day, arriving with a fanfare of trumpets and the
liquid flutter of hundreds of yellow silk banners.
Squadrons of heavy cavalry came first, riding around the
northern perimeter of the besieged city in a sinuous column of brightly coloured pennons. Silver pendants
worked into the horses' harnesses glittered icily in the
bright sunlight, contrasting with the strange, coal-black
scale shirts and greaves that the cavalrymen wore. Behind
the heavy horsemen rode smaller squadrons of horse
archers riding sleek, lean-limbed mounts. Short, powerful
horse bows rested across their wooden saddles, similar to
the fearsome weapons of the vanquished Bhagarites.

Behind the horse archers, long columns of spearmen
marched under various silk banners that announced the
identities of their noble patrons. The footmen wore dark

metal armour similar to the cavalry, and their swords and spear-tips were fashioned from the same ore.

At first glance, the final Lahmian infantry companies appeared to be spearmen as well, except that they bore no shields and were smaller in number than the standard foot companies. Each warrior marched with a long pole held against his shoulder, but upon closer observation it became apparent that these weapons were not spears. In fact, they hardly looked like weapons at all. One-third of the object was indeed a pole of hard wood, nearly as thick as a man's forearm and capped at the end by a bulb of dark metal. The rest of the object's length was made of unpolished bronze and held in place with more dark metal bands. Artisans had carved the bronze to resemble the scaly hide of a fearsome lizard, and the object's bronze tip resembled the leering, fanged mouth of a crocodile. The carved jaws were parted, opening to reveal dark hollows within.

The Zandrian outriders who met the Lahmians studied the strange warriors with a mixture of curiosity and dread. It was well-known that Lahmia was a distant and exotic place, and its people traded with mysterious barbarians in the Silk Lands in the far east. What they saw only confirmed their expectations.

The army came to a halt within only a few hundred yards of the Zandri positions and quickly began to stake out a perimeter as though preparing to make camp. Into their midst came a procession of brightly coloured wagons that no doubt contained the Lahmian king and his retainers. The newcomers appeared to take little notice of the gaunt, staring Zandrians, or the bone-covered plain stretching westwards from Mahrak's walls and the roiling clouds of darkness hanging in the sky beyond.

The same could not be said of the people inside the besieged city. When the first yellow banners were seen to the north, word spread like a desert storm through Mahrak's filthy, corpse-choked streets. By the time the

Lahmian army had drawn up before the Zandri encampment half a dozen tall Ushabti had climbed atop the city's northern wall, bearing a frail, robed figure who weighed little more than a child. Slowly and carefully, they set Nebunefer onto his feet and helped him lay his wrinkled hands upon the battlements for support. Then the withdrew to a respectful distance.

Nebunefer watched the wagons of the Lahmian king roll into view, followed by a long line of heavily laden supply wagons. The old priest's mind was still sharp, almost preternaturally so, these days. Starvation had a tendency to focus one's thoughts, he had come to learn, at least for a short time.

From the evidence, it was clear that Lamashizzar had no intention of lifting the siege. For ten long years the Lahmians had watched the war against Nagash unfold, refusing to commit to one side or the other. Nebunefer believed that they were waiting to see which side gained the upper hand before committing themselves. Now, apparently, they had made their decision.

An Ushabti approached and bowed to the priest, offering a small clay cup brimming with steaming liquid. Nebunefer took the cup in both hands, grateful for its warmth despite the bright, mid-morning sun. He took a small sip of the tea, Lahmian tea, he noted sadly, imported at great cost from the Silk Lands and purchased for the temple storehouses years before. The tea had a delicate, floral taste when combined with water from the Sundered Stone. It was all that the priesthood had left. They steeped the tiny leaves until nothing was left, and then ate those as well.

No one knew how many of Mahrak's citizens were left. Hundreds had died in riots as the food supplies dwindled, and many hundreds more succumbed after everyone became too weak to fight. Entire families had retreated into their homes, sending out the youngest and strongest in search of food, or when hope ran out, to loot an apothecary's shop for a fast-acting poison. There wasn't a single apothecary shop left intact anywhere in the city. It was only by the selfless efforts of the priests of Geheb and Asaph that a plague had not broken out years before.

Rumours were rife of cannibalism in the poorer districts of the city, as desperate, starving families fell upon the wasted corpses piled in the streets. The Hieratic Council declared such an offence punishable by death, but little effort was made to hunt for the perpetrators. No one really wanted to know if there was any truth to the tales.

Nebunefer sipped his tea slowly, wincing at the cramps that gripped his belly from time to time as he watched the Lahmians organising a royal procession to greet the Usurper. As he watched, his mind drifted back to the last time he'd spoken with the Rasetran king. He wondered what had become of Rakh-amn-hotep, and where he was now. Much could happen to a man in four years. Perhaps the king still intended to keep his old promise. If so, Neb-unefer feared that the Rasetrans would not arrive in time.

'I thought that I might find you here,' said a sepulchral voice close to Nebunefer's ear.

The old priest blinked for a few long moments, unable to puzzle out where the sound had come from. He turned his head in a daze and saw the pale, hollowed-out face of Atep-neru, the Hierophant of Djaf. The long siege had turned the priest even more cadaverous than he had been to start with, but the privations of hunger didn't seem to plague him as much as Nebunefer or the other priests.

'Atep-neru, it's good to see you,' Nebunefer said. His voice was a thready whisper, despite the Lahmian tea. 'It's been some time since you left the precincts of your temple. I had begun to fear the worst.' He gestured towards the north. 'You've come to see the arrival of the Lahmians, I expect.' The Hierophant of Djaf frowned worriedly at the old priest.

'Nothing of the kind,' he said. 'I've come to summon you to the Palace of the Gods. There are important decisions to be made.' Nebunefer sipped his tea and winced as another cramp seized his guts.

'I have nothing useful to add,' he said, shaking his head wearily. 'Nekh-amn-aten speaks for our temple, as always. He can decide for himself.'

'Nekh-amn-aten is dead,' Atep-neru said flatly. 'He took poison sometime during the night. By right of seniority, you are now the Hierophant of Ptra.'

Nebunefer could not bring himself to reply at first. He looked down at the cup in his hands and waited until the terrible pain in his heart subsided.

'I pray that Usirian will judge him kindly,' he said at last. Then the old priest took a deep breath and straightened. 'What decisions must be made?' Atep-neru folded his thin arms.

'Nekh-amn-aten insisted upon defiance against Nagash,' he said. 'Now that he is gone, Khansu is advocating a rash and destructive response.'

The old priest nodded in understanding. The Hierophant of Khsar had grown increasingly intemperate and erratic as the siege wore on.

'What does he suggest?' he asked.

'An attack, of course,' Atep-neru said. 'With not just the Ushabti, but every person left in the city. A last gesture of defiance, while we still have the strength to fight.'

Nebunefer shook his head, and said, 'That would be no fight. Just glorified mass suicide.'

'My thoughts exactly,' Atep-neru said. 'Khansu is a fool, but he's won a number of council members over to his side. I need your support to suggest a more rational course of action.'

'Such as?' the old priest asked.

'Why, surrender of course,' Atep-neru replied. 'Something we should have done long ago and spared our people much suffering.' The hierophant spread his hands. 'Nagash must see that we are at an impasse. Every day the Usurper lingers here, he and his allies see the fortunes of their home cities dwindle. I'm certain he would be willing to negotiate an end to the siege.'

'Assuming that were true, what of our allies? We would be betraying them.' Nebunefer replied with a sigh. Atep-neru's frown deepened.

'Our allies have abandoned us,' he snapped. 'It's been four years, Nebunefer. They are not coming. No one is going to save us but ourselves.'

Nebunefer stared up at Atep-neru and saw the absolute conviction in the hierophant's eyes. The old priest sighed, feeling more weary than he'd ever felt in his long life. He turned, looking out at the Lahmian camp once more, and shook his head sadly.

'Go on,' Nebunefer said. 'Convene the council at the Palace of the Gods. I…' He stared down at the depths of his cup. 'I'll just finish my tea.' The hierophant nodded curtly.

'I'll see you at the palace, then,' he said. 'Don't keep us waiting long. With Lamashizzar here, our position becomes more perilous by the moment.' Atep-neru turned on his heel and hastened towards the battlement stair.

Nebunefer watched the hierophant go, and then turned back to the Lahmian army. He watched their silk banners ripple in the desert wind, and sipped the last of his tea. The sense of loss he felt cut clean through him, like a flashing blade in the heat of battle.

This would be Mahrak's last day. The city's brave resistance was at an end, whether it be thrown away in a single, doomed charge or traded like cheap cloth in the marketplace. Those were the only options that remained.

The old priest drank the last, bitter dregs and studied the empty cup for a long moment. Then he stretched forth his hand and let it fly, casting it in a plunging arc over the city wall.

There was, Nebunefer realised, a third option.

* * *

THE LAHMIANS DID not bother sending a messenger to the tent of the Undying King and waiting to be invited to an audience. Within an hour of their arrival a procession was organised and set off towards the centre of Nagash's camp. They announced their coming with the blare of trumpets and the clash of cymbal and bell, filling the air with a riot of celebratory noise. The warriors of Zandri stood aside as the procession marched through their encampment, marvelling at the dark-armoured horsemen and the black lacquered palanquin, leading a procession of brightly clad retainers carrying dozens of bundles and wooden chests.

News of the army's arrival raced through the camp, drawing Nagash's remaining immortals from their posts to attend upon their master. The king's Tomb Guard, hastily mustered to full strength as the procession approached, stepped aside and allowed the pale-skinned nobles to file hurriedly into their master's cavernous tent.

Arkhan the Black slipped in among them and sidled towards the shadows in the far corner of the dimly lit chamber. He searched the growing crowd for any sign of Amn-nasir or the twin Kings of Numas, but Nagash's mortal vassals were nowhere to be seen.

The Undying King was already present, sitting upon Khemri's throne at the far end of the chamber and attended by his blind servant Ghazid. Neferem was absent. Even her small throne had been hastily removed.

Speculation was rampant. Arkhan listened to the sibilant whispers of his fellow immortals. Many reasoned that Lamashizzar had reached his majority and come to swear his allegiance to Nagash. Others speculated that the young king would challenge their master for the return of Neferem. Still others believed that Lamashizzar hoped to intercede on behalf of the priests of Mahrak. Arkhan folded his arms and settled down to watch the audience unfold.

The blaring horns and ringing cymbals drew near. A hush fell over Nagash's court. At a quiet order from the

Undying King, Ghazid limped down the aisle between the waiting immortals and made his way outside the tent.

The music outside stopped. Then, after a few moments, it began again, softer and more melodious. The tent flaps were drawn aside, and a score of colourful musicians entered, filling the dark chamber with the crystal notes of silver flutes, cymbals and bells. The Lahmians took no notice of the ghastly assemblage filling the shadowy expanse of the chamber. They spread quickly to either side of the opening and continued to play as the first courtiers began the long procession towards Nagash's throne.

Each silk-clad noble approached the Undying King with a handsome gift: bolts of the finest silk, chests of delicate jade or gilt necklaces decorated with gleaming gems. The courtiers bowed before the throne and stepped alternately left or right, forming ranks that ran the length of the aisle all the way back to the tent's entrance.

After several long minutes, when the last courtier had bowed and strode smoothly to his appointed place, there was another bright flare of trumpets and a rising crescendo from the musicians at the entrance. Then, in the silence that followed, Lamashizzar, the young Priest King of Lahmia, entered the crowded tent.

Word had reached the besieging army just last year that Lamasheptra, former King of the City of the Dawn, had finally succumbed to the strain of a long life of indolence and excess. Very late in life he had sired a son and daughter by one of his wives, and his heir, Lamashizzar, had only just reached adulthood. The young king walked straight-backed and proud towards Nagash's throne, clad in an ornate version of the dark scales worn by the rest of his army. The Lahmian king wore no helm, allowing his long, curly black hair to spill across his squared shoulders and frame his lean, handsome face. His large, brown eyes were sharp and bright, like a hawk's, and the young king favoured Nagash's court with a warm, dazzling smile. A curious wood and metal club was cradled in his left arm, like a sceptre. Like the objects carried by his men, the king's club was worked in the shape of a grinning crocodile with a gaping, polished maw.

The Lahmian king approached Nagash without the slightest sign of fear, and bowed respectfully at the foot of the throne. The Undying King regarded Lamashizzar with a cold, baleful stare.

Nagash's lip curled into a sneer. His ghostly retinue keened fearfully.

'You forget your place, boy,' Nagash said. 'Kneel in the presence of your betters.'

The hateful tone of the necromancer's voice cut through the air like a knife. Then a stir went through the immortals as the Lahmian king threw back his head and laughed.

'The years have treated you unkindly, cousin,' Lamashizzar said. 'Do your eyes fail you after so many centuries? I am no boy, but the king of a great city, the same as you, and so I greet you warmly, and offer these gifts to show you my esteem.'

Shocked hisses rose from the court. Many looked at Lamashizzar with frank astonishment, thinking the young man deranged. Arkhan sidled closer, now even more interested in the exchange. Nagash straightened. His hands closed on the arms of his throne.

'What is the meaning of this?' he asked coldly.

Lamashizzar looked surprised, and said, 'Meaning? Why, merely to reaffirm the close ties between our two cities. I have watched your campaigns with great interest, cousin. It shamed me to see you stymied so long here at Mahrak, so my first act as Lahmia's king was to raise an army and march to your aid.'

Arkhan saw Nagash's face drain of colour. The necromancer leaned forwards slightly. 'You are here to aid me?' he asked.

'Oh, yes,' Lamashizzar said. As he spoke, his demeanour changed slightly. The mirth drained from his features, and his voice took on a hard edge. 'For the love we have for

Khemri, and for my aunt, your queen, the warriors of Lahmia are prepared to deliver Mahrak into your hands. What the gods have denied you for four long years we will give you in the space of an afternoon.'

A shocked silence fell upon the court. Arkhan watched Nagash intently, expecting violence. Instead, the ghost of a smile touched the necromancer's lips.

'What is your price?' the Undying King asked.

Lamashizzar bowed once more.

'I wouldn't dream of taking advantage of you in such a dire circumstance,' the young king said. 'I merely want Khemri and Lahmia to enjoy the close relationship our cities have had since the time of mighty Settra.'

Nagash's expression hardened once more. 'Enough dissembling,' he growled. 'What is it you want?'

The young king spread his hands.

'What else is there worth sharing?' he asked, turning to survey the gathered immortals with a smile, but Arkhan saw the cold, calculating gleam in Lamashizzar's eye.

'We want power,' the Lahmian said, turning back to Nagash. 'Share with us the secret of eternal life, and Mahrak is yours.' The baldness of the demand shocked even Nagash.

'You forget yourself,' declared the Undying King.

Lamashizzar slowly shook his head.

'Oh, no,' he countered. 'I assure you, cousin. I have forgotten nothing. It is you who have lost your way and brought your kingdom to the brink of destruction.'

The young king pointed eastwards, towards Mahrak, before continuing, 'You have defeated one army after another, but this city of priests continues to defy you,' he said. 'The plain of bones outside testifies to their power. Eventually they will all starve, perhaps in another six months, perhaps in another two years, but even then the city will not fall. You won't be able to cast down its gates and loot its great temples, and your enemies will take heart from this and continue to resist you while your own cities fall to dust.'

'And you imagine that you can triumph where I cannot? You are a fool!' Nagash spat.

Lamashizzar smiled once more, but his eyes were intent.

'Then our bones will litter the field outside Mahrak, and you will have lost nothing,' he said.

The assembled immortals watched, rapt, as the two kings vied with one another. The Undying King was furious, but Lamashizzar was undaunted. The young king had considered his position carefully, and was confident he held the upper hand. Arkhan studied Nagash's expression closely, and was surprised to find a hint of tension that he'd never seen before. It was possible that Lamashizzar was right.

As Nagash considered the young king's offer, the tent flap was pulled aside and an immortal rushed into the chamber. Heedless of the tension in the room, the captain bowed to the king and said loudly, 'The Hieratic Council has sent a representative to treat with you under a flag of truce!'

Lamashizzar listened to the news and his eyes widened with surprise. His triumphant smile faltered. Behind him, Nagash's grip on the throne relaxed. His eyes glittered like a viper's.

'Your offer of assistance is noted,' the Undying King said to Lamashizzar, 'but will not be required.'

The Lahmian king turned back to Nagash and bowed.

'Then I shall take my leave of you,' Lamashizzar answered smoothly. 'Perhaps later we may speak again.'

Nagash smiled. The spirits surrounding him whirled about in fear.

'Oh, most assuredly,' he said. 'We shall speak again very soon.'

Lamashizzar spun on his heel and beat a dignified retreat with his retainers close behind him. Their rich gifts lay where they left them, forming crooked lines all the

way back to the tent's entrance. Nagash watched the Lahmians go, savouring their dismay.

When the last courtier had fled, the necromancer beckoned with a clawed hand.

'Bring me this emissary,' he commanded.

MINUTES LATER, THE tent flap swept aside again, and a pair
of immortals escorted a wrinkled old man into the chamber. They held the emissary by his arms as they led him
down the aisle towards the throne so that his sandalled
feet scarcely touched the ground. To Arkhan, the frail,
withered mortal looked like nothing more than a dust-
covered beggar, but Nagash took one look at the emissary
and rose swiftly to his feet.

The immortals reached the throne and forced the emissary to his knees before the Undying King. Nagash looked
down on the old man, his face lit with triumph.

'This is an unexpected gift,' he said. 'I thought to find
you cowering in some temple deep within the city, or hiding behind those fools who make up your so-called
council. Did they send you to me as some kind of peace
offering, Nebunefer? A gift to persuade me to stay my
wrath?'

Nebunefer put a hand on his bent knee and slowly,
painfully, levered himself to his feet. Once more, the
immortals reached for him, but this time the old priest
met them with a stern glare. Waves of heat radiated
from his skin, which glowed like metal drawn from the
forge. The two undead champions recoiled, hissing
warily.

The old priest turned his attention back to Nagash.

'I have come to negotiate on behalf of the people of
Mahrak,' he said in a voice that was little more than a
whisper.

Nagash's eyes narrowed thoughtfully. 'The citizens have
defied the council and wish to surrender?' he asked.

Nebunefer sneered at the Undying King.

'You pompous ass,' he rasped. 'I'm here to negotiate the terms of your surrender.'

Heads turned. The immortals gaped at the old priest's bravado. Then, one by one, they began to laugh, until the darkened chamber shook with the racket. Nagash silenced them with an unspoken command.

'Your precious city teeters on the brink of destruction, and you come here to mock me?' the necromancer hissed.

'You think this is a jest?' the old priest snapped. 'Think again. Your siege has been an utter failure. In four years you haven't got within ten yards of the city walls. There are hundreds of thousands of bones strewn between here and Mahrak's gates. Truth be told, we've lost count of the number of assaults we've defeated.' Nebunefer folded his arms. 'The city will not fall to the likes of you, Nagash. The gods will not allow it.'

'The gods,' Nagash sneered. 'Those disembodied charlatans. Their time is done. The empire to come, my empire, will be eternal.'

Nebunefer let out a wheezing laugh, and said, 'Settra thought the same thing, and now the beetles are burrowing into his guts. You won't be any different, Nagash. You're just another petty tyrant who will rise and fall like all the rest, and when you die the gods will await you in the place of judgement. No doubt they're looking forward to seeing you.'

'No god may stand in judgement over me!' Nagash roared. 'I have burned their temples and slain their priests! Soon their precious city will be mine, and then their names will be forgotten for all time!'

Nebunefer shook his head.

'You are a fool,' he said, 'an arrogant, deluded fool who thinks himself the equal of the gods. Yet you aren't clever enough to understand one simple fact: so long as the covenant exists, the gods cannot be overthrown. They are bound to us, just as we are bound to them, and nothing you can do will ever change that. Can't you see? Your pathetic crusade against the gods was doomed from the beginning!'

The old priest was goading the necromancer. Arkhan saw that at once, but could not understand the point to it. Nagash, however, was blind to this. How often had he dreamt of getting his hands on Nebunefer after the treachery that night in the royal palace? Now he had the old priest in his clutches, and Nebunefer had stoked the king's hatred to the boiling point.

Nagash's hands clenched. He took a step towards the priest, and then froze. His eyes widened, and his expression turned to one of dawning triumph.

'Of course,' he whispered. 'The answer was right in front of me all along.'

The Undying King let out a savage cry of joy and lunged forwards, seizing the old priest by the throat.

Nebunefer's eyes widened. He grabbed Nagash's wrists, trying to pry himself from the necromancer's grip, but he was no match for the king's unnatural strength. Nagash lifted the priest off the ground and shook him like a rag doll.

'I could not see it!' Nagash said, laughing like a devil. 'I had the power of the gods in my clutches and never realised it! Mahrak is doomed, Nebunefer, and you will die knowing that you made its destruction possible!'

Nebunefer continued to struggle, tearing at Nagash's wrists with his failing strength. Pure hatred glittered in the old priest's eyes. Then, there was a brittle *crack*, like the snapping of a rotted branch, and Nebunefer's head rolled back at an unnatural angle.

Nagash tossed the dead priest's body aside.

'Bring me the queen!' he roared. 'The fall of the old gods is at hand!'

At that moment the tent flap was pulled aside once again. A messenger staggered inside, stained with dust and half-dead with fatigue.

'The armies of Rasetra and Lybaras are coming!' he gasped. 'They will be here within the hour!'

Surprised hisses rose from the immortals. Nagash, the Undying King, merely smiled.

'They will be too late,' he said.

LITTLE MORE THAN a league to the south-east, the allied armies swept across the rolling plains like a storm wind, bearing down on the Numasi encampment. Eight thousand cavalrymen made up the host's vanguard, led by Ekhreb, with the rest of the army advancing close behind. Huge plumes of dust were kicked skywards by their advance, but stealth had been cast aside in favour of pure speed. If the gods were with them, the Numasi would not have time to form a proper defence.

Ekhreb felt the wind upon his face as the horses raced across the plain, and felt a surge of savage joy. The weight of all the bitter defeats seemed to fall from his shoulders at long last as they closed for one final battle with the enemy. Here, at last, the advantage was theirs. The battle would belong to them.

Riding in the midst of the allied horsemen, Ekhreb guided his powerful horse up a high, sandy dune and plunged down the other side. Beyond sat another broad plain, perhaps half a mile across, ending in another tall set of dunes. Dark clouds swirled past the distant slopes, and the tops of Mahrak's temples dotted the northern horizon.

In between, arrayed across the plain, were squadrons of Numasi horsemen: twelve thousand cavalry, drawn up and arrayed for battle around the standards of their twin kings.

At the sight of the allied vanguard the Numasi drew their swords. Sunlight glinted on a thicket of polished bronze. In an instant, Ekhreb's joy turned to ash. Somehow they had been discovered. Rakh-amn-hotep's gamble had failed.

In the centre of the enemy battle-line, the twin kings raised their hands. War-horns bellowed out a single note, and the Numasi began their advance.

* * *

HORNS WAILED ACROSS the vast camp of the besiegers, calling the undead host to war. Immortals scattered from the tent of the Undying King, almost too fast for the eye to follow. They leapt onto their skeletal horses and sped off in a dozen directions, already composing the intricate series of orders that would reposition tens of thousands of troops to deal with the sudden arrival of the enemy.

There had been no word from the Numasi kings to the south, but fragmentary reports indicated that the cavalry had already assembled and advanced to meet the foe. Nagash's captains chose a line of low ridges a few hundred yards behind the Numasi encampment to place their initial battle-line; companies of spearmen were hastily shifted south-east and formed up along the forward slope of the ridge line, while messengers were sent racing northwards to summon Zandri's archers for immediate action. Within minutes, the bulk of Nagash's army, fully a hundred thousand undead infantry and horsemen, was on the move, angling south-east to present a wall of bone and metal before the advancing eastern forces. Farther behind the battleline, siege engineers plied the lash against the backs of their slaves as they struggled to orient their massive catapults towards the attacking enemy.

Amid the chaos, eight huge companies of skeletal warriors, the army's entire reserve force of forty thousand troops, stirred beneath Nagash's furious will and began to march towards the shadow line. The Undying King stalked behind them, surrounded by his Tomb Guard and a large retinue of slaves. A score of the terrified servants carried the stone sarcophagus of Nagash's queen upon their bare shoulders.

Arkhan the Black trailed behind the grim procession, fiercely wishing for his armour and sword. He was tempted to race back to his threadbare tent and garb himself for battle despite Nagash's spiteful orders; better to be tortured again than to have his head cut off by a chance encounter with an enemy horseman.

Not that he had any idea what he might do if he were armed and armoured. Who would he fight? Part of him entertained the thought that he could still win back the Undying King's favour if he acquitted himself well in battle, but to what end? A return to slavery, begging at his master's hem for droplets of his terrible elixir?

Power crackled invisibly through the air. Horns wailed, and the earth shook beneath the tread of tens of thousands of marching feet. To Arkhan, it felt as though the world's foundations were shifting beneath him. Moving as though in a dream, the vizier was pulled along in his master's wake.

The army's reserve companies clattered to a halt mere inches from the shadow line, the warriors' rotting faces lit in shifting tides of light and darkness wrought by the warring sorceries. To the west, distant but growing ever nearer, came the heavy tread of giants.

Nagash appeared in the midst of the skeletal companies, his robes flapping in the charnel wind rising behind the undead army. In his left hand he held the mighty Staff of the Ages, wreathed with the tormented spirits of the king's ghostly retinue.

The necromancer stepped to the edge of the shadow line and felt the power of the city's wards seething across his skin. As the queen's sarcophagus was set upon the ground behind him, he turned and stretched forth his right hand. The spirits surrounding the staff flowed across the stone coffin and pulled aside the lid, and then drew out Neferem's withered body. She hung in their grasp like a broken doll, trailing scraps of filthy linen and tattered skin. Ghazid, standing close by the coffin, turned his blind face to the queen's drifting form and wailed in misery.

Nagash drew his queen to him. The shadow line roiled in response to Neferem's presence.

'You are the key,' he said, looking down upon the queen's tormented face. 'You are the covenant made flesh. Go, and open the gates of the city.'

The necromancer set Neferem on her feet. She swayed unsteadily, her shrivelled face turning this way and that, like a lost child. A tortured moan escaped her lips. Then, with a rough shove, Nagash drove her across the shadow line.

At once, a fierce wind sprang up around the queen, and the air crackled loudly with building tension. His face set in a hateful mask, Nagash followed a few steps behind Neferem. Moments later, his warriors followed suit, penetrating the wards in their thousands.

Arkhan bared his ruined teeth at the sudden surge of energies that rose from the sands around Nagash and his warriors. Even the slaves felt it, and they cried out and covered their faces, expecting to feel the merciless wrath of the gods at any moment. Ghazid let out another despairing wail and lurched forwards, his hands raised to the heavens.

The wind's fury rose with each step that Neferem took, scattering drifts of bleached bones and drawing plumes of sand and dirt into the air. Waves of heat began to rise from the ground, even as the building clouds covered the face of the sun.

Undaunted, Nagash drove Neferem and his troops forwards. He could sense the strain building on the city's wards as their carefully worded incantations were forced to deal with a paradox. The wards were made to protect the faithful from those who threatened the City of the Gods. By virtue of Nagash's bond, the undead queen was both.

Dark clouds seethed angrily overhead, and the stink of brimstone permeated the air. Flashes of orange light blazed within the clouds, and the first streaks of fire began to fall on the advancing companies. Fierce thunderclaps smote the sky with each falling stone, as though the wards were starting to crack beneath the strain.

Blazing stones carved fiery paths through the advancing companies. One burning projectile fell like an arrow directly at Neferem and Nagash, but even as it plummeted earthwards the rock began to break apart, until it exploded harmlessly a dozen yards from its intended target. A wave of fierce heat washed over the queen, curling her dried robes and parchment-like skin. Nagash raised his staff skywards and roared in triumph.

With every step, the roaring wind and blazing heat grew stronger. The churning motion of the clouds increased, and the hail of fire dwindled. The insides of the clouds were rent by successive concussions that shook the air over the advancing troops. Arcs of violet lightning lashed at the plain like a taskmaster's scourge.

They were nearly halfway to the city walls when the sphinxes appeared. They emerged like wraiths from the whirling dust, roaring and snapping their jaws fearfully at the terrible image of the queen. The scouring dust had shredded her priceless robes and torn away the queen's golden headdress, and her skin began to unravel like rotting thread. Still she pressed on, lashed by the storm and by Nagash's furious will. Her cries were lost in the roaring of the desert spirits and the fury of the wind. Tossing their fearsome heads, the sphinxes withdrew before her like whipped dogs.

The heat had grown intense, like standing at the very mouth of a great furnace. Nagash saw his robes begin to smoulder, and staggered to a halt. His troops came to a stop behind him, but Neferem he drove ever forwards, pressing relentlessly against the ancient wards. Behind the necromancer, the shadow line was contracting, its border fraying beneath the onslaught. Unholy darkness flowed like ink in its wake.

There was a peal of thunder, and for an instant Neferem was wreathed in a halo of savage lightning. Her body burst into flames, but Nagash's will drove her still onwards. Her arms drooped as fire ate through the tendons and leathery muscle, and her lustrous hair burned away in a sudden shower of sparks.

A figure lurched past the Undying King and staggered into the searing heat. Ghazid, faithful to the last, followed in his queen's wake. His skin blackened in moments and his robes caught fire, but the former vizier did not falter.

The sphinxes howled and writhed in torment as the magical wards began to shatter under the strain. The building heat grew so intense that the air itself seemed to glow. Neferem was visible only as a skeletal silhouette, wreathed in orange and violet fire.

From more than half a mile away, Arkhan felt the tension in the air like dull knives raking at his skin. The slaves around him fell dead, blood streaming from their ears and eyes.

Then, without warning, the pressure vanished, bursting like a bubble, and a deafening silence fell across the field of bones. Neferem was gone, her body turned to ash. Ghazid's blackened corpse lay just a few yards away, one outstretched hand still reaching for his beloved queen.

Drifts of dirt and sand fell in rattling curtains across the plain. With a last, dwindling roar, the sphinxes turned to ribbons of smoke and were scattered by the ebbing wind, and darkness fell upon Mahrak, the City of the Gods.

Out on the plain of bones, Nagash raised his hands to the sky and roared in triumph.

'The age of the gods is at an end!' he cried. 'From this day forwards, the people of Nehekhara will worship their Undying King!'

Nagash swept down his ancient staff and his skeletal warriors swept forwards. Among them marched three towering giants, who raised their massive clubs and advanced upon the city gate. Within minutes, the slaughter of Mahrak's citizens would begin.

A blare of trumpets sounded to the south-east, and Arkhan realised that the armies of the east had arrived, just in time to watch Mahrak's fall.

Suddenly the vizier staggered beneath the savage lash of his master's will. From across the charnel plain, Nagash commanded the immortal, *Seek out Amn-nasir and command him to attack the Lahmians at once.*

The vizier struggled to reply, but the necromancer had already turned his thoughts elsewhere. Arkhan found himself on his knees, surrounded by the bodies of dead slaves. Their tormented faces stared up at him, their expressions of fear and pain no doubt mirroring his own.

Arkhan the Black staggered to his feet and set off in search of the King of Zandri.

THE FINAL DESTRUCTION of the Daughter of the Sun reverberated across the City of the Gods and then spread outwards, across the warring armies and on to the far corners of Nehekhara. Every priest and acolyte, every bold Ushabti, felt it like a blade of ice, sinking without warning deep into his heart. When it withdrew they felt the power of the gods flow out of them like their life's blood, a wound that no healing hand could stanch. Helpless, horrified, they knew that the covenant had been broken, and they felt the gods receding from them forever.

It was the beginning of the end. Nehekhara was blessed no more.

Rakh-amn-hotep and Hekhmenukep also felt the breaking of the covenant, and knew what it portended. Their Ushabti cried out in horror, tearing at their beards and beating their breasts in vain as their god-given powers began to fade.

The kings guessed what the terrible change portended, but neither man said a word. Their warriors were still advancing, mere minutes away from clashing with the Usurper's undead horde.

It was the end of all things. All that remained was to fight until the darkness overwhelmed them.

A CHEER WENT up from Nagash's immortals as the bone giants reached the gates of the city to the north-east. The siege was over, and the final victory was at hand.

Across the killing ground in front of the undead battle-line, squadrons of swift Numasi horsemen were falling back before the advance of the eastern armies. A solid wall of Lybaran and Rasetran spearmen more than two miles long drove the enemy cavalry back through their own encampment and towards their own lines. When the advancing spearmen were fifty yards from the waiting skeletons, the twin kings signalled their men and the Numasi broke into a full retreat, falling swiftly back through narrow lanes between the undead infantry, and forming up to the army's rear.

As soon as the Numasi were out of the way, companies of undead archers stepped forwards and raised their black bows. Clouds of reed shafts darkened the skies over the killing ground, and the final battle was joined.

To THE NORTH, the Zandri encampment was a scene of pandemonium. Men fell to their knees and begged the gods for forgiveness, or shook their fists and shouted curses at the bone giants and skeletons assaulting Mahrak's walls. The ponderous blows of the giants echoed across the plain as they battered down the city gates.

Consumed with grief and rage, many of the Zandri fighting men turned on Arkhan with fists and knives as he tried to fight his way to the king's tent. Snarling with rage, he ignored their feeble blows and hurled the fools out of his path. Once or twice an arrow hissed past, but the vizier paid them no mind.

Another fight seemed to be brewing outside Amn-nasir's tent. Messengers from Nagash's captains were arguing furiously with the Zandri king's attendants and bodyguards, who were half-mad with anger. The vizier noticed a dozen silk-clad Lahmian retainers standing apart from the raging dispute. They eyed Arkhan warily as he shoved through the press and plunged through the tent entrance.

Amn-nasir and Lamashizzar stood in the main chamber, surrounded by a dozen stricken-looking Ushabti. The bodyguards turned on Arkhan at once, drawing their terrible blades, but both kings swiftly intervened.

As the Ushabti withdrew, Amn-nasir bowed his head gratefully to Arkhan. Lamashizzar regarded the immortal inscrutably. Arkhan sensed that he had interrupted another heated debate.

'Have you made your decision?' Amn-nasir asked. Arkhan turned to the King of Lahmia.

'You offered the might of your army in return for the gift of eternal life,' the immortal said. 'The Undying King will never reveal the secrets of his elixir to you, but I can.'

WITH A SPLINTERING crash, the gates of the city crashed inwards. As one, the surviving skeletons outside Mahrak's walls surged forwards, spilling clumsily through the opening as the giants turned their attention to climbing over the sandstone battlements.

Beyond the broken gates lay an open square, where the resolute figures of six hundred holy warriors stood. Mahrak's Ushabti commended their souls to gods that no longer heard their prayers, and rushed forwards to fight and die according to their vows. They struck the skeletal horde like a ravening wind, shattering the undead attackers by the hundreds. When the bone giants swung over the city walls the Ushabti hacked at their massive legs until one by one they collapsed to the ground.

The defenders of the city fought like heroes of legend, but their strength ebbed with every blow and more and more of the enemy spears found their marks. One by one, the great Ushabti fell, crushed by giant hands or bled dry by scores of terrible wounds. Slowly but surely the survivors were driven back from the gates by the relentless press of skeletal bodies. Nagash guided his warriors expertly, using alleys and side streets to isolate and surround the defenders, before burying them beneath a tide of metal and bone.

By the time the last Ushabti fell, all three giants and nearly fifteen thousand skeletons had fallen before their flashing blades, a last, doomed gesture of faith and honour in the face of all-consuming night.

Heedless of fallen heroes or forsaken gods, the thousands of remaining skeletons marched on the city temples. Nagash, surrounded by his Tomb Guard, made his way towards the Palace of the Gods.

SCREAMING SKULLS TRACED glowing arcs of sorcerous fire over the battlefield as the armies of east and west tore at one another with spear, axe and sword. The warriors of Rasetra and Lybaras fought like devils, carving deep into the ranks of the undead, but their companies were sorely outnumbered. The allied kings had committed every company available into the battle-line, and still the enemy troops were lapping inexorably around the companies fighting along the flanks. Slowly but surely, the undead army pressed forwards, closing around the allied troops like the jaws of a crocodile.

Sensing that they had the upper hand, the immortals sent half their number and their cavalry escorts galloping off to the right flank. The Numasi kings watched them go, and realised that the pivotal moment was at hand. Once the cavalry swept around the allied flank, the fate of the army was sealed.

Seheb and Nuneb took up their reins and waved to their captains. Without any fanfare the cavalry squadrons began to move, edging towards the army's right flank. As the immortals and their light horsemen crossed in front of the advancing Numasi cavalry, the twins sent another signal. Blades flashed from their scabbards, and the squadrons increased their speed to a canter.

Pale heads turned at the approach of the Numasi horsemen. The immortals grinned like jackals, raising their weapons in salute.

Seheb and Nuneb grinned back, returning the salute. Then their swords swept down in a vicious arc.

'Charge!' the twins cried, and their kinsmen replied with a bloodcurdling roar and the flare of trumpets.

The Numasi cavalry took the immortals and their horsemen in the flank, isolating the undead squadrons and smashing the warriors to the ground. For a few, crucial moments the immortals were caught off-guard by the sudden reversal, and their surprise was reflected by the lack of resistance by their warriors. The skeletons were reaped like wheat by the veteran horsemen, and the pale-skinned captains soon found themselves beset by dozens of flickering blades.

Snarling in fear and rage, the thirty immortals tried to hack their way free of the press and rejoin their comrades, who watched the battle helplessly more than a mile away. Little more than a handful succeeded.

ON THE OPPOSITE side of the battlefield, Ekhreb and the waiting allied cavalry stirred at the sound of the Numasi trumpets.

'That's the signal,' the champion told his lieutenants. 'Let's go.'

Ekhreb was still somewhat in shock over the Numasi kings' surprising offer of parley. He had been on the verge of ordering the allied vanguard to charge the enemy horsemen when the twin rulers suddenly lowered their weapons and rode forwards under a sign of truce. They told the Rasetran champion that they had seen enough horrors in service to Nagash, and had repudiated their oaths to serve him. The whole army was ready to switch sides, if the eastern kings would have them.

The trouble was that there was no time for discussions. The armies were on the move, and even with the support of the Numasi horsemen, the advantage of surprise was fast slipping away. Ekhreb had to decide whether the twin kings could be trusted. One look into their haunted eyes was enough to convince the scarred champion. He knew what they were feeling all too well.

The allied cavalry rode westwards along a shallow gully pointed out to them by the Numasi horsemen. It concealed their movement for more than a mile, emptying the squadrons out on the enemy army's far right flank. The skeletons had already advanced well forwards, sweeping inexorably around the flank of the smaller eastern army. That left their rear ranks exposed to the sudden appearance of the allied cavalry.

The Numasi were moving further east, sowing confusion along the rear of the enemy battleline. Seheb and Nuneb had been as good as their word. With a fierce grin, Ekhreb raised his heavy sword.

'For Rasetra! For Lybaras! For the glory of the gods! Charge!' he commanded.

With a wild roar the allied cavalry thundered forwards, their swords glimmering balefully in the gloom. The undead spearmen, focused on the enemy infantry in front of them with mindless zeal, did not realise their peril until it was far too late.

NAGASH FOUND HIMSELF at the edge of the great plaza that stretched before the Palace of the Gods when he heard the faint clamour of trumpets to the south-west and the exultant roar of thousands of living men. He paused, just as he was about to give the order for his Tomb Guard to storm the palace of the decadent priests, and focused his attention through the eyes of various undead champions in his host. What he saw brought a stream of blasphemous curses to his lips.

The Numasi had betrayed him! Already they had killed half of his immortals or put them to flight, and were bearing down hard upon the rest. The right flank of his vast army had been hit by a surprise charge of enemy cavalry and wavered on the brink of collapse. So far, his army's centre and left flanks were holding, but with his captains under direct attack they could not guide his mindless companies effectively.

Pure, venomous fury welled up within the necromancer. How he had longed to burst open the doors of the Palace of the Gods and watch those fools on the Hieratic Council come crawling on their bellies, pleading with him to spare their worthless lives. Now he was to be cheated of his rightful reward, a mere hundred yards from his goal!

There were, however, more pressing matters at hand than simple entertainment. His reserves were out of position, rampaging through Mahrak's streets and wrecking the city's temples. He would have to assume command of the companies on the battleline and then extricate his warriors from the city immediately. With their added numbers he would have more than enough troops to stop the attack on the right flank and regain the initiative against the enemy. First, however, he needed to restore his battered forces to full strength.

Drawing upon the power of the Black Pyramid, Nagash began the Incantation of Summoning. Across the city, Mahrak's dead citizens began to stir.

OUT ON THE charnel plain, the right flank of Nagash's army rallied briefly under the lash of the necromancer's will, but pressure from Ekhreb's cavalry and the Rasetran spearmen drove the skeletal companies back. The surviving immortals, freed from the strain of fighting and simultaneously directing the huge host, drove the Numasi horsemen off to the west and kept the allied troops from completely turning the right flank. Nagash's troops were effectively cut off from their camp, and slowly but surely they were being driven back against Mahrak's implacable walls.

The immortals stared furiously off to the north, wondering where the Zandri army was. Nearly a dozen messengers had been sent demanding their support, but none of the riders had returned.

In the swirling chaos of battle, the immortals failed to notice that the army's catapults had fallen silent, nor could they see the smoke rising from their tents in the sorcerous gloom.

WHILE THE WARRIORS of Zandri were overrunning Nagash's encampment, Lamashizzar's troops formed up and advanced southwards, closing in on the necromancer's forces from the north. The warriors had furled their brilliant yellow banners and smudged their faces with ash, concealing them somewhat under the pall of shadow covering the city. They had reached to within a hundred yards of the enemy's struggling right flank just as Nagash's first mob of reinforcements came stumbling through Mahrak's shattered gate.

Observing his army's progress from the back of a coal-black mare, Lamashizzar ordered his companies of dragon-men forwards.

NAGASH HURLED MAHRAK'S dead headlong at the advancing enemy troops, seeking to bog down their advance under the weight of thousands of shambling bodies. The wasted corpses of men, women and children stumbled through the gate and threw themselves upon the eastern spears, while the Undying King marshalled his skeletal companies inside the city and sent them back out through the gate in good order.

The king came last, leading his Tomb Guard. His immortals took heart at the sight of the Undying King, and redoubled the efforts of the companies on the centre and left. The battle had been raging for more than two hours, and the eastern troops were weakening steadily. Nagash gathered his reserves on the right and prepared for a counter-assault. Controlling such a huge force and maintaining the mantle of shadows overhead was fast draining his magical reserves, leaving him little in the way of power to devote to destructive spells. That would come later, once he'd hurled back the enemy assault and regained the offensive.

Then the king noticed the black-armoured troops advancing slowly from the north, nearly perpendicular to Mahrak's western wall.

The damned Lahmians! Either they had put the men of Zandri to flight, or else Amn-nasir's men had turned traitor like the cowardly Numasi. Regardless, the necromancer knew that they had to be dealt with immediately, or else they would leave his army with no room left to manoeuvre. They would be trapped against the walls of the city and ground to pieces by forces advancing on three sides.

Nagash shifted the army's reserve companies to the north, anchored in the centre by his elite Tomb Guard. With another set of unspoken commands he returned control of the main army to his immortals, and then headed north in the wake of his bodyguards. The Undying King drew on the last of his dwindling reserves and began to chant a fearsome incantation.

AT LAMASHIZZAR'S COMMAND, four companies of dragon-men rushed out in front of the set ranks of the spear companies and formed into tightly packed blocks, four ranks deep. The front rank of each company dropped to one knee, allowing the rank behind to rest their dragon-staves on the shoulders of the men in front.

Five companies of skeletal warriors advanced upon the dragon-men in a thunderous rattle of wood, metal and bone. It was a fearsome sight to behold, but the dragon-men were the elite of the Lahmian army, hand-picked for their intelligence and strength of will. Few people had the nerve to handle the deadly and unpredictable dragon powder made by the alchemists of the far east.

The skeletons approached in tight formation, advancing implacably upon the Lahmian lines. As they approached, the dragon-men drew lengths of smouldering cotton rope from bottles at their waists. They blew steadily upon the wicks to keep the burning ends lit as the distance to the enemy dwindled. Two of the four companies aimed the mouths of their dragon-staves at the centre of the enemy line. The white shields of the troops in the middle made for excellent targets in the faint light.

At fifty yards, Lamashizzar ordered the dragon-men into action. Each warrior touched his burning wick to a tiny hole drilled in the side of his stave. Two thousand dragons spat tongues of fire, and sent balls of lead the size of sling stones crashing through the enemy ranks in a wash of brimstone and an ear-splitting crescendo of man-made thunder.

THE SOUND WAS appalling. Nagash had never heard the like. It was followed by a terrible, rending clatter as a hail of invisible projectiles tore through the dense formations of his troops. Shields splintered, and limbs and torsos exploded in a shower of fragments. The terrible hail ripped through the companies from front to back, buzzing malevolently through the air like river hornets. A fearsome impact struck the king in the left shoulder, punching like a fist through cloth, muscle and bone. The words of his incantation were swept away in a furious tide of searing pain. Nagash staggered, his right hand rising to his shoulder and coming away slick with viscous blood. A hole the size of his thumb had been punched through his robe and vestments, and the cloth surrounding it was soaking with gore.

For a moment the necromancer's view was obscured by a pall of stinking black smoke. When it cleared, he was stunned to see the extent of the damage wrought by the Lahmian attack. His Tomb Guard had suffered the worst, nearly three-quarters of the heavy company having been blown apart. Nearly a third of his remaining companies had also been destroyed. The survivors were still moving doggedly forwards, but the enemy companies were moving, shifting so that their front two ranks traded places with those behind them, and more of the terrible staves were being brought to bear on his warriors.

Trumpets sounded in the north-east. Nagash could hear a rumble of hooves, and knew that the Lahmians had committed their cavalry. The black-armoured horsemen charged past their spear companies on the Lahmian right flank and slashed through the risen corpses of Mahrak, scattering the last of Nagash's reinforcements and sealing his army's doom.

Ahead of the king his skeletons had almost reached the front ranks of the Lahmian fire-throwers, but the enemy had readied their second volley. Furious, Nagash struggled to force the pain aside and summon forth his power, but even as he did so, he knew that he would be too late.

Overhead, the mantle of shadow was weakening, admitting thin shafts of bright, golden sunlight. Shouts of terror and dismay went up from the king's immortals. Nagash, the Undying King of Khemri, roared out a bitter curse as the world before him erupted in blooms of hungry flame.

⟨ EPILOGUE ⟩

The Casket of Souls

Khemri, the Living City, in the 63rd year of Djaf the Terrible (-1740 Imperial reckoning)

Two MONTHS AFTER the Battle of Mahrak, the Army of Seven Kings arrived at the outskirts of Khemri. There were no armies to contest their approach, nor cheering throngs with vessels of sacred water to welcome their liberators. The fields outside the great city were barren, and its gates open and untended. Vultures perched on the battlements, and jackals stole furtively down the sand-choked streets. It was a desolate, haunted place, marked by centuries of terror and steeped in innocent blood. The army's scouts, hardened veterans one and all, refused to enter the city at all except when the sun was high and bright overhead.

It had been a long and arduous pursuit from the charnel fields outside the City of the Gods. At Mahrak, the dragon-men of the Lahmian army had shattered Nagash's reserves and sent a terrible shock through the rest of the Usurper's host. As the allied armies began to tighten their grip around the undead horde, the pall of shadow hanging over the city began to unravel. Shafts of lambent sunlight pierced the gloom, heartening the allied warriors and filling their enemies with dread. The rumour spread among the eastern armies that Nagash had been slain, and a great shout of triumph went up from their ranks as they forced the Usurper's skeletal horrors back against the walls of the ravaged city.

When the sun burst through the failing shadows the surviving immortals in the Usurper's army knew that all was lost. Their only hope of survival was to break through the ever-tightening encirclement and try to get away. The immortals gathered their remaining cavalry, and with a wail of war-horns they threw themselves at the allied warriors stretched across the western edge of the plain. These were the spearmen and cavalry of the allied armies' right flank, who had seen the hardest fighting of the day and were on the verge of exhaustion.

The sudden enemy charge caught the warriors by surprise, and despite a bitter fight the immortals managed to punch through their lines and break out to the west. They fled through the chaos and flames of their encampment and raced for the Gates of the Dusk, hoping to lose themselves in the Valley of Kings before the mantle of darkness came completely apart.

The immortals sacrificed entire companies of infantry to hold their pursuers at bay. Fewer than ten thousand undead infantry and horsemen reached the Valley of Kings, leaving the bones of more than a hundred thousand warriors littering the fields to the east. By the end of the day the terrible army of the Usurper had been all but completely destroyed.

There were no thoughts of giving chase at first, for merely lifting the siege of Mahrak had been daunting enough. Their victory had been greater and more total than they had believed possible. Men were sent south to gather supplies for the long trek eastwards, and in the meantime, the kings turned their attention to the devastated city and its citizens.

They soon discovered that Mahrak was a city only in name. Its homes and marketplaces were empty, and fires burned out of control in many of its temples. Late in the evening after the battle had ended, the city's few survivors emerged from the Palace of the Gods and wept for their salvation. Half of the once-mighty Hieratic Council, plus a few hundred distraught priests and starving citizens were all that remained. A great many of the priests died on that first night, unable to bear the knowledge that their gods were lost to them forever.

Out on the charnel plain, companies of soldiers combed the battlefield in search of survivors. The bodies of the dead immortals were taken into the city and hurled into a roaring bonfire lit in the plaza outside the Palace of the Gods. The body of the Usurper could not be found, nor that of his vizier, Arkhan the Black.

So, the allied armies set off in pursuit of the last remnant of the Usurper's host. They chased the fleeing army down the Valley of Kings, encountering stubborn resistance from enemy rearguard troops and suffering constant ambushes from parties of skeletal horsemen. The bulk of the Usurper's surviving companies fought a bitter holding action at the Gates of the Dawn, but the allied troops forced their way through the ruins after three days of hard fighting. Outside the gates of Quatar the pursuers came upon the Usurper's terrible battle standard, woven from the living skin of King Nemuhareb. Someone had planted it so that it faced towards the city's deserted streets. Why it had been abandoned like that, none could say.

Some prisoners were taken on the trade roads west of Quatar, mostly terrified merchants carrying ingots of bronze from Ka-Sabar to Khemri. From them, the allied kings learned of the treachery of Memnet, the former Hierophant of Ka-Sabar, and of his nightmarish rule over the City of Bronze. They also learned that Raamket, one of the Usurper's chief lieutenants, still held the Living City with a small garrison of immortals and undead warriors. The host continued on, preparing for one final battle outside the walls of Khemri, only to discover a city of ghosts and silent, echoing streets.

Raamket and his garrison were nowhere to be found. The great palace of Settra was empty. There were signs that it had been looted more than once, and after the last attempt someone had tried to set it on fire. The allied scouts suspected that Raamket and his warriors had fled more than a week before, perhaps to Zandri, or to Numas, or even down the Spice Road towards Bel Aliad. None could say for certain. When the garrison left, the city's few remaining inhabitants had fled also, leaving the city to the scavengers.

On the second day after reaching Khemri, allied patrols were ambushed by skeletal warriors inside the city's necropolis. For the rest of the day, allied infantry forced their way into the city of the dead, fighting a bloody cat-and-mouse game with undead horrors lurking among the crypts.

Soon it became apparent that the Usurper's last remaining troops had established a ring of defences around the Black Pyramid. It took two more days of difficult fighting before the last of the undead warriors were destroyed, and the kings turned their attention to the pyramid and the secrets it contained.

SHOUTS AND BESTIAL snarls echoed up from the darkness. A warrior, his face gleaming with sweat beneath his conical helmet, turned away from the featureless entrance of the pyramid and shouted, 'They're bringing out another one!'

The seven kings rose from their chairs beneath the shade of a great pavilion tent erected a dozen yards from the entrance to the pyramid and stepped once more into the blazing sunlight. A thousand warriors filled the great marble-flagged plaza outside Nagash's pyramid. They had been standing watch outside the entrance since dawn, observing the heavily armed hunting parties and teams of engineers that had come and gone from the crypt over the course of the day. They straightened their tired shoulders and readied their weapons once more as the pyramid surrendered another of its monsters.

The immortal shrieked in pain as he was driven out into the sunlight. He was tall and powerfully built, with a bare chest and gaping jaws dripping ribbons of dark blood. The hunting party had bound the undead noble's arms behind his back with loops of heavy rope, and then driven the points of two stout spears into his back, just beneath the shoulder blades. With two men on each spear they drove the monster into the plaza, towards a bloodstained patch of paving stones near the centre. The decapitated bodies of twelve other immortals were laid out side-by-side nearby, their pale skin blackening in the heat of the day.

At the place of execution, the hunters bore down on their spears and forced the howling immortal to his knees. The kings approached, trailed by their bodyguards and champions. Hekhmenukep and Rakh-amn-hotep walked side-by-side, accompanied by Khansu, the Hierophant of Mahrak and de facto master of the ravaged city. The kings of the west, Seheb and Nuneb of Numas and Amn-nasir of Zandri, walked some distance apart from the eastern kings, each man lost in his thoughts. Lamashizzar, Priest King of Lahmia, kept entirely to himself, sipping wine from a golden cup and speaking softly to a number of veiled attendants. When they were close enough to clearly see the immortal's face, they came to a stop.

Rakh-amn-hotep studied the monster's features for several moments, and then shook his head.

'I don't know him,' he said. He turned to Amn-nasir. 'Who is he?'

The King of Zandri frowned. His body was more gaunt and wasted than ever, and his left eye twitched feebly.

Rumour had it that he was trying to wean himself off the black lotus, but the struggle was taking a fearful toll.

'Tekhmet, I think,' Amn-nasir croaked. 'He was one of the captains at Mahrak. A minor lord and an ally of Raamket. No one of importance.'

'Traitor!' the immortal hissed, spitting gobbets of blood onto the stones. 'The master will have his revenge upon you! You and the cowards of Numas! All of you will suffer an eternity of pain!'

Rakh-amn-hotep nodded curtly to Ekhreb. The champion stepped forwards, a huge, bloodstained khopesh resting against his shoulder. At the sight of the blade the immortal began to writhe and howl in fear, pushing back against the spears until the points burst through his chest. Ekhreb reached the immortal in four measured strides, and without ceremony he swung his heavy sword in a flashing arc. Tekhmet's head bounced twice along the stones, and came to rest near Amn-nasir's feet.

The men of the hunting party pulled their weapons from Tekhmet's body and bowed to the rulers, their chests heaving with strain.

'That is the last of them, great ones,' their leader said. 'We've emptied all the crypts at the base of the pyramid. Many looked like they had been abandoned some time ago.'

Rakh-amn-hotep nodded, and said, 'This was boldly done. Rest assured, you and your men will be well-rewarded for what you've done today.' The men of the hunting parties had all been volunteers, willing to brave the depths of Nagash's pyramid in search of the king and his servants. Over the course of the day more than half of them had met grisly ends in the confines of the brooding crypt.

Khansu studied the bodies stretched out on the paving stones.

'Thirteen,' the hierophant said. 'That still leaves more than a dozen of the fiends unaccounted for, including

Raamket and that devil Arkhan, to say nothing of Nagash.'

Rakh-amn-hotep saw Amn-nasir stir uncomfortably, and realised that the King of Zandri was staring at Lamashizzar. The Rasetran king scowled at the Lahmian.

'Were you going to say something?' he asked.

Lamashizzar shrugged. 'The rest of the immortals have no doubt gone into hiding elsewhere. Perhaps to Ka-Sabar, or even to Zandri or Numas. Didn't those merchants we caught on the trade road mention that Arkhan had a citadel somewhere north of Bel Aliad?' The young king shook his head. 'This war is far from over, my friends. Mark my words: we'll be hunting the last of Nagash's immortals for many decades to come.'

Hekhmenukep folded his arms thoughtfully, and said, 'But if that's true, then it's clear that Nagash is no longer in control. He must be dead, or at least gravely injured.'

'He was with the Tomb Guard outside Mahrak's gates,' Lamashizzar said. 'I would swear to it. The Usurper was struck down by my dragon-men, along with his body-guards. Either his immortals recovered his body and brought it back with them, or it's buried beneath heaps of bones outside the City of the Gods.'

'Nagash wasn't left behind at Mahrak,' Rakh-amn-hotep said doggedly. 'I had a thousand men searching at the foot of the walls. No. He's here somewhere. Tekhmet and the other immortals returned here for a reason.'

One of Hekhmenukep's engineers emerged from the depths of the pyramid and approached the assembled kings. The Lybaran bowed to Hekhmenukep and said nervously, 'We believe we've found the king's chamber, great one. It's in the upper levels, just beneath the ritual chamber at the centre of the pyramid.' The scholar pulled a cloth from his belt and wiped the sweat from his face. 'The approach to the chamber is guarded by a number of deadly traps. For your own safety, I beg you to reconsider entering the room. Surely a cadre of champions could accomplish the task just as well.' Hekhmenukep shook his head, but it was Rakh-amn-hotep who answered the engineer.

'Enough of our men have died inside that damned crypt today,' the Rasetran said. 'This one thing we must do ourselves.'

The engineer bowed again and backed away, returning to wait by the entrance to the pyramid.

Rakh-amn-hotep surveyed his fellow kings. 'Gather your swords,' he said gravely. 'It's time Nagash paid for his crimes.'

A servant stepped up to the Rasetran king and handed him his sword. Rakh-amn-hotep took it without a word and headed off to the pyramid's entrance with Ekhreb following a pace behind. When he was halfway there he felt a tug on his sleeve.

The king turned and saw Amn-nasir. The King of Zandri was unarmed, and his expression was grave. Amn-nasir cast a worried glance back at the other kings, still some distance away, and then said, 'There is something we must speak about, Rakh-amn-hotep.'

The Rasetran bit back a surge of anger, and said, 'I understand your reluctance, Amn-nasir, but it's important that we face Nagash together.'

'No!' the King of Zandri replied. 'It's not that! There is something you must know about Lamashizzar, and what happened during the battle at Mahrak. The Lahmian is not to be trusted!'

Rakh-amn-hotep scowled at Amn-nasir. 'What in the name of the gods are you talking about?' he asked.

Amn-nasir started to speak, but Ekhreb made a faint warning gesture. 'Lamashizzar is coming,' he said quietly.

The Zandrian nodded. 'We'll speak more tonight,' he told Rakh-amn-hotep, and then stepped aside as they were joined by the remaining kings.

For a moment, the Rasetran was tempted to press Amn-nasir further, but he noted that the sun was sinking towards the horizon and he had no desire to be caught in the pyramid after nightfall. Whatever the king wanted to tell him, it paled next to what waited for them in Nagash's sanctum.

'All right,' he said, gesturing to the engineer. 'Take us to the chamber.'

THE NERVOUS ENGINEER led the seven kings into the depths of the great crypt, navigating by virtue of an oil lamp and a complex map scrawled on a large piece of parchment. Rakh-amn-hotep was conscious of few details as they worked their way through the maze of corridors, dimly lit chambers and winding ramps. The darkness of the place had a weight to it, pushing back against the feeble light of the lamps and hanging like a shroud over the king. From the hunched shoulders and apprehensive expressions of the other rulers, the Rasetran could tell that they felt it, too.

After what seemed like an eternity, the engineer stopped at the foot of a long, sloping passage that angled upwards for almost sixty feet before ending at a pair of towering double doors. Lamps had been laid at ten-foot intervals along the passageway, illuminating dozens of chalk marks on the intricately carved walls and along the floor. A group of equally nervous Lybarans waited at the foot of the passageway, staring apprehensively up at the doors.

'The corridor is lined with many different kinds of traps,' the lead engineer said. 'We've marked all the triggers we can find with chalk, but...' He shrugged helplessly.

The Rasetran nodded, asking, 'And no one has been in the king's chamber?'

'Blessed Tahoth! Of course not!'

'Good,' Rakh-amn-hotep said. He drew his sword and began to carefully make his way up to the doors.

It was no small feat to avoid the telltale chalk marks inscribed on the floor, requiring a slow and careful dance along the passageway. The doors at the end of the corridor were made of basalt. Their surfaces had been carved in a bas-relief of Nagash, holding the Staff of the Ages and looming over a multitude of kneeling kings and priests. Scowling, Rakh-amn-hotep put a hand against the door on the left and pushed the heavy portal open.

Beyond was a four-sided chamber whose basalt walls angled inwards to form a second pyramid. Walls, floor and ceiling were inscribed with thousands of intricate hieroglyphs, inlaid with crushed gemstones that glittered balefully in the lamplight. An intricately carved marble sarcophagus rested upon a stone dais at the centre of the chamber.

Waves of magical energy pulsed inside the chamber, setting Rakh-amn-hotep's nerves on fire. Faint echoes, cries of terror and misery, rose and fell in his ears. Each step across the chamber sent waves of despair coursing up the king's spine.

Gripping his sword tightly, Rakh-amn-hotep approached the dark sarcophagus. Some instinct told him that the casket was not empty. The final reckoning with the Usurper had come at last.

The Rasetran king waited by the side of the sarcophagus until all seven kings stood by his side. All but Amn-nasir were armed, and they held their weapons ready.

Rakh-amn-hotep laid his hand on the edge of the casket's lid. Each of the other men did the same.

'For Ka-Sabar and Bhagar,' the Rasetran said. 'For Quatar, and Bel Aliad, and Mahrak.'

'For Akhmen-hotep and Nemuhareb,' Hekhmenukep added. 'For Thutep and Shahid ben Alcazzar.'

'For Nebunefer, loyal servant of Ptra,' Khansu said. 'And for Neferem, the Daughter of the Sun.'

Rakh-amn-hotep raised his sword.

'Let justice be done!' he cried, and heaved upon the casket's lid. The top of the sarcophagus slid aside, and a torrent of locusts and glittering beetles poured from the darkness, filling the air with the dry rustle of wings.

The kings staggered away from the casket, batting furiously at the rushing wall of insects. The sound of the swarm in the confined space was nearly deafening, Then, just as suddenly as it appeared, the cloud of insects was gone, racing down the passageway behind them.

Stunned, Rakh-amn-hotep ran a trembling hand across his face. For a moment he'd been transported back in time, when another swarm had swept over his sky-boat above the Fountains of Eternal Life. He shook away the awful memory and stepped back to the casket once more. This time he threw his full weight against the stone lid and sent it crashing to the floor. Sword ready, the Rasetran peered inside.

The sarcophagus of the Undying King was empty.

AN ENTIRE COMPANY of swordsmen was left to guard the pyramid once night had fallen. A bonfire had been built in the centre of the great plaza, and the bodies of the immortals had been consigned to the flames. Later, after the seven kings had given up and returned to their encampment outside haunted Khemri, a team of workmen barred the pyramid entrance with a massive block of granite that had been found elsewhere in the necropolis. It was merely a temporary measure, for on the morrow the Lybaran engineers would set to work sealing up the pyramid in earnest, ensuring that its evil powers could never be used again.

That mattered little to the small group of men who crept up to the far side of the pyramid shortly after midnight. There was more than one entrance into the great crypt, if one knew where to find them. The leader of the group touched a series of faint indentations on the pyramid's smooth surface and a narrow portal slid open with only the faintest grating of stone.

Once inside, the group lit small oil lamps and followed their guide through a maze of narrow passageways and vast, echoing chambers that led them inexorably towards the centre of the pyramid. Finally, their path ended when they came to a blank wall at the far end of a long, sloping corridor. The guide ran his fingers over the stone until he found a tiny indentation. There was a faint click, and a section of the wall swung inwards.

The cloaked figures slipped silently through the doorway. Their guide was already moving around the large chamber beyond, lighting a series of larger oil lamps with a practised ease born of long familiarity. The expanding glow revealed shelves heaped with scrolls and thick, leather-bound books, as well as broad tables cluttered with a plethora of arcane objects made from glass, metal and bone. Elaborate skeletons, some human, others bestial, were fixed together with wire and stood on display in various corners of the room. The men looked around the chamber in awe, amazed at the sheer wealth of knowledge contained within.

One man in the middle of the group reached up and pulled back his hood. Lamashizzar raised his oil lamp high above his head and stared covetously at the many bookshelves.

'You never said there would be so much,' he whispered. 'We'll never get them all out.'

'We don't need all of them,' Arkhan said. The immortal worked his way across Nagash's library until he stood before an apparently bare stretch of wall. He felt the stone carefully for the hidden lever, wary of the booby traps set in the wall around it. Finally he found what he was looking for, and with a gentle tug a part of the wall swung open, revealing a niche that contained four leather-bound tomes. The immortal's lips pulled back in a ghastly smile. 'The other books are just records of Nagash's experiments. These are the ones that contain all the things that he learned, including the secret of his elixir.'

Arkhan felt his pulse race as he closed his hands around the books. Here at last was the knowledge he craved. He would return to his tower with the books and unravel their secrets, starting with the formula for Nagash's life-giving elixir. Already the hunger was so great that it cut into his guts like a knife. Soon he would regain his full strength, and then he would plumb his master's more eso-teric spells. Who could say what might happen after that? The power of the old gods was broken, and the land dev-astated by war. The people of Nehekhara would need a new leader for the dark times to come.

'You said that the pyramid was to be sealed,' Arkhan said to the Lahmian king as he placed the books in a leather bag that hung from his shoulders. 'What will the kings do then?'

'The hunt will continue,' Lamashizzar replied. 'Rakh-amn-hotep intends to march on Ka-Sabar next. Seheb and Nuneb have said they intend to return to Numas and scour the city for signs of your fellow immor-tals, while Khansu and Hekhmenukep plan to return to Quatar. There is talk that one of the Lybaran king's sons may become king of the city.'

Arkhan nodded absently, still with his back to Lamashizzar and his men. There were only five of them, and with his preternatural senses he could place each and every one of them around the large room. His hand reached down and drew a narrow dagger that he'd con-cealed in his sleeve. Weak as he was, he was still a match for five normal men.

'What of Amn-nasir? Aren't you afraid he might tell someone about our little arrangement?' he asked.

Lamashizzar affected a sigh, and said, 'Unfortunately, the King of Zandri suffered a terrible accident as we were leaving the pyramid earlier today. I'm afraid I accidentally triggered one of Nagash's many traps, despite the chalk marks left by the Lybaran engineers. Tragically, Amn-nasir was right behind me. The poisoned darts missed me, but one of them struck him in the arm. He died before we could get him back to the surface.'

The vizier's smile widened. That was one loose end he had no need to worry about. Once Lamashizzar and his men were dead, he would take Nagash's tomes and disappear into the desert.

'Such exceptional treachery,' the vizier said approvingly. 'I suppose I shouldn't be surprised.'

Quick as a snake, the immortal spun and leapt for the first Lahmian. The man barely had time to shout before Arkhan seized him by the shoulder and spun him around. He slit the man's throat with a swipe of his dagger and started towards Lamashizzar.

Suddenly there was a flash of orange light and a clap of thunder. A heavy impact smashed into Arkhan's chest, just above his heart.

The immortal staggered. He looked to the Lahmian king, who was holding a miniature version of a dragon-stave in one outstretched hand. Smoke curled from the dragon's bronze jaws.

Arkhan's gaze fell to the blackened hole in his chest. Darkness pressed in at the corners of his vision. He tried to speak, but his lungs refused to draw breath. Slowly, the immortal sank to the floor.

The Lahmian king walked over to Arkhan's prone body and carefully studied his face. 'Take the monster and as many books as you can carry,' he said to his servants in a steely voice. 'I want to be on the way back to Lahmia by mid-morning.'

Lamashizzar reached down and pulled the books from Arkhan's bag. While his servants looted the necromancer's library he opened the first of Nagash's arcane tomes and began to read.

HUNDREDS OF LEAGUES to the north-east, where the Plains of Plenty gave way to the broken foothills of the Brittle Peaks, the boiling cloud of locusts used up the last of its strength and plunged earthwards on a trail of smoking insect husks. With a harsh, chittering buzz the last of the insects struck the wasted ground and burst apart in a hideous clatter of chitin and boiling fluids. Wreathed in the vapour of thousands of shattered locusts, a human figure staggered from the centre of the dying mass and stumbled forwards for a few, painful steps before collapsing to his knees.

He could not say for certain how he'd come to this wasteland. Memories flitted at the edge of his awareness like ghosts, haunting him with meaning and then vanishing when he tried to seize them.

Agony stabbed through him like a hot knife. His left arm was curled tightly against his chest, like a rope that had been wound too tight. A ragged hole had been blown through his upper arm, shattering the bone and causing the muscles to constrict. Two more holes had been driven into his chest, one to the right of his breastbone, just below the lung, and the other a hand's span above his navel. Bile and other fluids leaked from the wounds, reeking of corruption.

His face was burning with fever. He reached up with his good hand and pressed it to his forehead, where he found another awful wound. A ragged hole had been punched into his skull, close to the temple. The edges of the bone were splintered, sinking like needles into his fingertips. The touch set his head to pounding and sent more waves of hot agony pulsing through his brain.

There had been a battle. He could hear the sounds of it in his head: the clatter of bronze and the dry rattle of bones as dead men advanced towards the enemy; an army, his army, marching into a wall of orange flame and bursting into fragments, and then a series of invisible blows striking him one after another, plunging him into darkness.

He remembered hands pulling at him, dragging him through the blackness, and an eternity of shouting voices and the tumult of battle. When light finally returned, it was grey and unfocused. Dark figures flitted above him, and he could hear harsh whispers that once or twice rose into vicious shouts.

Look at him! His flesh doesn't heal, no matter how much blood we give him! What kind of sorcery is this?

We'll take him to the pyramid. There is power enough there to make him whole.

Slay him! Take his blood for our own! If we don't scatter, the eastern kings will kill us all!

Coward! Go, then, and be damned! When the master is whole again, how you will suffer!

The arguments continued until he could take no more, and he cursed at the voices with words of power until they fled like startled birds.

Later, much later, he was carried into cool, throbbing darkness. Power, soft and sensual, caressed his skin and sank into his wounds. The voices came back, whispering entreaties: *call upon the pyramid, master. Heal yourself. Please! The enemy draws near!*

He called, and the power flowed into him, but it lapped uselessly over his wounds. He tried to force it to heal him, but it would not obey no matter what he tried. It was as though the secrets to wielding the power had been taken from him somehow, leaving him bereft.

Much had been taken from him, of that he was certain.

Some time later there had been cries of fear, and the sounds of battle once more. A voice called out to him to flee, and then fell silent. For a long time afterwards, there was only darkness.

Then he heard strange voices, full of anger and the promise of destruction. His enemies had found him at last. Anger and terror consumed him, until the power building beneath his skin threatened to tear him apart. Stone grated on stone, letting in a blade of burning light, and then came the rising sound of wings.

Nagash turned his head this way and that, taking in the panoramic sweep of the wasteland. Nothing moved among the broken stones and lifeless sand. With a sound that was half-groan, half-growl, he forced himself painfully to his feet and turned around, looking back at the trail of broken husks that stretched towards the green horizon to the south-west.

His bones were cold and his muscles weak. Only the pain kept him going, denying him any chance of peace. Nagash sought the power that he'd felt in the cool darkness of the pyramid, but there was nothing there. He was as broken and empty as the smoking carapaces at his feet.

Clenching his one good hand, Nagash the sorcerer threw back his head and howled his rage at the heavens. He cursed the green land at the edge of the world that had once been his.

Reeling, exhausted, he spun around and glanced northwards, into the wastes. His foes had consigned him to this place somehow. No doubt they expected him to die, and his spirit to be lost forever in this empty land.

That was when he glimpsed it: a whisper of power, far off among the broken peaks to the north-east. It was faint and ephemeral, twisting effortlessly away from his mind as he tried to focus on it. Not that it mattered. The power was there, beckoning to him in the midst of the wasteland.

His face set in a grim mask, Nagash took one halting step forwards, and then another. Pain lanced through his frame, but he drew strength from it, driving his legs forwards with bitter strength. A cold wind wracked his body and sent fingers of ice into his wounds, but he embraced the pain gladly.

The wasteland would sustain him, and one day, he would revisit it upon his foes until all world was nothing but howling spirits and dry, bleached bones.

DRAMATIS PERSONAE

Khemri
The Living City, once the capital of Settra's Empire

Thutep: Priest King of Khemri.

Neferem: Daughter of the Sun, Queen of Khemri

Sukhet: Prince of Khemri, Thutep's son

Nagash: Firstborn of Khetep, Grand Hierophant of Khemri

Amamurti: Hierophant of Ptra

Khetep: Former priest king, slain in battle

Ghazid: Khetep's Grand Vizier

Arkhan: A dissolute minor noble: later Nagash's vizier

Raamket: A dissolute minor noble

Shepsu-hur: A dissolute minor noble

Khefru: Servant to Nagash

Malchior: Druchii warlock

Drutheira: Druchii witch

Ashniel: Druchii witch

Zandri
The City of the Waves, wealthy and powerful
   Nekumet: Priest King of Zandri
   Amn-nasir: Nekumet's son
   Shep-khet: Hierophant of Qu'aph

Lahmia
The City of the Dawn, strange and decadent
   Lamasheptra: Priest King of Lahmia and brother to Neferem
   Lamashizzar: The king's son

Ka-Sabar
The City of Bronze, industrial and militaristic
   Akhmen-hotep: Priest King of Ka-Sabar
   Suseb the Lion: the king's champion
   Pakh-amn, Master of Horse: a general in the army
   Memnet: Grand Hierophant of Ptra
   Hashepra: High Priest of Geheb
   Sukhet: High Priest of Phakth
   Khalifra: High Priestess of Neru

Rasetra
Former Khemri colony, now an independent city
   Rakh-amn-hotep: Priest King of Rasetra
   Guseb: Grand Hierophant of Ptra
   Ekhreb: Champion of Rasetra

Lybaras
City of Scholars and wondrous inventions
   Hekhmenukep: Priest King of Lybaras
   Shesh-amun: Champion of Lybaras

Mahrak
City of Hope, birthplace of the old religion

Nekh-amn-aten: Hierophant of Ptra, member of the Hieratic Council

Atep-neru: Hierophant of Djaf, member of the Hieratic Council

Khansu: Hierophant of Khsar, member of the Hieratic Council

Nebunefer: Priest of Ptra and emissary from Mahrak

Quatar
The White Palace, guardian of the Valley of Kings

Nemuhareb: Priest King of Quatar, Lord of the Tombs

Numas
Breadbasket of the Kingdom

Seheb and Nuneb: Twin Priest Kings of Numas

Ankh-memnet: Hierophant of Phakth

Bhagar
A trading town in the Great Desert

Shahid ben Alcazzar: Prince of Bhagar

Bel Aliad
A trading town on the Spice Road to the south

Suhedir al-Khazem: Keeper of the Hidden Paths, Prince of Bel Aliad

THE NEHEKHARAN
PANTHEON

THE PEOPLE OF the Blessed Land worship a number of gods and goddesses, both major and minor, as part of an ancient pact known as the Great Covenant. According to legend, the Nehekharans first encountered the gods at the site of what is now Mahrak, the City of Hope; the timeless spirits were moved by the suffering of the tribes, and gave them succour amid the wasteland of the desert. In return for the Nehekharans' eternal worship and devotion, the gods pledged to make them a great people, and would bless their lands until the end of time.

Each of the great cities of Nehekhara worships one of the great deities as its patron, though devotion to Ptra, the Great Father, is pre-eminent. The high priest of a Nehekharan temple is referred to as the *Hierophant*. In every city but Khemri, the high priest of Ptra is referred to as the *Grand Hierophant*.

In addition to the priesthood, each Nehekharan temple trains an order of holy warriors known as the *Ushabti*.

Each Ushabti devotes his life to the service of his patron deity, and is granted superhuman abilities in return. These gifts make the Ushabti among the mightiest warriors in all the Blessed Land. Since the time of Settra, the first and only Nehekharan emperor, the Ushabti of each city have served as bodyguards to the Priest King and his household.

The fourteen most prominent gods and goddesses of Nehekhara are:

Ptra: Also called the Great Father, Ptra is the first among the gods and the creator of mankind. Though worshipped all across Nehekhara, the cities of Khemri and Rasetra claim him as their patron.

Neru: Minor goddess of the moon and wife of Ptra. She protects all Nehekharans from the evils of the night.

Sakhmet: Minor goddess of the green moon, also called the Green Witch. Ptra's scheming and vindictive concubine, who is jealous of the Great Father's love of mankind.

Asaph: Goddess of beauty, magic and vengeance. Asaph is the patron goddess of Lahmia.

Djaf: The jackal-headed god of death. Djaf is the patron god of Quatar.

Khsar: The fierce and malign god of the desert. A cruel and hungry god worshipped by the tribes of the great desert.

Phakth: The hawk-faced god of the sky and the bringer of swift justice.

Qu'aph: The god of serpents and subtlety. Qu'aph is the patron god of Zandri.

Ualatp: The vulture-headed god of scavengers.

Sokth: The treacherous god of assassins and thieves.

Basth: The goddess of grace and love.

Geheb: The god of the earth and the giver of strength. Geheb is the patron god of Ka'Sabar.

Tahoth: The god of knowledge and the keeper of sacred lore. Tahoth is the patron god of Lybaras.

Usirian: The faceless god of the underworld. Usirian judges the souls of the dead and determines if they are fit to enter into the afterlife.

ABOUT THE AUTHOR

Together with Dan Abnett, Mike Lee wrote the five-volume Malus Darkblade series. Mike was the principal creator and developer for White Wolf Game Studio's *Demon: The Fallen*, and has contributed to almost two dozen role-playing games and supplements over the years.

An avid wargamer and devoted fan of pulp adventure, Mike lives in the United States.

BOOK ONE OF THE SIGMAR TRILOGY

TIME OF LEGENDS

HELDENHAMMER
The Legend of Sigmar

GRAHAM McNEILL

ISBN 978-1-84416-538-4

Wolfgart's horse pulled to a halt beside Sigmar, and his sword-brother put up his war horn to draw his great sword from the sheath across his back. Wolfgart's face was a mirror of his own, with a sheen of sweat and teeth bared in ferocious battle fury.

Pendrag rode alongside, his war axe unsheathed, and said, 'Time to get bloody!'

Sigmar raked back his heels and said, 'Remember, two blasts of the horn and we ride for the bridge!'

'It's not me you need worry about!' laughed Pendrag as Wolfgart urged his mount forward, his huge sword swinging around his head in wide decapitating arcs.

Sigmar and Pendrag thundered after their friend as the pursuing mob of orcs drew near. The re-formed Unberogen horsemen followed their leaders, charging with all the fury and power they were famed for, a howling war cry taken up by every warrior as they hurled their spears, before drawing swords or hefting axes.

More orcs fell, and Sigmar skewered a thick-bodied orc, who wore a great, antlered helmet, the spear punching down though the creature's breastplate and pinning it to the ground. Even as the spear quivered in the orc's chest, Sigmar reached down and swept up his hammer, Ghal-maraz, the mighty gift presented to him by Kurgan Ironbeard earlier that spring.

Then the two ancestral enemies slammed together in a thunderclap of iron and rage.

buy this book or read a further extract at
www.blacklibrary.com

COMING JANUARY 2009